A
Consequence
of Sin

An Archie Cavendish Mystery

Frederick James

BLURRY LINE BOOKS

A Consequence of Sin:
An Archie Cavendish Mystery
Copyright © 2020 C. Empett
All rights reserved.

ISBN 13: 978-0-578-76648-5

Author photo Copyright © 2020 Rosary Empett

ACKNOWLEDGMENTS

I thank my wife for her tireless editing and proofing of this book and her help and encouragement pushing it over the line.

My critical readers – Jesse, José, Lily and Nigel – have my gratitude for giving of their time to read, review and serve as the focus group to make sure Archie's first adventure was ready to be unveiled to the Public. My thanks go to Melissa Buell for her insight into the pathways to publication.

Most importantly, I thank my wife again - for her ongoing Love and inexhaustible support, and not just in this endeavour...

CHAPTER ONE

In a tiny office above a Front Street jewelry store where tourists imagined they were achieving duty-free bargains, Archer Cavendish was concluding that the man trying to hire him was not a very nice man at all. Ross Buchanan was freely confessing sins that surely rated high on the list of "things that will keep you out of heaven." He now found himself in a devilish predicament and clearly expected Cavendish to sympathize with his plight.

Buchanan was a man of medium height and build, fair complected beneath tropical sunburn, and indignant that his own bad choices might end his life as he knew it. He had come to the office in a state of extreme agitation. An island girl had picked him up, seduced him and then revealed that she was both beneath the age of consent and an aspiring Spielberg.

The ambitious young filmmaker had produced a film that was both graphic and damning and would put an extreme strain upon his marriage, at best, if it did not end it completely. The simple local girl persona used to lure Buchanan had proven to conceal that of a hard-edged businesswoman. She proposed a trade: in exchange for a sum of money she would make sure his wife never saw the film of their very brief encounter. Buchanan was in Cavendish's office now because he was determined not to pay the fee.

Cavendish let Buchanan ramble on because he wasn't blunt enough to come right out and tell him to shut up and go away. Cavendish was one of four private detectives on the island. Like the other three, his primary work was capturing evidence of infidelity. It was not the most glamorous occupation. In fact, he would confess it bordered on sleazy. But the subjects of his inquiries brought their fates upon themselves by betraying their significant others, so he could reconcile the work with his old-fashioned sensibilities. Choosing Cavendish as a detective likely to help conceal his infidelity was probably the worst choice Buchanan could have made.

Buchanan was reaching the part of the story where he had reacted to the girl's threats by grabbing her and threatening her with violence if she didn't hand over the video. That was when he discovered she had back-up standing by – a man burst into the room and tackled him. While they fought, the girl disappeared. Then her accomplice fled too. When Buchanan recovered from being knocked down, he found himself alone in the room pondering his next move.

Cavendish thought Buchanan ought to have paid up, hoped they didn't come back for more and count himself lucky. The blackmailers had home turf advantage. Moreover, by threatening the girl he might have angered her to the point of sending the incriminating video to his wife whether he paid up or not.

It took Cavendish a moment to realize that Buchanan's mouth had stopped moving and he was now looking at him expectantly. Despite his distaste for the man, his curiosity got the better of him.

"What did you do next, Mr. Buchanan?"

"I went into the hall, but the fight had drawn so much attention that there were people in the hall. I asked if anyone knew who owned the room but they all just stared at me – you know how these island people are, just covering each other's backs," he sneered knowingly. "Then I reckoned I needed professional help, so I looked you up in the book."

Cavendish was white, English, and although he had not lived on the Caribbean island of St. Lazarus for a long time, it already felt like home. The way Buchanan implied there was a greater kinship between Cavendish and himself than between Cavendish and the local community made Cavendish feel sullied.

"And presumably, you are here in the hope that I will track down this girl and this man?" queried Cavendish.

"Exactly."

"And then what?"

Buchanan was perplexed. "What do you mean?"

"We locate one or both of the people that conspired to blackmail you. Then what? You hardly seem likely to go to the police or you would have gone to them already to report this – blackmail is a crime and you could prefer charges. Instead, you are here. You want me to track the girl down and then what? You pay them?"

"Pay them? You give a blackmailer a dollar he'll come back for a hundred!" Buchanan looked at Cavendish like he couldn't be very good at his job if he didn't grasp such a fundamental precept. "You should never pay a blackmailer," he concluded helpfully.

"Then what? You're going to call the police? If not, you know there's only one more option, don't you? Try to get them not to blackmail you. You can steal the incriminating evidence – if you can find it. Or you can kill them and hope they haven't arranged for a care package to arrive at your house – and you did say they had your wallet and access to all your identification, right?"

"Yes."

"Then I ask again – what is your plan if you find them? Or haven't you thought that far ahead? Because if you do find them, you're going to be in the same predicament you were in when you were fighting with the guy."

Buchanan sputtered impatiently. "Find them for me. That's all I'm hiring you to do."

"Find them. A thin, lanky black guy with dreadlocks and

a pretty black girl who claimed she was sixteen years old – you know that if you do catch them she could cry 'rape' and get you slapped into jail. Even if she didn't, age of consent here is eighteen and you committed statutory rape. You should have paid up. Or maybe not go to a strange room with a strange girl in the first place."

"Look, I told you what I need you to do. What would it cost me?" demanded Buchanan.

"I don't know because I won't be the one billing you," Cavendish replied, suddenly feeling bored. "I'm not taking your case."

Buchanan looked dumbfounded. His redness was deepening, Cavendish guessed he was angry that money wasn't loud enough for Cavendish to hear. "What do you mean?"

"I know that there is a popular myth, mostly propagated by crime fiction, that private detectives are two pennies away from being late on the rent and will take any job to keep the bailiff at bay. And while I am not going to be buying a second house anytime soon, I earn a steady enough living that I don't have to take just any old case that comes through the door – I can be a little bit choosy. So, thank you for stopping by, but I won't be taking you on as a client. And if you find someone who will help you find these people and you do find them, I recommend you pay them, or go to the police and have them sort it out."

"What kind of a P.I. are you?" Buchanan was incredulous. "I need help. These people want to ruin my life. Don't you have any compassion?"

"For your wife, absolutely. I am sure it will be very hurtful to her when she realizes what she married, if she doesn't know already"

Buchanan shot to his feet, his voice spewing an angry torrent of words running one into the next while his body stretched like an angry cat puffing its hair to make itself look bigger; Demanding Cavendish wait just a minute, mind how he spoke to him or be ready to reel from the consequences.

Cavendish had been trained to be calm when people

around him were agitated, panicky, angry, or prone to violence. Buchanan's tantrum did not disturb him. In fact, it seemed a little ridiculous. He remained seated in his chair but angled his face to sustain eye-contact. "I feel sorry for the poor girl that dirtied herself touching your grubby little body for a buck. But for you – I don't feel so sorry. My primary job is usually catching people who cheat on their spouses. Busting people like you. You are normally my prey, not someone I would take on as a client. So, you should look in the yellow pages for someone else to go and try to find these people."

"Why'd you let me sit there and tell you my whole story, you limey jackass?"

"Morbid curiosity. And in case I see any headlines in the local paper about a young girl and a young man in dreadlocks who were the victims of assault. Then I could come forward and tell the police about our discussion today. Now, why don't you move along?"

Buchanan still stood there. Angry, stupefied. Just stupid. Cavendish could hardly tell and certainly didn't care. Buchanan tried one more thing.

"You don't understand, Cavendish – I could lose everything. My wife, she - if she divorces me, I'll have nothing. Her father made me sign an agreement because she owns part of his business!"

"Then you'd better get ready to grovel like hell to your good lady," said Cavendish mildly.

"You are a smug, arrogant bastard," hissed Buchanan. This made Cavendish smile, because his wife often critiqued him for both qualities and cajoled him to reel it in. Her tone tended to be more teasing than that of the hostile objectionable in his office. Even in disagreeable company, the thought of her brought momentary happiness.

Buchanan couldn't know the reason for Cavendish's little smile and his body was almost quivering in angry reaction to what he must have read as Cavendish mocking him with a grin. He could tell there was no point in continuing the conversation, though. He stormed out of the office and slammed the door. It was heavy island wood and the small office shuddered.

Cavendish had a small office because that was all he needed. It was about nine by ten and he had the desk sideways against the wall farthest from the door. This meant he could look to the left and look out the window and the person facing could do the same if they looked to their right. The view was smashing. The office was above a store on Front Street, which ran along the waterfront of Obstinate Bay, the main port of the island that was named after a ship that had been instrumental in liberating the island from the French during the Napoleonic wars. (Or seizing the island for the British, depending on your loyalties) Cavendish commonly kept the windows open because the mountainous arms of the bay usually funneled a refreshing breeze across the harbor and into his office.

Outside was noisy by day – cars and tour coaches and surrey buses passed in greater quantities than the road was ever designed for, and buildings crowded too close to the water to make room for expanding it. They honked at each other frequently and joining the chorus most days were throngs of tourists milling about. People chatting can be cacophonous when they number in their thousands. Days when cruise ships called were the busiest, with massive liners tying up at the pier or dropping anchor in the bay and sending tourists ashore in 2,500 person lots. His daughter, who kept pace with cruise ship construction told him the bigger ships would soon be bringing twice that many per ship. Most of the people, nearly all of them, were on holiday having a lovely time. A few nasty pieces of work like Ross Buchanan were inevitably and unavoidably scattered among them.

Cavendish knew the other three private detectives on the island. They had drinks and played pool at the bar once a month. They helped each other out from time to time. He considered ringing them up to warn them about Buchanan, but then thought better of it. He could afford to turn away a job but maybe they couldn't. Far be it from him to sit in judgment of their client lists.

He also thought about checking his email, but now that Buchanan was gone, he found the man loitering in his thoughts. The man was angry, upset and felt backed into a corner. He felt wronged, and probably vengeful. He was determined not to pay. He could easily find himself doing something really, really stupid in his quest to extricate himself from the mess he had concocted. Cavendish had alerted him that he would be paying attention for any news of violence against the people that blackmailed him, but would that be enough to discourage him?

Cavendish drew most of his business from referrals – with the help of another British ex-pat, one who was a lawyer, Cavendish had established a little network of law firms, mostly specializing in divorce, that referred him business. It was not a huge business, but it was enough, and it liberated him from the need to take on people like Buchanan as a client. But having met Buchanan and sending him out into the world, Cavendish was feeling concerned about the fallout should he find the girl. Perhaps he shouldn't have stood on his high horse and, instead, accepted him as a client for the singular purpose of keeping him out of trouble. Instead, knowing the man was a powder keg, Cavendish had struck a match and then shown him the door.

Cavendish stood up with a sigh of surrender and left his office, locking it behind him. He would try to find the girl and the man who had made blackmailing the nastier tourists into a going concern. Not to bring them to justice – he wasn't a police officer anymore - but to warn them they may have poked a bear.

The stairs leading down from his second-floor office opened behind the duty-free jewelry store, on the side of the building facing away from Obstinate Bay. This back street was cramped and narrow - more of an alley - and dating back to the 1700s. Aside from Front Street, many of the streets in the old part of Port Rose were ill-suited to twentieth century life. They were too small for trucks and there was an absolute dearth of parking. When delivery vans stopped to unload they left barely enough room for smart cars and bicycles to pass. Cavendish kept his car three blocks away, but he wasn't going to need it right now. If he was going to find the blackmailers and warn them, he had two leads. Buchanan had provided the address of the rooming house where he had been videoed with the girl, and the location of the rum bar where she had picked him up. Both were only a few blocks from his office. He wasn't sure what he would find but they were the only leads for him to follow.

It was eleven o'clock in the morning, but the air was already hot and humid and thick, and he could feel his shirt clinging to his torso. His attire today, as on most days, was simple: polo shirt, linen slacks, and boat shoes.

Unlike many people who came to the island from other places, it was not a quest for paradise or a need to escape an oppressive existence that brought him here. As a place to live, he was more ambivalent about St. Lazarus. He was not immune to the island's beauty and he loved the warmth of both climate and people, but he also missed the life he had enjoyed in London. Mostly, he missed his career in the Met, and thinking about the life that might have been often tinged his spirit with melancholy. Moving to St. Lazarus had always been part of the plans he and Elizabeth had made, but it was supposed to come later, much later, in retirement, and they were meant to be here together.

But Cavendish did not regret resigning from the Metropolitan Police. It had been the right choice, as was moving to St. Lazarus. It was just that he had once imagined himself as a detective-superintendent solving high profile murders, and would never in a million years have expected to retire as a detective-inspector and wind up on a small island, even one that was a tropical paradise, as a two-bit gumshoe. He felt self-righteous about exposing infidelities, but it was a long fall from working homicide investigations as an apprentice to the greats. Maybe his self-righteousness came from a desire to feel this work had some semblance of the importance he felt when doing policework. He had reached the address where Buchanan was blackmailed.

The main floor of the building was occupied with shops, though less chic than the ones at or near the main drag. Some t-shirt and souvenir shops, a pharmacist that catered to the local community, a news agent. He walked around the building until he found the inevitable door that opened onto a staircase that led to the rooms upstairs. At the foot of the stairs was a small lobby with mailboxes, a wastebasket and a table with a plant struggling for life. There was no one on the stairs and as he ascended, he caught the ghosts of normal life in the air – a TV turned up too loud, a baby crying, somebody dropping something in their kitchen.

At the top of the stairs a hallway led left and right. He turned right and as he looked at the numbers on the doors to track his progress, he made note of the general disrepair. The wall paint flaked, the air hung heavy and muggy around him and the lighting was sparse. A small window at each end of the hall and the glow coming up the stairs from the entry offered the only glimpses of sunshine.

Finding the room he was looking for, he paused and listened carefully. He heard no sounds from within. He then figured to himself *"What the hell?"* and knocked loudly. Still no sounds from within. He knocked again, to be sure. But even if they were here, would they answer the door when a stranger knocked?

He looked over his shoulder to confirm the hall was still empty. No one came out of their rooms. No one seemed to be coming up the stairs. Then he evaluated the doorknob and the lock. You needed a key for both the knob and the deadbolt. The latch would be easy enough to pick, but picking a deadbolt could be a pain – and this one was much younger than the building, still relatively shiny looking, even though it looked like a straight forward pin-and-tumbler cylinder lock. He looked around again.

"Really, Archie," he told himself, *"In the time you are spending thinking about this, you could be in there already."*

He unzipped the little pouch on his belt. This was just one of the items he carried. He usually wore his polo shirts loose and outside his slacks so no one could see the items he carried on his belt: Lock picks, a small four-inch Maglite flashlight, his mobile phone, a Swiss army knife. Tools of his trade. He squatted to his knees as he checked the clock.

He took the thin tension wrench from the lockpick kit and slipped it into the lock and turned it like a key. Expert lock pickers would pop in a pick and start lifting the pins until the lock yielded. Cavendish was no expert, so his next tool was a wide tipped one that he used to "rake" the pins. He inserted it all the way and then yanked it out. In theory, this would bounce many of the pins up, much like the key would displace them when pushed into a lock. As he pulled out the rake, he turned the tension wrench some more to turn the plug, the center piece of the lock assembly in the lock. A key pushes up some pins and not others, like entering the right combination on a keypad so that the lock can be opened. Cavendish was not surprised the lock did not give immediately. Raking is quick but it doesn't always move all the pins enough to line them up properly on the first attempt.

He looked quickly left and right, feeling sweat bead on his forehead in the hallway's stifling air. This was not an activity that came naturally to his law-abiding nature. He selected another pick, a thinner one this time, and eased it into the lock to try and move the remaining pins. It sounded easy, but locksmiths and thieves spent an eternity mastering this skill. You couldn't really see what you were doing so you had to concentrate and listen for a piece of metal so tiny it barely even had any weight to make a tiny noise as it slipped into position. It took concentration, just the right amount of pressure and a steady and delicate touch. If this were a place where people came and went every few minutes, he would be busted quickly. As it was, he was crouching in front of the door a good ten minutes and his legs were burning before he felt the last pin give and he was able to finish turning the wrench. He felt the bolt slide back with a reassuring clink. *"It's dogged as does it,"* his mentor always used to say.

Of course, that left the doorknob. He inserted the wrench. The process was the same, but it was often easier because the bolts in a doorknob were typically less heavy duty than in a deadbolt. Nevertheless, it was a good three minutes more before the knob was turning and he was able to get inside.

He scanned the room as he stepped over the threshold, wary of ambush but equally eager to escape risk of discovery in the hallway. They would certainly be expecting him after he spent half the morning playing with the lock! Reassured that no one was there to jump him, he closed the door behind him. The room was well lit from two windows with sheer curtains in them. The windows were open, but the curtains were still – the breeze from the bay didn't make its way around this alley. The room itself was still and hot, with a ceiling fan that was turned off right now. He flipped the switch on the wall. The fan struggled to move the stagnant air, but it was heavy work beyond the machine's abilities, and a rivulet of sweat snaked its way down Cavendish's back.

The room itself offered little to see. It was tiny, just a bedroom with no *en-suite* bathroom. There was a bed with a thin blanket, sheets, and pillows. Not overly large but probably when it was in use the occupants were in close proximity with each other. The walls were painted white and like the peeling hallways were in dire need of a fresh coat. There was a shabby five drawer bureau against one wall, the only piece of furniture aside from the bed. The ceiling had a mirror as did one wall, but there was no hanging wardrobe.

He started with the bureau. He opened the top drawer and found towels. He lifted the first one and found another and another. He counted ten deep and checked inside the folds of each one, but there were only towels and no secrets tucked within them.

The next drawer offered condoms and sex toys. Or rather, he assumed they were all sex toys. Some of the designs were self-evident but many of the objects were befuddling. He abandoned them because they weren't helping his cause. He was trying to find out who this girl and - her what? Partner? Pimp? Boyfriend? – was.

The next three drawers were all empty. He dropped to his hands and knees and looked under the bed. He retrieved his flashlight and stabbed around in the darkness and this time found a small reward – there was a photograph. It was within reach and he stood up looking at it. He recognized Ross Buchanan and next to him was a pretty young girl. Very young. His shorts were around his ankles and she was dressed in panties and the evidence of their recent activities was – apparent.

This picture must have ended up under the bed during the scuffle between Buchanan and her male accomplice. He wasn't sure he could walk around flashing this picture and asking people if they recognized the girl in question, but he pocketed it, nonetheless. It would help him identify her.

A walk around the bed to the windows yielded nothing helpful and he thought about the mirror. From what Buchanan had told him and from the angle the photograph was taken, that must be where the cameras were. The mirror was on the shared wall with the adjacent room. He contemplated picking the lock and investigating that room, too. He felt a little more comfortable breaking into the second room because if he heard anyone approaching, he could duck back into the first room. He went into the hall and crouched at the next door. It took him a few minutes, but again his work was undisturbed, except for a mother yelling at a child for some unclearly articulated transgression, and he was soon able to open the door and step inside.

Of course, he had so carefully considered his escape plan back into the first rom that he did not take other precautions, like listening first to see if there was anybody inside. Now he was slipping into this room before he could be seen. The door hinged at the right and he was looking to the left as he stepped in, glancing hurriedly to right and left to validate that he was alone in this second room. He was fully in the room when the man standing behind the door gave it an almighty kick and it slammed against him, knocking him sideways.

He knew it was a man because as he spun to respond the man was coming towards him, lifting a rattan chair high and looking intent upon smashing it down on Cavendish's head. There was nothing for it. The door was closed now, and the path was clear. There was no time to try to talk and de-escalate the situation. Cavendish dropped his head low and charged into his assailant, throwing his knee into the man's groin. The attacker had too much momentum to dodge and as Cavendish's knee connected with its target, the man doubled forward.

Now close, Cavendish was able to put a hand under each arm – they were raised to hold the chair in striking position – and swing the man past him. The chair didn't look heavy, but it was an awkward and ungainly shape and it threw the man's balance off. He fell in a heap on the floor and the chair came down on top of him. He pulled his knees up to his abdomen, clutched his privates in pain but was struggling bravely to regain his feet. He had fallen against the wall shared with the first room and a table with computers and cameras pointed toward the wall stood against it. Cavendish felt a little relieved that he hadn't mistakenly tackled an innocent tenant defending his home. The man put a hand on the table to pull himself up.

Cavendish tried to wave him off. "We can fight, or we can talk. I just want to talk."

The man paused his ascent and eyed Cavendish suspiciously through a curtain of dreadlocks. Clearly, having broken in, Cavendish was on the low moral ground. But Cavendish guessed that within the world this man orbited, ethics were measured somewhat differently.

"Who are you?" the man demanded. "What are you doing here?"

"Looking for you. And the young lady you work with" replied Cavendish, sizing up this room. No bed, a couple of chairs, the table that was made into a workspace. As he looked over the table laden with equipment and saw the monitors, he realized they were recording.

Surprise, Archie. You were just on candid camera. "You saw me in there?"

The man on the floor nodded. "But I don't remember you."

"I'm not a former customer. I'm actually here to warn you about a former customer."

"Why would you do that?"

"I'm not big on standing by and letting people get hurt,"

13

replied Cavendish. He was also a former cop. He wished he could call the police and turn this over to them. But he had broken in, and although the computers and recording equipment looked shady, there was no proof of wrongdoing. And who knew if the computers themselves held proof. Even if they had videos, there was only a crime if it could be proven the videos were being used to extort money. "One of your former customers tried to hire me to find you – although he could have done it himself pretty easily. I guess he didn't expect you to hang out here on a regular basis." A thought occurred to him. He reached for his mobile phone – man-on-the-floor flinched, and Cavendish rolled his eyes.

"It's a phone."

He made three brief phone calls to the island's other private investigators. Mr. Buchanan hadn't called any of them. The man, perhaps too confused to pick a fresh course of attack, waited on the floor almost patiently, as if waiting to see what happened next.

"Okay, Spielberg," Cavendish began as he pocketed the phone. "If you're here you were expecting the girl to bring someone up. Do you work with just one girl or do you have a stable?"

"What are you, man? A cop?"

"A private detective that's going to start kicking you if you don't stop answering my questions with questions. I just want to make sure you and the girl are on your guard. One girl or a group?"

"One girl, man. Just one. She's the boss."

"I'm sure she is," it seemed unlikely a girl would voluntarily run a scam like this, but he had seen stranger. "How does she pull blokes up here? Where does she go looking?"

"A few places, man. A few places. Can I get up now?"

Cavendish felt their relationship must have reached some level of trust if the man was asking permission.

He feared that Buchanan would retrace the steps of his own indiscretion. Would he try and go to wherever the girl picked him up, or would he come back here and wait for her?

Where would he have the best chance to intercept him? Cavendish dismissed this line of reasoning. He wasn't trying to intercept Buchanan; he was just trying to give the girl fair warning that she may have trodden in a wasp's nest.

"You can get up if you help me find her," decided Cavendish. "What's your name?"

"My name is Tyree. And I'm not taking you to her, man. I don't know what kind of psycho craziness you're planning for her," Tyree pulled his arms around his chest resolutely, bracing for the blows. "And even if you're on the level, she'd kill me for taking you to her."

"Spielberg, I found you here. You think I can't find her, given time? You two really pissed some guy off yesterday and he's looking for you. This guy." He jabbed the picture he had found in the other room towards Tyree's face. Tyree squinted, and then nodded with recognition.

"Yeah, he got a little crazy." Worry furrowed his brow. "How do I know he ain't who you're working for?"

"You don't. But there's an old saying I'm sure your mother used a hundred times. We can do this the easy way – you can give me the benefit of the doubt. Or we can do it the hard way, and you don't. I'm on my own time here and I am trying to do you a favour. And wherever she is, it's a public place. You rather I meet her there, or hunker down with you and meet her here – where there's a lot of privacy? If you're worried about her safety, better we find her in a public place, no?"

CHAPTER TWO

Tyree committed only to introduce Cavendish to one of the haunts where the girl trolled for men. He had steadfastly refused to reveal her name and he was mum on any personal information about her. What she wanted to share with Cavendish was down to her, but Tyree was not going to make any decisions about trusting Cavendish. Perhaps Buchanan was honest about the girl being the leader, he seemed more afraid of her than protective.

As they headed into the thickening crowds near Front Street, Cavendish expected Tyree to bolt. It would not be difficult to evaporate within the crowd, and Tyree did not strike him as someone bright enough to realize that such a move would only postpone the inevitable since Cavendish knew where their little nest was, and the money they had doubtless invested in it would make it a difficult place to abandon quickly. Maybe Tyree was brighter than he looked, maybe he was just curious about Cavendish's agenda, or maybe he took him at his word that he was acting in the best interests of the girl - but he didn't make a break for it. He led the way to Front Street and turned left. Shops were packed densely; their sidewalk displays of t-shirts and tchotchkes and postcards seeming to spill one into another. Many stores enhanced their garish signage with assurances that no better bargains could be found elsewhere; often with an employee charged with luring tourists into the store with enticements like a free gem. A free t-shirt. A free piece of rum cake.

He and Tyree stuck out like sore thumbs because among all the milling people, they were the only two moving with purpose, the only two not strolling along with the mixture of uncertainty and curiosity that propels tourists haphazardly through streets in strange lands around the world. Many of them were Caucasian and already suffering from overexposure to the sun or hiding from the glare under hats with ridiculous brims. Often in pairs, often with one grabbing the arm of their mate to point something exciting out to them. Holidaymakers, happily making the most of brief respites from lives and jobs that were probably boring and oppressive. Cavendish felt a twinge of jealousy but shrugged it aside and kept his focus on Tyree.

Tyree grabbed him by the elbow and pointed to a liquor store that promised free rum tastings. "A lot of women dump their husbands there when they go shopping and the men get drunk on the free shots. She goes there a lot."

"Lead on, MacDuff."

Tyree looked at him quizzically. "My name's Tyree."

"Well, lead on Tyree, then," Cavendish replied impatiently. An attractive young woman was at the door ushering them inside. Inside were several tables, half-moon shaped. In fact, judging from the height Cavendish imagined they began life having blackjack dealt on them. In the dealer's place at each table was a man or woman with an array of bottles and stacks of plastic thimble-sized shot glasses fanned out before them. Across from these bartenders, tourists sat down to swig the rum of this island and its neighbours. The tasters were mostly in couples or groups of friends, seemingly having a great time while the servers made a stoic impression of people having just as much fun as the people that were spending money here, not earning it. They laughed with the tourists; but laughed a little too hard and glanced at their watches a little too often. Several tables also had solitary men at them. Not all these men would be willing targets for the girl, but they would be her fishing grounds, where she would troll with her bait. Cavendish was surprised she could get in here. The store owners were usually adept at keeping locals out.

Tyree was looking around. When his eyes stopped, Cavendish followed his gaze and found the girl. She wore a sun-visor that had the logo of one of the cruise lines emblazoned across her brow, and a big straw purse that only tourists normally wear. She looked like a high school girl on summer vacation, and Cavendish understood how she could get in here.

Cavendish eyed Tyree warily; still concerned that he would make this task more tiresome by doing something unnecessary and stupid. He hadn't tried to run, but he could try to warn the girl and spook her, so Cavendish strode towards her briskly, leaving Tyree in his wake. As he hoped, someone with a nametag was already swooping towards Tyree because he did not look like a schoolgirl on vacation.

The girl was standing at the elbow of a middle-aged man, asking his opinion of whatever he had just drunk. She laughed at something the man said and placed her hand on his arm. The man glanced down at her hand and up at her face, and her smiled widened promisingly. His eyes widened and Cavendish could almost imagine the mark's heart rate accelerating and almost laughed aloud at the perpetual gullibility of the male of the species.

Cavendish caught her looking at him out of the corner of her eye, so he smiled in what he hoped was non-threatening way and edged up next to her. He could sense her guard rising but she stood her ground and looked him up and down. He felt she was sizing him up and he knew immediately that between herself and Tyree, she was the thinker.

"I'm terribly sorry to bother you, but I really need to speak with you for a few minutes. I have your friend with me."

Her look of curiosity dissolved into suspicion when she realized Cavendish was with Tyree. Cavendish didn't want her to run from him, so he said in a low voice: "I'm not here to cause you any aggravation. I just need a word. Then you can go about your business."

She patted the man at the table on the arm and promised she would see him later. He toasted her good naturedly with his glass as the girl stepped away from him and moved towards the door. Cavendish followed closely, still cautious that she could be mapping out her escape.

"An angry man tried to hire me today. I didn't take the job, but I thought I ought to warn you," he explained.

"Why don't we start with exactly who you are?" she demanded as they emerged onto the sidewalk. Tyree joined them and was about to say something to her when she withered his words with a glance full of daggers.

Cavendish now believed she was not just the smarter of the two but also the power holder in whatever twisted arrangement they had.

"Archie Cavendish. I'm a private detective. One of your victims – "

"What do you mean by one of my 'victims'?" she demanded with sharpened innocence.

"I've been to your apartment-cum-movie studio. You blackmail married men and one of them wants to try to find you and I suspect he may cause you some harm if he does. He is stupid, but you aren't hard to find. His name is Ross Buchanan. You met him yesterday. This man." He produced the picture of her and Buchanan, holding it so that she could see it but passersby could not.

After standing frostily for a minute, possible reactions and tactics seeming to scroll behind her eyes, she cracked a smile, and hooked one ankle behind the other coquettishly. "Ah, you saved a picture of me in all my glory. You got a dream of making it with a local girl while you're in the islands, mistah?"

Suddenly, Cavendish felt impatient. "You're playing with fire little girl. One of these guys is going to kill you one of these days. This guy is angry and he's looking for you. He may hire someone else or he may come looking himself. Angry and stupid are one of the worst combinations."

She waved her hand dismissively. "He'll be gone home

in a few days."

"That still gives him a few days. You're not exactly hard to track down. It took me a whopping hour to find you," Cavendish snapped back.

"Yeah, but you had a guide," she said, the daggers in her eyes were pointing at Tyree again. Tyree looked down at the street, then rallied himself to meet her gaze

"Buchanan did go a bit crazy," Tyree reminded her guardedly. For Cavendish's benefit he added: "Usually the guys are scared. In shock. This guy flew at me and we fought."

"So, we stay away from the studio a few days. He goes home. It blows over. Mistah, I'm more worried about you knowing about the studio," she said pointedly. "What do you want from me?"

"I'm not a cop. But one day somebody is going to go to the cops or go after you and get you. You are playing with fire and one of these guys is going to get you for it," Cavendish warned. "I am just trying to warn you, so you rethink your career choices before things get out of your control."

It was hard to reconcile this girl in front of him with the porn star in the photo. She looked fresh and innocent and ready to run to class or lean off her Daddy's arm and implore him to buy her some trinket. Her eyes were quick, intelligent, and fearless. She did not react to Cavendish impulsively or recklessly – she seemed strategic and measured. She did not look like a girl who would use her body to blackmail married tourists. It always saddened him to see a girl taking a path like this, but most of the young women he'd encountered in similar circumstances were fragile and broken, not proud and defiant. This girl made him both grateful that his Sophie was not on that path and fearful of the unexpected turns life could take that might send her down a similarly dark road.

"What are we gonna do?" Tyree asked her. He was looking back and forth between Cavendish and the girl uncertainly.

"Not discuss this in front of Dad the detective, for starters," she chastised him.

"How old are you?" Cavendish asked her.

Now it was her turn to be impatient. "Okay. You warned me. Thank you. Doesn't that mean you're done now? Don't you have murderers to catch or something?"

Cavendish smiled despite of himself. "Only TV detectives solve murders. My life is about catching cheating spouses, mostly."

She softened, but just very slightly. "Then we move in the same circles. But seriously, thank you, you warned me, but there's nothing else for you and me to talk about. Leave me alone, okay? And if you are on the up and up about not getting into my business, thank you and I wish you a good life."

She turned around, clipping him with her big old straw purse as she started heading away through the crowd. Tyree stood a moment, looking at Cavendish and perhaps wondering if he was released or not. Cavendish motioned with his thumb. "Go. I'm done with you. You held up your part of the deal and helped me find her. Just watch her back."

Tyree headed into the crowd without a word or even a nod of acknowledgement. Cavendish watched their receding heads moving purposefully away like fish moving through a sea of other moving heads. The heads of the tourists seemed to move around in random directions – except for the girl, Tyree, and a third head that Cavendish now realized was following the first two.

Cavendish mumbled a curse to himself. He was reasonably confident no one had followed them from the apartment, but if this bar was a normal pick up point then Buchanan may have been trolling the area looking for the girl. And he wasn't a hundred percent sure it was Buchanan under that baseball cap that seemed to be part of the uniform of the American male – but he caught a glimpse of fair hair on the back of his head and a sunburned neck which were factors this man had in common with Buchanan. And even if it wasn't Buchanan, the person most likely to be shadowing Tyree and the girl would be a vengeful victim. If this person was the police, they wouldn't need to follow the pair. They could just go straight to the apartment and wait. Someone intercepting them at the bar didn't have time to wait or lacked the patience. Cavendish did not stop to think about becoming the caboose in the strange little train snaking its way through an oblivious sea of happy people, because he really had no choice.

This was exactly the opposite of the behavior he should be exhibiting – in opposition with a big chunk of the motives and concerns that led him to abandon London and bring his daughter Sophie here. And in any other day and with any other people he might not have felt this compulsion to follow. But there was something so at odds in who this girl was, her outward appearance and what she was doing. She had none of the hard-edged roughness of the London prostitutes he had known; none of the skittishness of the damaged girls that had wound up trading their bodies for food and rent money. No signs that drugs were ravaging her person – she was in every external way a girl that could have been his daughter's classmate.

Maybe that was why he felt compelled to follow her. Maybe not so much concern for her but curiosity about how she came to be in this place and circumstance, a fear that she took a wrong turn any girl could follow – even his daughter. Or maybe it was that basic quality of being a cop – or at least of being what he thought of as a good cop. The compulsion to intervene in the name of the law; to protect the vulnerable. Not that this girl seemed all that vulnerable, but he felt certain she was headed into trouble and she was probably short on allies to come to her aid.

The girl and Tyree went back to the apartment. That made sense, they would probably grab what they needed and then go somewhere to regroup and ponder their next move. Tyree opened the door that led to the stairs up to their rooms, holding it open for the girl who passed through, her hands and arms still gesticulating angrily. Tyree seemed to have been telling the truth when he said he was the employee of the girl and not her keeper, and whether or not she thought Cavendish was a threat, she was admonishing Tyree heatedly.

Tyree followed her inside and the door swung closed.

Buchanan sped up and raced to the door, looking left and right, exposing his profile to Cavendish, and removing the element of doubt about his identity.

What should Cavendish do now? Rush up and stop him from going inside. On what grounds?

The point was moot. Cavendish was still a good thirty paces behind him, and Buchanan was already through the door. Cavendish quickened his pace and stood outside the door, arrested by uncertainty about what move he should make next. If Buchanan had noticed Cavendish shadowing him, he could be lurking on the other side of the door. Cavendish had glibly ignored the possibility of someone waiting for him when he broke into the room where Tyree was hiding earlier, so he tried to be more strategic now. But the sun-burned American had seemed too focused on his prey to think much about the likelihood of being followed. Cavendish allowed enough time to pass to permit Buchanan to reach the top of the stairs, and then cautiously pulled open the door. The foyer was no wider than the staircase, which was helpful since it meant there were no hiding places for an ambush.

Moving on the balls of his feet to minimize the danger of squeaking steps, Cavendish went up the steps two at a time until he was near the top. He was tall, skinny, and still in reasonable shape, so the ascent didn't put him out of breath. By the time he was at the top of the stairs he no longer feared being ambushed because he could hear that Buchanan had found his quarry, and it sounded like he had caught up with them down the hall, outside the doors to the adjoining rooms. There was no yelling, but there was the thumping you would hear when people were struggling and bouncing against walls, and then he could hear Buchanan's angry voice erupting triumphantly.

As he reached the top of the stairs himself and turned right, he saw the three fighting in the doorway of the second apartment, the one with the recording equipment. There was less yelling than Cavendish would have expected. Tyree was sitting in a crumpled heap in the doorway gripping his belly. Buchanan had the girl's throat in his left hand, and he was

23

getting ready to clock her with his right, all the while profane vitriol blazing forth from his mouth. Cavendish started down the hallway at a run, assessing as he went. He saw that Buchanan was wearing brass knuckles. Quaint but, as Tyree would surely bear witness, effective. Buchanan's back was to Cavendish and his hand was flashing towards the side of girl's head.

Cavendish erased the gap quickly. Buchanan stood with a wide stance, his arm crossing in front of him as it connected with the girl's head just above the ear, slamming her into the wall next to the doorway and if Buchanan had not been holding her throat she might have crumpled to the floor.

Cavendish stopped about a leg's length shy of Buchanan and kicked up with his right foot. Buchanan started to turn his sunburned neck, belatedly aware of the threat. Cavendish's foot slammed into Buchanan's testicles and for a moment Cavendish thought Buchanan was going to lift off the floor. His grip on the girl was lost and she stopped herself from falling by clutching at the door jamb, while Cavendish put a hand on each of Buchanan's shoulders and flung him towards the right-hand wall. Buchanan was totally off balance from the blow to his nether regions and it was almost like he was throwing himself. He met the wall with his face and put his hands against it to hold himself up.

By now, Tyree had recovered himself and struggled to his feet. Not clear on the alliances and overlapping goals he and Cavendish might share at this moment, he threw a punch.

Tyree was hardly on full power, so Cavendish deflected the blow easily with his left arm and shot a perfunctory right jab at Tyree's nose which sent him back to the floor in short order.

Cavendish looked at Buchanan whose head sagged face-first into the wall and was trying to catch his breath. The girl faced Cavendish, wary, like a cornered cat, but not showing signs of any impending violence. Her eyes were wide and blood shot and she looked dazed. Blood poured from her ear and a nasty laceration in the side of her head where the brass knuckles had smashed into it.

Cavendish took a step back so that he was no longer at

the heart of the triangular formation of people who would like a piece of him, and reached for his mobile phone, thumbing the speed dial for the police before these three had a chance to gather their wits and decide he was a common enemy.

CHAPTER THREE

The Central Town Square around which Port Rose grew was bounded by Front Street and the Bay on the seaward side. The bay opened toward the south. If you turned your back to the bay, you looked across the grass common at Government House, where the legislative chamber met, and the bureaucrats administered the island's affairs. Well, they actually administered the affairs of two islands. The smaller was called Laconia but collectively the pair were referred to as St. Lazarus, after this, the main island. To the left of the square were buildings once used by government administration in years gone by, but the government had burst their seams and now lived in a bland 1960s office building behind Government House. They also housed the island's solitary Starbucks, a place of frequent repose and replenishment for Cavendish.

However, it was the building to the right of the square that Cavendish and his little parcel of bleeding people were conveyed by the constables. (To the right if one still had their back turned to the bay) This building housed the police station and the short-term jail.

Cavendish had a relationship with several officers of the St. Lazarus Police Department, a positive relationship. He was an ex-copper himself and not the sort of detective to think an adversarial relationship with police officers was the preferred one. Besides, his experience with the St. Lazarus Police had shown them to be a highly competent and professional constabulary.

Specializing in busting unfaithful spouses sometimes led to unpleasant confrontations with the couples involved and being in good with the police meant his word was usually accepted and he made it home in time for dinner. This suited him.

That's why Tyree and Buchanan had both been cuffed, while Cavendish had not. When the police arrived at the apartment house, Buchanan had found his tongue, his lungs and his vocabulary and was trying to charge Cavendish with assault. Clutching his nose self-consciously, Tyree seemed to see merit in this strategy and made similar charges. It was two voices against one, but Cavendish's carried greater weight with the arresting officers whose attitudes towards Cavendish were more along the lines of "What have you gotten yourself into this time?"

Cavendish noticed with interest that the girl did not yell or participate in the cross current of accusations. She stood quietly, letting an EMT attend her head but otherwise content to wait out the storm of yelling from the two men. Biding her time and not taking precipitate action. For his own part, Cavendish did not engage in the shouting match either. He trusted the police would ask him his side of the story in good order, and since he was being treated with a degree of professional courtesy (and not handcuffed) he was content to let the Police do their jobs.

He explained everything that had happened that day. From Buchanan's visit to the office in the morning to the kick he gave him up the bollocks. The only thing he omitted was how he had gained admittance to the apartment by picking the lock. And the officers, led by Hardy Swain, a towering, ebony man built like three oak barrels stacked one atop the other and who could probably carry Cavendish under one arm and a medium sized bull under the other, refrained from asking him how he'd gotten into the apartment. Cavendish knew this wasn't because he was a sloppy officer.

Buchanan refused to confirm that he had tried to hire Cavendish, and instead tried to parlay an absurd story about chasing the girl and Tyree up because they had pickpocketed him. According to his story Cavendish was the third member of the gang. When challenged on this point because his wallet was in his pocket, he asserted with a solemn straight face that Cavendish had restored the wallet to his pocket in a bid to make him appear a liar before the police. Cavendish could only assume Buchanan was desperately trying to avoid the word of his transgression spreading as far as his wife and thought there might be a way to nip his potential ruin in the bud.

The studio set up in the apartment had excited great interest from Swain, Jenny Singh (his partner – Cavendish wondered if the Duty Sergeant found it amusing to assign the department's largest and smallest officers to work together) and the other pair of officers that had answered Cavendish's summons. They keenly studied the two-room set up for performance and recording, took extensive photographs and made many notes.

The girl's eyes fell to the floor as the studio was explored. Not in shame or submission, she still stood straight backed and defiant, but she seemed resigned that all the cards were on the table and chips were now falling where they may. Her calm demeanor was an intriguing contrast to the hostile testosterone being vented by the two men. Without resignation or embarrassment, she was simply waiting to get on with things. What next scheme for revenue making did she have percolating under her attractive but wicked little brow?

Police-Constable Swain looked like a disappointed father. Like Cavendish, he had a daughter, so maybe he was seeing the ghosts of his darker fears reflected in this young girl.

"You have identification?" he had asked her.

"I never carry any when I am working." She explained. "My purse is in that room. In the nightstand." She pointed at the recording room. Police-Constable Jenny Singh, barely an adult herself, went to retrieve it.

"Will you tell us your name before I look, or are you going to be difficult all along the road?" asked Swain.

"Why are you treating me like a suspect? I am the victim here. We both are. This man assaulted us for no reason and this – this kind gentleman came to help us." At least she was trying to pull Cavendish from under the bus where both Tyree and Buchanan were busy throwing him. He wasn't sure if she had finally recognized him as a potential ally, or if she was just trying to sort the cards she had been dealt in order to bolster the strength of her hand.

"This man accused you of one crime," said Swain. "Said you took his wallet. This man here," he indicated Cavendish, "says you might have been blackmailing the other one, but that this one," he gestured at Buchanan dismissively, "might have been planning you physical harm. I don't know what's going on, but there needs to be some unraveling done. This little movie studio – not illegal by itself, I guess, would be a good set-up for blackmail. We need to get you all down to the station and try to get this sorted –" Singh handed him the girl's i.d. Swain held it at arm's length and squinted – "Miss Amber – Geranabby? Is that how you say it?" He tried it with a hard g and emphasizing the first syllable.

"Yes." She looked at him shyly. "I don't know what this man" – she indicated Buchanan with a disdainful snort. "Told the nice gentleman." (That was how she cast Cavendish) "But he has been following me around for a couple days. I don't know what would have happened if these men weren't here to help me."

"That bitch is lying!" Buchanan barked. "You can't believe her, I'm an American!"

Swain handed the driver's license to Cavendish who read it with interest. Buchanan's eyes lit with indignation. "Why does he get to see the license? He's not a cop, he assaulted me!"

Cavendish looked at Amber's birth date on her license. "Take heart, Mr. Buchanan. At least you weren't committing statutory rape. She's of age." He looked at Amber. "You play a cold game with your prey."

Amber met his gaze and shrugged with feigned innocence. Her way of taking his remark as a compliment? "I don't know what you're talking about."

Thirty minutes later they were all at police headquarters, and two hours later Buchanan and Amber were each stewing in different interrogation rooms, Tyree was in a holding cell and Cavendish and Hardy Swain were drinking coffee together at one of the desks in the second story squad room.

Swain was shaking his head as he gave Cavendish a run down on the interrogations. "The girl started saying that she didn't know who this guy was, same as at the apartment. I showed her that picture you had, then she just didn't say anything. Kept asking if she was being charged with anything. And Buchanan won't say anything either, so the only crime I've got is a fight where you all have different stories." He shrugged apologetically. "What do you think I am most likely to do?"

"Kick us all out of here with a caution to behave better from now on," said Cavendish. Swain had seen the recording equipment, but everyone had a right to their hobby. The picture of Buchanan and Amber might prove Buchanan was cheating on his wife, but it did not prove blackmail. Probable cause to enter the room did not give the police the right to bag, tag and analyze its contents. And Buchanan didn't want to press charges for obvious reasons. Cavendish wondered if Buchanan's wife was missing him yet. "What about Tyree?"

"Well he's not the brains of the outfit. He's changing his story every time someone different talks to him - but so far it hasn't coincided with anybody else's story. I think he's just not very good at remembering the lies he told us five minutes ago."

"Do you know what hotel Buchanan is staying at?"

"He won't tell us. Jenny has a call into Customs; they'll have it on his declaration."

"You know what you could do," Cavendish offered carefully, sipping at his coffee. "You could offer Buchanan a choice. Come clean about what happened, and you let him walk home on his own. Or charge him with disorderly conduct and his wife can come pick him up."

"So, he got in a fight? Do you think he'll care about fighting with his wife about that if it buries the infidelity?"

"True. We could just show his wife the picture, though."

"Why?"

"What do you mean why? He was cheating on his wife."

"You're a private investigator, Archie, and you care about such things. But cheating is not a crime. And the girl turns out to be of age, so she is a consenting adult."

"She was blackmailing Buchanan. If they all go home tonight, she will continue blackmailing him. She will probably be pissed and increase the amount she is charging him – and he is not some stiff going quietly into the night after paying his bill. He came after her. He's probably going to be angrier too, so the stakes are higher for them both. He'll come after her again, and fiercer next time, too."

"Maybe if you hadn't gotten involved it would all be settled by now, eh?" suggested Swain. Cavendish just looked at him and Swain continued: "But neither of them wants to tell the truth. I can't charge them with assaulting each other. They'll get in front of the judge and start hurling these patently false statements at each other, and then you'll be called to the stand as a witness and participant in the fight and start spinning this grand tale of blackmail and no one will believe any of you. Waste of time and money. That room is set up like a private movie studio to record trysts, and I believe you, Archie, I'm not saying I don't – but nothing can be done about it today. I can hold Buchanan until the morning to let him cool off – but do you really want me letting his wife know what he's been up to and ratchet his fury at your girl Amber another five notches?"

Cavendish considered this and knew that Swain was right. Police involvement in this situation was a dead end unless Buchanan pressed charges, something he would never do. But he would certainly have another go at the girl as soon as he was released. As long as he felt threatened by her, and nothing had happened to defuse his fear.

"Can I speak with Amber?" asked Cavendish.

Swain rolled his eyes. "We give you a lot of consideration because you are an ex-cop…. But you are an EX-cop. And not even an island ex-cop…"

"I'm not trying to interview her as a witness. If you have no further interest, can't I visit her as a friend? I'm just going to see if she'll let Buchanan off the hook, so he won't go after her. Or to at least reduce the odds of him going after her."

"I'll tell you what. I'm giving her a ticket for disturbing the peace and sending her home. You," Swain jabbed at the air with his finger (one of his favorite gestures). Cavendish sat back in his chair despite himself – Swain jabbing a finger at you was like another man's fist coming at you.

"Drive her home. Talk to her if you want. If she charges you with rape because you're alone with her, it'll teach you a lesson for trying to be a bloody do-gooder. I'll hold Buchanan for a couple of hours and have a car take him to his hotel. Assuming the girl still lives at the address on her driver's license, she'll have plenty of security once she gets home. And I'll tell you when Buchanan leaves the island. Okay?"

≈

Amber settled warily into the passenger seat of Cavendish's car. It was a late model Dodge Charger and his daughter had laughed out loud when she saw it.

"Of course, you want an American cop car, Daddy!" it was white to help reflect the tropical heat and the interior was black. It was also leather – Cavendish had indulged in some of the luxury options. Swain had held Amber long enough for Cavendish to fetch it. Now Amber was settled into the passenger seat usually reserved for his daughter, clutching her knapsack purse to her chest protectively.

"Fasten your seatbelt," Cavendish instructed. She obeyed, all the while studying him. Wondering what his interest was? Why he cared about her? Maybe considering the possibility he just wanted to get her alone for less than honorable reasons?

"You're taking me home?" she sought to verify.

"Yes. 498 Swallow's Peak Drive. The Lance estate. Very

posh digs," Cavendish noted. The address was the second thing on the driver's license that had taken him aback. Swallow's Peak was a ribbon tracing a line that connected several of the swankier hilltop estates of the well to do. Lance was an island celebrity; his family had owned a rum distillery for over two hundred years. His lineage blended the enslaved with the colonizers and he was the nearest thing to home-grown royalty on St. Lazarus.

"My mother is a maid there," Amber explained. "We live in the servants' quarters." Her explanation carried more than a touch of disdain for her circumstances.

Cavendish put the car into drive and eased it between the police gates and onto the street. The parking at the station was in a courtyard that dated, like the rest of the building, to colonial times when horse and carts were the only traffic coming to and from the station. The gate was narrow, and it was a tricky turn getting onto the street. It was late afternoon, but the ships were still in harbor and the streets were a molasses of cars and people. Driving out of the town center was like walking through a muddy bog in flip flops. At least it meant they would have time to chat, if Amber was willing.

"Do you tell the men you're underage to make them more scared of you? So they'll pay more promptly?"

He watched her out of the corner of his eye. She had turned to look at him, still assessing. She was nineteen but could easily pass for three years younger. Her complexion was clear, a physique that was probably the envy of her girlfriends. Her dark eyes bright and intelligent. She looked like she could have everything going her way if she wanted. It struck Cavendish that many people who grow up in poor circumstances never think of school and a good job as a route to a better life. Much better to aim for being a supermodel or basketball star if your plans lay on the right side of the law, or drugs and prostitution if you were of a more criminal bent. And give up and assume your destiny is to live in the shadows if you can't latch on to one of those two dreams. What made them think their brains and effort couldn't pull them into a better world?

Amber was not acting like a victim. She was not

intimidated by her circumstances and there was nothing in her demeanor that signaled helplessness. Her reticence was the act of a smart girl in control of herself; waiting to see how things were going to play out. Cavendish recognized she was the brains and the fatted calf all in one package. But what would make her want to be with men in such a way, however much money she was able to extract?

"I'm not a cop," Cavendish reminded her. "Buchanan came looking to hire me to find you, and he seemed like a loose cannon. That's why I came to warn you."

"And led him right to me," Amber added pointedly.

"I don't think he was following me - I don't deny it's possible - But he was looking for you on his own. He doesn't control the money in his family and if you tell his wife, she could divorce him and cut him off. That's why he came after you. You could have told the police the truth and gotten some protection, but that's not how you wanted it to go. So now I'd encourage you to tell him he's off the hook."

"You're sure he's not your client? That's exactly what he would want me to do."

"I know you don't know me from a hole in the ground., but you saw for yourself he is a crazy bastard. He will come after you again. Even if you let him off the hook, he might still come after you, but at least there is a good chance he will back down if you do – he won't want to draw his wife's attention to what he did – what's the security like at your house?"

"Let me explain it to you so you can tell him the best way to get in, will I?" she shook her head. "Just take me home. I want a shower and to lay down. By myself. There is a guardhouse and security alarms, no one can get to me on the property. He'll be gone in a few days, I'm sure."

Cavendish shook his head to himself, contemplating the invincibility that young people always seemed to claim for their own with so much confidence. It never occurred to them how quickly fortune could turn against them – even though she had felt Buchanan's hand around her throat earlier. Even the evidence on her own face didn't convince her that Buchanan was a serious problem.

"Why do you do this?"

"Do what? I'm just minding my own business and –"

"Oh, stop it. I live here. I'm a private investigator. If you keep playing the games you're playing, our paths are bound to cross again and again. Cheating spouses are my primary type of case. We can dance around the truth the next ten years or until one of your 'clients' rips your guts out for blackmailing him. But sooner or later, I am going to learn more about you. Why don't you just tell me? I couldn't arrest you even if I wanted to. Anything you tell me you could retract later. Indulge me. Why do you do this?"

As they climbed out of the town and into the hills, he was able to pick up speed. She continued to stare at him curiously, pulling stray strands of her long, straightened hair away from her face. Her fingers probed through her hair, touching the injured side of her face. She seemed to reach a decision, and she turned her face towards the road in front of them and fixed her gaze through the windshield. Did she not want to face him as she explained?

"Guys'll pay you for all kinds of stuff. And it sure beats working. But this way I don't belong to some rich boyfriend that'll beat the crap out of me. And nobody holds power over me. What's mine is mine. That's it."

"That's it?"

"Why? You think I'm a whore? A slut?" She continued to stare at the road ahead. This was the first conversation they'd had since they met earlier today where she refrained from looking at him.

"Maybe I am. But in a couple of years I'll have enough money put by to live life the way I want to for a long time. I don't belong to any of those men. They belong to me. They're stupid, they're horny and they're lousy and I give them what they think they want, and they probably spend a long time regretting it afterwards. Maybe I am a whore. But I'm a whore with money." She scratched her good cheek pensively. "And you want to know something funny. I only get the bad guys. You'd be surprised how many guys won't take the bait. Almost makes me want to find their wives and tell them to count their blessings."

Cavendish chuckled despite himself. "I'm sure they'd appreciate that."

"As for the rest of them…" She didn't finish the thought aloud. She turned and looked at him, smoldering curiosity stealing back into her expression. "Why do you care what I do anyway? If you get paid finding cheating husbands, then I'm good for your business. Hell, we might be able to do business together."

"I have a daughter," he replied candidly. "And whenever I see a girl in your circumstances it makes me a little afraid."

"That your daughter will be a whore?"

Cavendish shook his head. "No. That she could get lost."

Amber laughed derisively. "I ain't lost, Mister. And I sure as hell don't need saving. I might be the only one that doesn't." She looked out her side window and took in the view of the harbor, now far below them and glimpsed through gaps in the trees as the road elbowed inland towards the summit of the spine of hills that split the island.

Cavendish tried again: "Amber, I can't make choices for you. But think about what I said about Buchanan. Get your friend Tyree to go to him and give him what you have on him and cut him loose. You don't want to take away what he has; he won't take it lying down. Trust me. I know his type. Reckless and stupid."

"Then why would I give him all my insurance? *That* would be reckless and stupid."

"At least stay away from your little movie studio apartment. Lie low. I'll let you know when he leaves the island. Would you do that at least?" persisted Cavendish.

She changed the subject. "So, you chase cheating spouses?"

Cavendish retrenched. "Will you at least lay low?"

Amber shrugged. "I don't know. But if you tell me when he leaves, that would be cool. You should slow down. It's not far and the gate is kind of hidden."

The road was a main one, but it was still narrow and windy with trees and dense vegetation crowding onto it aggressively from both sides. There was a narrow drive that broke a gap in the verdant wall and Cavendish tapped the brake and heaved the car onto the driveway. The asphalt yielded quickly to gravel that led between tall stone pillars. A heavy wrought iron gate with a large, intricate "L" welded into the design was open. Through the gate, the driveway climbed upwards and the trees abruptly gave way to a vast groomed lawn that Cavendish was surprised to see full of trucks.

They were cube trucks; most had their rear gates open and he could see different inventories inside. Metal scaffolding, cables, lights, stenciled equipment cases. Milling around and among them were people with communication headsets and technicians with fully laden utility belts. There was a trailer with several doors on its side – it looked like a mobile dressing room unit. Cavendish had not expected to drive Amber home to a film shoot. Most of the people out here were probably involved in initial set ups and teardowns. There were no cameras or rigged lights in immediate evidence, so the actual shooting must be taking place somewhere out of immediate view. As a young copper Cavendish had picked up extra shifts doing set security on film sets in London, so the tableau was familiar to him, but seemed out of place on the island. He was also struck by how the theme of movie production seemed to be running throughout his day.

The driveway climbed briefly about a hundred yards to a circular carriage-way styled driveway in front of the house which itself sat on the summit of the property. The house was more modest than one might expect for an island dynasty, but it was old and part of the family heritage and if the quotes Marvin Lance gave the papers could be trusted, he believed deeply in the heritage of his company, his family, and the old-world ethics that the well-to-do had obligations to their history and the community from which they drew their support. Not that the house was a tiny bungalow – it was two-stories tall with a broad traditional stance.

"Are they making a movie here or something?"

Amber didn't hear or didn't want to answer. "Turn right. I live down there."

A secondary drive, more of a track made by wheeled vehicles than a formal driveway, split almost secretively from the groomed, graveled carriage drive and slipped down the gentle slope to the right. Cavendish followed it as instructed. It wasn't a steep grade, just four or five degrees, and Cavendish could see three simple cottages nestled against the edge of the forest.

"How do you come to live here?" Cavendish wondered aloud.

"My Mom is a maid. While I am a cheap whore, she is a good moral woman – which means she cleans other people's disgusting toilets," her tone was not just mocking but vindictive. "I prefer being a whore. We both get other people's shit on us. I just get paid much better for it. Stop here."

CHAPTER FOUR

Cavendish's car rolled gently to the end of the track. Amber flung open her door and launched herself out of the car before it came to a complete halt. Cavendish took his time stopping, turning off the car and securing it, while using the opportunity to assess the three pretty cottages with their uniform coats of white paint and navy-blue trim. The grass was groomed as neatly down here as at the main house. Little tokens of customization hung from the gables or stood on the porches in the form of flowerpots and yard art. They were small but cozy looking. He wondered if he would get to meet Amber's mother and what he would say to her if he did.

Amber was reaching for the framed screen door of the middle cottage but before she grabbed it, it was flung open from within and slapped against the wall of the cottage. A young girl looking near his Sophie's age, maybe twelve or thirteen, burst excitedly onto the porch and then halted, looking from Amber to Cavendish and then back.

Her skin was a little darker than Amber but there was an obvious resemblance. Her eyes widened like saucers as she finished her assessment.

"Mom is going to kill you! He's *her* age! MOM!!!"

"Shut up stupid. He just drove me home. He's not a

date," Amber walked past the girl that Cavendish took to be her sister and opened the door.

Undeterred, the younger girl turned her back on Cavendish, grabbing Amber's arm and challenging her. "And why did he drive you home?"

Amber looked first at her sister and then Cavendish. "He thought I was lost. I think he likes to save things. Even when they don't need saving. But I appreciate the ride."

She went inside and the screen door bounced closed behind her. Cavendish stood uncertainly in front of his car, and Amber's sister stood halfway between him and the cottage.

"You're not Amber's boyfriend?" she wondered aloud, apparently dubious about her sister's word.

"No. I am old enough to be her father, don't you think?"

This didn't impress her. "Some of Amber's boyfriends are pretty old."

"Well I'm not a boyfriend," he reassured her. "Just a friend. What's your name?"

She seemed a little nervous now, after the initial rush of teasing her big sister had waned and she found herself alone with a strange man. She must have recently gotten home from school because she wore the yellow blouse and grey skirt that was the uniform of the St. Lazarus public schools. Like her sister's, her hair was straightened but it was scooped back into a ponytail bound with a yellow ribbon.

"My name's Mia."

"I'm Archer," he stepped towards her with an offered hand. "Archer Cavendish. My friends call me Archie."

She shook politely then, still suspicious, asked: "So how do you know my sister?"

Amber reappeared in the doorway. "Mia, get in here!"

Mia appeared reluctant to obey, but it was clear she was used to taking direction from her sister and less used to defying her. Discipline won out. "I have to go." She offered her hand again. "Nice meeting you."

"It was my pleasure."

Mia turned and disappeared inside. As the door closed, Cavendish saw Amber lurking in the doorway, still watching him.

He stood a beat or two longer there in the yard, feeling stupid and dissatisfied. Amber would heed no advice no matter how sound, and he feared for her. To be so cynical so early, to play with fire the way she did, it piled sadness on top of his concern.

But he was not her parent. He opened the door of his car and settled back into the seat. He again thought of meeting her mother and father but didn't know what good it would do. Being told by a man you'd never met that your daughter was hoeing it up in town to blackmail tourists with more money than sense was hardly a great conversation opener.

He was reaching for the ignition when he heard a woman's voice call out to him. He looked over his shoulder and saw a woman of about his age or a little older approaching from the main house.

"Excuse me!" she called again. Even at fifty feet distance, Cavendish could sense the protective growl of a mother stalking a potential threat. He got back out of the car and tried to look as non-threatening as possible, smiling with what he hoped was a pleasant approachability.

"Who are you? And why are you dropping off my daughter?" She was wearing a light grey maid's uniform and a dark scowl. She was a little out of breath and Cavendish could imagine her working in the main house, seeing, or being told that her daughter was being delivered by a tall man old enough to be her father. Broom or duster dropped where she stood and bustling herself outside to confront him and check on her daughter. Her complexion was slightly lighter than her daughters, but beyond that was basically an older and wearier version of Amber.

He offered his hand to shake. "My name is Archer Cavendish." He fished in his pocket with his left hand for one of his cards. "I'm a private investigator."

She wielded his hand for a cursory shake and then

snatched the business card suspiciously, matching the details on the card with the introduction he had offered. "What business do you have with my daughter?"

Confronted with an angry mother and harboring no way to prove what he knew and not wanting to throw the visual evidence in a mother's face, Cavendish came to the conclusion he must lie. Or at least, skirt some of the truth. Perhaps a lot of the truth. Amber's mother had the hands of a woman who had known hard work all her life, and suddenly Cavendish didn't want to be the one to disappoint her with the information about her daughter that he had.

"Your daughter was accosted by someone in town. I was nearby. I gave her a hand and brought her home."

She looked him up and down. Cavendish tried to look pleasant and approachable, mindful of his daughter's frequent laughing admonishment that when he tried to look pleasant, it often came across as creepy.

"Did she now? Got in some trouble and you came rescuing her? Then I'd best be giving you a cup of tea by way of saying thank you," she pointed towards the cottage. "Come in for a tea?"

"I'd be delighted!" He felt it was a command, not an invitation. This mother bear wanted to know what was going on with her cub.

"My name is Pamela, by the way," she led the way to the cottage and held open the screen door.

Cavendish stepped over the threshold. The multi-purpose room he entered was a living room, kitchen and dining room combined. The kitchen occupied one corner; a laminate surfaced table with vinyl chairs occupied the second. A love seat and two chairs took up the remainder of the space, with doors leading off the living area – presumably to the sleeping quarters. It was a crowded room, the size of a modest hotel room with a whole house worth of functions crammed in. But it was spotlessly clean and decorated with a simple but elegant taste. It was welcoming and comfortable without being overly personal. There was an older model TV but no books and no magazines.

Mia was sitting in one of the chairs. She was sitting properly and doing nothing, as if she had just been told to sit down and dutifully done so. Amber stood next to the chair, looking at him with hostility. Her hands were on the back of the chair, and she was flicking her thumbs against each other, the only tell that she might be nervous and evidence to Cavendish that her mother was in the dark about her activities.

He had already decided he would not tell the whole truth. Just lay some groundwork in the hope that Amber might find her way to sharing the truth on her own. He offered a pre-emptive explanation:

"I was just telling your mom about that guy that was hassling you. That drunk tourist."

He stood just inside the doorway and nudged the modified story forward. "I know you think you could have dealt with him, but I think it was lucky I was there all the same."

Amber seemed to tune in, but her tone was grudging. Like accepting him as an ally was a sign of weakness. "It could have gotten uglier, I guess."

"Did you call the police?" asked Amber's Mother. She seemed skeptical. Cavendish sensed an ongoing battle of wills between these two women. Each was proud and strong. Pamela gently probed the bandage on the side of Amber's face.

"He hit me but it doesn't hurt too much. There was no point calling the police, Mother. Mr. Cavendish scared him off,' she seemed to relax, drifted from the table to the living room area and settled herself into the small sofa with feline grace.

Pamela filled the kettle and put it on the little stove. She indicated the table. "Won't you sit down, Mr. Cavendish?"

"Thank you."

She put a teabag in the teapot and then took the chair opposite him. It seemed like she was accustomed to disbelieving her daughter and she looked like a woman measuring the truth that was being apportioned out before her.

Cavendish thought it might be worth steering away from the elephant in the room. "I noticed all those equipment trucks. Are they making a movie?"

Pamela shook her head. "A television program. I try to stay away from it all. Cables and annoying people all over the house, all full of their own importance. I do my work and I get out."

"What kind of TV show are they making?"

"You look like you have a couple of bruises there. You came to blows with this man?" Pamela wondered, not abandoning her concern about the bandage even though she now had her back to her daughter. Cavendish thought of how Amber had reacted to his intervention in her life methodically and strategically earlier that day and realized that the acorn had fallen very close to the tree.

"Well – one or two…"

"Amber, come here."

Cavendish noted that for all her worldliness outside the cottage, she darted to the table when summoned. Pamela looked at her daughter's face and reached up, turning it left and right by the chin. One of her eyes had a bit of a shiner.

"You're sure it wasn't one of your boyfriend's did that?"

"Yes, Mother. Bruno was the only one that ever hit me, and I haven't been with him in ages."

"So where were you at when this happened?"

"Just off Front Street in town," offered Cavendish. "He was a bit of a lout. I thought he might intend to try to take liberties with your daughter."

Pamela harrumphed. "My daughter may have encouraged him."

Amber offered no argument but cast her eyes at the floor for the first time Cavendish had seen. When the kettle started to whistle, she took over the tea making, which got her away from the table.

"And you're a private investigator?" Pamela was looking at him again, trying to put the puzzle together but Cavendish could tell she knew she wasn't being given all the pieces.

"That's right. Finding kids that ran away on school break, cheating spouses. That sort of thing," he explained blithely.

"But you aren't from here?"

"No England. London. Though I grew up in Bath. I came out here about a year ago."

"Tired of the clouds and rain?"

"Yes. Much nicer here."

"Milk and sugar?" asked Amber.

"Just sugar," said Cavendish. "Pamela, how long have you worked on the Lance estate?"

The Lance family went as far back in island history as paper and pen could record. Since the 1700s, they had farmed sugarcane and produced a popular and tasty rum that made them among the wealthiest families on St. Lazarus. Their product was not as ubiquitous as Bacardi, but it was well known among enthusiasts and to be found throughout the Caribbean and Eastern seaboard of the U.S. The current ruler of the family empire was working to expand the reach of his brand to the broader world. Cavendish himself enjoyed a glass of Lance and Coke to round out his day.

"Going on twenty years. It's a good job. Mr. Lance is fair. Fairer than most. Even lets the girls use the pool," said Pamela, taking the cup and saucer from her daughter's hands. Amber placed Cavendish's tea next. The cups were white with silver piping tracing the rim and a border of pink flowers. Pamela took a sip before continuing. The dainty cup was like a doll's cup in Pamela's work toughened grip. Pamela did not mention the presence or absence of Amber's father, but a plastic mat next to the door contained an assortment of shoes and flip flops. None of the shoes were styled or sized for a man.

"It's hard work but thanks to Mr. Lance the girls have never wanted," said Pamela. The words were philosophical, but her voice was not. Her eyes were on her tea, but Cavendish sensed her thoughts were on her daughter and this strange man that had brought her home. Cavendish knew some girls strayed from the straight and narrow because of negligent parents or absent ones. The order of this home and responsiveness of her daughters suggested Pamela Geranabby was neither.

"I'd better be going," Cavendish pushed his chair away from the table. If Pamela sensed a lie, then maybe she would probe more deeply once he had departed. He felt that he had done as much as he could do without exposing Amber's secrets, and he knew it would be better for both mother and daughter if those secrets were shared in private. "Thank you very much for the tea."

He shook hands with Pamela again, and was surprised that Mia sprung forward from the chair she'd been reclining in to bid him adieu also. "Goodbye Mr. Cavendish."

Amber did not offer her hand; she just said "thank you and goodbye" dourly.

Outside, it was pushing towards five o'clock and though the light was still full the dipping sun was painting the scattered cumulous with pink and orange hues. There were more people milling about in the grounds and equipment-laden trollies starting to make its way to the trucks. The workers generally wore shorts, t-shirts and hefty work belts laden with the tools of their trade. A group piled into a van that drove off, presumably ferrying them home or to a hotel where they were staying. One of the biggest trucks that couldn't turn around in the available space was backing its way down the narrow drive towards the gate, announcing its cautious progress with an incessant "beep, beep."

Cavendish got into his car and turned the key. He backed up as far as the main carriage drive and pointed the Charger at the gate, waiting for the reversing truck to get out onto the street and free up his own access to the gate. He glanced at his watch, wondering whether there would be time to stop in at the Barefoot Buccaneer for a quick libation on his way home. At the pace the lumbering truck was moving, he suspected not.

The road outside was not exactly wide and the turn in and out of the driveway was tight. The truck should back all the way onto the street, staying perpendicular to the gate, and then three-point its way into the direction it wanted to go. If the driver turned too soon when backing through the gate, he was liable to wedge himself in – the pillars were probably as old as the house and were meant for horse carriages, not juggernauts.

The driver did turn the wheel too soon and the truck started to angle awkwardly. It started scraping against the pillar on one side, the sound of metal grinding against stone with a shrill screech that made the nerves crawl. The driver kept easing backwards, as if the truck could force its way through if he didn't give up. The engine noise rose as the truck found it increasingly difficult to overcome the friction of the stone.

The driver stopped and tried to pull forward, but now was wedged between pillars. As it advanced, it became apparent it was also bending the metal gate against the other pillar. As the truck pulled forward there was just more grinding. The driver turned the wheels this way and that, shunting forward and back to free the truck but it seemed like every choice just pinioned the truck more snugly in place like a cork in a bottle. It probably wasn't helping the driver that the crew were now gathering around shouting varied words of encouragement and instruction at him. The poor guy was probably caught between realizing he'd made a mess of things and not knowing how to deal with the problem. Every suggestion getting thrown at him, he seemed to try. The net result seemed to be wedging the truck tighter and tighter between the pillars, effectively blocking the way out of the estate.

Cavendish propped his elbow on the door sill of his car and rested his head in his hand as the truck lurched forward with increasing diffidence. The grinding noises kept getting louder, like the strains of Ravel's Bolero. Scratching on one's nerves, building in intensity, but not seeming to go anywhere.

A crowd of non-film crew had joined the audience. Amber and her family had emerged from their cottage, a couple of house workers were out in the carriage drive. Nobody was telling the driver to just be still. Except for a squat little woman that suddenly trundled out of the main house like a pug.

"Stop it, man. What are you doing?" she yelled. The driver yelled something back and within seconds there was an energetic exchange of opinions and condemnations. Confronted with his sins, the driver instinctively defended himself by lunging to the offense and declaring all the reasons why it wasn't his fault he had ground his truck to a standstill while beginning to demolish the gate posts and gates.

Seeing the truck immobilized between the gates, Cavendish stopped wondering about the visit to the bar and instead telephoning his mother-in-law and telling her he wasn't going to make it for supper. The driver got out of the truck and the stocky little woman shook her fist at him. He leaned towards her and said something menacing, and then the film crew were swooping in from either side to prevent the incident from escalating to fisticuffs.

Cavendish had been in enough melées today, so he left the people to their own devices. He ambled towards the house. Maybe he could find someone who would call a tow truck or make the decision to let the truck finish ripping out the gates completely so the driveway would be unobstructed.

The gravel crunched under the soft souls of his boat shoes. There was a clutch of people standing in the portico of the house, and their attention shifted from the brouhaha at the gate to his approach. He smiled, again doing his best to appear affable. He wasn't sure how well it came off.

"Maybe someone should call a tow truck?" he suggested helpfully.

There were five people in the group; two of them were in uniforms similar to Pamela's. One of the remaining three was a woman who looked like she hoped the ground would open and swallow her up. She was a white woman, wearing a flowered dress and had long hair that he guessed was light to start with and further bleached by the tropical sun. Big-framed sunglasses dangled from her hand and she was regarding the gate with wide eyed horror. Unlike the two maids, she seemed not to register Cavendish's approach.

"Marvin will kill me," she muttered over and over. Applying the skills that made him a crackerjack detective and knowing that Marvin Lance was the current head of the little Lance empire, Cavendish deduced this was his wife Deirdre. He knew of her because you couldn't live on St. Lazarus and not know of her. Like Cavendish, she was an import to the island, but from Canada. Her shoulders were mottled with freckles multiplied by a cocktail of tropical sun and insufficient sun lotion. She was in the local paper a lot and never shy about it. He sensed she enjoyed her celebrity, even if it was limited to a small island most people outside of cruise liner passenger manifests had never even heard of.

"He'll kill me."

Would Marvin think she had been driving the truck? Or more likely, had her influence brought the film crews here. Standing at Deirdre's side was a tall, almost statuesque black woman dressed elegantly in a pale blue dress and holding a microphone pack in her hand. One of her hands was rested reassuringly on Deirdre's, but she was looking directly at Cavendish. The third person, a mousy man who had stood in her shadow now stepped forward protectively. "Mrs. Letourneaux does not give unsolicited interviews."

Cavendish guessed he was a man used to being listened to within the circles he normally moved, but he was not naturally authoritative. Maybe his relationship to Mrs. Letourneaux lent him some façade of authority. He was holding up his hand as if to guard against Cavendish's approach.

"I'm sure she doesn't. I'm not here to interview anyone, I just dropped someone off. I assure you, all I want to do now is leave."

Mrs. Letourneaux was the tall black woman, and she had a voice of her own. "That may be easier said than done Mister…?"

"Cavendish. Archer Cavendish."

She shook his hand, regarding him with interest. "You don't recognize me."

It seemed like a strange thing to say, and the mousy man ventured an explanation that struck Cavendish as both uninvited and irrelevant. "She's a psychic."

To which Cavendish responded. "She doesn't recognize me either. Does knowing that make me psychic?" he turned to shake hands with the mouse. "Or maybe it's just we've never met."

"She's the famous psychic, Martine Letourneaux," the mouse seemed irritated he had to explain her.

"And you are?" asked Cavendish.

"He is Hoyt Buxton, my agent," explained Martine.

"Nice to meet you Mr. Buxton," he released the mouse's hand, fearful that the brittle bones might snap if he shook too firmly.

"So, Mrs. Letourneaux," Cavendish jabbed a thumb at the truck in the gate good-humoredly. "Why didn't you warn the driver about that?"

Hoyt Buxton harrumphed, Mrs. Lance scowled, and Martine Letourneaux smiled tolerantly at his flippant skepticism. "It doesn't work like that."

Mrs. Deirdre Lance, who had been silent so far, was now joining the conversation. "I am Mrs. Lance. And I wonder what you are doing here."

"I dropped off Amber."

Mrs. Lance pursed her lips prudishly. "I see. I'll have to speak to her." Apparently, her fear of being killed by her husband had subsided, trumped by her annoyance that Amber was bringing strange men to the property. Cavendish decided to steer the conversation back to Deirdre's fear of death.

"Why did you say your husband will kill you?"

Panic flashed in her eyes. "He's in the study. I better go tell him, so he doesn't find out from someone else. He hated this whole idea!" She turned and fled.

Martine explained Deidre's anxiety. "Mr. Lance has been very polite, but I think he is accommodating us to indulge Mrs. Lance. She is a fan and our hostess" Martine had the ghost of a local accent, overlaid with inflections picked up elsewhere. Cavendish guessed she had been living off-island for many years.

"This is your television show they are making?" he speculated.

She nodded. "I am a psychic medium and clairvoyant."

"Her show is on the Living network in the United

States," explained Hoyt eagerly. "She's making a cycle of episodes bringing her back to her roots."

"I was a child here," said Martine, breezily delivering her self-biography like it was an advertisement to her show. "When I was nineteen, I went to the United States, and I haven't been back since. It is good to be back."

Cavendish didn't need to be psychic to recognize the first lie she had told him.

"Local girl done good. That must make for compelling television," Cavendish glanced at his watch and the gate. He really wished someone would call a tow truck. The argument seemed to have subsided and now twenty people were looking at the truck and the gate from different angles, as if a specific perspective might magically dislodge it.

"Oh My God!" The new voice boomed across the portico as Marvin Lance strode out, slapping his forehead in disbelief. Lance was tall, athletically built and dressed in slacks and shirt that were impeccably ironed with creases in all the right places. His features were a composite of his African and European heritage, and they were tightened in a grimace filled with fury. "These morons!"

Deirdre was carried along in his wake, white knuckling the sunglasses in her right hand.

"Where is that producer? You." Lance pointed at Hoyt. Hoyt, diminutive to begin with, shrank physically. He might be an authority on his home turf, but he withered in the face of someone who exuded power naturally. "Find that idiot producer. Tell her to get a tow truck and tell her I am going to give her a bill for the repairs." Buxton scurried away and Marvin Lance rounded on Cavendish. "Who is this?"

"He's a 'friend' of Amber," Deirdre sniped from the shadows.

"His name is Archer Cavendish. Mr. Cavendish, this is my gracious host, Marvin Lance," Martine exuded a state of patient grace. Cavendish couldn't tell if it was natural or manufactured.

Cavendish, weary of the arm shaking, offered his hand

to Marvin Lance with genuine pleasure. Psychics were a dime a dozen, but this man made his favorite rum and was truly a man of nobility and distinction! His professional demeanor fell aside and he was a fanboy for the moment: "Sir, I truly enjoy your rum and it's a pleasure to meet you."

"How are you a friend of Amber?" Lance asked skeptically.

"I drove her home. She had some trouble in town today."

Lance looked Cavendish up and down, and then at his Charger. "Your car?" Cavendish affirmed with a nod. For some reason, the Charger seemed to improve Lance's take on him. "What kind of trouble?"

"She was accosted. Some drunk tourist got a little out of hand," explained Cavendish. "I was just there to lend a hand."

"I see."

Cavendish sensed this wasn't the first trouble Amber had gotten into, and that Lance knew something of the kind of trouble she tended to attract.

Lance looked around.

"Well, as soon as that idiot producer turns up, we can get that truck moved. In the meantime, I need a drink. You want one Cavendish? You can tell me more about how you just happened to meet Amber when she was being 'accosted.'" He turned scornfully towards Martine Letourneaux. "Unless you can just read his mind and tell me?"

Cavendish felt flattered that Lance made the same joke that he had.

"Honey, please!" Deirdre was cowed but still felt the need to defend Martine's honor.

Martine was non-plussed, probably well-accustomed to the ways of unbelievers. Con-artists had to be patient to woo their victims into the proper state of gullibility, so her demeanor was exactly what Cavendish expected. He had no doubt that she was a confidence trickster.

"I have tried to explain to Mr. Lance that it doesn't work that way."

"Those gates have stood there since 1878," growled Marvin Lance, looking at the truck wedged between the ravaged stone.

"I need a drink."

CHAPTER FIVE

The party circled the outside of the house, led by a crabby Marvin Lance. Cavendish knew from his bio that his lineage was interwoven with African, Spanish, British and Danish blood. (An ancestral spouse had come from St. Thomas) His cheeks were shadowed with frustration.

For the first time that day, Cavendish was in a good mood and enjoyed the tour of the outside of the house. It was a traditional colonial home, very handsome although not as flashy as some of the homes built by celebrities as retreats. The exterior aspect was elegant and welcoming, and the view it was concealing was spectacular. As they came to the back of the house, they found themselves on a broad patio with a huge pool and a view of the Atlantic Ocean that was commanding and breathtaking. Cavendish could picture Wentworth's fleet swooping across the horizon to support the imperiled HMS *Obstinate,* for whom the bay his office overlooked was named. They were sheltered from the trade winds that could gust across the mountain top on this side of the island by a clear glass wall encircling the pool. The modernity of the glass seemed discordant with the traditional lines of the house. It was early enough that the wind was still strong and the glass panes rattled between their posts but the sky was so clear that Cavendish doubted they were bringing the mild rain squalls that were usually typical of the late afternoon.

The pool was a rectangular shape with a waterfall pouring into it at one end – a simple flat spout waterfall that added a pleasant gurgle to the atmosphere. The pool came close to the house on the inland side. The patio between the wall of the house and the pool was shaded by a sloped roof that projected outward from beneath the second story windows. Cavendish guessed them to be bedroom windows. There was ample space for sitting and relaxing both on the shaded side of the pool and the part that basked in the sun before the mountain sloped downward. Under this roofline were wicker chairs and settees in a sheltered conversation pit, with a built-in bar in the corner furthest from the one they had just rounded. The roofline covered the entire patio on the side of the house and the other three sides of the pool were exposed to the sky.

There was no barman or other staff immediately apparent, and Marvin Lance seemed to be setting about the task of making drinks himself. Bottles and glasses clinked as he mixed a fruity concoction for Deirdre without asking. Either she was a creature of habit or she was going to drink what she was given.

There was an awkward silence that Cavendish was unsure how to breach and wasn't sure he wanted to. His natural curiosity wanted to see how this little drama played out. Would Lance's temper cool and then he make the first overture? Would Deirdre try to talk him down, or would Martine ask someone from the spirit world to pacify the domestic disturbance?

The chill was gradually thawed through the mundane. Lance asked Martine what she would drink, and she took a white wine. Lane uncorked a bottle with aplomb, and then asked Cavendish the same thing.

"I'll take a rum and coke, Mr. Lance. Your dark rum, if you have it," asked Cavendish.

For the first time, Lance smiled. It was small but genuine, the simple pleasure of a proud man gratified that someone appreciated his wares.

"Some people call that a Cuba Libre," he observed as he up ended a bottle of rum with the familiar coat of arms on its neck. His bottles were shaped like the rum bottles of pirate movies from days of yore. "Those bastards at Bacardi claim to have invented it. I have never thought a drink with just two ingredients requires a formal name and simply call it a rum and coke myself, as you do." He mixed one for himself, then passed a second to Cavendish. He mixed a strong drink, a third rum to two thirds soda, allowed it one ice cube and added a lime wedge. Both drinks were made identically.

"Your health everybody," said Lance and they all drank. Cavendish wondered how Hoyt Buxton's expedition to find the producer was coming along, and what was going on in the little cottage Pamela Geranabby shared with her two daughters.

"You said you are a friend of Amber," said Lance abruptly. "You didn't say how you know her."

"I only made her acquaintance today," Cavendish said truthfully. "A tourist was accosting her in the street. After the tourist was taken in by the police, I offered to bring her home."

"Then you are not a visitor to the island yourself?" wondered Deirdre, enjoying the fact that the blessed historical gates no longer seemed to be her husband's focus.

"No, I've lived here almost a year. Out by Rogue's Point."

"Then this is out of the way for you," Marvin Lance noted. Like Pamela, he seemed skeptical of Cavendish's motives. "Generous of you to bring Amber all this way."

"Not at all," Cavendish was unoffended by the suspicion. It was natural enough. Although it piqued his curiosity that Lance would be concerned about Amber. Wasn't she just the daughter to a maid? Aloud he explained: "I have a daughter myself."

"I always forget how wonderful the air is here," Martine exclaimed suddenly, doing a slow and melodramatic twirl. Cavendish assumed she felt she had been excluded from the limelight long enough. "I do love it here so."

"Then why did you leave?" asked Cavendish.

"I was called away," she explained. Cavendish expected her to say she was called away by destiny or by spirits. "There just wasn't any opportunity for someone like me here. So, I went to America."

"But you're filming your TV show here. Is that sort of a home coming special or something?"

She nodded. "Partly. And partly there is a lot of history on this island. A lot of ghosts and unsettled souls still wandering the place. Some who don't want to leave, some with no place else to go - some afraid of where they'll go. We're shooting six episodes."

"Our house features prominently," Deirdre interjected proudly. "It's haunted."

Marvin Lance rolled his eyes, but Martine just smiled. "You don't believe, Marvin. But believe me when I tell you the pain that lives in this house will touch you.

"Having you here is exciting for Deirdre, and that's all I care about. This has always been a very happy home. For my lifetime, at least," Lance was almost done his drink. "I am going to see what happened to that fool Buxton and what they are doing about my gate. Help yourself to another, Cavendish. You might be stuck here for dinner."

It was not an unpleasant invitation, so Cavendish drained his glass and headed for the bar. "May I refresh your drinks, ladies?"

"Not me," said Martine. "I don't like to cloud my senses."

"I'll have another," Deirdre plopped her glass on the bar and hoisted herself onto one of the stools. Close up, she looked older than she should. Her fair skin was wearing poorly in the tropical sun. Cavendish looked at her glass helplessly. He had no idea what her drink had been.

"I take it you're a fan of Ms. Letourneaux' work?"

"A huge fan. I knew her before the world knew her. She read my future about ten years ago. She told me that my acting career wasn't going to work out – she was so kind and gentle about it – and said I should find a new path," explained Deirdre.

Cavendish refrained from commenting on Martine's powers of clairvoyance.

"And what path did she suggest?"

"She told me to take a trip, to spend some time to find myself and my destiny, and I took a vacation here to St. Lazarus – Martine told me about it and how beautiful it was, so I did. And I met Marvin. Destiny." She smiled and clinked half empty glass against Archer's and emptied it. She guided Cavendish through the construction of a refill through a combination of pointing out bottles and holding her hand in a "when" pose as the right amount of each liquid had been added.

"When I saw her show on TV, I didn't think she would remember me, but I wanted to let her know how important she had been to my life. I mean - My God she led me to my husband. And I actually talked to her husband, Peter, and he was really nice, and we got to talking about her show, and how I lived where she grew up. Then he had the idea to come and film some episodes here in her home and I thought it was brilliant and I asked Marvin if she could stay – the house is so big - and then it ended up being the production headquarters. Marvin is too good to me. Just too good. Where is Peter, anyway?"

Martine waved one of her hands about. "He's around here somewhere. He got very excited about this project. He did a lot of research on the history and some of the buildings here. This house has known more sadness than Marvin likes to admit. It started out with white owners and slaves that were brutalized. There was a slave revolt at one point and the white owners were brutalized in their turn. And then one day, long after the slaves were free in name yet living in bondage practically, the Mr. Lance of the day took a young black girl as his bride and murdered her when she was unfaithful to him. There are still a lot of angry spirits. And a lot of sad ones. I am going to help them move on. We are doing a full episode on this place."

Cavendish considered that historians and psychics were probably the only two kinds of people that researched the historical background of places.

"Come on," Archer said impishly. "I won't tell – I love

that you have a great show and you are so successful – but between us. You don't really see or hear spirits, do you?"

"Yes. I do, Mr. Cavendish. Just not on command." She did not seem irked. Skepticism drained off her back like water. She was very professional. The best cons were.

"Have you met Amber?" he wondered aloud. "I think she would love to say goodbye to the island life. Maybe you could give her some tips."

"A few times. Mr. Lance lets her use the pool, so I have seen her swimming and taking the sun. She and her sister both."

Deirdre swigged her drink. "He lets the children of all the staff run all over the house like it's their own." She tapped her drink with her sunglasses and said: "You make it almost as well as Marvin."

"He feels responsible for them," explained Martine. "He cares for them. Try to be understanding of that, my dear."

The door to the house opened suddenly and Marvin Lance appeared again. "It's not going to be a quick fix. Cavendish, I think you definitely are going to be staying for dinner."

≈

Cavendish phoned home to let everyone know where he was and that he was going to be missing dinner, then finished enjoying his second drink but abstained from a third. He and Lance and the ladies remained by the pool for about another quarter of an hour. The light changed from setting sun to magic hour, but on this side of the island they could not see the sunset. Then a servant in a crisp white shirt came outside and announced that dinner was ready.

They filed into the house and thence the dining room. Not surprisingly, the furnishings and décor were British colonial, a legacy of the British desire to take every aspect of their cold little island home with them to whatever far flung outpost of the empire they were heading to. Although first settled by Spain, this island had changed hands during the War of the Spanish Succession. Then the French seized it during the French Revolutionary wars and then the British took it back. Its early decades as a British colony did not tell a particularly original tale. Plantations and sugarcane, slavery and disease, piracy and treasure, and moments when this was as close to home as British sailors could get during one of the interminable wars with France or other European nations. Men had fought to own this island and died to keep others from stealing it. Others had died under the harsh ownership of it, while many more had just fallen victim to the natural curses of its geography. Hurricanes and pestilence sent by God to tarnish the scent and sight of a place that was in every other way idyllic.

Sugarcane and rum were still cornerstones of the island's economy, with tourism now bringing more revenue but the governor was eager to further diversify the economy of the island for the betterment of all its citizens, most of whom lived at or below the poverty line. A new casino was proposed and what the Americans would call a "junior college" (albeit of modest scale) was under construction. The legislature also talked about everything from becoming a banking outpost like the Caymans to the more fanciful goal of being the first Caribbean state to be a manufacturing center.

The dining room was double the size it needed to be for the table, which could have accommodated twelve but was laid for seven, grouped at one end of the table with Marvin Lance taking the head position. Two big ceiling fans at each end of the room gently churned the air, but whereas a century past they may have been solely responsible for cooling the room, air conditioning now kept it almost overly chilled and their responsibility seemed more attuned to creating the proper ambience. The windows in this room were small, white framed against pale yellow walls. The table was covered in a simple white tablecloth and a dark sideboard rested against the wall at Marvin Lance's back.

The diners arrived in two groupings. Deirdre, Cavendish, Martine Letourneaux and Marvin Lance arrived first. Deirdre directed them to their assigned seats. Martine was seated to Marvin's right, and next to her Cavendish. An empty place setting was laid to his right. To Lance's left, Deirdre, then two open seats.

It was only a moment before the second party arrived, two faces unknown to Cavendish and the third belonging to the still edgy Hoyt Buxton. One of the newcomers was a tall, swaggering fellow that looked like he fancied himself a bit of a John Wayne. He had a sandy thatch of hair, combed but restless, and if forced to a physical description Cavendish would have taken shelter in a cliché and said his face looked chiseled. He was all sharp angles, well-tanned and handsome. And he struck Cavendish as the sort of smug bastard who knew it.

Martine went around the table to welcome him with a kiss and brought him to Cavendish.

"Mr. Cavendish, this is Peter Pennington, my husband," the measured patience that had characterized her voice so far during her acquaintance with Cavendish was displaced with a genuine warmth and enthusiasm for her husband. Because she loved him, or because he showed well? Cavendish allowed his hand to be encompassed by Pennington's massive fist. The man was such a stereotype that Cavendish almost broke a smile when he spoke, for Pennington had the echo of a Texas drawl to perfectly complement his physical appearance.

"Nice to meet you, Mr. Cavendish."

"Please call me Archie. Pleasure to meet you."

"Mr. Cavendish is a private detective," volunteered Martine, looking suddenly short in the shadow of her husband. She patted his arm and pushed him back towards his side of the table. Buxton made the second introduction.

"Mr. Cavendish, this is Megan Shepard, she produces our program."

Megan shook hands slowly, studying Cavendish. She was perhaps a year or two older than him, but still handsome, and looking very together. The hand she extended was manicured and tipped with long pink talons that Cavendish would have expected to find shredding society enemies in a drawing room, not producing television programs in the Caribbean.

"You're a private detective? What brings you here?"

"I got trapped by one of your vehicles – the truck that got stuck in the gate," explained Cavendish. Her hand was delicate and fragile, but he felt the vise like grip of Peter Pennington much less unnerving. Pennington hardly seemed interested in him, but Megan started dissecting him with her eyes the moment his occupation was mentioned. And she was taking the seat on his right.

"I've known a few private detectives," explained Megan. "I've used them for shows a lot. How come you're sniffing around our show?"

"I am not sniffing around your show. I didn't even know there was a show until an hour ago," he explained. A maid and footman filed in and delivered appetizers – a single skewer of prawns in a rich buttery garlic sauce.

"You've never heard of our show?" Megan dismissed the absurdity of the very notion and rolled on. "What brought you up here, if not us?"

"Myself. I drive a car."

"I mean what was your motive for coming? Are you a friend of Marvin?"

Lance answered for him. "Never laid eyes on him before in my life. He brought one of the servant's children home. Please pass the bread."

"He doesn't believe in my gift," added Martine provocatively. "I doubt he takes my show very seriously."

"Well many have tried to prove that Martine's gifts are insincere," Megan warned him. "None have been able to. Because she is the genuine article."

"She has a real gift," Deirdre affirmed.

"Mr. Cavendish is entitled to his skepticism. In his line of work, I am sure he sees the darker side of human nature a lot. Probably more than any of us could cope with, perhaps more than he wanted to deal with. I imagine that's why he left the police," said Martine, her voice reverting to the measured serenity she had displayed earlier in the evening.

"Your psychic powers lead you to believe I was once a

policeman?" queried Cavendish.

"You are an Englishman living on a Caribbean island. My powers of observation suggest you left the life you were living for a new one here," Martine rejoined with a gleaming eye. "I didn't need my spirit guide to tell me you probably disliked the life you were leading. And I believe many private detectives were once policemen?"

"I believe most of the good ones are," allowed Cavendish. "And I actually loved being a police officer. Family responsibilities led me here."

The starter plates were taken away by the same two servers. Cavendish hadn't expected to see Pamela Geranabby again, but he overheard Lance whispering a question about her to one of the servers, and the discreet reply explaining her absence seemed to satisfy him. Apparently, the maid helping with dinner this evening was covering for her. It didn't surprise Cavendish that Pamela would need to take off the evening to deal with her daughter. He hoped they were having a long and heartfelt mother-daughter talk.

"What kind of family responsibilities?" wondered Megan. "Most people flee to paradise to escape responsibilities. What brought you here?"

"A large airplane followed by a smaller one. At the risk of sounding rude, I really don't want to discuss my personal life with a TV producer I have known for two minutes," he knew he was being rude, and most of the time he was very open about his reasons for coming here. It was easier to get the conversation over with than leave the door open to endless speculation. But Megan put him on the defensive.

"Oh, don't be so grouchy," Megan slapped his arm with her left hand and hoisted her wine glass for a hearty swig with the other. "I am always looking for good stories. If you have a good story, I could make you some money. Maybe a lot of it. Wouldn't you love to have your own TV show?"

Peter, quietly munching until now, seemed to come on the alert. "But you have Martine's show."

"Martine's show is airborne. I can step back from the

day to day and her success – sweetie," She focused doe eyes on Martine. "Your success, sweetie, gives me some leverage. You made me successful, and right now I can use that to get another show, another couple of shows, off the ground. If I can find the right concepts we can be riding pretty for a few years. I might be able to start my own company and do it under my own banner - Sweetie; your show might not last forever. I can make you an executive producer on new shows and you can own some product outside of your own. It will help you feather your nest for the future."

"I know I am a simple rum producer, but don't executive producers usually have to come up with some of the money?" wondered Lance.

"Yes, often they do," agreed Megan. "But don't worry, Marvin, I wouldn't object to including you in the project. It would be good to diversify your holdings. What if people stop drinking rum?"

Lance and Cavendish both laughed. Lance looked at him approvingly and lifted his glass. Cavendish felt childishly pleased that he was bonding with the maker of his favorite rum.

"To your private detective show, Archer," and they clinked glasses. "If you do it, I might just invest."

Megan brightened. Everything had been hypothetical a few minutes ago. "Really? I didn't think I would have the money to start my own company for a few years, but – "

Cavendish held up his hand. "I am sorry, Megan, but I have no interest in appearing on television. Thank you, but no thank you."

Megan deflated before his eyes, "Well, maybe in a year or two…"

"I think Martine's projects will keep you pretty busy for a while," asserted Peter, looking miffed that Megan was already looking past his wife in search of the next great thing. Megan was instantly conciliatory.

"You know Martine is my star, and I would never neglect her," she smiled and took a sip of water and Cavendish saw in her eyes that she was still mulling opportunities. She did not seem to be the type of person to count on a gravy train to last forever. Peter probably thought his wife would always be a star and maybe she would, but public tastes changed. Cavendish understood that and he wasn't even in television. He was sure Megan had worked on shows that didn't involve supernatural communication before, and that she would do so again. But it wasn't going to be about him.

"I'm not familiar with your wife's program, but I have noticed there are many psychic TV shows and books out there. I guess it behooves you to cash in on it as much as you can while the popularity endures."

Peter didn't disappoint. "I think my wife is more than a flash in the pan."

Martine did not react to Cavendish's jibe; she just maintained a face of serenity. Probably a mask she mastered after years of people trying to derail her or prove that she was a fraud.

"I'm sure she is. And now that I have met her, I will certainly have to watch her on television," he promised. He looked at Hoyt Buxton, who had been largely silent through the meal and kept his face relatively near the plate to minimize the journey the food had to make. He was not at all a match for the mental image Cavendish had of agents as a class of people. He expected loud, brash, salesy people full of bravura and chutzpah and demanding that people "show them the money". How could this mouse of a man hustle the studio execs or the lawyers or the producers or whoever else he had to hustle to get Martine the best dressing room filled with M & Ms in her favorite color? When introduced he demonstrated an expectation to be taken seriously, but his authority was co-opted from the success of his charges. It did not come from within.

"Martine, how did you go from St. Lazarus to television?"

Martine did not launch immediately into a bio; she seemed to wade cautiously into the waters of her life. Not suspicious that Archer was showing interest in her story, but perhaps curious as to why.

"Once I learned about my gift, I started helping people here on the island. Mostly local people. But the truth was it is a small place and my very good friend and I learned to marshal our gift from a very gifted woman. She was the person most people wanted to go to for advice, and she was older, so her gift was more mature than mine. There wasn't really any need here for me to answer."

"So," Cavendish thought to himself. "Naturally, you went to Hollywood." Outwardly, he just remained attentive.

"I went to America, and I was amazed to discover there was a hunger for the kind of understanding I could bring into people's lives," she looked at Hoyt. "I was giving readings in a small theatre in Los Angeles when Hoyt came to me for help. And he became a regular. We started talking a lot, and I learned he worked at an agency. He introduced me to Megan."

Megan took up the tale. "John Edward was popular at the time; Kim Russo was recapping celebrity ghost stories. And when I met Martine it was perfect – the Caribbean woman who can speak to spirits, it just gave it that little bit of difference in the spin to set her apart," Megan motioned for someone – anyone – to refill her wine glass. "We hit a bump when that infomercial psychic turned out to be from Brooklyn, but the publicity actually helped draw a lot of attention to Martine's show, and between the people turning to her for help and the people wanting to bring her down and expose her as a fraud, the ratings went through the roof!"

Now Cavendish turned to Buxton. "Who are some of your other clients?"

Buxton looked up from his plate uncomfortably. "Martine is my most important client; I am dedicated to her career and I don't like to distract from – I don't like to spread myself too thin. If can't give personal support, I can't give my best, if I have too many clients because I can't take really good care of any of them, I am constantly distracted by the needs of the next client, so I am really focused just on Martine right now. She is my client; she is my star."

"So, you're from the Jerry Maguire school of agenting?"

Cavendish observed agreeably. TV was foreign to him but movies, he could speak.

Dessert was a Caribbean Syllabub made with dark rum that was house appropriate. An extremely sweet dish, it went down well with the excellent coffee that was served with it. The conversation shifted to Caribbean cuisine, and the revelation that the coffee was Jamaican Blue Mountain spurred a debate about the beans grown on St. Lazarus, how favorably they compared and if Lance was unpatriotic for buying Jamaican coffee. After all, how did he feel when he saw locals drinking Bacardi or Myers?

The party began to break up as people finished dessert. Megan was the first to excuse herself. She had drunk so much wine she was probably called away by the needs of nature. And Cavendish was feeling the pull of home. It was unusual for him to stay out this late. It was only about nine o'clock, but it was his normal routine to go straight home at the end of the workday. One of the advantages of being a private detective on a Caribbean island was that the infidelity usually happened right in the middle of the day – the whole time on the island was an assignation. Not like a PI in New York who might have to traipse after extra marital trysts taking place in the evening, when people are "working late."

The truck had been shifted so it was time to say goodbyes, express gratitude for the meal and go home. Cavendish also hit the head prior to his departure. When he emerged from the restroom, he was surprised by Peter Pennington lurking in the otherwise empty hallway. Peter was not waiting for a turn in the restroom, he was waiting for Archer and he was antsy.

"So why are you here, Cavendish?" he demanded in a quiet tone laced with anxious anger.

"You know why I'm here. My car got blocked in," Cavendish was taken aback to be confronted outside the restroom, but he did not back away as Peter got into his face.

"Who are you working for?"

"No one at the moment. But if I was, you must have

seen enough movies to know I couldn't and wouldn't tell you who."

"Was it Buxton?"

"Why would Buxton want to hire a private detective?" and then a thought occurred to Cavendish to add. "You do realize that my work primarily involves catching unfaithful spouses in the act. Are you the sort of person that could be the subject of my work?"

Pennington bounced edgily from foot to foot. It seemed like he was deciding this conversation had been a bad choice. He shook his head. "Good night, Mr. Cavendish." And skulked away down the hall.

CHAPTER SIX

When Archer Cavendish sold up everything and moved his daughter to the Caribbean, it was not the need for a fresh start, or a place not filled with memories that drove the choice. While Cavendish certainly wanted distance from the grief for both his daughter and himself, he felt no need to separate them from places that held memories of the woman they both loved so much. Places they had frequented together brought pangs of sadness, but they also provided touchstones to her memory, touchstones he missed. A way to connect with the memory and spirit of her, even if her arms were no longer within reach. In fact, one of the hardest things for Cavendish was selling the flat where they had made a home for their family. Putting away pictures and bric-a-brac and leaving bare the shelves they had painted together. They had spent hours debating the color for the shelves in one of those conversations about trivial matters that can become some of the sweetest memories. The little odds and ends of life that glue a marriage, or a family.

He remembered watching the furniture being taken away by the consignment dealer, because taking furniture to an island in the Caribbean was prohibitively expensive. Wondering what the next family would bring in their place. What colors they would pick, as they erased the evidence of the Cavendish household and made the flat into something new for their family.

No, Cavendish felt no desire to escape the past. He wanted to crawl into it and pull it around his shoulders. To hug Sophie and wrap her in it too, hide in a bubble from the need to make a new life together for the future.

If it had been him alone, he might not have bothered. But he was by nature a family man, and in the absence of his wife, his daughter had become his whole universe. She needed a future, not an eternal past.

His wife, Elizabeth had moved to London from the Caribbean island of St. Lazarus. His family had little interest in Elizabeth or Sophie, so when they lost Elizabeth it was just Cavendish and Sophie, suddenly and violently on their own. Being a Detective-Inspector in the CID meant long and strange hours for him, and potentially long absences from Sophie. He did not want Sophie alone in a house while he was out working a case in the middle of the night. He didn't want her sleeping in the flat alone; or arriving home from school to make her own meal and manage herself like a miniature adult. What did Americans call it? A latch-key kid? No, he didn't want her to be one of those. She was eleven, and if she had to deal with the loss of her mother she should at least be able to have a year or two more where she could live like a kid, and have a father that was a constant presence.

He loved being a policeman, but it took him only a moment to realize that he had to leave the force. He loved his daughter more so there was no question and he harbored no regret from the moment he made the decision.

Secondly, without a mother he still wanted her to have a mother figure in her life. Someone she could talk to about all those things that he would certainly be willing to discuss, but that she might prefer to share with her Mum than her Dad. There were friends that could act as surrogates, but family was in St. Lazarus – Elizabeth's own Mum and Dad.

Thirdly, there was the question of a living. What could an ex-policeman do to earn a pound or two? He could take a lot of different jobs, but it was a mate of his that gave him the idea to be a private detective. A chap named Charlie Blake that he had met when he arrested him for spying on a couple through a bedroom window. It transpired that Blake was trying to catch an unfaithful couple in the act and had succeeded. There was money in wickedness; money was almost naturally a consequence of sin. The adulterer lost it in the settlement, the lawyers got more of it in the uglier separation battles, and the private eye who collected the damning evidence got a bit to put in his pocket. Even Amber, the girl he met today, was earning her keep from the sin of men whose lust blinded them to the consequences. Cavendish decided he could make a living as a private detective.

His Mother and father-in-law were both more than amenable to the idea of him moving to the island with Sophie. They would have been excited to have their granddaughter so close in any event, but doubtless as they dealt with the death of their daughter the closeness of their kin took on extra meaning. They decided to sell their modest bungalow and pool resources with him to buy a bigger house. Cavendish didn't remember how the idea came up or whose idea it was. He did remember Glenda, mother-in-law, assuring him that it would be okay with them when he was ready to start seeing other women. A kindly offered gesture, but one that just struck him as bizarre. The only love he had left in him was the love he felt for his daughter. The rest of his heart had been burned away.

They shared a home perched on a steep slope about two hundred feet above the Caribbean Sea with three bedrooms and two bathrooms. Built on the slope as it was, the driveway was aligned with the upper level. The upper level was also the main level, and one descended to the lower floor with bedrooms and patio access from there. They were able to afford a property with a pool, and their westward facing views from Rogue's Point favored them with some beautiful sunsets. Arriving home from his unscheduled dinner at the Lance estate, he nestled his Dodge between the well-worn Ford pick-up truck of his father-in-law, Paul, and Glenda's newer Honda CRV.

The main entrance to the house opened directly into the kitchen which spilled over into the dining area and family room. The common area of the house was reminiscent of Pamela Geranabby's cottage, but much bigger. It was all open plan so the areas were defined by use, furniture, and décor. Glenda had acquired an interest in Southwest American design from somewhere, so the space could easily be transplanted to Arizona and seem at home. Bookshelves lined the walls and they were overflowing with her library. Austen, Hardy, Dickens, Faulkner, Steinbeck, Buck, Christie, Bronte, James – it was an easy and correct assumption to guess there was an English literature teacher in the house.

Glenda was marking papers at the kitchen table and looked up at him with a smile. "You're quite late," she ventured hopefully. Cavendish thought it took a remarkable woman to be so accepting of the idea that her son-in-law should move away from the memory of her dead daughter. And a quality completely wasted on him.

"It was interesting. My car got blocked in when I was dropping someone off at the Lance Estate, and they invited me for dinner."

Sophie had clambered out of the couch where she had been watching *Hannah Montana* and came over to give her father a hug and a kiss. She was already wearing the shorts and t-shirt she favoured as pajamas. The three of them made an interesting spectrum, he looked like Casper the ghost next to Glenda's African-American skin, and Sophie's caramel skin tone bridged the difference between them.

"I met someone famous," he told his daughter.

"Who?"

"Do you know Martine Letourneaux, the psychic?"

"Some of the kids at school watch her," said Sophie. She shared her father's skepticism about psychics. "How did you meet her?"

"She's on the island filming some episodes, and she is staying at the Lance house, and I had dinner there tonight." He sat down at the kitchen table and Sophie sat down between him and Glenda.

"Can you take me to meet her?" wondered Sophie. Skeptical or not, she was curious about celebrities. Cavendish shook his head.

"You know I can't take you to meet people that I know through work."

"You have Hardy Swain and Jenny Singh over to the house," she complained.

"That's different. They're police officers and they aren't part of a job."

"There's a job? Is Martine cheating on her husband?" demanded Sophie. "I'm sure her husband isn't cheating on her because Martine's spirit guide would tell her about it!"

Cavendish had to smile at the faultless logic. "No, Martine isn't the matter I am working on –" he seldom used the word 'case', it sounded cheesy to hear himself say that about the tawdry matters he investigated – "But she sort of came into the edge of the matter because of someone else that is involved."

"How come she came here to film episodes?" Glenda wondered. "Why come to a little Caribbean island? Is she doing a bikini episode?"

"Apparently she is from here originally, so it is something of a 'returning to her roots' story. And I think they are playing up local ghost stories."

"As long as they don't talk about voodoo. There was never any voodoo on St. Lazarus, and I hate it when people talk like there was." Cavendish felt sorry for the student whose paper was in front of her right now because it suffered a long, sharp stroke from her red pen and he wondered if she would have been more generous had she not been feeling that moment of pique. She taught High School History as well as English and it frustrated her when the traditions and history of different islands were blended with St. Lazarus' own by people with homogenized concepts of the Caribbean.

Sophie pulled at one of the papers and started reading it. Glenda slapped her hand and pulled the paper away from her. "This work is private for the students."

"You should let me grade some grandma; I could save you a lot of time."

"I'm sure you could. But there will be plenty of time for you to grade papers when you are older. Now just do your homework and watch your Holly Maine or whoever she is."

Sophie rolled her eyes. "*Hannah Montana* grandma. You do that on purpose."

Sophie stood up and wandered back to the couch, flumping down to catch the final act. She amazed Cavendish. He knew she missed her mother, but she had been able to move forward without growing bitter or angry or mean. Sometimes it worried him that she never lashed out. What if a ball of grief and anger was simmering deep inside her, She had cried, she had screamed, she had gone through the steps of grief the pamphlets and counselors told him to watch for and expect. But somehow, she seemed to have emerged on the other side still whole. Maybe it was the resilience of youth. Maybe it was the strength of her mother's genes. Cavendish, who was far from spiritual or religious, sometimes surrendered to the fanciful but comforting notion that maybe, just maybe, her mother was able to reach into Sophie's heart from wherever she was and soothe it. If only he could believe in someone like Martine Letourneaux and ask.

He went and sat next to her on the couch and watched *Hannah Montana* and *Witches of Waverly Place* with her, and she snuggled up next to him and leaned against his shoulder and he felt the only peace he had felt since he kissed her goodbye after breakfast that morning, and reflected that he could never allow her to see how much he needed her to preserve his sanity for that was surely a bigger load than any child should have to carry. But for the moment, here in front of the TV he could enjoy the fact that she hadn't outgrown him yet, and she couldn't tell how much he needed her.

≈

When the alarm went off in the morning, Cavendish was already awake. The nightmares had passed for the most part, but his sleep was still fitful and restive at best, and he wakened frequently to look at the red digital numbers on the clock as they taunted him. He always felt like crap in the mornings, and his body resisted as he dragged it out of bed and moved it into the bathroom. There were two in the house. His in-laws had one *en-suite* with their bedroom, because he had deferred to them and let them have the master. The other was between his room and Sophie's. All three bedrooms were located on the bottom floor of the house, and they had windows that looked over the patio and pool. They had a routine, and by now she would be finished in the bathroom and he could hear her singing along with her radio in her bedroom as she dressed. Thanks to Sophie he was well versed in the songs of Selena Gomez and T-Swift, and embarrassedly caught himself singing along to them more often than was respectable for a middle-aged male.

He showered and dressed. He wore a polo today, typical for him, and lathered on sunscreen. Like most redheads his skin was extremely fair, and he was prone to burn easily, especially under a tropical sun.

He banged on Sophie's door as he headed for the stairs. "It's 7.30, Sophie!" and continued upstairs even as she called out that she would be ready in a minute. It was just part of their routine. He loved their routines.

In the kitchen, Glenda divvied scrambled eggs across three garishly coloured plates.

"Paul's not eating?" wondered Cavendish, inquiring after his father-in-law.

Glenda shook her head. "Gone already. One of the fuel filters on the boat got gummed up and he wants to try and get it replaced first thing, so he doesn't have to cancel his ten o'clock charter."

Paul owned a 54-foot Bertram dating to the 1980s that he used for day charters. Only pride had prevented Cavendish from accepting Paul's offer to become a partner in the small charter business. Pride and a sense that while one sport fishing convertible could sustain an income for one adult, it was unlikely that it could sufficiently support two. He did crew on occasion, but it was more like a relaxing vacation for him when he did so.

Glenda added sausage links and toast to his plate and

put it on the table. He added some HP sauce to his eggs before reaching for the newspaper which was next to Paul's normal seat. Not surprisingly, The *St. Lazarus Chronicle* was not the largest paper physically. It was tabloid format, very thin, and as he unfolded it, he was drawn to a secondary headline below the fold. His felt like his eyes might have bugged out of their sockets.

"Local Girl Blackmails Married Tourists In Sex Den."

He scanned the article quickly; part of his mind wondering how it could be a news item when it was just yesterday that he had stumbled upon it himself, the other part wondering who would have leaked such a story to the newspaper at all. It seemed inconsistent with the interests of everyone involved. *"...lured men to an apartment wired with sound and video equipment ... engaged in wide array of sexual debauchery ... pretended to be a minor... police became aware of the alleged pornographic blackmail scheme when the latest alleged victim assaulted her..."* Ross Buchanan was named. Amber Geranabby was named. The fact that her mother worked for Marvin Lance, the closest the island had to a mogul, was also named, and gave the incident a tinge of celebrity. The scandalous nature of the crime gave it the sex. It was a compelling read, the headline bolded in the largest font he had ever seen the *Chronicle* use.

How was it all over the paper within twenty-four hours? The answer seemed obvious. Someone at the police department must have tipped the reporter. Ross Buchanan would never have said anything to the papers, and there was no reason for Amber to kill the golden goose. If she wanted to punish Buchanan, she had the means to do it without burning herself in the process. As of yesterday, there was no question of prosecuting her. Buchanan wouldn't sign a complaint and without that, there wasn't much of a case. She had no reason to tip the papers, even though she held the strongest evidence. The island cops made decent money, especially by island standards, so at first blush it was hard to imagine a cop selling out a story for what would probably only have been a couple hundred bucks, if that. But you never knew what was under the surface. A cop with a gambling problem or an expensive girlfriend could weigh the pros and cons of corruption differently than his colleagues.

He would call Hardy Swain or Jenny Singh later today to ask them about it. He knew them pretty well and neither of them was likely to trade their own virtue so cheaply. They were probably reading the headlines with similar levels of astonishment.

"Whatcha reading?" Sophie demanded, plopping herself gracelessly across from him and leaning over the table. Cavendish folded the headline and cover story inside the paper. He wanted to keep Sophie twelve as long as possible.

"Just the paper. Nothing that would interest you. What do you have happening at school today?"

"You're so goofy Dad," she laughed, stabbing at a sausage on her plate, hiding her point behind a playful tone. "Whatever you're trying to hide… they have these things all over town where you put money in, and a newspaper comes out. Not to mention the stuff I can find on the internet. You can't hide the world from me forever."

"For as long as I can," he replied simply, softly. That was something her mother would say, and almost how she would say it.

"What is it? Was there a murder?" she grabbed for the paper and he slid it away from her.

"No," he decided sharing the generalities may curb her interest in finding a copy and reading it for herself and seeing the lurid details. He knew if he didn't offer her something her curiosity would compel her to find a copy of the newspaper. She wouldn't be able to help herself. With two detectives as parents, she was more or less destined to have a genetic compulsion for truth seeking. "There was a girl who is being accused of blackmailing married men. She would meet them and kiss them and stuff and take pictures and threaten to show their wives, so they gave her money."

"Did she get a lot of money?"

"I don't know. It's just a newspaper article making allegations. They may not be true," while he knew they were, he wanted to instill in his daughter a healthy skepticism about anything she read or heard in the media, especially when they were rushing to judgment.

"What was the 'stuff'?" inquired Sophie.

"'Stuff'?"

"You said she kissed them and 'stuff'…"

Cavendish stood up. "On that note, I need to get to work. So, hurry up and eat your breakfast."

The morning air was already heavy with heat and humidity. White puffy clouds scudded across a gorgeous blue sky. They drove with the windows down because they both enjoyed the movement of the fresh air, even if it was hot. The air was rich with earthy smells as the sun's rays stirred the jungle's fragrances. The vegetation that flashed by was rich and verdant and part of a radiant palette of greens that made the whole island seem like it was made in Technicolor. It still amazed Cavendish that so many shades and textures of green were possible. Red roofs, buildings of white and rich pastels, all under that amazing cerulean canopy that hovered above the backdrop of lush forest completed the vivid and beautiful tapestry.

The first part of the drive was always relatively painless, but traffic started to thicken and slow as one descended into the township of Port Rose. Most of the roads had not seen much widening or improvement since they were carved through the forests as trails for donkey carts. Sophie surfed the radio stations and offered education on which songs were cool and the which were boring, while sharing her anxieties about her English paper. Cavendish promised to help her. English had been one of his strengths and he remembered *Macbeth* (the subject of her paper) quite well, and fondly. More importantly, her grandma was clearly a stronger authority on the material so the fact she was turning to her father for help moved his heart to be the best English tutor he could possibly be.

Sophie craned to see the cruise ship coming into the pier. It was the *Albert Ballin,* a weekly visitor. She had an intense interest in ships and the mid-sized *Ballin* was one of her favorites, both for her lines and for the fact she had such a distinctive name that set her apart from the endless flow ships with repetitive corporate names like *Ocean Voyager, Sun Voyager, Dream Voyager, Ocean Dream Voyager, Big Glorious Voyager* etc.

She looked into the back seat. Cavendish could see her in the corner of his eye and his parental radar registered an alarm. A focus had crept into her face and her left arm lunged. A second later she had the newspaper in her hands and was unfolding it, consciously doing it towards the passenger door so it would be more difficult for her father to intercept or grab it back from her.

Cavendish thought of chastising her, but he also knew the danger of making fruit too forbidden. Besides, her general nosiness was a chip off the old block. Part of him was pleased to see it.

Sophie's eyes grew wide as she exclaimed dramatically. "This girl's a ho!"

Cavendish laughed aloud at the emphatic verdict of his worldly tween.

"Wait – she lives on the Lance estate – that's where you were yesterday...." She touched the mark on his forehead where Buchanan had managed to plant a useful blow during their melee the prior day. "That's why you didn't want me reading this. You can't blow it off as the newspaper writing something crazy because you know it's true."

Cavendish nodded grudgingly and decided to forestall further interrogation. "But that's all we are going to say about it. We're not going to talk about it anymore."

"Okay. I mostly wondered why you wanted to hide the paper from me," explained Sophie. Now her principal question was addressed, she was content to return the newspaper to the back seat and go back to chatting about school.

They pulled into the lane outside the school a few minutes later. Most children were bussed or walked to school, so there was only a short queue of vehicles unloading. One of the cars ahead was a town car he had seen before. He paid attention today because he recognized the little girl hopping out of the back – Mia Geranabby, Amber's little sister. He doubted the car was her mother's. Marvin Lance must provide it.

Cavendish wondered if it was a regular service, or if it was a particular favour today. Perhaps they had seen the news story up at the Lance home. Cavendish wondered what Mia's day at school would be like today as she flung her small backpack easily over her shoulder. How would it have hit Amber's mother? Or the household?

He restrained himself from asking Sophie any questions about Mia – inquiring if she knew her, for example, because he didn't want to add fuel to her natural sparks of inquisitiveness.

He eased his car through the gate, and it was soon their turn to unload. Sophie gave him a kiss on the cheek and lunged out of the car. He watched her climb the front steps to the main door and waved when she turned back to look at him. She responded by wagging her arm with ingenuous enthusiasm, half bidding him adieu and half reassuring him that she was safely in school and he could stand down for a few hours. He blew her a kiss and eased back into traffic.

He left the car in his regular parking lot a few blocks from his office and walked the last portion of his commute. His shirt already tugged at his flesh as humidity and heat did their work. It was not uncommon for islanders here to take two or three showers a day. His building even had shower facilities for its tenants, for which he was grateful.

The walk from the carpark took him through Guerra Square and past the Starbucks where he fetched a venti Americano. Despite the heat, he had to drink his coffee. In fact, he often felt the warm climate somehow enhanced the flavor. He climbed the stairs to his second-floor office and went inside. He put his coffee and newspaper down on the desk and fired up the computer.

When he didn't have an active case to work on, he spent his time finding law firms in the United States that specialized in divorce and family law, as well as private detective firms. He had form emails that he methodically fired out to everyone that he could find, soliciting business. Sometimes he even cold-called them to offer his services. He had stirred up enough business this way to pay the bills, and it promised to grow into a pretty healthy little business.

He didn't try to reach Swain or Singh immediately, although he wanted to ask them who else knew about the altercation between Buchanan, Tyree, the girl and himself yesterday. He also knew the Chief Constable of the island's police force and he imagined that if the Chief shared his suspicions about how the story of Amber was released to the newspaper, heads would be a-rolling down the block in Guerra Square. Chief Constable Borden Boxer ran a tight ship and there was nothing slack about the St. Lazarus Police Department's professionalism.

He wondered if the *Chronicle* was the newspaper of choice at the Lance Estate. How would this story go down with the Lances? How would Amber feel about her business being splashed across the newspaper? Did she care about her public image? And Deirdre had been scornful of her husband's kindness towards the staff – this article might shore up her condemnation of his indulgence.

What about tourists? Or Buchanan and his wife? Did their hotel deliver the *Chronicle* with their breakfast? As if cued by his thoughts, the sound of the building's main door slamming echoed up the stairwell. Someone stormed up the stairs, across the hallway and into Cavendish's small office. Suddenly Ross Buchanan filled the bottom two thirds of his doorway and then was fully inside the office.

There wasn't much room for Buchanan to maneuver in here, so Cavendish sat behind his desk expectantly. He had letter openers and staplers, and a solidly built telephone, so he was well armed to receive his guest.

There were scratch marks on one side of Buchanan's face that hadn't come from yesterday's fight. Someone else had given those to him. His shirt was soaked with sweat and he was out of breath. He hurled a newspaper at Cavendish, who swatted it aside with the back of his hand.

"My life is ruined, Cavendish. My life is ruined!"

Buchanan was furious and red faced, but also completely out of breath and wheezing like a broken-down steam engine.

Cavendish remained impassive, said nothing. Buchanan took a step closer to his desk.

"Well, what do you have to say about it? First you won't take my case then you help that fucking evil little whore and now this!!" He pointed at where the newspaper had ended up, in the corner. "What do you have to say?"

Cavendish allowed no emotion into his face or his tone when he said: "Get out."

Buchanan seemed incredulous. Did he really think he had made a stronger impression on Cavendish? "Get out? That's all you have to say?"

"That's already a longer conversation with you than I want. So, get out."

Buchanan took a step deeper into the office and Cavendish started calculating distances in his mind in conjunction with the relative weights of his weapons.

"How did this get in the newspaper?"

"I don't know. Would you like to hire me to find out? That's a case I would take."

Buchanan seemed to physically darken. "*Now* you want me to hire you? I tried yesterday and you treated me like some shit you stepped in. Today you want me to hire you? Fuck you!"

"I take it Mrs. Buchanan read the *Chronicle*?"

"You take right. And she believes it. She believes it!" this seemed incomprehensible to him. "How did this get in the paper?"

"What does it matter? Now why don't you leave and try to make up with your wife?"

"Didn't you hear me? My wife believes that this girl is blackmailing me. My life is ruined."

"Why are you puzzled that your wife believes the paper? I don't know how the paper got the story, but the story is true."

"I think you told the paper." Buchanan took one more step.

"Why would I do that?"

82

"Because you sit on some stupid moral high horse. You wouldn't take my case, and then you protect that girl from me. For all I know she gives you a cut of her income to pay you for your protection."

Cavendish nodded equitably. "You're right. For all you know I do. You should take your suspicions to the police. Because I am not interested in hearing them."

"Does that mean you are you admitting it?" Buchanan looked confused. Cavendish concluded he had two expressions: anger and confusion. He wasn't sure there was enough brain capacity behind those seedy little eyes to process much else.

"I'm saying I am not discussing it with you, but it is a fair suspicion. Based on the information you have; you have reached a reasonable hypothesis. The proper people to test your hypothesis would be the St. Lazarus Police. Now why don't you calm down – maybe your wife has calmed down. Maybe you can talk it out."

Buchanan shook his head. He was still angry, but there was a subtle change in his timbre. "I never saw her so mad. Like she hates me. She believes it because when she read it… and she started yelling at me… - I'm fucked." Buchanan's anger faltered and then recouped its edge. "If you had helped me find that whore, I could have got the pictures and put an end to it!"

"Maybe you could have put an end to it by never starting it in the first place. Why are people always upset about being caught and confronted with their actions? Nobody thinks back and says to themselves – 'gee, I really shouldn't have nailed a girl that wasn't my wife'," Cavendish shook his head angrily at Buchanan. His anger and judgement were amplified because he once had a wife that he loved and was devoted to and she had been taken away from him. And here was a scumbag with a living, healthy wife and he was banging the first bit of skirt that walked up to him in a bar. "What did you come here for? To kick my ass because you thought I gave your story to the newspaper? To get revenge on me for your own actions? What? Because one thing I am pretty sure of – if you came looking for a fight, it's not going to be very long and I am a little irritable today so you might wind up in the hospital."

Cavendish had still not risen from his chair but was mentally adding items to his inventory of potential weapons. In addition to the stapler, he had a heavy marble pen set that Glenda had given him as an office warming gift, wire mesh in-trays, a computer monitor, mouse, and keyboard. The marble pen set was probably the best weapon. Might kill the bastard too, and that was overshooting the mark somewhat. There was also the cup of hot coffee, but that just seemed a sinful waste of good brew.

Buchanan had made only the initial three steps into the office. He knew Cavendish had taken him on yesterday and come out on top, and he was probably smart enough to think twice before engaging in a rematch. He was just so full of anger that he was letting it blow him this way and that, but with no focus, just rage looking for a shore to smash upon. He had clearly come here thinking this would be a good shore, thinking Cavendish had sold the story. Fury and anger had driven him here but maybe Cavendish's calm disdain had chilled his ardor. He seemed less certain now.

Cavendish waited for Buchanan to decide how this meeting was going to play out. Was he going to leave or were they going to fight? He could feel his dislike for the man simmering near the surface, could feel the latent anger at losing his wife connecting to the simmering hostility and recognizing a potential outlet. His temper could get him into more trouble – but seeing the destructive path Buchanan's temper was taking him on helped Cavendish harness his own. And the voice he heard in his head, the voice of the wife who had always steadied him in life, admonished him against letting his emotions rule his decisions unwisely.

"Mr. Buchanan, I live on this island. If you want to fight me, I will fight you. But until you are sure about whether or not you want to fight me, why don't you just leave. Just turn around and leave."

Buchanan stood there dumbly; caught between his anger and his uncertainty about the outcome of a fight should he start one. He fell into the foxhole of the emasculated man. The vague "if" threat. He blustered:

"If I can prove you did it, I will tear you apart." He stabbed the air with his finger angrily. "I will rip you a new one!"

He turned around and stormed down the stairs as noisily as he had ascended them. Cavendish reached for his coffee, and the phone rang just as he heard the heavy slam of the door downstairs. He let it ring while he enjoyed a mouthful of coffee before he answered it. "Archer Cavendish."

It was the police department. A constable he had met but didn't know well was calling on behalf of the Chief Constable. They had some questions about a news story and his involvement in it. They would like his help with their inquiries. Could he please come over to Police Headquarters immediately?

Cavendish sighed. He had assumed the police would reach the same conclusion he had – that the news story made it into the paper as a result of an internal leak. Instead, they had reached the same conclusion that Ross Buchanan had. They thought it was him who had given the news story to the *Chronicle*.

CHAPTER SEVEN

The walk to the police station was near his office and the carpark where he kept his Charger during the day. The shops were mostly open to receive the passengers from the ships. The morning air was still and heavy though the temperature was far from its zenith. He walked along Front Street, on the side close to the water simply because he enjoyed being near the water and seeing all the boats tugging at their mooring buoys. The cruise ships across the bay and the steep verdant spine of the mountains beyond them made an impressive backdrop, and he liked to imagine the bay through years passed. A lot of different craft had dropped their hook here.

In the Second World War, British and Canadian corvettes had been known to call here between voyages shepherding oil tankers ferrying crude oil from South America, Texas, and Mexico north to England. Before that ships of Nelson's Day were based here to protect King George's interests in the Caribbean, not long after the island of St. Lazarus had been snatched from French occupation in Napoleon's time, one of the more famous episodes in the island's history. Earlier still were pirate ships, and before that the canoes of the Arawak, a people long since erased from Caribbean memories. Seeing all the boats and ships in the harbor made him feel the transitory nature of the islands, the people passing through and never stopping. It sometimes felt strange to think he had put down roots in a place that for most people was a vacation destination they would touch once and never again, remembered in photographs and faulty memories.

His mobile phone rang and he answered it grudgingly. He was already feeling annoyed to be going to the police station and his musings on the watercraft that had called here over the years was a welcome distraction from his irritation. A distraction that had been broken by the tinny digital ring.

"Hello?"

"Mr. Archer Cavendish?" It was a woman's voice. Caribbean lilt, but very professional. He confirmed that she had reached Archer Cavendish. "I have Mr. Marvin Lance for you."

Lance came on the phone without any salutation. "Cavendish, have you seen the morning papers?"

"Yes, Mr. Lance, I have."

"This garbage they are printing about Amber – is there any truth to it?"

"Mr. Lance, I really think that if you want to know something about Amber, then Amber is the person you should be speaking to," Cavendish replied carefully. "I'm certainly not going to speak for her."

"Where did this story come from? How did it get in the paper?" demanded Lance. "Who would want it in the paper anyway?"

Cavendish sighed. Was Lance going to join the growing bandwagon of people who thought Cavendish had given the story to the *Chronicle* for a hundred bucks or two? Did everybody think that infidelity paid so poorly that he would need to take bribes and back handers and sell people out? And did Lance's sense of responsibility to his staff extend to concern about their extracurricular activities?

"I really don't know who would want to print such a story," was what he said out loud.

"Are you busy this morning? I would really like to speak with you in person."

Cavendish had reached Guerra Square and was looking at the polished white colonial edifice that housed the police department. "I am going into a meeting right now; I'm not sure how long it will take. But I can meet with you later."

"Come by the house at eleven. We can talk. I am very concerned about Amber," said Lance, sounding a little wary, almost nervous, as he shared what he obviously felt was a confidence. Sounding more psychic than Martine Letourneaux, he expounded: "I know you might think it strange of me to take such an interest in the daughter of one of my maids, but Pamela has worked here for many, many years. I have known Amber since she was a toddler, seen her grown up. I've known her family a long time, which is why I am so concerned about what I read today and the problems she might be creating for herself. And it makes me see your sudden appearance in her life in a new light. I would be interested to hear more about how you came to meet her and to be the one who brought her home yesterday."

Cavendish didn't want to make any promises, but he didn't object to meeting Lance again and speaking with him and he told him so.

"Thank you, Mr. Cavendish. I will expect you around eleven then." Lance rang off without saying goodbye, and Cavendish pocketed his phone and headed into the police station. He nodded to the officer working the front desk, Ekkel, a chap he had a nodding acquaintance with, and headed upstairs. The squad room was up there, so were the interrogation rooms where he had been yesterday, and the offices of the senior department officers.

He didn't see Swain or Singh and assumed they were out patrolling their beat. Near the corner of the floor was a civilian employee in a floral dress that Cavendish knew to be the secretary of the Chief Constable. He plotted his course to her and saw her pick up her phone and speak into it while she was looking at him. She obviously recognized him and was letting the chief know he was there so that when he reached her desk, she simply smiled at him and said, "Please go right in."

Cavendish pushed open the outer door – it had no

window and neither did the walls of the office because this was an old, scarcely updated building – and stepped through. It was a big office, about twenty by twenty feet, dominated by a big desk backed against the far wall. The Chief Constable sat behind that desk and was looking at him expectantly. This would be the first time he had met Chief Constable Borden Boxer. He knew him by reputation and had seen his picture but had never had the chance to say so much as 'hello'. Boxer stood up and reached across the desk to shake hands with Cavendish. His torso was heavy and thick and his legs made it look like he was walking on tree trunks. He was slightly overweight but looked like he could still pack a solid punch if he needed too. He was taller than Cavendish but not as tall as Hardy Swain. His head was almost shaved, and his hands seemed inconsistent with the general thickness of the man's body and legs – they were long with sinewy fingers that put Cavendish in mind of ET. His greeting was formal, his tone serious and his appraising look more than a little suspicious. Many police officers held private detectives in low esteem. Cavendish sensed that Boxer was one of them.

"Sit down, Mr. Cavendish." The lack of pleasantry seemed deliberate. Cavendish wasn't put off. He dropped into the offered chair with exaggerated casualness. Boxer wanted him to feel guarded and ill at ease, so he acted nonchalant. "You know why I asked you here?"

Cavendish was an ex-policeman who still had the soul of a lawman. This made him want to help the police. But like any citizen, when he felt he was being treated as a suspect in something he had no complicity in, he felt affronted and wanted to put the Chief Constable in his place. Part of him felt that, as a former police officer, and as a former – he knew it was arrogance that made him feel this way, but so be bit – officer of Scotland Yard, that he deserved a little extra measure of respect from someone he deemed almost a colleague. He got this from the St. Lazarus patrol officers, and he didn't see why he shouldn't expect it from the Chief Constable, too.

"I'll let you tell me."

In the same motion that Boxer used to sit down he slid

a newspaper across his expansive desk. Aside from the paper and a case folder, its vast surface was clean. "This story. You read it?"

Cavendish glanced at the paper and recognized the article about Amber Geranabby, so he nodded affirmatively.

"You came in with this girl yesterday. You were in a fight with one of her alleged victims."

"That's right."

"How do you know her?"

"I met her yesterday. The man I was in a fight with attempted to hire me. He wanted me to track her down for him. I thought he was dangerous, so I tried to find her myself to warn her. I found her about the same time he did."

"You never knew her before yesterday?"

Cavendish shook his head. "No."

"At the rooms where you fought this Ross Buchanan, you discovered she had set up a little pornographic movie studio?"

"I did."

"Did Buchanan pay you for helping him find the girl? Did she pay you for saving her from him?"

"I never took money from Buchanan or the girl."

"Did you take money from the *Chronicle*?"

"I never discussed this with anyone at the paper. I don't know anyone there," he decided to tweak the Chief Constable's nose. "I assumed that story had been leaked by one of your officers." Boxer reacted predictably.

"What? Because we are a third world country you think all my officers must be corrupt? Is that your opinion Mr. Scotland Yard wash-out?" He maintained a conversational tone, but the undercurrent of hostility was unmistakable. Cavendish was a little shocked by the "wash-out" - did Boxer think he was fired from Scotland Yard? And why should he care if he did? Or was he just trying to unsettle him? Cavendish tried to keep his words focused and on point.

"Because no one else knew. Amber had no interest in bringing attention to herself. I thought maybe one of your constables on duty yesterday might have an excessively expensive girlfriend."

"My officers are well paid enough they don't have to take bribes or sell stories to the newspaper," asserted Boxer.

"The best paid man in the world can live beyond his means. Besides, money isn't the only motivator. What if one of your people is sleeping with the author who wrote this story? Helping them out with a good story out of the love in the heart? It must be a boon for the writer – there hasn't been a news story like that since I got here. Usually the most exciting article covers the opening of a new seafood restaurant or something."

"Do you know how many men this girl victimized?"

"I'm not sure that's a fair characterization. I mean, I know she blackmailed them – but they were grown men choosing to behave in a self-destructive way."

"The answer is we don't know how many men this girl preyed on," continued Boxer, ambivalent about Cavendish's observation. "What we do know is our island newspaper was filled with a story about how men came here and cheated on their wives and were blackmailed by a local girl. And that this story is being picked up all over the world. It was on the Drudge Report, the LA Times, BBC – they all love this story. Sin and debauchery in paradise. And the governor is pissed. He wants to know how this story got in the paper, he wants to know how this girl did this, and he wants to make sure she never does it again. That no one does it again. Which brings me back to you. Do you know how this story got released to the *St. Lazarus Chronicle*?"

Cavendish shook his head. "No."

"You have lived here less than a year so you may not be familiar with what the governor is trying to do. Our little island produces rum and has nice beaches. He is trying to build up tourism. Wives won't want to bring their husbands to an island where local girls are going to steal them," said Boxer. "He is also trying to bring foreign banks and financial institutions here – and they don't like scandals and the idea that this island could be some kind of sex playground."

Cavendish had met some bankers who would be drawn to exactly that notion but thought it might be best not to say so.

"Why did you drive Amber Geranabby home?"

"She needed a ride."

"You say you never met her before, yet you go out of your way to take her home. Why?"

"She's a young girl making mistakes. I'm a father. I hope if my daughter was out there making mistakes and I couldn't help her that there might be some male that offers help instead of trying to take advantage of her. I wanted to talk to her a little bit. I wanted to know why she was doing this, selling herself in this way. I don't know if there is any help I could offer her, or that she would accept but – she's playing with fire. It was always just a matter of time until someone like Ross Buchanan showed up. Someone who wasn't willing to pay the toll, who would try to shut her up instead. I think she could get herself in serious trouble one day. I wanted her to see that."

Boxer regarded him skeptically. "And did your silver-tongued eloquence bring her to her senses?"

"I don't think so," Cavendish conceded. "I think she believes she is young and invincible. But I wanted to try, nonetheless."

"Out of the kindness of your heart?"

"For want of a better explanation that you might find satisfactory, yes," shrugged Cavendish belligerently.

Boxer opened the case file and pulled out a sheet of paper. "Do you know how much money she had in her bank accounts?"

Cavendish shook his head. Boxer held up the sheet. "Two-hundred and fourteen thousand dollars. That's a lot of money for a nineteen-year-old whore."

Cavendish whistled appreciatively in spite of himself. He had not expected her to have made so much.

Boxer was prompt to disparage Amber, but Cavendish reflected more on the nature of the men falling for her trap. He had frequently heard the refrain that a man was just a man and would take any sexual offer he was given, as if he had no ability to consider or reject such an offer, as if giving into sexual temptation was as natural for him as giving into the temptations of hunger or a bathroom visit, and as impossible to resist. Cavendish had met men who behaved this way, and most women seemed angrier at a woman trying to poach her man than the man acting like the mangiest street dog. It was a strange phenomenon, that with all the advances in technology and social mores, that as far as humans had advanced and evolved, women did not expect men to be anything more than creatures of the basest instinct and most men didn't call upon themselves to be more than that either. He had seen many Ross Buchanans, quick to give into temptation and quicker to blame the woman who had tempted him as if all the fault was hers and he had no responsibility because, after all, he was a man, and what else could one expect? Since Eve had taken the apple, she had taken the heat for all the sins of man and shared that blame with the women of every generation thereafter, it seemed.

He also wondered how much money Amber planned to make before she quit. Or did she figure roping men with her wiles and blackmailing them was a train that would never stop running? Until she crossed a Ross Buchanan that was a little better organized and a little more ruthless.

Cavendish reached for the sheet and Boxer let him take it. There were multiple bank accounts – she spread her money around and any one bank might look at her profile and think she was unusually good at saving for a girl of her generation, but there was nothing dramatically suspicious. Taken individually there was nothing about any of her bank relationships to draw extra attention. She was smart enough to fly under the radar, or else someone was giving her good counsel.

"Does she have a day job?" asked Cavendish, relinquishing the paper to Boxer.

"This is her day job," groaned Boxer, restoring the financial information to the folder. "Or at least it was."

"How are you going to stop her if you can't get the men to make any complaints against her?"

"This isn't New York, Mr. Cavendish. We aren't

hamstrung by Miranda rights and the ACLU. We can put a stop to it. We will put a stop to it. And if you can't help me determine who released the news story to the paper, and since I have no proof to show it was you, then you are free to go."

Cavendish was surprised that the interview was being halted so abruptly, but having determined whatever he hoped to determine, Boxer was clearly moving on to the next item in his agenda. Cavendish was not going to provoke him and had a meeting with Marvin Lance to get to, so he took advantage of Boxer's dismissal and fled.

≈

Cavendish enjoyed the drive up to the Lance plantation. The winding roads led away from the congestion of the town and he made good time, the car swooping with confidence through the corners. He passed a couple of surrey buses loaded with tourists, driving almost as fast as him. The views alternated as he drove. Panoramas down the mountainside to the sea, corridors of green trees, clusters of shacks and sugar cane fields.

It was almost exactly eleven as he pulled up to the entrance of the Lance House. The broken gate hung impotently but a guard waited to register his arrival and usher him into the yard. A pair of men in jeans were contemplating the damage to the gates and pillars, and their work truck sat just inside the opening so Cavendish guessed they were either preparing a bid to repair it or getting ready to start the work. The yard was empty of production vehicles this morning. Maybe it wasn't a shooting day, maybe they were shooting elsewhere or maybe Lance's anger had sent them away.

Cavendish parked his car and headed up to the main door of the house. He hoped he would have a chance to speak with Amber. He had questions, and he wanted to warn her, too. But first he would see what Marvin Lance had to say.

Pamela Geranabby opened the door to him. It was plain she now knew a lot more about what her daughter had been up to yesterday than the last time they'd met, and her tear reddened eyes condemned him roundly. "You knew what my baby girl was doing yesterday, and you didn't tell me."

"I was hoping she would tell you herself," Cavendish felt like he was the one being caught by surprise, and he tried to explain. "I was hoping yesterday might make her think about making changes in her life."

"You don't think her Mother had a right to know what she was up to?"

"Yes – but she's over eighteen. If she was a minor, I surely would have." He knew it sounded hollow, and he knew it hadn't been his place to tell Pamela, but he found himself feeling guilty anyway.

"That's different then," she barked caustically. "I didn't realize you knew it was time for me to stop caring about my daughter. Why don't you go through and see Mr. Lance? He's waiting for you in his study," she stepped aside, eyeing him cynically. "Maybe you don't talk to me about it because you think there's some way for you to use her, too?"

Cavendish took a tentative step forward. "That's not the case. Maybe we can talk a little bit after I've spoken with Mr. Lance?"

"Yesterday would have been a good day for you to talk with me. Today I don't see any point," she stared at the floor. She was ignoring him, not kowtowing. "I ain't got nothing to say to you. And you can't tell me anything I want to hear."

Cavendish nodded and moved into the house. He understood her sentiments. He would probably have the same reaction if, god forbid, it was his daughter. He found his way to the study easily because it opened from the main hallway, as the dining room did. The study was finished in anachronistic dark wood but was brightened by vast, seamless floor to ceiling glass windows that had been retrofitted to bring the vista of the Atlantic Ocean into the house.

Lance was seated at his desk, but eagerly rose to greet him.

"Thank you for coming, Mr. Cavendish." He moved around the desk and offered his hand. They shook; he gestured to one of the chairs and returned to his own as Cavendish sat and threw his ankle over his knee. Cavendish had been answering questions all morning. That was not the natural role of a detective, and he was tired of it already. Even though Lance had summoned him, he decided to try and start with a question or two of his own.

"Mr. Lance, is Amber a popular girl in your household?"

"What do you mean popular?"

"I mean, if anyone here found out what she was up to, would they have a vested interest in publicly exposing her and humiliating her? Is there anyone that hates her that much? That's jealous of her?"

"She and Mia are the only children that live here now... I think the staff like her. She can be rambunctious - I think all teenagers can - but she is always courteous and friendly to everyone. Besides, I don't think anyone knew what she was doing. Lord knows I didn't." He shook his head as if to emphasize his level of shock.

"Do you believe what you read in the newspaper about her?"

Lance looked at him sadly, nodding. "The first thing I did was confront her. It was the first time I have ever seen her angry, defiant. She said it was all true. And asked me – asked me if I wish she had given me a chance to be with her. I don't understand it."

"I don't understand it myself, Mr. Lance. She seems like a bright girl. Maybe she thought it was easy money." Cavendish wondered if other children lived on the property, would Lance have taken such an immediate and personal interest in their actions?

"She's a criminal." He sounded laden with regret.

"She's an alleged criminal," Cavendish clarified. "A newspaper report doesn't mean she is guilty of anything. It doesn't even mean charges will be filed. I am a little surprised though – why you are taking such an interest in her..."

"She grew up here. I've known her since she was small; I try to take care of my staff and their families. It shocked the hell out of me to see this happen. I'm sorry, where are my manners? I forgot to offer you coffee…"

"I'm fine, Mr. Lance. Thank you, though. I saw Mia being dropped off at school. You sent her in the town car. That seems like a pretty generous thing for you to do."

"The car is there whether I am riding in it or not, why shouldn't it give the girl a ride to school?" Lance sounded offended. "Her mother has worked here for years and worked very hard and shown tremendous loyalty. I don't think an employee deserves to be treated like a commodity." In fairness to Mr. Lance, Cavendish had to acknowledge that he had a reputation for fairness and generosity towards all his employees. "I would have paid for Amber to go to college if that was what she wanted. Why would she do this?"

"The only person that can answer that question is Amber. But I will tell you this, if you care about her the way you say, one thing she may need help with is legal counsel. I don't suppose she's around is she? I would really like to ask her a question or two."

"Yesterday a man became violent with her and you were there to intervene. I thank you for that."

For a moment Cavendish thought Lance might whip out a checkbook to offer a token of his gratitude, and in that moment, Cavendish was already imagining figures and ways to graciously accept the generosity without appearing mercenary. Alas, Lance did not reach for his check book. Maybe Cavendish's detection instincts were rusty.

"I imagine that Amber could be in danger. If that man is still on the island – "

"He is," Cavendish affirmed.

"Then he could be very angry – especially since his wife might know about this now."

"She does."

"And who knows what other victims who are out there could come looking for her?"

"You might get more media attention, too," Cavendish warned him. "So far, the news story is just local, but it is the kind of story that can garner attention from outside the island. You may want to get all your security alarms and your fences checked."

"That producer, Megan Shepard? She already pitched her on trying to sell her story as a movie of the week," Lance shook his head. "Pamela is devastated. She worked so hard to show her girls the right way to live their lives. She spent fifteen years cleaning our house to teach her daughters to make an honest living. She could have easily taken an easier route - and then this is the path Amber takes. It almost makes me feel happy I was never so blessed."

"Mia may not make the same mistakes," suggested Cavendish.

"So far, so good," agreed Lance. "But you need to understand, Amber was never a bad girl. She was bright, friendly. She struggled in school, but she was no dummy. There was nothing to suggest she would do something like this – Do you think she needs to worry about criminal charges?"

Cavendish liked Marvin Lance, both with and without the context of his rum. But he had known him less than twenty-four hours and wasn't sure about sharing confidences that could affect Amber's life. For all Cavendish knew, the benevolent, fatherly Marvin Lance could number among Amber's victims. He fit the profile. Monied and married.

"I think that the police will probably take a look at her, but I'm no lawyer. I don't know if they will bring charges. They might just be eager for the scandal to subside."

"Who would leak this to the newspapers?"

"Somebody who knew. Somebody who could gain." The reasons for doing it were obvious. Less obvious was determining who would benefit.

Lance just shook his head. "I just can't imagine why she would do something like this. She was never a bad girl. To think of her doing this – with how many men? It's hard to imagine. She didn't have to do this. She didn't have to make this choice."

"Sometimes those are the kinds of choices that are hardest to make sense of Mr. Lance," observed Cavendish. He was a little intrigued by the depth of concern Lance seemed to have. He knew of employers with a fondness for employees, but Lance seemed deeply distressed. A man having trouble reconciling his image of a little girl with the reality of the woman? A man who may have coveted that girl himself, or even had her himself and was jealous to think it could have been a non-exclusive arrangement? Monied and married.

"Mr. Lance, the police questioned me because aside from the possibility of a police officer leaking the story, there don't seem to be any other suspects with the knowledge of the situation or the motive to give it to the newspaper," began Cavendish. Curiosity is the curse of the detective, and in the next breath Cavendish had let his curiosity lead him into an inquiry for which he had no client to bill. "Starting with motive, can you think of anyone that would want to publicly 'out' and humiliate her like this?"

"I see her around the property. I see whether she looks happy or not. I see the friends she is on good terms with, but when they stop being her friends, I stop seeing them. I've never really heard huge fights or arguments or anything."

"Does she go through friends quickly?"

"What counts as quickly? I would see the same faces for a year or two when she was growing up. That's normal for a young girl, isn't it?" he stopped short, struck by a fresh realization. "But I haven't seen her bring any friends around for a year or two. Probably since she graduated high school."

"Did anything happen in her life at that time – the time when she stopped bringing friends around? Anything that was a big deal to her, even if maybe it didn't seem such a big deal to the adults around her?"

"Not that I know about. Her mother might know better. Or maybe even her sister although I don't think I like the idea of dragging Mia into this…"

Cavendish wasn't sure if it was wise to dig his nose any deeper into the mystery of the published article. He wasn't getting paid and the person he was most sympathetic too probably was less than enthusiastic about seeing him anymore involved. Lance seemed to be reaching out for help, but

Cavendish wasn't sure if he should trust him.

And yet it couldn't hurt to talk to Amber a little bit more and see if she would be more forthcoming now that the news had broken.

"Mr. Lance, is Amber around today? Is there any chance I could speak with her?"

Lance regarded him appraisingly. "What for?"

"Maybe she might be able to shed some light on who might have the motive to sell the story. Or who else knew."

Lance nodded. "Okay. But who are you working for?"

It occurred to Cavendish that with $214,000.00 in the bank Amber could easily afford his daily rate for a few days.

"I'm not working, I'm just having a conversation," he replied.

Lance gestured towards the seaward side of the house. "She was lying by the pool. She seems very - she seems to be taking this all very much in stride. I find it all very hard to process."

He shook his head, tired, resigned and confused. Much like Pamela Geranabby had seemed.

CHAPTER EIGHT

Amber was lying by the pool, flat on her back with a purple and gold baseball cap protecting her face from the blast of the sun of the almost midday sun She was wearing a one-piece and had a small pool-bag with a towel and water bottle sticking out of it. He walked up to where she was laying, wondering if she was aware of him and deliberately ignoring him. He sat gracelessly on the chaise lounge adjacent to hers, but she still gave no indication that she was aware of his presence.

He noted the rhythm of her breathing, and the pace of her rising and falling chest suggested she was awake and feigning ignorance. He decided to be direct. He grabbed her cap by its peak and flipped it off her head.

She blinked in the glare of her sun and snatched for the hat irritably. "You're blinding me!"

He relinquished the hat. "I wanted to talk to you."

"God, is that all you do?" she covered her face with her hat again. "What's the deal with you anyway? Why are you sticking your nose all over my life?"

"Nosiness is an occupational hazard for me. And I am concerned about you... I think you are getting into a lot more trouble than you need or want."

She pushed the cap up onto her forehead and looked at

him through squinting eyes. "Did you sell me out to the newspapers?"

Cavendish shook his head. "I was going to ask you if you knew anyone who might want to expose you."

"Nobody knew. Except a bunch of husbands with no reason to tell anyone. I'm sure there are people that hate me, but the only people that knew all the details that were in that article were Tyree, me, you, Buchanan and the cops. I'm thinking Buchanan wouldn't have gone to the paper and Tyree wouldn't. This could put a dent in our gig." She eyed him momentarily. "And I am thinking you wouldn't have gone to the paper, however much you disapprove of me."

"It's not you I disapprove of," he replied gently. "It's what you're doing. Why don't you think I would have outed you?"

She shifted on to her side and propped herself on an elbow. "You know something that I learned luring all those guys into my web? Some guys can't wait to nail you. But not all guys. There are some nice guys out there and you get pretty good at telling them apart. I don't think you would've outed me because I don't think it's your style. It's an asshole move."

"Thank you for the compliment. But that leaves you and the police..."

"Well I wouldn't have outed myself. I used to think I was going to do it for a while and then quit, but I don't have a husband or a boyfriend so I'm not hurting anybody in my life and let's face it, the money is easy. You just lie there and let the guy do whatever and then you take all his money and you make him feel like a scared little piece of crap that nearly wets himself. I love watching them go all shaky." She seemed a little embarrassed. "I know they think they have all the power and then they realize I have it, and they freak. Maybe it's bad that I like that so much."

"Is that how you see yourself? An avenging angel screwing the guys that screw around on their wives?"

"I don't pretend there's anything good about what I do. I'm not pretending I am the moral justice police or anything. But those men that go with me, none of them are drugged; they know what they're doing. They deserve what they get."

"You never worry about someone like Buchanan?"

She shrugged. "I didn't read him as someone that would go violent. I try to pick my marks very carefully. The guy who'll cheat but who will turn to jelly when you shove the pictures in his face and make him think he's going to jail after he gets out of divorce court. Buchanan was a bad call. I misjudged him."

"He could have really hurt you. Maybe even killed you."

Amber smiled mischievously and clutched her hands together under her chin like a mock Disney princess. "But then you came along, my knight in shining armor. You saved me." She pursed her lips and looked down at herself provocatively. "How will I ever thank you?"

Cavendish ignored her, tried not to look embarrassed because he knew it would amuse her. "How did you start doing this anyway?"

"Didn't you hear? I might have a deal for a movie of the week. Megan says I shouldn't talk to anyone about my story because somebody could steal it. 'This' could be my meal ticket."

"Is Hoyt Buxton going to be your agent?"

"Maybe. He offered," she smiled coquettishly and batted her eyelids. "I might become a star."

"Was that the master plan?"

"No. The plan was just the money. This is unexpected. But I'll take it. I might not have a choice. With my name all over the place I might not be able to lure men to my lair anymore..."

"How did you get that whole studio set up arranged?"

"Earlier customers financed the upgrades."

"You don't seem very concerned. Aren't you worried that being out in the public eye could draw unwanted attention from some of your victims?"

"I still have pictures and video. Anybody who came after me would be outed."

"Yes, but now they are just philanderers. They aren't going to be afraid of going to jail for statutory rape," he observed. "They thought you were a minor, but the newspaper printed your true age.

"The worst thing that is going to happen is I have to stop doing what I was doing, but another door is already opening."

"When you were growing up - you never wanted to be a teacher or a lawyer or a dentist or anything like that?" wondered Cavendish.

"My stupid mother was a maid. And I didn't want to have my tuition paid for by the Marvin Lance charitable organization. Besides, I hated school. I can't see myself spending any more time in it than I had to. And look where we live. Even if I did tough it out and get a degree – where am I going to get a job? There's like 150,000 people on this stupid island. All the good jobs are taken and anytime anyone dies and frees up a decent job, there are thirty people lined up to take their place. People with A averages would have a better shot at landing jobs than someone who barely managed Cs. I would end up being a maid, or a stupid tour guide. Hate me for being shallow or being a whore if you feel like it, but I wanted more. I want a good life with all the stuff I want to buy. My mom didn't want to set me up – maid – so I had to figure out a way to set myself up. And I may not be super-hot, but I was hot enough to lure horny middle-aged married men to their demise."

"And having sex with so many men didn't bother you?"

"You mean do I feel bad about being slutty?" She flopped onto her back again. "Why didn't I save my womanly delights for that special someone? And live in wedded, acceptable bliss while working as a maid and sleeping with a man who will probably end up leaving anyway. Or he's cheating on you with a dozen other women because you've borne his babies and your figure goes to pot? And then that special someone leaves, and you have another special someone, and then another. How is that different from being a whore? You're still sleeping with a bunch of people, just at a different pace. Sex isn't special to anyone anymore. Look at how many one-night stands people have. In a way, I am just more honest about it. And I used it. It was the straight line to the life I wanted." She tugged the cap down over her eyes again. "And if you do try and do it the right way, what happens? You just end up living your life as a maid raising your daughters and having no life of your own."

How did this girl become so jaded and cynical? Or was she right? Had the world discarded all the old values and she was just interpreting the new world order more honestly. Cavendish had seen much of the unseemly aspects of life, but even his jaundiced eyes were a little shocked by Amber's cavalier outlook.

"I think it's a shame you see the world that way," he said finally. "I think it's a shame you don't see how much you could contribute to the world in a more positive way. If you get a kick out of exposing these guys for their misdeeds, you might make a good cop. Or private detective. You are strong and bright and there might be a man out there who really appreciates those qualities."

"Well, after I get my movie deal, I don't think I'll need to worry much about contributing. Just collecting!"

Cavendish thought she might be overestimating the remuneration she could expect from a movie of the week, but he was hardly an expert so there was little reason to dispute her optimism.

"If you think of anyone else that might have known what you were up to yesterday, whether or not you think they had a motive to expose you, give me a call, okay?"

The cap was shoved back on her forehead again. "Is Lance paying you?"

"No."

"Then why do you care?"

"I'll tell you when you tell me how you decided to get mixed up in this business in the first place."

He stood up and walked away, heading around the exterior of the house in the reverse course of the route that had brought him here last night. He heard Amber adjust herself more comfortably on the chaise lounge. In his guts he felt she was in worse trouble than she thought and her lighthearted regard for the threat worried him. His path took him under the angled roofline that shaded the patio. People with rooms above it would have had a commanding view over the pool and sea from their windows.

As he came around to the front of the house, he had a clear view of Pamela's cottage at the foot of the short embankment. He expected she was probably still on duty in the house since she'd answered the front door less than an hour earlier. The thought of trying to restart a conversation with her fizzled as fast as it formulated. She was in no mood to speak with him, and as a parent he could empathize.

He got into his car and headed back into town, taking the winding roads slowly as his mind picked through the conversations and encounters of the day. The publication of the revelatory news story was starting to irk him. Who could have wanted to smear her reputation that way? Maybe a lot of people, but none, it seemed, with access to the comprehensive details that were published in the paper. Who had access to the information? Cavendish, Tyree, Buchanan and Amber, and the police. None among the first four seemed to have a motive. That left the police. It was certainly conceivable for a corrupt policeman to sell the story. But how would that have worked? Someone in the paper with an open-ended agreement to buy any dirt that the police could provide?

It would be interesting to see the police report and compare it to the article. He wondered if Hardy Swain or Jenny Singh would be obliging enough to give him a copy, or if that would be too ambitious a favour to ask. He could always talk to the newspaper writer to see what her source was, but experience taught him that was likely to be a worse than fruitless venture.

It was about one o'clock already by the time he neared the office, so he ditched his car in the usual spot and then walked down the back alleys of Port Rose where the tourist throngs seldom reached. He went to a little coffee shop where the food was fresh, and the grill was kept clean. He liked it because the food tasted like itself and not like the twelve other dishes that were cooked on the grill previously. His mother-in-law's cooking was bountiful and had an expansive effect on his abdomen, so he opted for half a tuna sandwich and salad. He was still in good shape but staying lean and fit no longer came as easily as when he was in his twenties. He made a mental note that he should go for a run that night.

He turned the morning's events over in his mind as he crunched through his luncheon. He had left a voicemail for Swain to see if they could meet for a drink after Swain's shift – he didn't want to ask about the police report on the telephone. And he thought about trying to pursue some real, paying work in the meantime. He didn't know what else to do. Amber didn't want help and despite his misgivings he wasn't really sure what kind of help she needed or if he could offer it. Maybe she needed psychoanalysis to find out why the most intimate behaviors were so unimportant to her. He had known prostitutes. Girls abused in their youth, girls who stopped caring about their bodies after they had been consumed by cravings for drugs and alcohol. And from time to time there was the girl who just figured she was sitting on a gold mine and might as well make use of it.

He dropped enough cash to cover the meal and tip, then left and walked back his office. His curiosity prodded him to try and find out who had leaked the story about Amber to the press, and how much it had been worth. But it was most likely a cop and in a small island nation provoking the police by unearthing corruption in their midst may not be the best away to assure himself of the quiet life he wanted to provide his daughter.

On the other hand, if the police decided to hang the blame on him as the only interested outsider with a motive, that could be equally disruptive. They could hassle him, pull his investigator's license, or even charge him with a crime. It was doubtful he would get convicted – third world or not, St. Lazarus was not known for kangaroo courts – but revoking his license could be done almost arbitrarily. Its renewal was at the whim of the police. While it was worth proving that he wasn't the one bringing embarrassment and bad publicity down on the island, he could paint himself into a fresh corner if he proved it was a policeman who was corrupt.

As he walked back to the office with the intention to

check his email for invitations of gainful employment, he pulled out his mobile phone and tried to call the reporter who had written the story but she was unavailable. He wondered if the police had gotten to her yet. If it was a corrupt copper who spilled the beans, maybe she would spill the beans to the police and his problems would go away. He hoped she wasn't the sort of sanctimonious and principled journalist who protected her sources – but knew she probably was.

Climbing the stairs to his office, he wondered what kind of reporter would consider this story newsworthy anyway. The only victims were men who, let's face it, deserved what they got. And their wives, Cavendish supposed. But as news it was hardly relevant beyond the lives of those immediately involved. The only value it had as news beyond that was its ability to sell newspapers. Perhaps very many. St. Lazarus was not known for its raging sex scandals.

At the top of the stairs, he was surprised to discover he had someone patiently waiting in the hallway outside his office. There was no waiting room but there were three simple stick and wicker chairs spaced along the hallway that was a shared waiting area for all the offices on the floor, and Hoyt was adjusting his pear-shaped frame uncomfortably on one.

"Mr. Buxton?"

Buxton seemed almost relieved to stand up. "Hello, Mr. Cavendish. I hope you don't mind me looking you up."

"Not at all. But if you had stayed at Mr. Lance's house, you would have seen me sooner. I just came from there." They shook hands, and despite the Caribbean warmth outside, Buxton's hand felt like a packet of wieners taken fresh from the fridge. Cavendish unlocked his office and motioned for Buxton to precede him inside.

"I knew you were there this morning, but I didn't want to speak to you there," Buxton said furtively.

Buxton sat without bidding in one of the two visitor's chairs, perching on the edge of the cushion. Cavendish squeezed around behind his desk – it really was too big for this room – and plopped into the big leather chair, the only piece of furniture in the office that wasn't weather beaten and ancient and picked up third or fourth hand.

"Why not?"

"Mr. Lance has a very nice house, but every time you go around a corner you bump into someone. Maids. Other guests. You never know who is listening."

The pear was a good metaphor for Buxton's overall physique as well as certain parts thereof. He had a pear-shaped head on top of a pair-shaped torso. He seemed to wobble and barely balance on the edge of the chair, because his legs were quite skinny. He was like a cartoon parody of a man.

"What would you be afraid of them hearing?"

"Mr. Cavendish, I know you might think I am crazy, but I think my life could be in danger."

"Your life?" Cavendish tried to keep his voice from sounding incredulous, but it was such an unexpected statement, and so out of sync with his morning that he was taken aback. "Why on earth would your life be in danger?"

"I think – I think Martine's husband would like me out of the way," said Buxton warily. He seemed afraid of sharing this confidence, like he was telling tales on the schoolyard bully who might be listening outside the door at this very moment. And who might punish him later for exposing him. But even as Cavendish processed Buxton's unlikely fear, his mind flashed back to the brief and strange encounter with a distinctly edgy Peter Pennington. *Who are you working for? Was it Buxton?*

"Why would Martine's husband want you out of the way?"

"Peter wants to run her career himself. He wants to cut me out," said Buxton, concluding ominously: "He has threatened me in the past."

"Why would he want to manage Martine's career?"

"To control her money. Right now, he basically lives on an allowance, Martine is very jealous, and keeps him on a short leash by controlling the money. But Peter is not the kind of man who likes to live on an allowance. He wants to call the shots. He thinks if he can convince Martine to get rid of me, he can become her agent and get control of her money because he would be calling the shots on her career."

"Do you call the shots on her career now?"

"Of course not. I advise her and help her — but Peter would tell her what to do in every respect. He thinks he is the smartest man in any room."

"And you don't?"

"Not even if he is alone in the room. He is a pile of arrogance and testosterone, but Martine loves him, and he has been trying to convince her I am holding her back and that she should fire me."

"Is that what you mean by your life being in danger? Are you really just talking about your livelihood?"

Buxton shook his head. "Last night he took me by the throat and shoved me against the wall and told me if I knew what was good for me, I would quit…. He accused me of hiring you, too and was very angry about it."

"That seems a bit extreme, if he is going to be able to convince his wife to fire you, why threaten you?"

"Because I know he just wants to spend her money until it's all gone, and I called him off on that."

"What makes you have such a low opinion of him? Have they been married long?"

Buxton shook his head. "Only a couple of years. He is younger than her. I know he doesn't look it, but she looks young for her age," Buxton paused as if puzzling over an internal question he'd considered before and never resolved. "I don't know what makes certain women trust certain men. But she trusts him more all the time, even though I have been with her since she was working school carnivals for two dollars a reading. She has been tight with his allowance, like I said, but she is getting more and more trusting. And when Peter started hinting I should leave, I stood up to him and said I wouldn't go and he just got angry and threatened me and started trying to make me look bad to Martine every chance he gets. Last night he thought I had hired you to try to dig up dirt on him and he held me against a wall."

"He thought you hired me?" Cavendish repeated quizzically. What dirt was there in Pennington's background that worried him so much? Clearly there was something for him to have reacted with such heat. "Have you any idea what secrets he could be afraid of coming out?"

"That's the thing. I don't. If I did, believe me I would have hired someone to dig them up before now to try to get rid of him. Or at least get Martine's guard up. I didn't think there was anything except for him being a jerk, until last night when he pinned me to the wall, and I thought he wanted to put my head through it."

"So are you looking to hire me for protection because I have to tell you I am not a bodyguard."

"No, Mr. Cavendish. I can lock my door and stay where there are other people. I don't think he is stupid. If we were by ourselves on a cliff, he might give me a push, but in the house, I think I am safe. But I do want to know what secret he is afraid of me finding out. Maybe I can use it against him, or at least keep myself safe."

"Mr. Buxton, whatever his secret is, I doubt it's something here on the island. You've been here what – a couple of weeks?"

"But you can start. You can check his background. And you're the only detective I know. What is your rate? I can pay you very well you know. Martine has made me very comfortable financially."

Cavendish *was* in need of a client. He mentally doubled his daily fee. It was a brazen sum, but he was curious to see if Buxton would go for it. He only did it because Buxton was boasting about his bankroll. "Mr. Buxton, you have to understand I am not cheap. I charge one-thousand dollars a day, plus expenses, with a five-day minimum."

Wordlessly, Buxton reached into his pocket and with some difficulty extracted a wad of bills. He sorted and straightened them on the desk. "That's a thousand. Can you take a cheque on an American bank for the difference?"

With a thousand dollars cash laid out before him,

Cavendish felt that he could chance the time lag in seeing the balance clear. "A cheque is fine."

Buxton pulled a cheque book from his other pants pocket. It was twisted from where it was bent against his body when he walked. He scribbled quickly and ripped the cheque from the book quickly and carelessly. The corner tore.

"You really feel that scared of Peter Pennington?"

"Look at me, Mr. Cavendish. You can tell I am not the kind of man who laughs in the face of danger. I even get scared negotiating deals. I am not an agent's agent, it's a miracle I have such a great client and I am smart enough to know it. Peter is probably right. I probably could have gotten her better deals if I was more of a fighter. But I'm not. And I am desperate to keep her as a client. Just because he scares me doesn't make me a bad person, and just because I am not the best agent in the world doesn't mean he should be able to get rid of me. And there must be a skeleton in his closet if he is so scared of me hiring a detective – that's why I want to hire you. Maybe it's time for me to fight for something."

"I'll do some digging. And if I find any leads, and you don't mind paying for travel or for me subcontracting to local investigators, maybe we can find something out. And I agree, from what you describe there seems to be something he is afraid to see come out."

Buxton looked relieved that he was being taken seriously.

"How long have you represented Martine?"

"About ten years?"

"How did you meet?"

"She gave me a reading at my nephew's school carnival," said Buxton. "She had a way – it was that whole island flair. She was so convincing – "

"You don't sound like you believe in her gift?"

"Of course, I do. I believe in her gift to get a client to handover fistfuls of money to hear her commune with his dead relatives. I believe in her gift to get an audience to sit on the edge of their seats wondering whose relative will be the next one to try to reach through the barrier from the next world. I believe in her ability to sell advertising space on the Her Life network, and sell books, and sell out personal appearances. I believe in her ability to pay for my mortgage on the Sherman Oaks house I own and the St. Lazarus condo I am looking at. I believe in her gift completely."

Cavendish smiled. "At least you're honest about her."

"And who says she isn't the real thing?" Buxton expounded. "I've seen her have some pretty amazing insights. Whether she was told by spirits or just made a very lucky guess, she has a gift. And yes, it's a gift that made a lot of money for her and for me. I know she is my gravy train and I am riding her coattails. Sue me."

"You said Peter came along after she was successful already. How did they meet?"

"At a book signing. He was in line to get a book signed for his mother," Buxton shook his head. "Sometimes a hundred people pass by in a blur and you can't tell one from the other. Somehow, he managed to get her talking and set himself apart. I don't know how, but he charmed her. When I met him, it was back at the hotel bar. She was having a cocktail with him and telling him about his father.

"Then they were dating, and he was taking time off from work and showing up two towns further up the tour... she never talked a lot about the relationship, but suddenly he was around all the time. I guess he went on furlough from work, if he even was working," Buxton noted bitterly. "And she started spending money. She had never been a big spender. She liked to be comfortable, but nothing crazy. And then suddenly, she is buying him a black Maserati for him to cruise around Beverly Hills. He's a con artist."

Cavendish reflected upon Martine's chosen profession. "Sometimes con artists themselves make the easiest marks."

Buxton either didn't register the jibe or chose to ignore it. He stuffed the cheque book back in his pocket. "I'd better get back."

Did he fear extra punishment if his absence was

detected? They both stood up and shook hands. His was still cold and nervous. If nothing else, his fear of Peter Pennington was sincere.

"Thank you for helping me, Mr. Cavendish. I know you probably think I am just being foolish and nervous for no reason."

"It's not for me to judge. I'll do the job you asked. But remember that I might turn up nothing. Or if I do find something, the secret Pennington is so afraid of might end up being useless to you or meaningless to Martine."

"I understand. But I have to do something. I don't know how to fight Peter. And Martine is my gravy train. Call me whatever you want, but I don't want the gravy train to end. I know I am not going to find another one and maybe I am selfish, but at least I am honest about that. And I have always stood by her and done my best for her."

Buxton left the office and his quick, nervous steps receded down the stairs. Cavendish pushed aside the shadow of guilt he felt for overcharging Buxton, consoling his conscience with the thought that Buxton was flush with cash. If it later turned out he was exerting a hardship over the poor sap, he could always give him a refund.

He glanced at his watch. It was half past one. He compartmentalized the question of the newspaper story about Amber's sins and started doing some preliminary research on Peter Pennington and the question of the mysterious secret he seemed so sensitive about.

CHAPTER NINE

After leaving another message for the newspaper writer who had outed Amber Universal Pictures, Cavendish started researching Peter Pennington.

Aside from Hoyt Buxton's allegations, Cavendish knew few things about him. He knew he was married to Martine Letourneaux. He knew that Pennington disliked or feared Buxton and that Pennington was impulsive, possibly foolish and violently so— his emotional outburst in the hallway after dinner established the first point. Buxton could have been lying about the physical threat to himself, but Cavendish thought it was consistent with his own observations of Pennington. Third, Pennington had no apparent professional interests outside his wife's career. Buxton could have been exaggerating, misreading, or lying about Pennington wanting to push him out of the picture – but his conversation at the dinner table was exclusively about his wife's career. He didn't talk of anything else.

The internet was always a handy place to start researching people. In the new millennium people were often publicly boastful of who they were or, more precisely, who they wanted you to think they were. Cavendish soon discovered that Pennington did not fall into that camp. Facebook and LinkedIn searches were fruitless.

He did find Pennington referenced in a lot of biographical articles about Martine Letourneaux and on her own website. The official bio read as Hoyt had described it. A big fan meeting his favorite psychic medium at a book signing. Except in the P.R. blurbs he stood out from the line of adoring fans because of something especially compelling in his aura, something she couldn't ignore. Something that resonated with her as if they had been together before, perhaps many times before in different lives and times. Perhaps Martine's spirit animal pointed him out to her, Cavendish speculated.

He also started to learn more about Martine Letourneaux' personal perspective on being a psychic and the other world as she understood it. Or rather, how she sold it. She claimed she believed in reincarnation. She believed that spirits could come back to this world as many times as they wanted while they sought to achieve whatever long-term goals of understanding they sought. This life, this mortal life that Archer Cavendish plodded through, seemed to be a school ground for spirits, in the mythology Martine spun for herself and her followers. Or a laboratory. Where experiences could be savored in a way apparently impossible in the world of infinite enlightenment that lay beyond the doors that sealed us off from death. She also believed that the world beyond co-existed with the world we live in, and that when we believed we saw ghosts it was because for whatever reason we were able to peep into that other dimension. As a psychic medium, it seemed that to her the barriers between the two worlds were pretty much transparent.

Reading through Martine Letourneaux' official website, the lore she had crafted for herself seemed to start from a place of Caribbean mysticism. She had folded in a healthy dose of Hindu spirituality and tied it up for modern audiences with concepts and ideas Cavendish himself had seen in a dozen episodes of Doctor Who or Star Trek. He was certain it was all a bunch of hooey. He guessed that she was very good at reading people and exceptionally adroit at teasing information from them and feeding it back her victims as if she had come by the knowledge through spiritual revelation. And after his first meeting with Peter Pennington, who was clearly afraid that Hoyt was scheming something against him, he was inclined to think that Peter's beliefs were along the same lines. It was hard to believe in him as a true believer and a number one fan. If he really believed in her gifts, would he think he could get away with scheming behind her back? Yet he had been able to differentiate himself from the stream of adoring fans scrolling past the table where Martine Letourneaux was signing copies of her book. He had made an impression. Maybe he, too, was very good at reading people and teasing information from them.

He started googling for news stories tying together arrest reports or court cases with Peter Pennington. To woo a con artist from the autograph line took charm, a lot of it. To know the author and know what buttons to push to make such an impression took research. And if he wasn't a true believer – and Cavendish conceded to his inner voice that he did not know with certainty if Pennington was a true believer or not yet, though he doubted it – Pennington came across as a con artist looking for a gravy train. If you conned your way into the heart of a celebrity, the next objective is to cleave her away from the other people she trusts and who benefit from their relationship with her. Enter Pennington, exit Hoyt Buxton.

Cavendish found the lead he was looking for on one of the many websites dedicated to skepticism about psychics. He didn't realize that as much of the internet was devoted to websites of experts trying to debunk psychics as was occupied by those who truly believed.

He took a detour into an explanation of cold reading, something he was vaguely familiar with and kind of wished he could learn to do. Cold reading was the free association game that fake mediums used to create the illusion that they were communicating with the other side. "I see a J name... does that mean anything to you?" – "why yes, my Uncle was named John." – "Ah-ha! That must be who is trying to come through... I feel like John made an impression on you when you were very young" … "Actually, I didn't meet Uncle John until I was thirty-six" …. "Exactly, his absence is what made the impression on you as a child!"

It was a game where vague questions were used as bait to get the victim to unwittingly provide the facts that drove the narrative. The subject convinced themselves that the psychic was communicating with the dead instead of realizing that they, the subject, were feeding the messages from beyond the grave to the psychic.

There were several pictures of Martine with subjects, many famous, scattered among the websites of friend, foe and even her own website. Celebrities she had helped, talk show hosts who reveled in her powers and helped promote her to the unsuspecting masses that adored them. Pictures of her humble beginnings here in St. Lazarus, a poor island girl of eight or nine.

There was a photo of a woman she claimed gave her guidance on her first journeys "to understand a gift that had haunted and terrified her as a child." No name in the caption of the picture that showed an ancient looking woman sitting behind a table full of candles, but Cavendish wondered if that woman was still around and could be found. He printed the picture on the off chance. There was another young girl in the picture, of about Martine's age, and Cavendish thought her maybe a friend, sibling, or fellow pupil. Cavendish wondered if she was reading palms in some carnival somewhere. If there were two famous psychics from St. Lazarus, he was sure his internet search would have stumbled across this information, so perhaps the fickle finger of fame had focused exclusively on Martine.

He would show the picture to Pennington and gauge a reaction. An alternative to charm or con artistry in snagging Martine could be blackmail. Someone who knew Martine from the old days might be someone Pennington could leverage. Did he have a hold on her that was about more than romantic chemistry? A scorned partner in mysticism from her early days with an axe to grind that Peter had found and made use of?

Or was Cavendish's cynicism reading too much

nefarious activity into the lives of Martine and Peter. Even if he was a con, and she was a fake, it didn't mean either of them were criminals.

He found videos of Martine ministering to her clients, interviewing subjects in a room that looked like a cross between a psychiatrist's office and a voodoo temple. People crying with joy and happiness as they felt that Dad or Mom or Cousin Bette were reaching out to them from the beyond. The people left happy, and Cavendish was reminded of the line from the movie *The Brothers Bloom* that said the perfect con is the one where everybody gets what they want. The psychic gets her money, and the victims get the closure or emotional relief that they were looking for. It was the perfect con.

Cavendish wished he could believe in people like Martine, but he was incapable of believing in communication with the other side. He believed in facts and evidence and clues and leads and truth.

But what would it do for his soul to have someone tell him that Elizabeth blacked out long before she died? To tell him that she couldn't feel what they were doing to her body when she was hanging from that pipe, her body whirling as they took turns swinging at her. Not content to kill her, they wanted to make an example of the policewoman who had brought their organization down. He hadn't been allowed into the crime scene, and his colleagues refused to tell him about it to his face. They didn't need to. He could read their expressions. Jaded crime scene workers that were shaken and pale.

Later he had accessed the files. Her body was hanging by chain-bound wrists, arms almost pulled from the sockets. The M.E. expressed confidence that one of the earlier blows had rendered her unconscious, even killed her, and Cavendish clung to the hope this was true. But his wife had been determined woman, and she was a fighter. He could imagine her struggling to hang on regardless of the cost. Hanging on for Sophie, for him.

What he would give for a word from her to tell him that she had not been aware of the pain. Not been aware of her bones snapping under the successive blows. And what he would give to hear in her own voice that she forgave him for everything that he did next.

He suddenly realized he had been staring through the computer screen into the shadows for about half an hour. The past was not a place he could safely go because he became trapped there. He stood up, mentally shook himself off and focused on moving forwards.

He ran downstairs to the local coffee place for something tall, hot, and black and then went walking. The walk and the aroma helped clear the cobwebby ghosts out of his mind. The air was hot and heavy, but he didn't mind. He enjoyed it; besides, a late afternoon breeze was struggling to pick itself up off the bay and promised to stir life into the sultry afternoon.

Refreshed and back at his computer, he reviewed what he had learned about Pennington from an unlikely source. The skeptic websites that took great delight in picking apart Martine Letourneaux and her fellow mediums also had a few choice opinions about Peter Pennington. And since they had been trying to break down the medium myth for far longer than Cavendish, there was already a fair amount of background information published on their sites, because they approached psychics like defense attorneys – attacking the credibility of every witness that came into contact with the case.

The story of Martine meeting Peter Pennington was described consistently. No one knew or presented a theory as to how exactly they made that first connection, but they didn't refute the official narrative, either. What they did report consistently was that Pennington had been a long-time celebrity medium chaser. He had popped up in receiving lines at other book signings, had emailed, phoned, and written to all the skeptics with the purpose of defending psychics and mediums in general and specific psychics in particular. Did he want to hook up with a medium and just cast a wide net until he found one he could reel in?

Why chase psychics and mediums? Cavendish read further. He had popped on the scene about ten years ago. He would have been about thirty. He talked about lonely jobs before that, having lost his parents when he was a child and being alone. He had used psychics to reach out to his parents, and only Martine had been able to communicate with them… He could see the con being baited, but it seemed like a lot of work with a very specific target audience.

He wondered if Pennington had a criminal background. So did the skeptics. They hadn't published anything for certain on the subject. Criminal records were confidential under United States Law. However, individual arrest and conviction reports were not. People could petition to get them sealed, but in Cavendish's experience it seldom occurred to them to do so. They knew the criminal history report was private and assumed that arrest records were part of the same file. They didn't realize the administrative complexities of public record keeping. Cavendish finished out the day requesting arrest and conviction records on Peter Pennington in all the jurisdictions where he could place him. After punching *send* on the last email, he leaned back in his chair and rubbed his strained eyes with the palms of his hands.

He turned his chair around and looked out his windows. One of the cruise liners was easing herself gracefully out to sea through the channel. He watched the boats in the harbor – the myriad anchored vessels bobbed and tugged impatiently on their rode and mooring lines. A few pleasure craft were returning to their moorings from a day of adventure on the high seas, a dinner cruise boat headed out to provide its passengers with the romantic grouping of a sea cruise, fine meal and a Caribbean sunset.

He often thought of Elizabeth's childhood spent on this island. He had never been here with Elizabeth; his in-laws had visited them in London. Although they had taken him around and showed him her favorite spots - her school, the beach she loved the best, where her best friend had lived – it always made him sad that she hadn't had the chance to show him these things herself.

It was four-thirty and since he had missed dinner

yesterday, he wanted to be sure to be home in time to share the family meal tonight. He picked up Hoyt's cheque from his desk, folded it twice and slid it into his pocket. He locked the office door and descended the stairs, still turning over all the events of the day in his head.

He walked to the Credit Union and went inside. He deposited the cheque through the ATM. The ATM was a crass and heartless businessman who put the bulk of his deposit on hold. He could almost feel the machine snort its distrust, even though he was reasonably good with money and managed to keep the incoming amounts in excess of the outgoing most of the time. The tellers knew him through his parents-in-law – opening an account with their Credit Union seemed logical and convenient – and would have probably waived the hold for him, but they would have also wanted to chit chat with him, and when he was stewing over a problem or a case, even the smallest one, he liked to be able to lose himself in his own mind. He had always achieved a lot by just ambling through his thoughts, picking at ideas like stones on a pebble beach, turning them over, considering what was underneath, replacing them and moving in another direction.

It was his reluctance to go inside and leave his internal zone that rang an alarm bell within him. He was introspective because something today had caught his attention. Not something conscious or obvious, but something just beneath the surface. Like a sliver in his finger. It was there, he could feel it. He just couldn't see it. And something made him believe it was significant.

Replaying the day in his head was not doing any good. It just wouldn't come. He tried to shake off thoughts of today and thought of getting home to his family. He needed to get today out of his head and the sliver would work itself out. He knew it would, his brain worked that way, but he still struggled to find the patience to wait. The drive became pleasant once he escaped the morass of traffic on the narrow colonial roads of the Port Rose Township. He lost himself in the contours of the landscape as the road wound its way up and along the west face of the mountains toward Rogue's Point. The sun set early this time of year, so the magic hour was covering the island in its blanket of half-light before he was even halfway home. He thought of seeing if everyone might want to go out to dinner, or maybe he could pick up pizza and they'd watch a movie – but if that was the plan he would have to swing by the house and pick up Sophie first because she wouldn't forgive him for picking a video without her input.

It was in these moments of having finally shed the last clinging tendrils of work that his phone rang. He pushed the button on the steering wheel that answered the call.

"Hello?"

"Mr. Cavendish?" he recognized the voice. It was the female assistant from the Lance mansion he'd spoken to on the phone earlier that day. He confirmed that he was Cavendish and the voice continued: "Mr. Cavendish, Mr. Lance apologizes for calling you twice in one day, but he wonders if you could come by the estate right away. Something has happened."

"Something? What kind of something?" he asked.

"Mr. Lance would prefer that we don't speak about it on the phone. But he did ask me to tell you that he realizes he has been calling on you for professional services and he does intend to compensate you for those."

Cavendish thought about the pizza and video, and he thought about the prospect of having two paying clients at once, both affluent. And he thought about the twin mysteries unfolding at Lance House, the case of the promiscuous videographer and the case of the nervous agent and reached his decision.

"I'm about twenty minutes away." He hung up and dialed the house and made guilty excuses. Neither Sophie nor Glenda seemed to be upset that he was calling in late for the second evening in a row, but he still felt guilty. He should be home with his daughter. She wouldn't be twelve indefinitely. As he thought of ways to make it up to her, he thought of the number of fathers who paved their passages to hell with promises to make up their shortcomings to their children.

≈

It was dark as he cruised up Swallow's Peak and he almost missed the entrance to Lance House. His car half skidded to a halt outside the gate and then he turned in slowly. The gates were open but the damaged one seemed to be hanging a little straighter than it had this morning. A man in a security officer's uniform came forward from a temporary security booth to shine a light in Cavendish's face. He asked for and reviewed Cavendish's identification. He returned it and waved Cavendish up the drive.

There was a police car by the front door, easing into gear and leaving the house just as Cavendish pulled up in front of it. They passed each other slowly and he glanced into the car. The officers were Carter and Brickner, men he knew but not as well as Swain and Singh. Brickner raised his hand to Cavendish sociably. In the backseat of the car: Ross Buchanan. The nature of the summons to Lance House started to make sense. Somehow, he must have found Amber and come here to make trouble for her, and by extension for her mother and the Lance household.

The front door opened to receive him when he was still five steps away. The maid stepped back to let him pass and said: "Mr. Lance is waiting for you in the drawing room, the second door on the left."

The maid looked a little distressed. Cavendish followed the directions into the drawing room and found a small party gathered. The way they were assembled was most surprising. Pamela Geranabby was there, in her housekeeping uniform, sitting on the couch with a glass in her hand that looked to contain brandy or sherry. Her hair was disheveled, and she was breathing heavily, clearly upset.

At her left, with her arm around her mother protectively in a most unexpected way, sat Amber. Consoling or comforting her. Standing in front of her, his back to the door, was Marvin Lance. And standing slightly but deliberately separate from this party was his wife, Deirdre.

"What happened?" asked Cavendish.

Lance turned around. He looked concerned. "Ross Buchanan came here tonight. He was very angry, and he got past the gate before the guard could stop him. He stormed around the place like a madman and found Amber by the pool. He was drunk and angry and very noisy, so Pamela heard him and came out of the house. He was threatening Amber, Pamela got in his face and he pushed her out of the way – she fell over the chaise and then she got up and went for him with one of the little end tables. She cracked him across the side of the head with it."

"He dropped like a rock," Amber observed approvingly. Cavendish wanted to applaud Pamela, but Deirdre expressed her disapproval before he could.

"We had paramedics out here *and* the police. I'm just glad Martine wasn't here to see it."

"I didn't do a very good job with security," explained Lance apologetically. "We've never really needed it before…"

"He called my daughter a whore," said Pamela softly, staring bleakly into her glass. "He called her a dirty filthy whore is what he called my little girl."

Deirdre sniffed with the haughtiness of someone who lived in a glass house. "Well the man was no angel, but how would you describe Amber's activities?"

Pamela flinched physically at the rebuke. Lance tried to be the peacemaker. "Dear, none of this is Pamela's fault. There's no reason to make her feel worse."

Amber looked up with a flash of anger and hurt that seemed targeted towards Marvin. Perhaps because she read the undertone in Marvin's sidestep suggesting he did lay blame on Amber. Maybe she was disappointed he hadn't spoken up more directly in her own behalf. Pamela's eyes shifted down from her glass to her shoes.

Cavendish looked between Pamela and Amber. "Are either of you ladies hurt?"

They both shook their heads.

Cavendish turned towards Lance. "I see the gates are getting repaired."

"And I have a guard posted. We always got by with just

the cameras and alarm system before. Even with Martine here we didn't have so many issues – I suppose she is more famous in the States than here but now – we have been getting telephone calls today. Calls from tabloid television shows and newsmagazines. The story of Amber has reached America and I think there is going to be a hailstorm of publicity coming down on us and I don't know what to do about it. This is outside my experience."

"It's outside any normal person's experience!" Deirdre sneered angrily. "Why are the servants sitting on our couch and drinking our brandy after they started a fight in our living room?"

"They didn't start the fight and it's my fault that man came in here because I didn't set up the security properly," Lance retorted.

"They did start the fight. The man was only calling that tramp names until her mother picked up that table!"

"Wouldn't you defend your daughter if she was being called names?" Lance wondered aloud.

"Maybe," Deirdre allowed. "But she's not my daughter. So why are you sticking up for her like she's your child and I'm not your wife? Why aren't you throwing them both out for being such a disruption to our home?"

"Darling, you know Pamela has been here for years and Amber grew up here!"

"So you think she'd be grateful for a nice place to grow up so she doesn't have to live in some shanty on the north shore, instead of whoring herself around with every man with money who comes through this town. So what is it, Marvin? Why do you want her here – is she paying for the rent some other way. Or maybe it's her Mom. Maybe she does the sort of depraved things for you that I won't to keep her and her slut daughter in the house?"

"Deirdre!" Marvin's shout cracked the air like a whip. Deirdre was startled by the sound, clearly unaccustomed to such an eruption of anger. But if she was surprised, Cavendish could see her anger was not cooled or subdued by it. She glared with a mix of anger and defiance at her husband.

Amber had jumped to her feet near the end of Deirdre's tirade, but Lance's intervention forestalled her from lobbing whatever verbal grenade she was readying. Pamela, who had been sitting in quiet sadness reached up for her daughter's hand.

"We should go."

"To your home?" asked Deirdre icily. "The one my husband provides for you and that you crap all over."

Pamela stood up. Cavendish could see her visibly mustering herself. Gathering her shredded dignity, suppressing her anger.

"Mrs. Lance, I am truly, truly sorry for the trouble my daughter has brought to this house, especially because your husband has always been kind to us, as he is to all his employees," she said carefully.

"You don't owe her any apology," said Amber in a stage whisper. "She's just another poor girl spreading her legs to get into a nice big house. She's no better than me. The only difference is she married her john."

Deirdre blanched with hostility and Cavendish imagined that Lance gulped, but his eyes hardened, too. "That's enough Amber. You need to go get some sleep."

But it was too late for Amber to beat a retreat, even if she had wanted to. In three strident steps Deirdre was at arms' length from Amber and the palm of her hand was connecting with Amber's cheek. Amber's head snapped to the right, the sound of the slap like a branch snapping in the forest.

"Don't ever speak to me like that again, you little bitch!" Deirdre hissed. Amber's eyes blazed with venom, but Pamela who had so vigorously attacked Ross Buchanan looked lost and subdued and sad as she wrapped her arm around her daughter as an obvious precursor to trying to scurry away. She probably wondered if she was still going to have a job in the morning.

"Amber, let's go."

Amber was still focused on Deirdre. "You think I'm a slut and whore because I trade in sex. But what you don't get is that it isn't my business; it's just one of the hooks I use. I trade in secrets and lies and those men paid me to hide their lies and betrayals. But secrets of men cheating on their husbands aren't the only secrets I deal in, so you better think again before you ever lay a hand on me, you self-righteous hypocrite! Do you hear me?"

Deirdre was incredulous. "You have the gall to threaten me? In my own house? Just because my husband isn't man enough to put you in your place doesn't mean I won't put you in the gutter where you belong."

Cavendish stepped forward so that he was abreast of Deirdre, facing Pamela and stretching an arm in front of Deirdre to create a barrier between her and Amber. Part of him was fascinated, and eager to hear whatever secrets were about to be spilled and see what light they could cast on the mysteries of the last twenty-four hours. But it looked like an all-out fight would erupt before the useful information started coming out.

"I think everybody needs to take a step back," he suggested.

"Who the hell are you? You brought all this mess on our doorstep," Deirdre shoved him away, but took a step back in the same movement which built a small buffer zone between herself and Amber. "And you!" She rounded on her husband. "Just standing there letting her talk to me like that. Am I your wife or what? Or do your servants get special loyalty because you knew them longer." She shook her head. Her bobbed blonde coif was looking as ragged as her nerves.

The sound of commotion from the hallway distracted everyone but Amber. Her right arm shot up from her side in a viper-like motion, fingers clenched in a fist that was targeted at Deirdre's head.

Cavendish saw it from the corner of his eye and was too slow to block it, but he lunged out with both hands and was able to grab her by the wrist and pull her arm to the left so that she would not connect with her target. His sudden yank on her arm threw Amber off balance, and when Cavendish released her wrist her momentum carried her down into the sofa. Her momentum spent; it took her a minute to gather her balance.

Meanwhile, Martine Letourneaux, Megan Shepard and Peter Pennington materialized in the doorway. Taking in the scene with widening eyes as her glance jumped from Amber landing on the couch to Deirdre to Cavendish to Lance to Pamela Geranabby, Martine gasped and cried:

"Holy Mother of God!" and fainted dead away.

CHAPTER TEN

Later, Marvin Lance and Archer Cavendish ended up at the little wet bar outside by the pool sharing rather strong rum and cokes. A full moon filtered through scudding clouds bathed the property in ghostly luminescence. Lance had poured the beverages without discussion, shoved one into Archer's hand and then sat down on one of the chaise-lounges. He put his glass on the little side table and wearily swung his legs one by one onto the lounge chair. Then he reached for the drink and downed half of it in a single swallow.

After Martine hit the floor like a ton of bricks, Deirdre had been distracted from her rage by the health of her celebrity guest and spiritual adviser. Martine easily trumped the importance of Amber Geranabby. Deirdre had rushed to her side and there was talk of smelling salts or water or fresh air or helping her sit or helping her stand.

With Deirdre and the newcomers attending Martine Letourneaux, Cavendish had checked Amber, asked if she was all right and apologized for dropping her onto the sofa all in the same breath. The wind was knocked out of her and she couldn't speak, but her eyes communicated her feelings plainly enough. *Everything was going according to plan until yesterday. Until you stuck your nose into my life. This is all your fault.*

Lance put a hand on Pamela's shoulder. "Get her to your cottage and try to keep her in tonight. We'll figure everything out tomorrow."

Megan shouldered past the Penningtons and Deirdre joined Lance, Cavendish et al. She was wide eyed with enthusiasm "Wow. What happened here tonight?"

Lance put his hand up. "Not now, Ms. Shepard, I implore you. The night is a disaster already; it can only get worse - so please, not tonight."

Megan looked both curious and delighted. Maybe she envisaged another scene for her movie of the week. Thinking of the anger in Amber's eyes, Cavendish consoled himself with the notion that even if he had brought a lot of trouble into her life, he had also brought an agent and a movie deal, so it could hardly be all bad.

Cavendish sat down on the lounge chair next to Lance and swung his legs up, sipping at his drink and finding appreciation for the beautiful moonlit view of the vast Atlantic even as he reviewed the events of the evening. Deirdre had helped Peter take Martine to her room. Pamela made a quick inspection of Amber to make sure she wasn't injured before hustling her out of the room. Cavendish wasn't sure which way Megan had gone, whether she had followed one of her clients or just gone her own way. He just knew that within a few minutes he and Marvin Lance were abandoned, and Lance was motioning that he should follow him.

Lance had emptied his glass wordlessly and now hauled himself up and went to the bar to pour himself another. He had not yelled or cussed, but his anger played out in the rigid movements of his limbs, moving in snaps and lunges, with none of the relaxed ease Cavendish had seen just a day earlier.

Lance returned to the lounge chair and was half-way through his second drink before he spoke.

"When staff work for you a long time, Mr. Cavendish,

it's not exactly that they become family but they – they're more than staff." Was he rehearsing what he would say to try and mend bridges with Deirdre? "I've known Amber since she was a few months old. I can't just dismiss her as my wife would like me to. It's not that I think it's okay for Amber to – well, I don't know how to explain it to Deirdre."

"What you said makes sense to me," observed Cavendish slowly, hoping to coax Lance along. His visit this evening so far had been brief and dramatic, and he still didn't know why Lance had wanted him to come.

"It doesn't make sense to Deirdre. Another?" Cavendish declined a second drink and was still only half-way through his first as Lance started on his third.

"My wife doesn't – some people have a different attitude about staff and servants. They don't see them as people. But they are people with all the problems of people, and it might not be a family, per se, but it's a community. A small community where you just don't turn your back or throw someone out when they are going off the rails. I know Amber is out of control, but am I supposed to fire her mother for that? What am I supposed to do? I think Deirdre would like me to fire her... I know she would..." St. Lazarus did not have the kind of economy that supported people finding new jobs quickly, and the social support nets provided by the government were scarce.

"If she is sufficiently embarrassed, Pamela might quit on her own," suggested Cavendish.

"That wouldn't be right. It's not fair to her. Or Mia, or Amber."

"It's not my business, Mr. Lance, but shouldn't your first loyalty be to Mrs. Lance? If she doesn't want someone here, why keep her on? Doesn't it make your life more difficult?"

"So, I should fire an innocent woman to make my life easier? Is that your philosophy Mr. Cavendish?"

"A lot of people would," observed Cavendish.

"Maybe so. But I am not going to punish Pamela Geranabby for her daughter's behavior," he rubbed the back of his hand across his eyes. "But I know I have to do something about this – Amber can't behave this way to Deirdre."

Cavendish was itching to ask what secret Amber could possibly know about his wife but thought it better not to explore that point of the conversation with Marvin Lance while he was so upset. He might try to find out from Amber first – After all, it could have been an idle boast hurled in anger.

Cavendish heard movement in the yard, the crunch of gravel on one of the paths. How many people in the house had heard the commotion? Or loitered in adjacent hallways to get a better point of view?

"I don't understand why Amber has so much anger in her," Lance explained after a lengthy lull in the conversation, his words beginning to slur. "She was never an unhappy child. I allow the staff to use the pool and the tennis courts so they have a lot of facilities growing up that they wouldn't have had otherwise."

Cavendish didn't think he was betraying a confidence to share a thought that he considered relatively self-evident anyway. "Maybe it bothered her to have access to all those things but for them not to be her own. They were never her own. She knew they could be given and taken at whim. Sometimes people aren't grateful when you expect them to be. If they feel like you can take something away from them at any time, they can resent the power you have over them."

"Her mother is a good woman; she could have done a lot worse than to bring her daughter here. And now she's breaking her mother's heart."

"Pamela had Amber before she came to work for you?"

Lance nodded as he struggled to ascend from his lounge chair with increasing difficulty and diminishing coordination. "She was about a year old." It was only about seven feet between the lounge chairs and the bar, but Lance's route to it was becoming less direct as he poured his fourth drink. Cavendish declined the offer of another drink yet again; he was still working on his first.

"Amber was over the top. She was so out of line I can't really blame Deirdre for wanting me to get her off the property.

But I can't do that to Pamela. She doesn't deserve it."

Cavendish looked at Lance hitting his fourth drink. He had probably done as much, for good or ill, as he was going to achieve tonight. "I need to be going, Mr. Lance. We haven't spoken about why you wanted me to come out here tonight, though?"

Lance had slowed his pace on the fourth drink and was moving at sipping speed. "When Buchanan showed up at the house, it occurred to me that the publicity could bring other angry men out of the woodwork. I wanted some professional advice. But I think, if it's all right with you, we'll postpone that conversation."

"Certainly. Can I give you a hand to get back into the house?"

Lance waived his hand dismissively. "I think I am going to stay out here for a while." He laughed bitterly. "I'm not sure I'll even be able to get into the bedroom."

Cavendish felt bad for him, and wished he could offer some useful advice, but this situation was beyond his experience. He had never been forced to juggle his loyalty to his servants with his loyalty to his family, although if he and Sophie had staff, he was sure she would be more understanding than Deirdre was being.

"I wish I could tell you something helpful, Mr. Lance." He stood up and offered his hand, which Lance shook without standing up. "I'll give you a call tomorrow."

"Thank you for coming up here, Mr. Cavendish. I appreciate your help," Lance gestured toward the bar. "Be a good fellow and just bring me the bottle, and the bottle of Coca-Cola."

Cavendish obliged. "You're certain you'll be okay?"

"You may be shocked to learn this is not the first time I got completely smashed," replied Lance. He poured equal measures of rum and coke into a glass and sipped at it. Since he had slowed his pace. His first two drinks had vanished in two gulps. At least now he'd slowed down enough that it required several swallows to reach the bottom of the glass. Cavendish felt there was no reason to stay any longer.

Cavendish walked toward the house and as he stepped across the threshold, he decided that he better arrange for someone to keep an eye on Lance; in case he fell asleep by the pool. He checked the study, the dining room, the drawing room – neither staff nor guests were in evidence.

He considered going upstairs and looking for Deirdre to see if her anger had cooled enough for her to be worried about her husband. He wasn't sure that his knock would be the most welcome one on her bedroom door. Well, Lance was a grown up. He should probably just go.

He went out the front door, glancing at his wristwatch he was surprised to see that despite the eventful nature of the evening, it was only a little after nine. He looked at where his car was parked on the driveway and his eyes drifted down the narrow,gravel path to the cottage where Pamela and her family lived and thought he heard footfalls crunching on the gravel, and then a shadow crossed in front of their illuminated windows.

Motivated by two things, he started toward the cottage. If the light was on Pamela or Amber might still be awake and he thought he would look in on them before he left to make sure they were okay. Secondly, he was curious about the identity of the shadowy figure coming up the path towards the house.

The footfalls on the path broke their rhythm, as if the walker became aware of his presence and was startled by it. Cavendish paused too, and momentarily the footsteps resumed their rapid cadence quickly and as he started along the path and moved out of the range of the porch light the figure started to assume clarity in the moonlight. They met in a few paces.

"Ms. Letourneaux?" Cavendish was surprised that she was the one walking the pathway from the servant's quarters. "I thought they took you to your room."

"They did," she confirmed. "But I felt better, and very foolish for passing out like that. Ridiculous. I see spirits every day and I faint at the sight of a little fight. How ridiculous is that?" Her hands were folded into each other and he saw her fingers were fumbling with each other. Why was she so nervous?

"What took you out and about after you regained consciousness?" he asked lightly.

"That young girl took a heavy fall. I wanted to check on her. They live in that cottage," she motioned to Pamela's cottage behind her. "I am just coming back from there."

"How was Amber?"

"I didn't see her. She was asleep. Pamela – her mother- was very, very upset. I can understand why. She has been through so much. It's horrible for her."

"Were you able to bring her any helpful messages from loved ones on the other side?" he asked glibly.

Her tone iced over. "Some would be wary of scoffing at the spirit world, Mr. Cavendish. Just because you don't believe in it doesn't make it less real to millions of people. Good night."

She shoved past him and walked into the house. He hadn't seen her enduring serenity shaken loose before. It made him wonder about her interest in Amber and in Pamela. Surely Amber didn't know a secret about Martine? Proof that she was a fraud or that she had skeletons in her own closet?

In the brief time that had elapsed, the light in the cottage window had gone out. Cavendish changed course for his car and headed home. It had been a busy and eventful evening, and if he could get Amber to speak with him again, he was extremely curious to find out what kind of secrets she had harvested on Deirdre Lance. Not that Amber would share. And there was his new case and his new client, Hoyt Buxton, and his inquiry into the dealings of Martine's husband.

These were all thoughts that he tried to shed with some Iron Maiden tunes as he headed home, wondering if Sophie was still up and thinking how it would be nice to make plans for some daddy - daughter time this weekend. There was a movie she wanted to see, something with the latest 'tween heart throb in it. He expected the plot involved youngsters saving the world from corrupt adults.

≈

While Archer Cavendish let his thoughts drift towards pleasant familial activities, Marvin Lance drank himself the rest of the way into a stupor in the lounge chair by his pool. The bottle of rum, in its entirety, was consumed and the bottle rolled off the chair and landed on the paving stones with a cracking sound but did not break.

In the night, he rolled over on the chair and regained consciousness enough to vomit on the floor beside it, but not enough to hear, let alone recognize, the sound of a single heavy splash as something rolled off the roof and plunged into the pool.

The Caribbean air grows heavy early as the sun heats the thick and humid air. When the sun crept above the eastern horizon and melted the darkness with a brightening dawn, the light in the sky became bolder and strong enough to pierce even tightly closed eyelids. With a bottle of rum inside one's belly, those pricks of light felt like scalpels that had been shoved through Lance's eyeballs, into his brain and were now scraping against the back of his skull the way one might scrape out the insides of a Hallowe'en pumpkin.

He wanted to be sick again, his head hurt, he had forgotten where he was and that unfamiliarity prompted him to sit up with unwise speed and he winced as the scalpels jiggled in his jellyish brain and the world tilted first one way and then the other. His mouth was ashy and dry. He had to look away from the bright horizon with its rising ball of fire front and center and as he looked down into the pool, he saw someone swimming. Except their legs weren't kicking and their arms were flaccid alongside their torso. He saw the back of long, healthy, and fit brown legs. The girl was wearing white underpants and bra but nothing else.

Lance had no idea how long the girl had been there, but he knew with sudden shock that she was not swimming. The pain in his head momentarily brushed aside, he sprung to his feet. The hangover was still there so instead of a heroic lunge into the pool he stumbled and fell sideways into the water, tripping over a chair that almost followed him in. He thrashed crazily to the side of the body in the pool and was chilled when he felt the skin. It was like brushing against a fish, it was so cold.

He grabbed an arm and hauled her towards the shallow end of the pool. He stumbled and fell backwards on the steps as he tried to pull the corpse free of the water. He ended up on his backside on the side of the pool, struggling to turn the body onto its back.

The face was no longer fiery or angry, though it was still pretty but in a quiet, gentle way he had never seen when she was alive. He knew there was shouting and screaming, and it hurt his head and he wished it would stop until he realized the yells were coming out of his own mouth, summoning help. Help that couldn't possibly make any difference, because there was no chance of saving her now. Amber Geranabby had been dead for hours.

CHAPTER ELEVEN

Archer was awoken roughly by Sophie jostling his shoulder.

"Dad, phooonnne!!" she shoved the handset against the side of his face. He was turning over as he strained towards consciousness and she had trouble lining the earpiece up. The voice at the other end of the phone sounded like it was coming through a basin of water.

"Who is it?" he demanded, grouchy and certain it was far too early to be taking calls.

"Someone named Marvin Lance. Its seven o'clock," she added helpfully.

He grabbed at the phone. "Archer Cavendish."

"Mr. Cavendish, you need to get here right away." Lance sounded strange. Insistent, nervous, a little frantic.

"What happened, Mr. Lance? What's wrong?"

"I already called the police," Lance was burbling, just spewing his information randomly and not listening. "They'll be here soon, and they might not let me call you after they get here so please come right away. I woke up and she was there, she was there in the water…"

"Who was there? Who was in the water?" Cavendish

was already wide awake and jumping out of bed, alarmed enough by Lance's demeanor to be triggered fully alert. Sophie was looking at him, not knowing what was going on but clearly tuning into the general excitement. He snapped his fingers at her and pointed for the door. She obeyed, grudgingly but promptly. "Who was in the water, Mr. Lance?"

"I passed out by the pool; I'd had too much to drink..."

Cavendish snatched the first pair of slacks from the wardrobe that his hand fell upon, gripping the phone between his face and his shoulder as he half jumped into them.

"At first I thought maybe she fell in the pool but there are these bruises on her throat – "

"Mr. Lance, who was it?" he thought about the sense of foreboding he had felt since he first met her, his fear that she was going to burn herself with the fire she was playing with. "Was it Amber?"

There was a long pause from the other side. He could envisage Lance standing there, reluctant to put a name to the body because then there was no denying the event, the finality, the end of a life that he had witnessed for eighteen years. Naming her made her dead.

"Yes."

Cavendish pulled a dark blue polo shirt out of his drawer and tugged it over his head, maneuvering the phone through one of the sleeves.

"I don't know how she got there – I must have been here when it happened – but I didn't hear a thing."

"Mr. Lance, you've called the police. Call your attorney, too," even as a cop Cavendish knew it was never a bad idea for the person who discovered a dead body in his swimming pool to have good counsel at hand. "I'm on my way."

He hung up the phone, pulled on socks and heavy oxfords that were hot but comfortable despite the Caribbean heat. (And darn good for kicking people and doing damage when you were in a pinch). He grabbed his wallet, mobile phone and keys and took the steps upstairs two at a time. Sophie was on his heels and he realized she must have been lurking outside his room.

"What happened, Dad?"

He turned at the top of the stairs. There was no reason for her not to know, but it alarmed him to see her mother's eyes burning with curiosity. Sometimes the last thing a parent wanted for their child was to be just like them. Maybe her curiosity would make her a scientist, because when he saw her like this, he saw her future and he imagined sleepless nights worrying about her as she was patrolling some crap-hole neighborhood.

"It looks like someone was murdered," he told her. "I have to go."

He kissed her on the cheek and raced out the door. The drive to the Lance house was quicker from his house because he didn't have to dilly dally working his way in or out of Port Rose. There was a main road that allowed Cavendish to race up and across the mountainous spine of the island. The Charger responded well to the urgency as he raced up to the bumper of the car ahead and waited for the opportune moment to leap into the opposite lane and roar past it. It was like the car heard the call of duty and was responding loyally.

He glanced at his watch, imagining that if Lance had phoned the police first then they would likely beat him to the scene and might bar him from entering. It took him fifteen minutes of blinding passes around slower traffic, ducking back into his lane before oncoming cars came too close to reach his destination. Blasting horns echoed in his ears most of the way but the Charger just growled at them defiantly as he raced to the Lance house.

He was driving so fast that the gate to the Lance estate caught him by surprise. His car slewed sideways as he jammed on the brakes and nosed between the stone pillars. A guard stood next to it but as soon as he saw Cavendish's driver's license, he waved him through. The police were here, but only one squad car so far. He pulled to a halt alongside it, jumped out of his own car and raced around the perimeter of the house to the pool.

There was a cluster of people a few feet removed from

the edge of the pool. Marvin Lance was there, still in the trousers he was wearing last night but with neither jacket nor shirt. His houseguests gaggled around him. Martine Letourneaux, Hoyt Buxton, Megan Shepard, and Peter Pennington. All pretending not to look at tableaux on the opposite side of the pool. Aside from Lance's strangely shirtless costume, the second thing Cavendish noticed was that his wife was not in attendance. Nor were any of the staff.

Laid alongside the pool, a bright yellow police blanket covering her, was the corpse of Amber Geranabby. Two uniformed officers hovered near her. Cavendish mentally chastised the local plod for covering her before the M.E. or the crime scene team got there to gather evidence. But this island wasn't overrun with murders and this may be the first such crime scene the officers had worked, and they may have understandably caved into their more human impulses to protect the dignity of the young girl. They might still see her body as a part of her personhood. Unable to think of it now as an empty casing, abandoned by its soul, with no dignity left, and no purpose, except perhaps to yield the crucial clues that might lead those who would seek justice for her to the person who removed the soul from its shell.

The officers were not inspecting the body; they were just standing guard and looking around, probably trying to maintain some kind of a perimeter around the pool. Cavendish didn't want to make their job any more difficult, so he kept as close to the wall of the house as he could; making his way to Lance's party.

One of the officers called out to him. "You there, who are you?"

"Archer Cavendish," he called back confidently. He didn't recognize either officer.

The officers regarded each other with uncertainty. Should they monitor the body or go talk to this newcomer and make sure he doesn't taint the crime scene? Cavendish took advantage of their indecision to make terse recommendations to the gathering of houseguests.

"Everybody, please don't discuss anything that happened last night or anything that you might have seen or heard with each other. Sharing ideas can confuse you about what you actually saw or heard, and the police will need the clearest and most basic recollections you can give them." Everyone nodded but also exchanged sidelong glances. It hadn't occurred to them that not only were they witnessing a tragedy; they might be witnesses to a crime. He wondered when it would occur to the innocent among them that they might also be suspects. Pennington looked resentful that Cavendish was giving instruction, but he suffered in silence.

Cavendish recognized that the only facts he had in hand were that Amber was dead, and that Lance said he had discovered her floating in the pool and she had bruises around her neck. Those facts alone did not add up to homicide. But Cavendish could not imagine a girl filled with so much defiance and fire offing herself. The third possibility was an accidental death – but it just seemed too co-incidental to Archer's naturally suspicious brain to let that possibility gain much traction in his psyche. He thought about who wasn't here. Amber's mother, her sister, Deirdre Lance.

"Does her mother know?" asked Cavendish, naively imagining that Deirdre might be comforting Pamela in the cottage or inside the house. No matter how much one woman might hate another, the loss of a daughter would speak to her compassion.

Lance nodded gravely. "She was screaming and shouting – a couple of the other maids took her to her cottage to try to calm her down, I sent for the doctor."

"And Mrs. Lance?"

"Still asleep. I haven't gone upstairs yet, and she hasn't come down," Lance's eyes were fixated not on the corpse, but on the pool. Where he had discovered the body.

It was only a matter of time before more senior police officers with more confidence than the two first responders showed up and shooed him away from their inquiry. He looked at the yellow police blanket concealing the youthful silhouette of

Amber Geranabby and decided if he was going to ask questions, he had better start quickly.

"Tell me how you found her, Mr. Lance," he asked, hoping his memory would be reliable enough to store whatever information he was about to glean. He didn't want to pull out his notebook because even the most uncertain of policemen were bound to chase away someone taking notes and interviewing suspects before the official investigators arrived.

Lance recounted waking, his head exploding – and his bleary red soaked eyes didn't tell the story of a man who was feeling any better now – and how he saw her floating in the pool.

"It didn't occur to me that she was dead, I didn't even think she could be. I just saw her floating face down and knew I had to get her out before she drowned – but when I grabbed her, I could feel how cold she was, and it wasn't just from the water. And she was so stiff and hard. Like she had no joints and her limbs were all rigid…"

Martine reached out for him, "You poor man."

Cavendish ignored her and took Lance by the elbow, cutting him out from the little herd. "You didn't see how she got into the water?"

Lance shook his head. "No. I didn't hear anything – I woke up because the sun was coming up, not because of anything I heard – but I don't know how I couldn't have heard – something. She must have screamed or cried out or something and I was just passed out on the lounge oblivious. She's just a kid, Cavendish. Screwed up for sure, but she's just a kid…"

Cavendish was aware Lance's guests were following them with their eyes, doubtless straining their ears, and the policemen still wrestling over what action to take in view of this new interloper. He tried to pull Lance far enough away to gain privacy from the other guests without triggering police intervention of his interview.

"Tell me what happened after you found her this morning. Step by step – "

"I woke up. The sun was coming up and it was getting hot and my head was hurting, and I was just getting my bearings and I saw her there – I saw her there in the water. The way she was floating – I should have known she was dead but I just jumped into the pool to pull her to the side – I don't know what I thought I would achieve, I was just reacting…"

Cavendish faced Lance squarely and held his arms rigidly by the elbow. Lance was looking at the ground, but the proximity of Cavendish's face made him react and he looked up into Cavendish's eyes.

"Mr. Lance," Cavendish began, speaking in a deliberately slow cadence. "You can still help her. You can't bring her back to life, but you can help us find out who did this to her and bring them to justice. But you need to calm down and focus. You pulled her out of the water. Then what?"

Lance started again, more slowly this time, mimicking the rhythm Cavendish had spoken to him with. Cavendish concentrated on his words to remember them as precisely as he could. This was a police matter. It would be a police investigation and it was not his place to start an inquiry. If he were the investigating officer and a private detective was doing what Cavendish was himself doing, he would throw him out on his ear and charge him with interfering in police business. But he felt a personal responsibility for what had happened. He didn't plan to get in the way of the police, but he certainly wanted to make sure that there were no rushes to judgement and that Amber received her share of justice.

"I must have been calling out, or people heard the commotion – because I didn't pull her all the way out on my own. Suddenly the gardener, Ridley, was there, helping me. And one of the housemaids – I didn't see which one. We got her out. I tried to do CPR. And I checked her pulse. She didn't have one, her body was all stiff and rigid and then I noticed – I noticed she had these horrible bruises on her neck, and I knew someone had killed her. I ordered that the police be called. And I … she was in her underwear, so I laid my jacket over her."

Well, putting his jacket on Amber could distort the meaning of any biological evidence the medical examiner might find on Amber's body. But he could understand the motivation to cover her, to protect her even in death. Something about her had elicited the same impulse from him when she was alive. It was a cruel truth that Cavendish's skills were better suited to helping her now that it was too late and really didn't matter to her anymore.

The policemen had clearly had enough, and one of them was coming around the pool towards them.

"Mr. Lance, the police are about to kick me out of here."

Lance seemed suddenly alarmed. "No, Mr. Cavendish, I want you to find out who did this. She is just an embarrassment to the police and the government; they will want to get it all quiet as quickly as possible. I can trust you to find the truth – and you have the training and background from your time with the CID at Scotland Yard… I read about the museum murders-"

Cavendish was startled that Lance was able to reference the case that got him promoted to Detective-Inspector, and immediately chided himself. Of course, Lance would have done a little research into the background of this strange interloper that was bringing Amber home. Friend or foe? What would his motivations be? His allegiances? It was an obvious thing for anyone to do, especially an affluent businessman, and it was a sign of Cavendish letting his instincts get bleached by the tropical sun that it hadn't seemed obvious to him when Lance first telephoned him. Just like the initial invitation to dinner. He could have left Cavendish to wait in the kitchen until his car was freed. Instead, he'd invited him to join the dinner party and learn something of who and what he was.

"Mr. Lance," he said. "I will help. But the police have their procedures and they are going to sideline me for the moment. But please do the following. As soon as you can, write down everything you can remember. Who came to the pool first this morning after you found the body, what they said. Write down *everything*, no matter how trivial or insignificant it might seem. Let me decide what's important, ok?"

"Sir, this is a crime scene. I need to ask you who you are," the policeman who'd been sent to challenge him stood with his feet anchored and hands militantly braced on his hips in a vaguely ridiculous Superman pose.

"I'm a private detective," explained Cavendish. "I also had a passing acquaintance with the victim."

Cavendish heard sirens as more vehicles neared the estate. The officer seemed unsure what to do with him. Cavendish decided to give him some unsolicited advice. The officer would either be offended, in which case it didn't matter, or he might accept it in the spirit that it was given.

"Officer, until your back-up gets here, you should keep all these people together and you should stand close to them. You want to want to make sure they aren't discussing the crime or comparing notes. It could taint their recollections and their statements.."

Cavendish saw the words go into the officer's head; but saw no evidence they were really registering on any level.

"What kind of private detective?" demanded the officer, still stuck on the previous sentences.

Cavendish rolled his eyes. "I'll be in the house if you need me. Keep an eye on these people. And listen. And pay attention. You don't mind if I go in the house, do you?"

The officer wasn't sure if he minded. Conflicting thoughts passed almost visibly across the fronts of his eyes, bumping into each other and knocking others aside.

"You didn't want me here anyway, did you?" Cavendish followed up.

"Well, no, sir," agreed the officer. "But I think you should stay here now that you are here."

"No, you don't want me here interfering with your investigation. I won't leave; I'll just be in the house if you need anything. Here's my card," he pulled the thin leather cardholder from his pocket and handed a card to the officer. "I have my mobile so you can just ring me. I'll be inside. There's a good chap." He turned to look at Lance as he walked away. "Write?"

Lance nodded gravely. The officer was going to say something, but his radio was crackling. Cavendish went around the house, so that he didn't pass through the cluster of houseguests. Striding quickly along the front of the house toward the portico he saw the first fresh unit skidding to a halt on the main road before reeling into the drive, kicking up gravel and debris as the brakes lost grip on the loose material of the driveway. Cavendish was pleased he wasn't the only one that came to an abrupt halt on the road outside the gate.

A van followed closely on its heels, and another car. Cavendish tried the front door and found it unlocked. With the escalating commotion in front of the house his visibility had shrunk markedly. He closed the door behind him and watched through the window as a third car came into the yard. The van was the crime scene team, and there was a sergeant in the third car that started detailing tasks. An officer marched back to the main gate, controlling any further access or departure from the estate. None of these officers were Jenny Singh or Hardy Swain, which vexed Cavendish because he was really hoping that they or one of his few other friends with the local plod would be assigned to this case so he could get some inside scoop on the investigation.

"Can I help you Mr. Cavendish?"

Cavendish spun to put his back to the front door and saw Deirdre Lance standing in the hallway. Unlike the grouping outside she was fully dressed and put together. She wore white Capri pants and a blouse that was nautically themed with broad blue and white horizontal stripes. She was wearing dark glasses that were shoved high on her head, an impromptu hairband pushing her blonde hair off her face.

"Good morning, Mrs. Lance."

"Good morning. Are you here because that horrible little slut was finally put down?"

CHAPTER TWELVE

"I don't suppose you have any coffee?" asked Cavendish, doing his best to sound light and cheerful. He was pleased with the opportunity to speak with her. There would soon be a lot of commotion outside and he hoped it would take some time for the investigating policemen to realize that he was busy interfering with potential witnesses inside.

"There'll be some laid out in the dining room," Deirdre assured him. "The staff is well trained. Once they hear people stirring, they will put out coffee and pastries – regardless of corpses floating in the swimming pool." She smiled. "I'd ask them to add mimosas, but that might seem in poor taste. Shall we?"

She motioned to the dining room door invitationally. Cavendish followed her to the sideboard where morning coffee and Danish were elegantly laid out. The coffee pot and cups and saucers looked very delicate with finely painted swoops and swirls in pinks and blues.

"What did Amber do to you to make you so dislike her?" wondered Cavendish aloud. He started with general questions. Asking her to account for her movements last night might be too direct and he wanted her to vent every angry thought and feeling she had about Amber to him right here and now. He knew she wouldn't be shy about it.

Deirdre concentrated on her task in hand, pouring coffee into two cups. "Milk and sugar?"

"Neither," said Cavendish. It was his first cup of the day, and it smelled rich and good. He watched Deirdre minutely – and the cups did not rattle even a little bit in their saucers. Her hands were steady as rocks. She was either as totally non-plussed by the body in the pool as she seemed, or she had resolute acting skills. "Did she do something to make you hate her?"

"She did all kinds of things to make me hate her. I count my blessings this morning. She is a thorn that has been pulled from my side," she stirred her coffee vaguely, a tinge of sadness creeping into the corner of her eyes. "Of course, there is going to be some fallout from all of this, but I have been in tougher fixes and done okay. All in all, it's a good morning. God is smiling upon me."

"Was it because your husband seemed to have a fondness for her?" pressed Cavendish.

"He *was* very fond of her, wasn't he? And she liked older men – or shall we say, preyed upon them," she framed her face with exaggerated demureness. "Do you think it's silly or childish of me to be suspicious of that?"

"You think something may have happened between her and your husband?"

"If only that was the case," sighed Deirdre, dismissing her look of demureness from the field of play. "I could have gone toe to toe with her. I can go toe to toe with any bitch moving in on my territory."

"Then what was it?"

"He took care of Amber because of Pamela," she sipped at her coffee. "If God really loves me, Pamela will be the next one in the pool."

"You think there is something between your husband and Pamela?"

"Of course not. He tells me that I am stupid to think such a thing, so why would I?"

She pulled a Danish from under a glass cover and

started pulling at it. Cavendish watched her eat. She was taking very tiny bites, like someone having trouble swallowing.

"And you didn't hear anything unusual last night?" asked Cavendish.

She shook her head, almost playfully. "Nope. You?"

"I left your husband at about nine o'clock – he was by the pool. Did you see him at all last night?"

Deirdre nodded. "Yes. I looked for him. He was snoring by the pool and drooling on himself so I thought I would leave him there."

"What time was this?"

"About 9:30. Maybe ten o'clock. I wasn't paying attention to the time; I just wondered where he was. When I found him, I left him there and went to bed. I figured he was exactly where he wanted to be."

"When you went to see him, did you see anybody else at all?"

Deirdre looked at him quizzically. "Are you interrogating me? Isn't that something that professional policemen should be doing?"

"Yes, it is," acknowledged Cavendish. "But I…" How to explain? He hardly knew the girl. She was chasing damnation from the moment he had met her and spurned every olive branch of assistance he had extended toward her. And yet – there was something fragile about her too. Something that spoke to him. And none of these thoughts would mean a damn thing to Deirdre Lance who hated her and her mother.

"She got her hooks into you too, is that it?" Deirdre shook her head. "I don't get it. You didn't want to sleep with her, did you?"

Cavendish shook his head. "No. But I am a former police officer. I have some experience with wayward souls making tragically stupid decisions."

"You think she was stupid? Men are so naïve. But if you want to play avenging angel to her, I guess that's your business," she pointed at his hands, occupied with holding the cup. "But shouldn't you be writing this all down?"

Cavendish feigned a sheepish smile. He had not wanted to produce his notebook outside in front of the officers, and it had become a ploy to inspire Deirdre's confidence. He hadn't yet realized just how freely she would share her opinions. "I left home in a rush. I didn't grab my notebook."

Deirdre pursed her lips. "Come with me."

She turned around with swishing hips and left the dining room. Cavendish followed her into her husband's study. She plonked her cup and saucer on the desk, using a leather-bound book that looked quite expensive as a coaster. Cavendish didn't think it was accidental. She didn't need to root through the drawers; she knew exactly where to find what she was looking for. He suspected her husband's desk was not virgin territory to her. She procured a steno pad with one hand and offered a selection of writing implements with the other.

"Pen or pencil?"

Cavendish took a pen and the pad with his free hand, setting down his cup on the desk. "Thank you." He heard uncertainty in his own voice as he expressed his gratitude, thrown off course by Deirdre's sudden helpfulness. He flipped open the cover. It was a brand-new book, the first page fresh and untouched, no indentions made from a pen pressing on pages above it.

Deirdre smiled, sitting down in her husband's chair, and reaching for her coffee. "There. Now you look the part." She leaned back and put her feet up on the desk. "No."

"Pardon me?"

"You asked if I ran into anybody else when I was looking for my husband," she expanded. "The answer to that question is … no."

He decided that her being playful with her answers was less annoying than being obstructive. He carefully recorded the answer to his question in the notebook and smiled at her. She smiled back.

"When you started looking for him – what time was it?"

She furrowed her brow. "I don't know. I found him pretty quickly and you weren't with him, so if you left about nine, it had to be at least later than that. I don't know exactly what time I got back to my room, but I know I was there at 10:15 because that's when I looked at the clock."

"And the route you took?"

She sighed. "I went down the main staircase, stuck my nose in the living room, the dining room and the study – all empty. I went out to the pool and there he was…I didn't look in the pool, but I think I would have noticed if a body was floating in it."

"And you went back the same way, to your room?"

"Yes."

"Now, back to your feelings about Amber…"

"I hated the little bitch but not enough to be hanged for her or spend my life rotting in jail. I like my comforts," she folder her hands behind her head and slunk down in the chair. "So, are you going to find out who killed her?"

"Somebody is," Cavendish promised.

"Who cares enough about her to pay you to investigate her murder?" Deirdre wondered theatrically, pretending to ponder it like a complex puzzle. "Ah, yes! My husband. Is he paying you? I am sure he will spare no expense."

Based on Lance's efforts to find a way to be conciliatory toward her last night, Cavendish thought she was underestimating her importance to her husband, but she was monologuing now and that was good for him. The talker will always reveal a nugget or two that is useful amongst the chaff. One just had to be careful not to tune them out while they were rambling.

"Don't get me wrong, Mr. Cavendish. I can spend as much as I want, and he certainly indulged me by helping woo Martine to stay here with us – he is good to me. I just can't help thinking –"

She pulled her feet off the desk and they landed on the floor with a graceless thump as she leaned forward in the chair, looking really serious for the first time. Not just the first time she looked serious today, but the first time she had looked serious in the days since Cavendish had met her.

"Tell me something, Mr. Cavendish. My husband took a lot of interest in Amber. Defending her, offering to send her to college, wanting to protect her from the police, from herself... based on your experience with people. Wouldn't you say his level of interest was – was downright paternal?"

Cavendish had expected her dislike and jealousy to be predicated by many things. He had even imagined Lance may have enjoyed Amber Geranabby in the biblical sense. When Lance had focused so much on Pamela's loyalty last night, he had considered the possibility of a bond there that ran beyond a loyal employer caring for staff. Deirdre had followed that line of conjecture to its natural conclusion. Aloud, he said: "You think Amber might be your husband's daughter?"

"Why else care about her so much?"

Having harbored darker thoughts of his own, Cavendish was reluctant to put voice to them and give them life beyond the dark recesses of his own jaded imagination. "He did see her grow up."

"Pah," Deirdre pushed the ridiculous idea away from her with a physical gesture. "I know men. They don't take a liking to a girl for no reason. And he liked her too much for it to be the other possibility. And Pamela liked him too – No, I wonder if maybe once upon a time he spent some time in the maid's cottage. I'm not saying he cheated on me – both her girls are too old for that. But even in this day and age, the wealthy landowner doesn't acknowledge the bastards he sired in the maid's cottage. Or would he?"

It was a possibility, but still not one he would reinforce to her directly. "Not all men fit the common mold, any more than all women do. Does the thought of your husband having children before he married you bother you?"

"Not as much as the thought of him hiding it from me," Deirdre admitted. "You'll laugh. I thought of stealing some of her hair and sending a sample of hers and his to one of those labs that do DNA testing for paternity cases. Is that pathetic?"

Cavendish ignored her question. Let her wonder if he was judging her, that might make her try to prove that she wasn't pathetic which meant she would talk more. The more she talked, the better. "Did you ever ask him about Amber? Or if he had children?"

She shook her head. "Something as big as that, I don't think you should have to ask your husband if he has children."

Cavendish had to agree with her there. "But were his feelings of kindness toward her the solitary basis of your suspicions?"

"It wasn't just that he was kind. It was that he was so very kind. Always praising her, always offering to help her go to school. It just seemed - too much. And if I did ask him why he cared about her so much he would get defensive, like I was being overly suspicious."

"Could there be another reason for him to have a particular fondness for Amber? He has no other children, right? Are there any other children of staff on the property?"

"No," said Deirdre skeptically. "You're saying she wasn't his daughter; she was just the daughter he always wished he had? I could believe that if he had shown more interest in having a real daughter or son with me."

Cavendish tried to imagine her in the context of motherhood, sticky little palms pawing at her crisply pressed capris, and found it hard for the image to form even at the periphery of his imagination. She was more the martinis with the girls at the club type of wife. She was attractive and shapely, but Cavendish hadn't seen much in the way of emotional or intellectual depth – and the jealousy of Amber could be more about a sense of ownership than about a wounded heart.

"Did you want to have children then?" Cavendish felt that he ought to give her the benefit of asking rather than making a judgment based on his observational prejudices. Deirdre pursed her lips.

"No," she admitted. "I guess I never really wanted to have kids. But he's never asked, either." She cocked her head to the side and Cavendish heard the same thing she did: Heavy footsteps clomping in from the back of the house. Quick paced, and a little hostile, if it was possible for footsteps to sound hostile. Cavendish and Deirdre both looked at the doorway as a shadow filled it, the burly bulk of Chief Constable Borden Boxer. In a community as small as St. Lazarus, it followed naturally that the Chief Constable would be involved in homicide investigations. Especially if they occurred at the private residence of one of the island's leading citizens. It followed just as naturally that Boxer was not going to be very happy that Cavendish was here running an investigation in parallel with the official police inquiry.

"Good morning, Chief Constable," said Cavendish in his best effort to put forward a convincing charm offensive. He let the notebook and pen in his left hand drop as unobtrusively to his side as possible and stepped forward extending his right.

Boxer did not offer a hand in return and looked at Cavendish's hand with distaste. He looked Cavendish in the eye. "Why are you here?"

"Mr. Lance called me shortly after he called you."

"Why?"

"I think you are aware that my work has become entwined with Mr. Lance and his – household – over the last few days. I think he thought I might be of help."

"Help? What kind of help?" wondered Boxer, his eye zeroing in on Cavendish's notebook. "Are you interviewing people?"

"I have been talking with Mrs. Lance, but I haven't been close to the body or doing anything that would constitute interfering with the crime scene, if that is your concern.'

"Interviewing witnesses to a crime is interference."

"Is there a statute that says so?"

"Is there a law that says I can't talk to Archie if I want to?" interjected Deirdre.

"Cavendish, go home," said Boxer. "You're in our way."

Cavendish was not going to get into a direct confrontation with the Chief Constable. He bowed out. "Thank you for your time, Mrs. Lance."

"You can have more of my time anytime you want, Mr.

Cavendish," she smiled mischievously at Borden Boxer. Cavendish decided it was probably best to head out and not provoke the Chief any further. He stepped towards the doorway but had to stop since Boxer's bulk was still filling the portal. There was an awkward beat while he and Boxer were looking at each other almost eye to eye, except that Cavendish had to tilt his head slightly up. Then Boxer backed up slowly.

"Watch where you stick your nose, Cavendish," warned Boxer.

"I always do, Chief Constable. And if you need any help–"

"I don't need any help from some two-bit gumshoe who makes his dime by sticking a camera through peoples' bedroom windows."

Cavendish decided to presume Boxer didn't realize that Cavendish was previously a Scotland Yard detective with stellar prospects who could be quite helpful. He didn't make that assumption because he knew the Chief was an intelligent man and he felt like the insult was designed to get a rise from him and that Boxer knew his background quite well. "Good day, Chief Constable."

A uniformed officer was standing just inside the front door, holding it open for him. There was to be no confusion about the route he was to take as he left - Cavendish went outside and felt a wind gust as the door slammed against his back.

Standing on the porch he paused. There was another officer at the front gate, and the yard had several police vehicles in it but most of the officers must be in the back by the pool, with the body.

Cavendish looked towards the cottage where Pamela Geranabby lived. It might be a while before the police got down there, with the victim's corpse and a cluster of witnesses by the pool that might keep them busy for a time. There might be a window of opportunity for him to speak to Pamela, always assuming she was in a state fit for receiving and talking to visitors. She had just lost her daughter, after all. Cavendish couldn't imagine a worse thing than losing your daughter.

He decided to try. He wished he could gather more fresh impressions and spend time poking around the pool and the house, but he was not an official investigator on the case. Boxer was right to dismiss him as an interloper.

Nevertheless, even as the interloper, Cavendish thought an exception should be made for him as long as he did his best to stay out from under the feet of the police. He felt justified in making this rationalization because it supported the course of action he intended to pursue. He crunched down the short gravel track and knocked on the door to Pamela's cottage.

Standing under the bright sky, it was hard to see inside the cottage. He was aware of two shadows; one of them approached the door warily, telling the other shadow - whom Cavendish took to be Pamela - the identity of their unexpected caller.

"Let him in," he heard Pamela say. The door swung open and he found himself facing the suspicious face of one of Pamela's fellow house maids, one that had helped serve dinner. He smiled in a way that he hoped was disarming, but the face did not soften.

"I'm going up to the house Pamela, but I will come back in a little while," she regarded Cavendish darkly. "Just to be sure you okay."

Like a cold wind, the shadow squeezed past him as he stepped inside the cottage. Pamela sat at the same little laminate kitchen table, a cup on its surface clasped between her hands. She did not look up to see her friend depart or to see Cavendish arrive, her eyes remained focused on the cup. Her eyes were narrowed, circled in black, and fixated like she couldn't look away. As if something about that cup was a lifeline her sanity clung to while her heart and mind processed the darkness of what had transpired in the night.

Amber's little sister Mia was not in evidence, but the doors to the bedrooms were both closed. Cavendish wondered if she knew yet. She must. What a bloody awful thing for any girl to deal with. Not just losing a sister but knowing someone had deliberately taken her life away. What would hurt more? Knowing that someone hated the person you loved so much that they had to wipe her off the earth or thinking of her being a victim of happenstance? Wrong place and wrong time?

He didn't think he was going to be invited to sit down, so after glancing in the cup to make sure it wasn't empty – making her a fresh cup could have been an icebreaker, but it was still almost full – he pulled out a vinyl chair and sat down facing her.

A face that was handsome yesterday looked creased and ancient today. Like the soul inside was broken, and the cracks had torn her open all the way to the surface.

"I'm very sorry about what happened to your daughter," he said. Pamela didn't look up.

"I still don't know where you fit into all this, Mr. Cavendish. I don't know how much fault is yours. If any of it is."

"I honestly don't know if I could have done anything to stop this, Mrs. Geranabby. I don't know. All I do know is I want to help. I want to help find out who did this to your daughter."

"It must have been that crazy man," she said. Her voice was dull, listless. There was no strength for venom. Just loss and tiredness. "When he came here last night, he could have killed her right then."

Cavendish didn't know if Ross Buchanan had spent the night in jail or not. And he didn't know when he would be able to talk to Pamela again. He had to cover as many bases as he could.

"Maybe it was him," allowed Cavendish. "But your daughter may have had other enemies. Especially after the news broke and her name was out there… we need to think about every possibility. And I know it is horrible to be answering questions about her right now, but the police won't want me talking to you and your memories of last night will be freshest right now."

"Why wouldn't they want you talking to me?"

"Because I'm not a police officer," he explained.

"Then why are you talking to me?"

"I only met your daughter a couple of days ago. And she was doing something dangerous, and stupid, and nasty. But she was feisty and too smart to be doing what she was doing, and I liked her. I wanted to help her. I couldn't help her when she was alive, at least not that I know of. I'd like to try to help her now."

Pamela's eyes still hadn't moved from the cup. Her body hadn't moved since Cavendish arrived, whereas he was already adjusting himself on the uncomfortable chair.

"She's past help. Probably past it awhile. I tried to raise my girls right, Mr. Cavendish," the assertion was her first flicker of emotion. "I tried to raise 'em right and she went so far off the tracks and I never saw it. How could I never see it?"

"When she left here, where did she say she was?"

"She said she was working. Always working. Selling t-shirts at one of the stores in town."

"And did you ever know her to lie to you?"

A shadow of a smile as a memory snuck through the cloud of sadness. "She got into trouble more than a bit, but she never lied. I thought she never lied. I was pretty far wrong about that, it turns out."

"Then you had no reason to expect her to be lying to you about where she was, did you?" he offered gently. "So, don't ask yourself those questions."

One thing he hadn't missed about the Yard was conversations like these. Looking into the eyes of the ones left behind as they wonder what they could have done to change the outcome. Why had this happened? What could they have done differently? Nothing or everything. There was no answer you could honestly give. Everything looked different when you were looking back on it. Patterns revealed themselves that are invisible when you are in the midst of the situation, doing the best that you can.

Her head stayed still, but her eyes rolled up, shifting their laser like focus away from the cup and into his own eyes.

He felt like she was drilling through his eyes, into his soul.

"You never ask yourself those questions, Mr. Cavendish? You never ask what you could have done different?"

Cavendish felt chilled. The way she looked at him, into him, her eyes boring through him. She had been so far away one moment, and now she was studying him in a way that frankly, he found very unnerving.

"When they told you they found her," she persisted. "You never asked those questions? What didn't you see? What didn't you know that you should be knowing? Your wife, Mr. Cavendish. I am talking about your wife."

Cavendish leaned back, away from her, involuntarily. There was an edge of craziness in her glare and the thought that she had been googling him unnerved him. It didn't surprise him that Lance had investigated him, maybe it was prejudice against the working class to think she wouldn't have done a little digging into his past, too. She had more of a vested interest in knowing about the man bringing her daughter home than Lance would have done.

"Of course, I asked those questions. That's why I know they don't get you anywhere."

"Are you going to avenge my daughter, Mr. Cavendish? Is that why you want to talk to me?"

"I want to help find who did this to her. To bring the perpetrator to justice."

"Justice?"

He didn't know how to address this query which sounded like an accusation, so he persevered with his line of questioning. "When you and Amber left the drawing room in the house – you came straight here?"

"Yes."

"Did she go out? Did she go to bed...?"

"She went to her room. She was upset. She was upset there'd been such a scene. Upset that Mia knew about it."

"And what did you do when she went to her room?"

"I made some tea. I took her a cup. She was sitting on her bed and I let her be, then there was a knock at the door, and

161

I came to see who it was. It was Martine."

"Martine Letourneaux?"

The eyes frosted. "Yes. This tea is cold," she pushed back from the table and took her cup to the sink, tossing out the contents. She reached for the kettle. "Would you like a cup, Mr. Cavendish?"

"No thank you. So, Martine came to visit you?"

"Yes. She has seen Amber about the place – Mr. Lance lets her use the pool you know. He's always been a very generous employer. We were very lucky," She put the kettle on the stove. She turned the knob and it clicked several times before Cavendish heard the "whoosh" of the flame. She stood there, staring at the wall. Even with her back to him, Cavendish could sense her heart scraping against the bottom of her soul.

"Poor Amber never thought we were lucky. She never looked around at this nice cottage –– so much nicer than I could've paid for myself – and thought what a nice home she had. She never thought about the pool she got to swim in or the view of the ocean she had or the fact she could have gone to college even without a scholarship... all she knew was her mama was a maid. And it wasn't good enough for her. I wanted to teach her the value of being an honest person doing an honest day's work. She never agreed with my choices. Up to the day she died, I wasn't good enough for her."

Cavendish filed through the possible bromides – he was sure Amber loved her mother deep down, appreciated her sacrifices on her behalf - but he couldn't summon them to his lips. Maybe because he knew these platitudes would be lies. Amber didn't appreciate her Mother; Amber thought her mother was a fool. Maybe if she had lived longer and grown wiser she would have grown to appreciate her – it had made an impact on her when her Mom took out Buchanan with a piece of patio furniture – but full reconciliation would have needed more time. Time that had been stolen from them both.

"So, Martine came to see Amber because she'd seen her around the place? Did she want to make sure she was okay?"

Pamela nodded. "But Amber had gone to sleep.

Martine was very nice. We talked. And she left around nine. Amber came out of her room a little after that. I thought maybe she would want to talk – but we argued. I was so mad, Mr. Cavendish. I don't know if my daughter was a criminal or a whore or some of each but she wasn't what I raised her to be and I'll tell you I had been quiet about it, I tried to talk to her from the time you came home but I didn't push and I didn't yell but last night, after that man came here, and it caused trouble between Mr. Lance and Mrs. Lance and she brought it all on their doorstep I was just so disappointed and mad that I let her have it. Both barrels. And my Amber – she wasn't one to stand there all quiet while you yelled at her. She made it plain things would've been different if I'd been different."

Tears were building in her eyes now, but she smeared them away with a rough brush of her forearm and put a teabag in the pot and added water from the kettle. "Then she went in her room and I went in mine and – and I bet Mia heard all of it and the last memory she has of her sister is probably her mama calling her a whore."

She stood in limbo for an instant, teapot poised while her eyes reviewed the scene that had played out in this little cottage just hours in the past, yet in a different reality.

"Tea?" she offered automatically again. Cavendish declined for a second time.

"Did you hear her leave the cottage?"

"No. I didn't know she wasn't here. I cried a while, and I fell asleep. I was mad at her, sad at her – choices I made so she had a good life, a right life."

She fell silent for a long while, turning the cup around and around between her fingers, feeling it grow cold like the first one.

"When I woke up, it was because Martha was banging on the door. She came in and – well she told me they found Amber."

"How is Mia holding up?" asked Cavendish.

"As well as can be expected – isn't that what you say?" She buried her face in her hands. "How did I let this happen?"

"Don't blame yourself…" Began Cavendish.

The fire was back when she dropped her hands away. "Then who do I blame? Tell me? Who do I blame for her going so far away from the path I taught her to follow? I kept her away from bad kids I kept her nose in her schoolbooks and still – this is where we end up. Who do I blame?"

"Blame the person who took her life. Your daughter was still half-way a child. There was plenty of time for her to change directions, go a different way. And you were there for her when she needed your help making those choices. Someone else took those chances away. Not you."

"You think so?" she was clearly unconvinced. "If you don't want to kill the one that took my daughter, why is it any better for you to chase the killer than for the police?"

"Maybe it's not. But I am a trained homicide detective. I can help."

"If not that crazy man, how many men do you think she blackmailed? How many men could there be wanting and planning to come get their revenge? You really think you can ever find out who did this?"

Cavendish rocked his head from side to side modestly. "I was a pretty good cop in my day. I have as good a chance as any. A little better than some. I would like to help." And he knew someone that could probably give him a reasonably accurate tally of how many men she had blackmailed. His ears pricked at the sound of footsteps crunching on the gravel, a sound he usually enjoyed hearing, and even now it was useful. From his place at the kitchen table he glanced at the screen door and saw the approaching figures beyond it. They were dressed in the black, pressed trousers and starched white tunics of the Island Police Force. In the lead, rumbling forward like a two-legged Saturn V rocket, was Chief Constable Borden Boxer.

Cavendish turned hastily to Pamela. "Does your cottage have a back door?"

CHAPTER THIRTEEN

Cavendish wished he could prowl the estate, speak to other witnesses, and get a sense of the crime scene. All those familiar rituals that he hadn't thought about in ages seemed like long lost friends as he skulked away from the estate like the unwelcome interloper he was. Now he understood the frustration of the bereaved who wanted action and were cast aside and told to let the professionals do their job. Even in the case of his wife, while he wasn't allowed on the case directly his colleagues kept him closely in the loop.

There was also a nostalgia factor. He hadn't been around a crime scene since he left the Met, so there had been no opportunity to miss it. Seeing the mounting level of activity around Amber's corpse reminded him of those days. Not that being around a murdered soul was a pleasure, but there was a satisfactory element in assessing the scene, understanding the language of death and evidence, reading the signs and starting to assemble the story of the victim's last moments, building the trail that could help you bring the murderer to account. Cavendish liked to think that a homicide cop was the last friend a murder victim ever made. Sometimes he thought a copper could get to know the deceased better than the people that loved them in life, or that hated them. You learned who they were, the secrets that shamed them, and anxieties they concealed. You found out what people really thought about them. Most of the time, not always but more often than people would believe, you could bring the people that stole their lives to justice.

Amber's crime scene had reawakened some of those sensibilities. To be certain, Cavendish felt a particular fondness for Amber and had done so from the beginning, which might explain why, from the instant his feet hit the gravel of the drive he felt his instincts sharpen, observing everything he could, filing the images even if he couldn't digest them yet. Recording the way the house guests were milling about. Nervous? Guilty? Curious, or not curious enough? Was Marvin Lance as torn up as he acted, or was he just acting well? Could Cavendish trust Lance's observation about the bruising on Amber's neck? If she was passed out, how did she get in the pool? Was she killed in the pool, or put there after? Why was she in her underwear, instead of being dressed or naked? If she had been killed by a blackmail victim, it seemed unlikely the killer would only half-undress her. If the goal was to give the crime the look of a rape/murder he would strip her naked. Likewise, if it was a sex crime then she would have been left naked. It wasn't unknown for a sex criminal to dress his victim after the fact, but if that was part of his *modus operandi*, the killer invariably dressed her fully. Of course, in either scenario the murderer could have been interrupted – or it was even possible she had been snatched from the cottage while she was getting ready for bed.

But who would risk carrying her half naked body around the estate and tossing her in the pool a few feet from where Marvin Lance was snoozing off his drunken stupor?

Cavendish should be working the crime scene. He wished he was. Instead, he had crept out the back door of Pamela's cottage and hot stepped it to his car before Chief Constable Borden Boxer had a chance to arrest him for interfering in a criminal inquiry.

Maybe after the police had finished their work, Lance would let him go back and do a follow up inspection of the scene of the crime. In the meantime, he turned his attention to the leads he could chase up outside of the estate. If he couldn't narrow down the means or the opportunity of the murder, he would start with the motive. A girl like Amber might have more enemies with more motives than he could shake a stick at, but as she was dead almost immediately after her secret life was published in the local paper, the former customer who seemed the most likely suspect was Ross Buchanan.

He called Hardy Swain on his cell phone. It rang a very long time before a woman answered. "Hello?"

"Bella? It's Archie," Cavendish and Sophie had been dinner guests of the Swains. Hardy was the closest thing to a friend on the island that Cavendish had outside of the bartender at the Barefoot Buccaneer. "Can I talk to Hardy please?"

"He's asleep Archie, he just came off a night shift."

"It's important Bella, please."

She acquiesced and he heard the muffled exchange of words as she dragged Hardy far enough into consciousness to take the phone.

"Archie? What's the matter?"

"Remember that girl you picked me up with the other day. She had the film studio and she was blackmailing married tourists?"

"Hard to forget. That's turned into the biggest scandal since Governor Bledsoe ran naked through the street grabbing crotches," Hardy replied, laughing at the memory. "Of course, in his defense, that was some *very* bad coke."

"Hardy, she's dead. She was murdered last night."

Hardy did not have to say anything for Cavendish to know that he had just snapped fully awake. "What happened?"

"What I know for sure is that Marvin Lance called me this morning saying he found her body floating in the pool. He pulled her out, says he saw bruising on her neck. I didn't get to see her body, so I am taking his word for now," Cavendish paused warily. Swain was a good bloke, but Cavendish didn't know if his friendship extended to discussing an ongoing investigation. "Then your Chief Constable showed up and chased me away."

"Well, you're not with Scotland Yard anymore," Hardy observed reasonably. There was a long pause. Cavendish didn't want him to think for too long in case he was thinking of not helping.

"Remember the guy she was videoing that day? Ross Buchanan?" Cavendish gently nudged him.

Hardy was thinking along similar lines. "You know, there was a disturbance call at the Lance place last night. It was before I went on duty, but the guys that answered it were in the locker room when I was suiting up. Crazy sunburned American white guy. So, I went to see out of curiosity. It was Buchanan."

Cavendish smiled. Curiosity, nosiness. Maybe Swain was a frustrated detective. And he was volunteering information, which made Cavendish's life enormously easier.

"Do you know if he was held overnight?"

Another pause. This was not a bustling metropolis and Hardy Swain had probably never evaluated his loyalties or where they should lie. He probably never had to. "Archie, I know you were with Scotland Yard and you were a good cop and I know you are a smart guy, but this is a murder case. This is police business. You shouldn't be getting in the way."

"Hardy, I promise I'm not going to get in the way."

Hardy sighed. "I can't see you, so I don't know if you said that with a straight face or not," but he was already helping. "If you wanted to speak with him, I think you would still find him there. He asked for a court appointed lawyer and he'll be up before the judge this morning; he didn't make any calls last night."

If he'd spent the night in jail that made it unlikely in the extreme that he could have killed Amber. Still, it would be worth having a follow up chat with him. It would probably be easier to meet him outside or inside the courthouse than to meet him at the police station. Cavendish was also thinking about who else he could speak with, but most of the key participants were under the watchful custodianship of Chief Constable Boxer. The only other person not under lock and police observation was Tyree.

He was both a suspect and someone, Cavendish hoped, that could lend some insight into Amber, the decisions she made and the little business she ran. His brief encounters with her did not give him the impression she was a helpless pawn of a brutal pimp. She seemed the dominant personality, even if she gave herself the dirtiest part of the job.

He would start at the courthouse, and then move onto Tyree.

≈

The courts were located at the head of Guerra Square, in Government House. There were only two courtrooms. The larger, more formal chamber was the original courtroom where most of the actual trial work transpired. The second was once a large dining hall; back in the days when Government House was both seat and residence of the Governor. Now, it mostly hosted arraignments. The spectators in the gallery sat on simple plastic chairs and a wooden balustrade bisected the room to separate onlookers from proceedings. Since most of the décor was still that of a grand dining room, the balustrade seemed bizarrely out of place. Simple but elegant dark wood tables served both defense and prosecution counsels. The judge sat on a simple riser about a foot off the ground, behind a desk that was ornate, but not more so than you would find in any CPA's office. Everything seemed a little out of place with the Regency era pastels that suggested elegant dinners and recitals, not carriages of justice.

Presiding today was Judge Meldon – St. Lazarus had two judges, both elected to their positions. Judge Meldon had been a crown prosecutor until recently and aspired to the senior judgeship which would allow him a cosseted life in the primary courtroom where he could preside, draw a grand salary, and get lots of perks. The role of the judiciary in St. Lazarus was not overly challenging.

For now, Judge Meldon seemed vaguely bored by the actual business of judging. To allow bail or deny it, to release on one's own recognizance or detain in jail. Who really cared? As long as he made his tee time. He didn't try to hide his boredom, resting his chin in the palm of a sleek and well-manicured hand, watching the tiresome attorneys with shuttered eyes. He did not look at the door when Cavendish slid into the courtroom and took a seat near the back. It had been a hike from his parking spot, and he was both sweaty and a little out of breath. Nevertheless, when he settled noisily in the chair, the judge didn't even seem to notice the interruption. No scathing glare like the ones that had met him countless times in the Old Bailey. Not very Judge Bullingham of him at all.

A list of the subjects to be arraigned was posted near the door. Buchanan was fifth in the list, but Cavendish was unsure what number the person in the dock was or if he'd missed Buchanan. When the current man on the stand was remanded in custody and the next defendant was announced, he was able to deduce that there would be two more arraigned before Buchanan. He settled in to wait and observe the proceedings. He looked at the other eight people sitting in the public gallery for anyone that might look like Buchanan's wife. If his assumption that she was Caucasian was correct, then she wasn't here. One matronly looking woman was taking notes on a yellow legal pad, but her hand moved lazily and with little interest.

Cavendish hoped Buchanan was allowed to post bail, because then it would be easier to intercept him and speak with him. If they took him back to jail he wasn't going to have access to him unless Boxer allowed it, which was unlikely. Not likely at all, Cavendish thought.

The gavel fell with an indifferent thud on the table and the person in the dock was dismissed with a fine to be paid at the clerk's office. Two of the observers stood up and followed him out of the courtroom. The prosecutor and defense attorneys both remained, they were the Crown Prosecutor and Crown Defender and would be providing counsel for most of the people that passed through this courtroom. From the exchanges between them and the judge he knew the Prosecutor was Mr. Hordern and the Defender was Ms. Teller. He waited impatiently as the next person was brought in, a young woman with tear ravaged make up who had been charged with prostitution. It was a repeat offense, and the judge asked questions directly to measure the accused's demeanor.

"We let you go with a fine last time," Meldon intoned gravely. "The court's expectation was that you would take the opportunity to learn a lesson and make changes in your lifestyle that ensured you did not come back before me again. I am not inclined to discharge you with a slap on the wrist again."

"Your Honor," Teller rose to her feet and advocated for her client. There were children at home who would go hungry were their mother jailed. She had no family or support system. Could the court be merciful? As Meldon chewed on this plea like gristly meat, Cavendish wondered about Pamela and her children. The choices she had made, Amber's ambivalence about the relative privilege they enjoyed. She was humiliated that her mother was a maid, but wasn't it so much better than the choices this young mother was making?

"Ms. Teller, I took those things into consideration the last time your client appeared before me. She will be held over for trial and I set bail at one thousand dollars." The gavel thumped and the young woman burst into tears as the bailiff led her out of the dock by her elbow and guided her gently from the courtroom. Cavendish guessed the bail could have been a million dollars, and she would have as much chance of making it as she was a thousand.

None of the observers left the courtroom – no one was here for the young prostitute – and Ms. Teller closed one folder and opened the next. She moved with brisk professionalism, but Cavendish saw she kept her eyes latched to the tabletop in front of her. This was not personal to her, she was just clearing her desk, one obligation at a time.

The door opened and a uniformed officer brought Ross Buchanan in as the clerk started reading the charges. "Mr. Ross Buchanan, American citizen, charged with assault, trespassing and drunken disorderliness."

Buchanan seemed to have shrunk to half his original size since first storming out of Cavendish's office. His life, as he knew it, was over. He stood in the dock, slumping forward, and looked to the judge with begging eyes. Cavendish evaluated the remaining six people watching the hearing, still looking for Buchanan's wife. None of them seemed any more or less interested in this case than any of the others – except for the woman with the notepad, who had straightened on her bench and began writing with the urgency of someone trying to keep up with the words being spoken and not miss anything.

Mr. Hordern stood up. "Mr. Buchanan went to the property, the private house, of one of our island's leading citizens last night. At the Lance estate, he entered the property and the house without permission. He found the minor daughter of one of the maids by the pool and physically assaulted her. Only the prompt and decisive intervention of her mother prevented him from committing egregious physical harm to the young girl. The police were called and were forced to handcuff and overcome significant resistance before taking him away." Hordern sat down.

The Judge looked at Buchanan. "Well, sir. You did have a busy evening." Teller did not object to the highly prejudicial statement from the judge, but she probably chose her battles. There weren't as many mechanisms for judicial oversight in St. Lazarus as England.

Ms. Teller stood up and leaned forward on her desk. "Your Honor, my client wishes to enter a plea of not guilty. He understands that he went to the Lance property uninvited but feels that he wasn't asked plainly to leave. Instead he was assaulted by one of Mr. Lance's staff. He was struck in the head by a maid. A maid armed with a patio table. This caused him to become disoriented and he does not recall anything that happened afterwards. Had the members of the household asked him to leave – instead of violently assaulting him – he would certainly have done so."

The Judge interrupted with a chuckle. "Maid hit 'im with a table?"

"Assaulted him, Your Honor," Ms. Teller said, making a point of emphasizing the term. "It was an unnecessary and unprovoked attack. Mr. Lance's property has gates, but they were open. Nobody was there to ask permission to enter – so he went looking for someone and was brutally attacked for his trouble."

"Your Honor," Hordern had taken his own feet. "Ms. Teller is leaving out an important part of the story – the suspect was yelling at the maid's daughter and threatening her with physical violence at the time the staff member interceded to defend her."

"Mr. Buchanan was very upset," Teller's tone made it sound extremely reasonable for him to be so. "The Maid's daughter had used her wiles to entice him into a sexual rendezvous. A rendezvous she recorded and was using to blackmail him. This was not an innocent girl - she was a blackmailer, and blackmail is a crime."

"Perhaps my learned friend would be so kind as to refer me to the case where this girl was convicted? Or the charge docket where a complainant filed a charge against her?" sniped Hordern.

"Mr. Buchanan refrained from pressing charges in the hope of avoiding public attention," Teller explained patiently. "Your Honor, Mr. Buchanan is deeply embarrassed by the poor judgment he showed, but he wanted it to be kept quiet. Then this girl released her story to the newspapers in a cynical publicity grab –"

Hordern cut her off. "The newspaper is irrelevant to the facts of the case."

"If it provoked my client to make an unwise trip to the Lance estate and explains how upset he was, it is relevant. If it goes to show that this girl was not an innocent victim but a criminal that had provoked Mr. Buchanan to defend himself, it is very relevant," insisted Teller.

Judge Meldon held his hand up. "Let me ask the accused a question or two. Mr. Buchanan, if the allegations against the girl are true, why did you not press charges?"

"Like my lawyer said. I didn't want my wife to find out."

A woman in business attire stole into the room and

delivered a note to Mr. Hordern. He said nothing to her, unfolded it, looked at it and put it in his pocket. His back was to Cavendish so he could not measure the man's reaction.

The judge nodded. "And when the story was in the paper, she did find out?"

Buchanan nodded. "I saw the newspaper on the morning breakfast tray at our hotel. I took it off the tray. I was in a panic – I was trying to think what to do. I didn't know that someone had placed more pictures on the tray. When my wife turned over the coffee cups, a folded-up copy of the newspaper article had been clipped and put inside. Underneath the plate were some physical photographs. She kicked me out of the hotel room there and then. I went to the house because – "

"Your Honor," Ms. Teller interjected quickly. She was professional enough to avoid letting her client hang him himself with too much transparency. "You asked my client if his wife had learned about his transgressions. I think he has answered that question."

Meldon snorted assent. He looked over at Hordern. "Does that note contain something you would like to share with the whole class, Mr. Hordern?"

Hordern nodded. "Thank you, Your Honor. I think it is relevant to your disposition of the accused to know that Miss Amber Geranabby died last night. While no postmortem has yet been made, the Police investigators on site have reported physical signs of assault and are proceeding on the assumption she was murdered."

Ms. Teller snapped impatiently. "Well, my client didn't kill her because he spent the night in lock up."

"Yes, that's true but he could be a material witness to a murder," argued Hordern.

"That's irrelevant to this case. What is relevant is the charges against him," exclaimed the judge. He tapped the file in front of him with his finger. "And they are serious. This tourist showed complete disrespect for our laws and discourtesy for one of the island's leading citizens. He attempted to commit a physical assault that was prevented by the mother of his victim;

Whether he would have continued the assault without that interference is a matter for a trial to decide. Furthermore, this man is a visitor to our island and a flight risk. He shall be held in jail pending trial and his bail is set at $100,000.00. Next case, please." The gavel slapped the desk and the bailiff moved in to grab Buchanan's elbow. The American did not resist or complain – if the money was his wife's he probably didn't have the means to make bail, but he probably no longer cared where he was or what was happening to him.

As they had after the prior case, both lawyers slapped closed the folders for this case to pick up the next one. Prosecution and defense moving harmoniously together through their caseloads. Teller seemed less perturbed by her defeat than Cavendish. He was annoyed because now Buchanan would be off limits to him - but at least he had learned how his wife had learned of his actions and seen that someone had worked quite diligently to make sure she found out.

He also saw the note taker was closing her notebook and jamming it into an oversized purse. Cavendish was sitting behind her so when she turned to leave it was his first chance to see her face. He recognized it as the face that was above the byline on the newspaper article unmasking Amber Geranabby. Her last name was Wynn.

He hopped up from his seat and almost leapt in front of her, startling the woman. "You wrote the article that exposed Amber Geranabby." It came out accusingly, and her hackles rose in response.

"You are in my way, sir."

"Ms. Wynn. My name is Archie Cavendish. I've been leaving messages for you," he explained, backing a step away from her to seem less threatening.

"Yes, and if I wanted to speak with you, I would have returned them. Excuse me," she moved to step past him, and Cavendish took a second step back, but also to the side, blocking her without invading her space.

"I need to speak with you urgently. It's about Amber Geranabby. She's been murdered," he explained. He was startled to hear the gavel slam loudly on the judge's desk. He and Gail Wynn both looked to the bench.

"I hope we're not distracting you too much with the business of the court?" Judge Meldon grunted derisively. Hordern and Teller had turned their back to the judge for the first time, looking at Cavendish and Wynn. "Perhaps you could take your business into the hallway?"

Both of them muttered apologies and departed the courtroom with alacrity. Ms. Wynn made haste for the main door, trying to escape Cavendish's inquisition.

"Ms. Wynn, I know you won't want to give up a source but that story you printed is having a lot of ramifications. A girl is dead. You're clearly interested in what happened to her—"

Wynn stopped, turned, and cut him off with a swish of her hand. She looked like a mother or stern auntie about to administer discipline, not like a professional journalist. She wore a loose-fitting floral dress and a broad brimmed straw hat on her head.

"I'm interested in reporting the story. And my story isn't having ramifications, the choices and decisions of all these people involved are having ramifications. I don't know whose interests you represent, and I don't care. I am not going to tell you my source, I am just going to keep reporting the story."

"Because that's more important than lives being shredded left and right?" suggested Cavendish.

"I didn't put *your* name in my story, but it doesn't mean I didn't know who you were before you phoned me. Did you read the article? It was pretty thorough, wasn't it?"

"Alarmingly so."

"I left your name out for a reason. You keep bugging me, I'll start including it and tying you to all these events and it might not be pretty for you. So, you run along and go do whatever it is you're going to do and leave me alone to do my job." She waggled her fingers at him in a gesture that suggested "walk away" and turned and shuffled her portly frame out of Government house and down the steps to Guerra Square. Cavendish stood speechless in her wake.

He did not let his condition hinder him long, though. There were two people he very much wanted to speak to and hoped to get first impressions from. This would require him to stay ahead of the police who would still be compiling their list of "persons of interest," but time was of the essence. He hot stepped it to his car.

CHAPTER FOURTEEN

Cavendish wanted to speak with Tyree to learn more about Amber and the blackmail scheme, and he wanted to speak with Buchanan's wife to see if she fit the profile of a potential suspect. However angry she may have been at Ross Buchanan, it was still plausible that she would follow in the footsteps of the countless women who had come before her, women who blamed the jezebel for the transgressions of their husbands, instead of blaming the men.

There was a strange mystique about the female view of the world, and how many women regarded men as helpless pawns. Even Elizabeth used to caution him that if you put a naked woman in front of any man, he would partake. Like the scorpion stinging the turtle as it conveyed him across the river in Æsop's fable, it was a function of the male nature. True, Mrs. Buchanan had ejected her husband from their hotel, but that may have been an immediate reaction that didn't reflect her long-term plans.

Cavendish was less charitable to his own gender. He put it down to weakness, flawed character, and vanity. It seemed like a bizarre holdover from Victorian times to hold women accountable for every turpitude that males committed, liberating men from responsibility for their choices or the consequences of their sins.

Finding Lorna Buchanan was time-consuming but straightforward. Cavendish sat in his car calling hotels, starting with the five-star properties. There were about twenty-five properties that he thought likely candidates based on his limited knowledge of her – she had the money. He started with her because he knew her first and last name – Tyree he knew by that name alone, and it might be first, last or nick. Swain would tell him, but he felt guilty about prying a second piece of information about the policeman so closely on the heels of the first.

He dialed hotel after hotel, asking to speak to one of their guests, Lorna Buchanan, poised to hang up if they acknowledged her as a guest. He had pulled the notebook he kept in the glove box onto his knee and wrote the name and phone number of each hotel as he called. Partly to keep track, and partly to strike the name off the list as he eliminated it. This practice gave him the illusion that he was making some headway. He was going through the list alphabetically and he was about halfway through when he struck upon a hotel operator that offered to put him straight through to Mrs. Buchanan's room. He ended the call and copied the address from the browser in his phone onto the notepad.

He started his Charger and fought his way into the beeping stream of traffic with fits and starts. He headed east out of town in a sluggish procession, trapped in the stagnant and toxic wake of an ancient bus. Two-way roads full of cars afforded few opportunities for passing so he had to hope the bus would turn off, while trying not to think about the sooty fumes he was ingesting from its exhaust.

It still seemed surreal that he was investigating a murder. Cheating spouses were his lot, and he'd built up a fairly healthy little practice around the simple routine of following and photographing.

He wondered how long the police would be at Lance House. He really wanted to go back and spend some time cultivating a sense for the crime scene and measuring up the people at the house, trying to build up a timeline of who was in what place at what time. Had there been a splash when Amber was tossed in the pool? Had anyone heard anything? Seen anything? He wanted to tap their memories before things started to shade and fizzle and lose their cohesion.

At least it wouldn't be a long drive from Lorna Buchanan's hotel to the Lance house. If he survived sucking in this accursed bus exhaust. The bus never obliged him by turning off the main road, and many of the sharp switch-backs were too tight for the bus, causing it to slow and crawl around the corner at speeds nearing a full-stop. In the end, he was the first to turn off, into a driveway framed by neat brick pillars and an oasis-like column of carbon monoxide free air.

The hotel was luxurious, but it was not one of the beach hotels. It was set in a meadow that lay in the shadows of this island's hilltops, on the grounds of an old sugar plantation. The cane was long gone, a neatly groomed golf course in its place. Cavendish imagined Judge Meldon meeting the two attorneys here for a round later this afternoon. The driveway courted the edge of the golf course framing the boundary of the property. The hotel was a modern, vanilla looking structure that could be an Airport Marriott or downtown Hyatt as easily as a tropical resort hotel. Swanky, but beige.

He left his car in the self-park. It meant a bit of a walk, but he preferred not to surrender his car to the mysteries of valet parking and the interminable wait when he was ready to leave the property.

The carpark was small because it was mostly off islanders that came here. Cavendish walked past about thirty stalls as he headed into the hotel pondering the fact that while he knew Lorna Buchanan was staying here, he had no idea of her room number. If he called her room from the lobby, she might decline to see him. Some hotel clerks could be quietly bribed, but this hotel tended to hire staff with annoyingly taut morals. The other problem with this hotel was that Cavendish was not exactly unfamiliar to the staff of the Hilltop Hideaway Inn. He had caught several of his subjects in *flagrante delecto* in these very rooms, and there had been an occasion or two that developed into quite a row. If observed, he might be quietly asked to leave. Or physically ejected if a man named Steve was working.

Focused on masking himself with an aura of unobtrusive nonchalance, he climbed the steps to the front portico. It had been a few months since he was last here, so maybe he would not stand out. Fortunately, his experiences had taught him the layout, so he moved through the lobby with rapid confidence. He veered right and aimed himself at an alcove between the tiny gift shop – more of a gift counter – and the restrooms. In this alcove was the house phone.

He plucked the phone off the receiver and dialed the hotel operator, asking for Lorna Buchanan's room. This time he did not ring off but let the phone switch over and listened to the rings. He always felt a gnawing in his stomach at moments like these. It was ridiculous, because there were probably a hundred different ways to approach her if she shunned him in this moment, but he always worried that he would say the wrong thing, fail to win her confidence enough to get a face to face meeting with his subject. She answered.

"Hello?" her voice was sadness and weariness blended together.

He went with a vaguely direct approach. Sometimes by offering a person a few facts, they would fill in the missing words according to their own expectations. He went for his best posh and official tones. "Mrs. Buchanan? My name is Archer Cavendish; I am a detective here in St. Lazarus – formerly of Scotland Yard in the UK. I was hoping I might have a few moments of your time."

"Scotland Yard?" she repeated.

"Yes, I was with the CID." He hoped she would assume he still served law enforcement in some official capacity.

"Um – okay. When?"

"I'm in the lobby of your hotel now. We could meet in the lobby and talk over coffee, or I could come up to your room if you prefer."

There was a long enough pause that Cavendish thought she might have abandoned the phone. Then: "You can come up. I'm in two-oh-eight."

He had to cross in front of the reception counter to reach the stairs, so he moved speedily and kept his face turned away from reception then ascended the stairs rapidly. He relaxed on the second floor and followed the signs to room two-oh-eight, pulling his wallet from his pocket and retrieving his private investigator's license with the intent of flashing it and hoping she didn't ask for a closer look or wonder why he didn't have a badge.

He caught a glimpse of himself in a hallway mirror, hair ginger, almost red, his navy polo shirt, and realized he didn't look at all the part of a cop. At least, not a cop that Mrs. Buchanan would have seen. Maybe she would assume that's how plain clothes officers dressed in St. Lazarus. His reverie was disrupted by the opening of a service entrance next to the mirror. A startled maid apologized and scurried past. Beyond her another maid was shoving an oversized bundle of sheets down a laundry chute. He resumed his search for Lorna Buchanan's room – it was only about fifty yards from the service room. He rapped on her door thrice with the knuckles of his right hand.

The door opened – she didn't have the latch secured so the door swung back all the way and Lorna Buchanan stood there looking him up and down with an appraisal that went beyond deciding if he was a cop. She half leaned on the door and it wobbled so she let go and then she wobbled a little bit of her own accord. She was not drunk – anymore – but she had only traveled a short distance from that state. She didn't look like a woman who felt well according to any metric that might be used as a gauge. Her hair was fair, shoulder length and a positive rat's nest. She wore a long dressing gown that was carelessly belted and left little to the imagination. She didn't seem to care and her carelessness about it filled him with pity, not interest.

Her eyes were blue and strangely hollow, like someone

had reached into them from behind and removed the soul they were once windows to. They were also bloodshot and hovered over deep dark bags in a pale, almost ghostly white face. She had grown tanned on her vacation, and she was probably pretty but here, now, she looked like a building that had caved in on itself. Cavendish felt sorry for her and liked her husband less in the same instant.

"I'm sorry to bother you, Mrs. Buchanan. I am sure you have been through enough over the last couple of days."

"What do you want to talk to me about? It's not like he committed a crime," she turned away from the door and walked into the room. Cavendish took it as an invitation, following her inside but carefully and conspicuously left the door open.

"Is it a crime to be a bastard in St. Lazarus?" she wondered aloud.

"Did you know that your husband was arrested again last night?" Cavendish wanted to keep to the facts and move through them quickly, both for Lorna Buchanan's benefit and because he wanted to move on from here. The scorned wife was a natural suspect in the murder of Amber Geranabby. The police would be here soon, he wanted to gather his impressions and move on. He set aside the sympathy he felt for her as a betrayed woman and steeled himself to find out what he needed to know.

She turned abruptly; brow furrowed in surprise. "No. What did he do now?"

"You know about the girl he was with – "

"The little slut who blackmails horny American tourists? Yes, I read about this little island's special treasure in the newspaper. And she sent me some snaps to enjoy. And a clipping in case I missed the paper You can see them if you like – few things warm a girl's heart like seeing her husband shoving himself into another girl's mouth," she slumped into one of two upright chairs at a round table by the window, the flaps of her robe landing such that more of her skin was now displayed. She was oblivious to it. A tray of coffee things was on a table next to her and she sipped from a half empty cup.

"Your husband went to see her last night," began

Cavendish. "He threatened her."

"Well he has to blame somebody, doesn't he? Can't blame himself. Did he hurt her?" it was the first time she'd used a hopeful tone.

"Um – no, the homeowner called the police and he was taken away."

"Pity. I would have liked it if she had the shit slapped out of her," she turned the cup in its saucer idly. "This is not how I thought this vacation would go. Maybe I can catch her somewhere and break a few of her teeth or something."

"The girl was murdered last night, Mrs. Buchanan."

Her eyes flew wide with pleasure, unabashed and unashamed. "Oh My God there IS a God and he is Just and he answers prayers. Who killed her? Another husband? A wife?"

Cavendish had to think a murderer would be less brazen in taking public delight in their victim's demise, and surely only an experienced crook would have the moxie to let joy in the crime runneth over as a ruse to throw investigators onto the trail of a false scent.

"That, Mrs. Buchanan is the million-dollar question," said Cavendish, concentrating on the carpet a little self-consciously because her robe was working itself looser and more of her pallid thigh was spilling out. Lorna seemed still not to notice, or she was playing Cavendish with a capable performance as the betrayed but longing wife. She was more attentive to the pleasing news that her husband's partner in dalliance had received her ultimate comeuppance.

"How was she killed?" she wanted to know.

"Mrs. Buchanan, I understand why you might be very angry at this girl – her name is Amber, by the way – but she didn't hit your husband over the head and take him against his will."

"That's supposed to make me feel better? I know my husband is an asshole. I was pretty clear on that point already. But that bitch put pictures of my husband and her outside my room to rub my nose in it."

"It's not likely that she put the pictures out for you to

find," interjected Cavendish. "She was very bitter about men, but she wasn't trying to hurt women. More like she wanted to punish men for hurting their women. Besides which, publicizing her activities would have threatened her business."

Lorna's mouth fell open a little bit. "What? Avenging adultery by luring men into it?"

"Your husband could have refused."

"Are you this girl's lawyer?" she demanded angrily. "I'm pretty clear that my husband made a choice, that he's a louse. I don't think he was a helpless victim. But this girl is deliberately luring men into a trap to make them commit adultery so she can blackmail them – so she's a blackmailer and she's basically a whore because what is she doing? She's fucking men for money. That's a whore. Ruining my life was a joint project she and my husband did together and they did a damn good job of it - so don't expect me to feel all sad that she's dead – I hope she died slowly and I hope my husband did it so you guillotine him or draw and quarter him or whatever you do on this stupid island." Spent, she coughed and sipped at the coffee. She dropped the empty cup into its saucer with a clatter.

She looked markedly disappointed when Cavendish informed her: "St. Lazarus doesn't have the death penalty, Mrs. Buchanan, and it seems very unlikely your husband could be the murderer since he spent the night in jail."

Cavendish felt relieved when Lorna leaned forward in her chair and pulled the dressing gown closer around herself. There was a second chair, so he pulled it away from the table and slid into it.

She looked at him across the table. "Why are you here again?"

"I'm a private investigator, Mrs. Buchanan, and your husband tried to hire me two days ago – to find Amber Geranabby, as it happens. I declined him as a client. But he looked for her himself. He found her. He also was arrested for an altercation he had with Amber, me and an associate of hers."

Light dawned and Lorna jabbed at the air with a fingertip. "Yeah, you were in the article in the paper. I remember now. 'the bystander that became involved', right? So, you are her friend? What's the deal with you?"

"I met her through that episode. And now I find myself making inquiries about her death…"

"Am I a suspect?" Lorna sounded amused, almost hopeful. Then her pale face darkened with thunderclouds of rage. "Oh, I would have killed her. I would have punched her in the face over and over 'til every finger in both of my hands were broken and every tooth in her little head was smashed and her face was a jelly." Her eyes gleamed as she rubbed her hands together, washing them in imagined basins of blood.

Cavendish chose to breeze past her murder fantasy and answer her about whether she was a suspect or not: "That depends on a few things. For instance, where were you last night?"

"I was here. Do you need a witness?" she moved a napkin aside on the table to find a room service receipt. She shoved it towards him without shame or embarrassment. "You can probably find him from this. I didn't ask his name. And he didn't offer it."

Cavendish looked at the time stamp – 8.57 PM. Then, however long it took for the room service waiter to get the food to the room.

"That only accounts for a few minutes."

Lorna shook her head slyly and crossed her legs in the first deliberate move she had made to show off her body. "It accounts for an hour. I was hospitable. I figured I would take a slutty lifestyle for a test drive. And he was receptive…"

The sly spark flickered and dimmed, and her eyes darkened once more. Cavendish guessed that her adventure had not settled her heart or her mind. He moved on: "So he was here for an hour? And then?" he pocketed the receipt so he could follow up with the waiter.

"I watched the eleven o'clock news on TV and he left a little bit before that… then I went to sleep. What time was she murdered?" Then something seemed to occur to her. "Aren't you a private investigator? Shouldn't it be a policeman here asking these questions?"

"They might come to speak with you too. But there are some people who are concerned that the nature of the victim might lead the police to pursue her killer less seriously than if she was – well, than if she was a respectable girl."

"Someone cares enough about her to hire you?"

"Everybody knows someone that cares about them, Mrs. Buchanan," observed Cavendish. "Amber may have made some bad choices, but she had a mother, a little sister, and friends that are all grieving for her right now."

Lorna accepted this. "I guess everyone has a mother. Ross'll be moving back in with his – you don't think he killed her?"

"I think he could have. But he was in a holding cell overnight."

"And I'm a suspect – I don't know exactly what time he left. But I didn't go anywhere. I ate my food – my food that went cold, and I showered, and I got in bed and watched TV. My beautiful Caribbean vacation. Besides, I could hurt her, but I couldn't kill her." She seemed to reflect on her earlier, more rabid vision of beating her to death. "I don't think I could go that far."

"A lot of murders happen when angry people go too far," observed Cavendish, thinking how often strangulations were crimes of passion. "Going too far can happen almost before you know it's happening. You stayed in overnight. What time did you get up this morning?"

"About nine. I didn't order breakfast until 10.30 or so, I just made coffee in the pot that comes in the room… I just – I didn't feel good this morning. Feel free to check my bathroom for signs that I washed off blood or anything."

Cavendish pushed back from the table and started wandering the perimeters of the comfortable room, happy for the invitation to indulge his nosiness. "You have children?"

"A daughter. She's twelve."

Cavendish smiled in genuine connection. "Mine too. Though she thinks she's twenty-one."

Lorna reciprocated the smile. "I think that's standard for their age."

The room had the normal paraphernalia of a married couple on holiday. Jackie Collins paperbacks and tour pamphlets on the nightstand, some of her jewelry clustered in an ashtray. There was a bra and panties discarded on the floor at the foot of the bed – not to the side as one might have expected, and Cavendish linked that to the party she had with the room service waiter last night. He wondered how she was feeling about that now. Some women could have casual sex or revenge sex and feel liberated. Other women were like people that got carried away drinking themselves into oblivion at a party, except the hangover was emotional rather than physical.

There was also a big crack in the mirrored door of the hanging closet. He pointed at it and looked quizzically at her. He didn't need to draw her attention because her eyes had been following him.

"I did that with the chair when I first found out." Now, she pulled her robe even more closely about her, like she felt a chill. "I smashed all the glassware, too. But they cleaned it up. The hotel staff has been really nice. I think they feel sorry for me. I'm sure they all read the paper."

"I don't think Amber sent you the clipping or the picture," offered Cavendish. "It wasn't in her interest to expose herself."

He stepped into the bathroom and saw toiletries arrayed around the sink, all women's products. Make-up remover, No 7 face cream, a cosmetics pouch. Secret brand deodorant and only one toothbrush. Used towels littered the floor. All the towels were used. He suspected she had binned Buchanan's belongings because she said she sent him packing without anything.

"I had them take all his clothes to goodwill," Lorna called from the other room, as if sensing his train of thought. Cavendish didn't see any medications, no sleeping pills or even vitamins. He didn't know the cause of death yet, not officially, and although it looked like strangulation and/or drowning there was always the possibility of being drugged first. May as well start cataloguing means to pair with motives.

He stepped back into the main room. "Have you decided what you are going to do?"

"About Ross? Divorce him. And minimize his exposure to our daughter and make sure he doesn't have a penny to his name. And if I can make his name mud everywhere, he goes, then I'll do that too."

Cavendish nodded. "Here is my card." He felt he had learned everything he was going to from the bitter, broken blonde in front of him. "If you think of anything else, whether or not you think it will directly shed light on the matter in hand – please call me."

She shook her head. "I'm not going to call you. I don't know anything about the murder, and I don't care if the killer gets away with it."

"Take it anyway. I just wanted to meet you and speak with you a little bit, and I appreciate the time you gave me, because you didn't have to let me in."

"That means the interview is over?"

"I think so," he extended his hand to shake hers and she took it in a limp grip without rising from her chair.

"Not like I had anything else to do. Zip lining doesn't seem as fun to me as it did a couple of days ago," she accepted his hand and shook it, then looked him up and down. "Do you think you would want to have some dinner or something later?" she let the invitation linger before adding: "Apparently I'm easy."

Cavendish pulled his hand away from hers self-consciously, and sure his fair complexion was fully flushed. "Um - Thank you," he said, aiming for a tone of confident gentleness and hearing his voice crack like a flustered junior high school boy. "But I don't think that would be a good idea. I better get going and talk to your room service waiter. Thank you for your time."

She looked down at herself, thrown by his embarrassment and seeming embarrassed herself for the first time. "He probably had a good time telling all his buddies about the good time girl in 208."

Cavendish said kindly: "I'm sure no one would believe him."

"Part of me would like to send pictures to Ross. Part of me."

Cavendish walked to the door. There was nothing more to learn here and now he was just feeling awkward. He opened the door and paused, looking back at her. She was still sitting in the chair watching him.

"Mrs. Buchanan, put some clothes on and go for a walk on the beach. Just go for a walk. One step at a time."

She smiled and nodded. He waited, thinking she would say something else, but she didn't. The pause just expanded and became more awkward as she looked at him, expecting him to leave. He closed the door and headed downstairs.

CHAPTER FIFTEEN

The residence of Tyree Fick was the sort of home that reminded one living in St. Lazarus was not necessarily paradise for all its citizens.

The Fick home was a shanty, eighth in a row of twenty or so, that had begun life as cute little cottages. The tropics are beautiful and bountiful in many ways, but they love to eat human constructions. Rain, humidity, mildew, hurricanes, and insects all pulled, chewed, and pawed at the buildings. These cottages were old, and poor islanders seldom had the resources to repair their homes and maintain their pristine, colorful newness. Most of the people born here were born in poverty, or close to it, and rarely rose above that level in life. That's why people like Archie's wife Elizabeth fled the island in search of better economic opportunity – although she loved her home and always aspired to return, once they had saved enough money to make a comfortable go of it. Some people like Pamela stuck out jobs in service to provide for their children. People like Martine used their skills as con-artists to rise above the poverty and fly to the lofty elevations of celebrity. Many followed education and legitimate opportunities abroad, gradually and steadily draining the island of talent and diminishing the prospect for the economy to diversify. The rest remained trapped here, on the outside of paradise. Pressed up to the glass and peering in.

Cavendish squinted at the shacks searching for Tyree Fick's. There were few house numbers, so he was counting the houses and doing the math. After speaking with the room service waiter - who *had* spoken widely and proudly about his conquest of the sad and lonely lady in 208, Cavendish had reached out to Hardy Swain again. Swain had obliged him with Fick's last name and address and cautioned him to keep a low profile.

Tyree's house – or more precisely, his mother's house - had lost large swathes of its roof, and these holes had been patched with corrugated iron sheets that were rusting and probably very noisy during the island's heavy rains. Shutters that once would have given a quaint and cozy air were barren of paint except for a few stubborn peeling licks of yellow, and glass was completely absent from one window. People here repaired their homes with whatever they could find, making houses into patchwork quilts of salvaged material: Corrugated metal, wood from shipping containers, tarpaulins. The bargain Pamela Geranabby made to bring her daughters up in a nice home while she worked in service made a lot of sense compared to some of the alternatives.

The stucco siding was dirty but had weathered better than the wood accessories of the design, but the porch creaked and bowed ominously when Cavendish stepped onto it. The termites had taken as much as they could from this house and even they seemed to have moved onto greener pastures.

The door had been painted more recently than the shutters, but it still needed to be painted again. Cavendish knocked on it and waited, looking up and down the tree-shrouded lane. It was a school day, so no children played, but there were a few men hanging out on the porch of one of the neighbours' cottages, drinking beer and sally wine (the local home brewed hooch, a brutal sugar alcohol created by the sally of its name, according to legend).

He could hear the TV playing in a couple of houses, including Tyree's, and noted with irony the small satellite dishes lashed to the roofs of many of these cottages. It was not just a case of people with nothing spending what little they had on idiot boxes. The governor shrewdly realized that subsidizing 500 channels for his constituents helped keep most of them a little quieter and more compliant than they might otherwise be. (It was both cheaper and easier to provide free cable than it was to create jobs, and a good way to gather votes at the same time.).

Cavendish heard someone stirring inside the house. Floorboards moaned as they moved about. The door was opened by a tall, skeletal woman who hardly seemed heavy enough to make the noises Cavendish had heard. Some women who were old and had lived tough lives still carried echoes of their youthful beauty in the shadows of their eyes. This woman did not look like she had ever been beautiful or young. She was a downright ugly husk of a woman that didn't even have the memories of a glorious youth to comfort her in her shabby existence. She was so used to being suspicious that her cautious appraisal of the pale, red haired white man on her porch seemed more bored than anything. She didn't even say "hello" or challenge him to speak his business. She just waited. She figured if he had driven out into the sticks to visit her home, he would feel compelled to explain his purpose eventually. And she had nothing better to do. She could wait.

"Is Tyree at home?"

"You a newsman?"

Cavendish shook his head. He was surprised that would be her first thought. Had reporters preceded him here? About the murder, or about the blackmail article?

She drew herself up and her face became more guarded. "He's not here."

Cavendish wondered what she had concluded about him just from learning he wasn't a reporter. She wasn't likely to think he was a cop, because there were no Caucasians on the force.

"I knew Amber."

"I bet you did. But my boy didn't have nothing to do with no blackmail. That was all that little slut's doing, so you need to move along yourself." She spoke firmly but without haste.

"I'm not one of Amber's victims, either." Had Buchanan visited out here as well? "I am a friend, and she was murdered last night."

Mother Fick was not so bored and disenchanted with life to let that go by without reacting. There was a flicker of surprise, and then the wall came down and her focus went straight to thoughts of her son. From what Cavendish had seen, he couldn't be much of a son. But for this poor woman in her broken-down cottage, he might be everything she had. "Was it one of her victims that did it? You think they might blame Tyree?"

"At this point we don't know who did it." Cavendish used the plural on purpose to try to bind himself to the idea that he was in law enforcement. After all, maybe he was a recent hire? "I am just trying to gather information."

"My son didn't do it."

"It would be unlikely for him to kill Amber, she was his meal ticket," agreed Cavendish. Unless the opportunities to do movies of the week about her life had inspired her to leave the business of blackmailing tourists. That might change the complexion of things a tad, but voicing that thought was hardly likely to win him an interview with this woman's son.

"But murder is bad for tourism – especially murder of someone that became very scandalous very quickly. And there might be those that want to pin the blame on an easy target – a target such as your son. The sooner we can get to the truth, the better for all concerned."

Mother Fick stood blankly in the doorway, ruminating these words. She expressed her decision by opening the door wider and pointing to the back. "Second door is his bedroom."

Tyree's room was shared. Two beds lined each lateral wall, with a window at the head and the door at the feet. The left-hand bed was unmade and unoccupied. Tyree slept on top of the sheets on the other bed. The room was hot and muggy despite the agitated stirring of the air by a squeaky ceiling fan. The large window was double hung and fully open, but no sea breeze penetrated this deeply into the rainforest to help liven up the air.

Mother Fick was at Cavendish's elbow, and she called to her son. "Up, Tyree! Man to see you."

Tyree rolled over and tuned into the universe reluctantly. His eyes widened as they focused on his visitor and Cavendish sensed he was about to bolt out of bed and attack or flee or fall down because he didn't know which to do. He held up his hand in what he hoped was a disarming gesture. "I am just here to talk, Tyree. This has nothing to do with the last time we saw each other."

Cavendish could feel Mother Fick looking at him suspiciously and wondered if he could take the two of them if they both attacked. Tyree was sitting up in the bed, but he was still.

"What do you want?"

"Amber was murdered last night."

Tyree snorted derisively. "Shut up, Cavendish. She ain't dead. That girl will never be dead. She too alive to ever be dead."

"Well, someone aimed to prove you wrong because her very dead body was found floating in a swimming pool this morning."

"No, you're lying man. She can't be dead. Where was she? What swimming pool?" He lobbed the questions like grenades, defying Cavendish to give him answers.

"The one at the Lance Estate."

"You kidding me? That stupid old man loved her!"

Since Lance was probably only three- or four-years senior to Cavendish, he tried not to be irritated by the characterization of his age. "Someone killed her and threw her body in the swimming pool. Dead. If you don't believe me, the news will be talking about it soon enough."

It seemed like the news was sinking in. "But who would kill her?" Tyree seemed puzzled but not distraught.

Feeling that the flight or fight impulse had receded, Cavendish stepped into the room and sat on the bed opposite Tyree. He leaned forward on the bed, so he could still move quickly if he needed to. "How many men did you two blackmail, Tyree? They would all be suspects, for a start."

"They wouldn't be that stupid, man. She had it set up for their wives to get all the dirt on them if anything happened to her. Someone hurt her and everybody we ever caught gonna be having some big marital problems. Amber was smart."

Cavendish pondered the flight of packages winging their way to unsuspecting spouses and imagined the fallout about to rain across Middle America. It didn't sound like Tyree was responsible for shipping the packages, talking about them as casually as he was. He knew about them in principle but not in detail. So, who had Amber entrusted that task with?

"What about men who became divorced and still harbored a grudge? What about men that got busted another way? What about men that got tired of paying?" he suggested.

"No, man, we never did it like that. One-time cash payment and leave them alone. She thought about that stuff and said if we kept going after them, they might get tired of it or get a backbone or try something. She said get as much as you can while you got them like a deer in the headlights and they are freaking out and they don't know what to do. Squeeze them and let them go. Whenever I told her we could get more from them by going back to ask them again, she always said I shouldn't be stupid and leave the thinking to her."

"What about Buchanan? There may have been other situations like him. People who put up a fight."

"No sir, first time we had that problem. First time. But he could've killed her! He was crazy – you saw."

"He was in jail last night. He threatened Amber – did he ever threaten you? – aside from the day when I was there?"

"Only when you were there, and you saw him threaten us."

It made sense for Buchanan to have gone after Amber on two counts. Only her place of residence had been listed in the article and Buchanan was a bullying type who was more likely to harass the girl than the guy.

"When was the last time you talked to Amber?"

Tyree lied, and he wasn't very good at it. "The same time you did. At the police station."

"You didn't talk to her after she saw the newspapers exposing you? Or after you did?"

"We don't have a phone in the house. She gave me a cellphone but the signal here is crappy."

"So how did you find out about the newspaper story?" asked Cavendish. Tyree rubbed his hand across the crown of his head, trying to buy time for an answer. If he'd read the paper himself or been told by someone other than Amber, he would have answered quickly. Cavendish was sure Amber had told him and he couldn't think of an alternative to shore up his lie that he hadn't spoken to her. "Maybe it was your Mom?" Cavendish suggested. Tyree nodded agreeably.

"Yes. She told me."

"Good. I can talk to her and get her to corroborate your story."

"It's not a story, it's the truth."

"If you say so," smiled Cavendish tolerantly. "I can't pull phone records, but the police can, you know. It will look really bad to them that you are lying. Might make them jump to conclusions"

Tyree shrugged. "Police are always hassling me anyway. They won't be able to prove anything."

"Because you're that good at covering your tracks?"

Tyree frowned at him. "Because I didn't kill her. Why would I? She's my paycheck."

"Were you happy with the pay?"

"It was enough for me. I'm not like her, I don't have grand wishes to be somebody," he spread his arms in an expansive gesture mockingly. "I have a place to sleep, money for my smokes. My belly is full. I got all I need taken care of."

"Yet you tried to convince Amber to try to go back to the well," Cavendish said pointedly. Tyree looked puzzled.

"Well?"

"You told her you should be trying to continue blackmailing the men after they went home. Why would you want to get more money if you have what you need?"

Tyree shrugged. "It didn't matter. She wasn't big on taking advice. She did the thinking; I worked the equipment and I was there as back up to keep the guys under control."

"How did you and Amber meet?" asked Cavendish, changing tack.

Tyree rubbed his hands together nervously. "She was coming out of a funeral. Old lady Montrose. I grabbed her purse. She held onto it tight and kicked me in the knee. She dropped me, then she got me in the privates and... well, and then she actually felt bad." He stared at the floor, looking embarrassed. "She made me cry."

Cavendish laughed despite himself. "She took pity on you?"

The word "pity" triggered a hostile glare. "She felt bad she hurt me, and we talked. We talked about everything wrong in our lives and said she had an idea she was trying to work out. She didn't tell me what it was then, but we started hanging out time to time, until she told me." He smiled at the memory. "I thought she maybe wanted to get with me. She was all fancy and everything and I thought she wanted to go slumming. But it never happened."

"And you became her employee?"

Tyree nodded.

"Did you like her?"

"I liked her a lot, sure. She was pretty, smart, funny. She was kind to me, even though I stole her purse," Tyree wasn't taking time to think about his words now, they were rolling off his tongue as the memories rolled pleasantly over him in waves. "When she listened to me complain about stuff, I felt like she cared."

"How did you feel when she told you what the job was going to be?"

"Surprised. I thought she was weird and I thought it was dangerous and she wasn't the kind of girl I thought she was – the first time she picked up a guy, I was sure she'd never go through with it," he looked up at Cavendish. "She just didn't seem like she could."

"And did she?"

Tyree stood up and prowled the small space between the beds like a caged animal. "She never blinked she never hesitated."

"So, she wasn't the girl you thought she was?"

"No," Tyree disagreed. "I knew she was tough and when she made up her mind, she was going to do what her mind was made up to do. She was exactly the girl I thought she was."

But not the girl you wanted her to be, conjectured Cavendish. "And then your relationship shifted from people hanging out to an employee and his employer?"

"Yes. When I saw how much the money meant to her, I knew I was never going to be her type," explained Tyree. "Instead, I helped. I knew she wanted to make a lot of money."

"How did she react to the newspaper article?" asked Cavendish mildly.

"She was pissed – she," Tyree stopped himself and slumped back down on the bed opposite Cavendish. "Asshole."

"Come on, Tyree, it was a pretty obvious lie. She must have reacted to her project being exposed and who else would she call? How did she react? You said she was pissed."

Tyree sighed, frustrated. "Yes. She was pissed. She couldn't think who had told the newspaper -the information they had was really good. I told her it must have been you. But she didn't buy that. She didn't think it was your style or something, for what it's worth. She thought it was a cop with access to the police reports."

"Who do you think did it?"

"Dirty cop seems likely to me, too" said Tyree slowly.

"Did she say what her plans were, now that the story was out in the open?" asked Cavendish.

Tyree shook his head, speaking more quickly again. "No. Her bank accounts got frozen so she couldn't touch her money. She didn't know what she could do, or if she could start over again. She didn't want to start over again."

Aloud he asked: "How much did she pay you?"

"Two hundred bucks each time. And we did two or three jobs a month."

"Cash?"

"Yes."

"Is that your only source of income?"

"I get odd jobs here and there, but mostly, yeah. Not bad money for two or three days of work."

"Not at all," agreed Cavendish. A person might kill if they thought they were going to be cut out of such a cushy gig. Cavendish had seen people kill for less. He couldn't see Tyree as a murderer though. Not in this context – not sneaking in and strangling Amber and dumping her in the pool right next to Marvin Lance. Moving on.

"Did you give her any suggestions?"

"Yeah, that dude she lives with offered to pay for her to go to university. I told her what the heck, go to university. Get a career or something. She was smart, she coulda – but she called me again later. After she figured out what she was gonna do."

Cavendish wanted to know about the second conversation, but he wanted to know about Tyree's plans, too. "What about you? What were you planning to do next?"

"I dunno. I have a little money put by, I already told you I don't need much. I can get odd jobs," he laughed a little. "Steal the odd purse."

"No school for you?"

Tyree laughed. "Look at me Mr. Cavendish. What you see is what you get. I ain't nothing and I ain't going to be."

"Now that she's gone – who controls the photographs and other materials you took?"

He shrugged briskly. "No idea. She never told me. I think she kept that from me on purpose. She didn't really trust anyone, me included. I asked about it and never got an answer. It wasn't my business. She was pretty clear about that."

"But you had access to the studio," objected Cavendish.

"Yeah but she didn't keep anything there. I'd have the pictures we shoved in the mark's face but that was all. And then she even took those from me. She wanted to control all that stuff," explained Tyree. "She said she didn't want to find herself or the marks on the internet."

Or maybe she didn't want Tyree trying to double-dip their victims for more money.

"You told me she called you a second time?"

"Yes - She was excited because that producer lady thought they could make a movie about her for some TV network. And she said Mr. Lance was going to help her get an attorney to fight the government for seizing her money."

Cavendish was sure Tyree could read the look of surprise on his face. That was a fact that Marvin Lance had omitted. It made Cavendish think again about the allegations Deirdre had made regarding the relationship between Amber and her husband.

"Where would that leave you?"

"I don't know. I figure if she was making money out of a movie, or she wrote some book about her life that she wouldn't be needing or wanting to blackmail guys anymore. Although sometimes I think she would have done it anyway – she really seemed to get off on watching them squirm when they realized they were on the hook. Like she was getting revenge for all the women that got cheated on by their men." He laughed suddenly. "I always was surprised how they were just paying, like they was afraid of their women. If it was me, I'd be like 'that's right, bitch, I nailed that piece of ass. So you better treat me right or else I'll be stepping out a lot.'" He rolled back the curtains on a massive grin full of ugly yellow and white teeth that seemed to point in every direction. "Them dudes was scared of their women."

"Not you, eh, Tyree?" Cavendish smiled conspiratorially, noting how often the men who fancy themselves as manly and powerful seemed to live under their mother's roof.

"No sir."

"On the second call; she seemed to be feeling better?"

"Yep. Thought everything was coming up sunshine.

She was still mad about the newspaper article, she still wanted to figure out who spilled the beans, but she thought everything was going to turn out just fine."

"Where was that going to leave you?"

"Out of a job. I was hoping I could get her to cut me in on some of her deals or introduce me to her producer friend. Maybe they could write a movie about me. Or maybe when her book came out, I could do interviews. I could go on TMZ and Larry King and talk about how we nailed these guys, y'know? And if she didn't – well, I got a place to sleep and money for my smokes."

Now Tyree was lying again. He wasn't dumb enough to imagine that anyone was going to want to see him on TV. And whatever the reality of the relationship between he and Amber, the world would see him as the man pimping her out. He would be the villain. There was no need to call him on his lies, though. They were natural enough – he knew he was a likely suspect and was only looking to make himself look less likely – and Cavendish and Tyree mutually recognized the lies for what they were.

"Girl was playing with fire," Tyree shook his head. "No good was ever gonna come from it. She was really smart, but maybe not as smart as she needed to be."

Cavendish was still imagining the packets of dirty pictures wending their way to wives innocently going about their daily business, oblivious to the havoc about to be wrought upon them by a dead girl they'd never met. "So, if you're not the one sending the pictures to the victims, who do you think Amber would have trusted to do that?"

Tyree shrugged. "I don't know. I told you, she didn't seem to trust anyone. I don't think she did. Whoever it is, I bet they don't know what they got or what they're sending out."

Cavendish had trouble wrapping his head around the idea of a girl wanting to start in the first place. As many girls on the game as he had met, he had trouble imagining the state their lives must have reached to make them choose such a path. It made less sense for Amber, who had a safe home, a hardworking mom, even a sponsor of sorts in the form of Marvin Lance. Unless Lance wasn't as beneficent as he seemed.

"I don't know. I never came around her at her place. Once we started working together, friendly visits were over. She didn't want to see me after we were done," lamented Tyree. "And she wasn't big on small talk, either. It was like someone threw a switch. Only person I can think would be her Mom."

"Her Mom?"

"Yeah. Her Mom is a maid. Maybe she didn't want to work until she dropped dead. Maybe she wanted a nice retirement. I know a lady who put her daughter to work to make a nice life for her. Don't look so shocked."

Cavendish had seen the same, but not when the mother was working her fingers to the bone in a menial job. Usually the mom who stooped to pimping her daughter was chronically lazy, or a junkie. Not a proud, hard working woman like Pamela Geranabby.

"Did you ever get jealous?"

"Of the guys?" Tyree did not try to disguise the truth, even though he might realize he was casting himself in the role of suspect. "Yeah I was jealous. I hated every one of them." As if it occurred to him belatedly that he was providing a motive, he added: "But if I was gonna kill anybody, I would have killed them. Not her."

Cavendish was bugged by the pictures that showed up on Mrs. Buchanan's doorstep. Things hadn't gone according to plan with Ross Buchanan. The police were in the studio room, Tyree could have gone back afterwards. He was there himself. Amber kept tight control of the pictures, but Buchanan introduced some chaos into the carefully managed blackmail project. The picture he found under the bed might not have been the only one that she lost track of. Who could have tipped the paper? Would the same person have taken the pictures to Lorna?

Tyree confessed that he had gone back to the studio after they had all been discharged by the police. "But the memory cards from the camera were gone, so was the video camera. I was making sure if the cops had got everything and they had."

"Did Amber go back with you?"

"Not with me. She might have done herself."

"Who would've taken the pictures to the paper? Or to Mrs. Buchanan?"

"Not me. I don't know."

Cavendish felt confident he knew who had given the news story to the newspaper and who had taken the picture to Lorna Buchanan. It only made sense for one person to have done it, although he didn't have all the pieces yet. For now, he needed to be moving along so he wrapped up the interview. Cavendish was handing Tyree his business card when he heard a militant hammering on the front door. Tyree was pocketing the card but looked up in alarm as they both heard Mrs. Fick speaking through the screen to someone on the porch. It was the Police – Cavendish recognized the deep bass of Constable Hardy Swain.

Tyree froze, and Cavendish regarded him calmly. "You know the police will want to talk to you. Just tell them the truth. And if they take you in, they might lean on you because of your history – just remember they must let you go in twenty-four hours if they don't charge you. I'll check to make sure you're out in twenty-four hours." Discovering that Tyree was helplessly besotted with Amber softened Cavendish to him. For his part, Tyree's eyes were wide and stark with fear of the police.

Tyree's mother was letting the police come into the house. Tyree seemed to be shrinking. Not in fear but coiling like a spring the way a cat does, about to launch.

Cavendish read his intentions. "Don't do it, mate, - not worth it."

Mrs. Fick was bringing the policemen towards Tyree's room. Tyree lunged for the window. There was no glass, just a big opening that could be covered by shutters when need be. He dove through it like he was diving into a pool just as the police loomed in the doorway. Cavendish was facing the window, giving him the same perspective on the view as the officers – the soles of feet disappearing through the frame. Tyree hit the ground sloppily and clawed at the earth to push himself up. He stumbled to his feet and sprinted up the narrow slope of grass towards the thicker vegetation of the rainforest.

One of the cops charged through the room and hopped through the window. It was Jenny Singh. It made sense for her to go first; she was smaller, younger, and faster than Swain who was a burly barge of a man. He also came into the room more cautiously. They knew Tyree was with someone, but Jenny never got a look at Cavendish and Swain came in more slowly to make sure Tyree's companion wasn't someone that might shoot or stab Jenny in the back. He looked at Swain and pointed to the window helpfully.

"He went thataway."

"Are you going to help?" demanded Swain grumpily, filling the door with his bulk.

"Why? I got what I need," Cavendish observed glibly.

"I'll remember that next time you need to peek at a file," warned Swain.

Cavendish sighed. "Chasing a hood through the jungle? What fun."

CHAPTER SIXTEEN

Branches and roots snagged and pulled at him as he tried to duck and weave, pursuing the flashes of white and black of Jenny Singh's uniform running ahead of him through the trees. He couldn't even see Tyree, but assumed that Jenny had him in her sights, so he just trailed her through the thickening brush.

Running, but tripping and stumbling over the thick undergrowth made his forward progress inconsistent. Sometimes the stumbles seemed to accelerate him forward in random bounds. He had been a long-distance runner in school, but usually the tracks were clear and the sport didn't include obstacles one had to jump over, duck under and swerve around.

His legs were soon aching. He was in worse shape than he thought. His speed was still pretty good, and he consoled himself with this thought as he pushed himself up the hill. He applied intelligence to his run. Tyree smoked heavily and was racing up hill. He would run out of gas. If Cavendish could maintain his pace and get his breathing under control, his endurance would win out. Not that it was going to be needed, Jenny was maintaining her distance ahead of him quite well!

Swain had foregone the foot chase completely. He had fetched the patrol car with the idea of heading off Tyree upslope at the next road. Meanwhile, Cavendish ducked under tree limbs and swung around their trunks. He was keeping up with Jenny at least, and she had to be about fifteen or twenty years younger, so that wasn't too bad. Was she keeping up with Tyree? He was in better shape than Cavendish had thought if he was able to maintain the distance in front of her while heading uphill. The incline was steepening as they went.

Cavendish wasn't familiar with this part of the island, so he wasn't sure how the landscape would evolve – but as he wheezed more rapidly, he began to worry about his capacity to stay in the chase at all.

From ahead he heard Jenny calling out for Tyree to stop. She seemed to be running out of air too. Cavendish wondered if she was calling to Tyree because she was close to him or close to giving up. His own legs felt like pillars of clay sticking to the ground, but he doggedly lifted each one in turn, pushed it forward and dropped it down to the ground and picked up the next foot and repeated. He grabbed branches and used them as extra leverage to pull himself along. He thought he heard the rumble of a truck and guessed they must be nearing the road Swain was planning to use for interception. With luck Swain would be waiting because Cavendish seriously doubted he had the energy to tackle Tyree if he caught him.

He lost sight of Jenny – then he heard grunts and rustling in the brush, like two people struggling. He forged ahead toward the noise, gasping like a beached fish. His own noises almost drowned out the sounds he was chasing.

Then he saw the bodies rolling in the ground. Tyree lay on his back. Jenny was underneath him, her arms locked around his knees and her face being squished by his butt. Cavendish surmised that she had rugby tackled him from behind, her shoulder buried in the crook of his knees, and taken him down. Then he must have rolled over. He was not a big fellow, but he still had a weight advantage. He was flailing his arms and trying to kick his legs, but Jenny was hanging on to her man like a terrier with a rat.

Cavendish walked the last few paces, trying to center his remaining strength and slow the pounding of his chest. He wanted to tell Tyree to give up, to stop fighting the inevitable, but he could not speak, he was too winded; his lungs were pumping like bellows just to get air into them.

Cavendish walked up to one of Tyree's outstretched arms as they scrabbled around on the dirt and stood on the wrist and applied his weight to it. He intended to immobilize, not hurt or injure. Tyree stopped and looked up at him, betrayed. Cavendish still didn't have enough air for words, so he just wagged his hand at Tyree as if to say: "that's enough."

Tyree thought about it, and then started flailing with his one free arm. Cavendish was starting to feel better now so he stepped off the pinned wrist and stood above Tyree's head. He reached down and took one of Tyree's ears in each hand and pulled.

Tyree yelled and reached up to grab Cavendish's arms as the latter tried to haul him off PC Singh. Meanwhile, Singh let go of Tyree's legs and scrabbled from under him. Once she was free, Cavendish released his ears. Tyree immediately tried to roll over to his front, and once on hands and knees was trying to regain his feet. While he was still on all fours, Jenny stood next to him and unceremoniously put her foot on his side and gave a hefty nudge. Since he was trying to get on his feet her shove caught him off balance and he fell on his side.

Cavendish nudged Tyree's shoulder with his foot and Tyree rolled onto his belly. Singh dropped to her knees on his back and yanked his arm back. She was strong for such a little thing and bent his arm well back until he yelped. With her free hand she tugged her handcuffs from her belt and within seconds her prisoner laid face down in the dirt, neatly secured.

She stepped off him and rose to her feet. She and Cavendish stood looking down at the ground, lungs and throats burning as their breathing slowed to more normal rhythms. Tyree lay prone, his own chest puffing and deflating, the fight gone and flight impossible.

Cavendish wanted to kick him for being such a dumbass. "You just gave them something to charge you with, you daft bugger."

"What do you want with me?" Tyree moaned from the ground, breathing heavily and expelling breath that smelled putrid.

Singh was wrinkling her nose as she pulled out her radio, ignoring his query. "You need a shower very badly. And that breath!" She called for Swain who was waiting on the road Cavendish had heard. She hauled Tyree to his feet, and they marched him upslope - it was about one hundred feet before they emerged from the trees. The police cruiser was there on the roadside, Swain swaggered towards them looking far too relaxed.

As they handed Tyree over to Swain, Cavendish leaned forward and rested his hands on his knees. His clothes were stuck to his skin by a gluey layer of sweat, and as the adrenaline drained from his system, he felt the ache of a pain in his side. Jenny was plucking at her tunic. As Swain guided Tyree into the back seat of the car, the bedraggled youth looked forlornly to Cavendish. Cavendish shrugged at him. "You ran."

"What do they want with me?" he whined.

"You're going to help us with our inquiries into the murder of Amber Geranabby," Swain explained. Slamming the door. He looked at Singh. "You want to hit him a few times first? I think there's a phone book in the trunk."

"No, that's okay. But I think I need a shower."

Swain looked at Cavendish. "Boxer'll want to know what you and Mr. Tyree Fick were talking about."

"He told me to stay out of it. I am sure he doesn't want to see me at all. But maybe you can give me a ride back down to my car?"

"If you don't come with us, I bet you he'll call you in later."

"Then I'll come later. Jenny can take my statement in the car."

His statement started from the moment the officers joined him and Tyree in the bedroom. He didn't volunteer any information about his reason for being there, and neither Jenny nor Swain asked. They were beat cops. They didn't especially care if Boxer had questions about what brought him there in the first place, they were happy to let him ask those questions himself. The only thing Cavendish did volunteer was that he was there in conjunction with the altercation he had with Tyree and Amber earlier in the week.

Back in front of the Fick house, Cavendish patted Tyree on the arm. "Just be honest. Answer their questions. If you get scared for any reason, tell them you won't talk anymore without a lawyer. They can't make you."

Cavendish unfolded himself from the backseat of the car, hearing Tyree behind him. "I can't tell if you're on my side or not."

Cavendish didn't reply. He just thanked Jenny and Swain for the lift and headed toward his car as the police cruiser headed away down the dirt road.

He should have expected Mrs. Fick to come running out of the house, wondering what was happening to her son, but he hadn't given her any thought since he plunged through the bedroom window. He remembered her the instant he heard the screen door slap against the flimsy side of her cottage and saw her charging towards them.

"Where they take him? Why they take him?"

She ran headlong towards him at such speed that he had to step out of her path because she could not stop fast enough. Her eyes darted between Cavendish and the receding police car.

"Why are they taking him?"

"Because he is a friend of Amber, a girl who was murdered. He ran away so they arrested him," Cavendish omitted the likelihood that they were going to haul him down to the police station for questioning anyway.

"But you said she died last night? He was here last night. He had his friends over. They were all drunk by the fire pit."

"You should probably get a list of the friends together and provide it to the police. That will help eliminate him as a suspect."

"How can they suspect him?"

"He has motive. You know what he and Amber were

doing?"

Mrs. Fick folded her arms across her chest, nodding reluctantly. Afraid to acknowledge anything incriminating about her son.

"That stopped. When it became public, it was over. Amber was on the verge of getting a movie of the week deal and who knows – she could have sold a book too. But your son – he was just her helper. She was the gravy train and while she was off getting a movie deal – he was back home with empty pockets. He could have wanted her to share the money. She could have refused. He could have killed her in anger."

"But he didn't kill her. I can swear it."

"A mother's word is never the most convincing testimony. Get the names of his friends together. I don't think your son has anything to worry about, I am pretty sure that the police are just trying to eliminate him as a suspect. I think it would have been more than a little tricky for him to get in and out of the house unseen. But witnesses will help."

She nodded. "I will."

Cavendish looked up and down the row of broken-down cottages. "Have you lived here long?"

"Since I was a child. This was my Momma's house."

Cavendish wondered how much Tyree's mother knew about his business partnership with Amber. "Did you know his friend Amber?"

"Met her couple times," said Mother Fick. "She didn't think much of around here."

"Tyree said he met Amber at a funeral for Lydia Montrose. Did you know her?"

"Everybody knows her. She had the sight. She could see your past and your future. Everyone around these parts went to her, hoping they could see something about them. What was in their future, what their loved ones would tell them from the other side."

"Hoping?" Cavendish was surprised by the word choice.

"She were no fraud. If she seen nothing, she'd tell you

211

nothing. She didn't see for everybody. She helped a lot of folk and you didn't cross her. She sees right through you."

"And Amber came to her funeral?"

"Probably got dragged. Amber's Mama grew up in that house right there. Right next door to Lydia. We all knew each other then, ran around up and down these streets. Pamela used to spend a lot of time with Lydia. Lydia thought Pamela might have the gift herself, taught her how to use it but I don't think Pam wanted any part of it. She were like Lydia in one way. Lydia never made herself rich off her gifts because they wouldn't come on demand. She used to say you needed to lie three quarters of the time to make a living. She didn't want to be lying to people. Pamela was like that too. Honest woman, she was an honest woman."

The common place of origin would have given Tyree and Amber a shared past, at least in small measure. It might have made her feel she could trust Tyree, that they came from the same roots and might share similar dreams and ambitions,

"Did you know Amber's father as well?"

"No. But Pamela moved away before she had her kids. Her mama died. Her Dad took up with some new lady that Pamela couldn't stand, and she left. I think maybe Pamela's step daddy took a shine to her, if you know what I mean. Her Dad and that lady are both gone now," she added.

Cavendish looked around the shabby little community. A scattering of people lurked on stoops and in doorways, wondering about the police car that came and went, and about this strange man standing in the street with Tyree's mother.

"Get that list together," Cavendish reminded her. "Thank you for your time."

She shook his hand and he eased his strained limbs into his Charger. So, Lydia Montrose was the local witch doctor and she had tried to teach Pamela how to read the locals and convince them that she truly saw their relatives on the other side. Pamela didn't want to pursue that path because she had too much integrity. She'd rather be an honest maid than a wealthy charlatan like Martine Letourneaux.

He was grabbed by a thought. He glanced around and saw Mrs. Fick stepping up to her door. He called out to her. She turned and drifted towards his car. He was only parked a few feet from her door.

"Mrs. Fick, you know that celebrity psychic, Martine Letourneaux? She's from St. Lazarus."

Mrs. Fick nodded. "She grew up over there." She pointed to a shack down the road a way. "I reckon she didn't have the same scruples as Pam. Pretty famous now, ain't she?"

CHAPTER SEVENTEEN

Cavendish was driving back to the estate at Swallows Peak Drive by five thirty. When he left Mrs. Fick at two-thirty he wanted to go directly for a shower and change of clothes because he could smell himself after the chase through the woods and felt more than a little pungent. Instead, he drove into town. Sophie finished school at three and since he might not be able to spend the evening with her, he wanted to drive her home and have a little time with her. After a shower and shave he could get back to the Lance house and resume his inquiries.

He spent the time until Sophies school let out sitting in his office above the front street and the throngs of tourists parading by, he pored over the article that blew the lid off Amber's cover and had probably been the trigger for the whole chain of events that left her floating dead in the pool. The paper did not give graphic descriptions of the acts she had performed, just used lots of words like "lewd", "depraved" and sentences like "Snaring unsuspecting men like American tourist Ross Buchanan in a sin trap baited with honey" – and a general overview of the whole scam. How she identified a potential mark, how she enticed him into betraying the vows he made before God or the justice of the peace, the rabbi or whomever. The moment when the trap was sprung. The money that changed hands and the threat that followed him home. The story culminated with an editorial note about how this smeared the island's reputation and made it seem like a Caribbean red-light district; a plague on couples who might be trying to revive troubled marriages in a perfect setting. Instead, the writer opined, wives would fear their husbands would be snared in the clutches of wicked tropical sirens. Or worse, grow prejudiced against all the women of the island, dismissing them all as vulgar and brazen temptresses poised to lure their men to ruinous ends.

The piece was written by Gail Wynn, she who would not speak to him except to warn him he should mind his business unless he wanted to see his own name in the paper. Her source was very well informed.

Cavendish disagreed with the notion that Amber had singlehandedly turned the island into a den of sin, but she sure had drawn some attention to it – he had seen TV Camera crews clustered around the police station entrance as he made his way back to the office. A sex scandal compounded by a murder. These were paparazzi times for St. Lazarus.

He folded the paper and put it in the top drawer of his desk before heading out to fetch Sophie from school. He was already feeling a little run down from the day. Remorseful over Amber's death and physically tired from the pursuit and apprehension of Tyree. Sophie on the other hand, was a dynamo with that fresh burst of energy that puts afterburners in a twelve-year-old's socks when the school bell signals the release of the inmates. She yelled farewells at her school mates and bounded down the path towards the row of waiting cars.

That was why Cavendish still made a point of picking her up at school. She was still excited to see him each day, and he knew well enough that nothing lasted forever and was determined to relish every last moment he was still the apple of her eye.

She hurled her backpack into the backseat while her other arm yanked open the front door and somehow she managed to lean across the car and kiss her Dad on the cheek while pulling the door closed behind her. Then her nose wrinkled. "You need a shower, Dad!"

"I know," he apologized. "Next stop."

"That girl in the paper yesterday was murdered," she said abruptly. After all the actions she accomplished in the last heartbeat, it was taking forever for her to do her seatbelt up. He motioned impatiently until she clicked the buckle.

"Yes, she was. It was very sad," said Cavendish, putting the car into drive and waiting for the cars ahead to move along.

"I can't believe she was with all those old men. So gross. If I ever did that I would do it with no one older than a senior."

Cavendish eyes almost popped in their sockets. Aloud he said: "You ever do what she did, and I will ground you forever and thrash you every other day and twice on Sundays."

She laughed. She was just trying to get his goat, and when she laughed her "gotcha" laugh her mother's voice echoed in its music.

"Are you trying to find out who killed her?"

Cavendish didn't want to answer. His work was seedy at the best of times and he didn't like Sophie knowing much about it. Seediness she could discover when she outgrew her Disney tween stars. He didn't like lying to her either, so the alternative was brushing over it towards other topics.

"The police are investigating. But her Mother works for a man who asked me to look into it," he said at last.

"Is he paying you in rum?" she grinned. She knew her Daddy's tastes.

Truthfully, Cavendish didn't know if he was getting paid or not. He and Lance had never discussed terms – but he was getting paid by Buxton to dig up dirt on Peter Pennington, so at least there was positive cash flow from somewhere.

Working their way out of town seemed to take forever, as it always did. Sophie poked and prodded with questions about the case. Cavendish gave short answers, staying clear of details.

"No, but he might give me some with dinner," he looked at her apologetically. "I need to go over there after I drop you off at the house." They drove in silence for a while.

"Her sister is in my class," said Sophie abruptly.

Cavendish could feel her eyes on him. She had been saving that comment. "But she wasn't there today." She paused, pretending to let her mind wander as she blithely took in the surrounding scenery while they worked their way up into the hills. It could only last so long. Cavendish was impressed how long she contained herself before the question burst out of her chest like a belch.

"Who do you think did it?"

Cavendish laughed at his daughter. She was oblivious to the tragedy and the life lost; she was just agog at the thought of her Dad capturing the bad guy. "I don't know."

"Have you interviewed all the suspects yet?"

"No. I think I've met them all, but I haven't spoken to all of them since the murder happened. And I don't know the sequence of events at the crime scene."

"Then what have you been doing all day?" she demanded impatiently.

"Sophie, I'm not a policeman anymore. I am not allowed to run around investigating a murder. All I can do is talk to the people involved and see what they have to say and see if that points me anywhere."

Sophie grudgingly accepted this explanation for his laggardly performance. She looked past him and down at the receding bay, then back at him. "So why are you investigating? If you're not supposed to?"

There was a question he didn't know how to answer. Didn't know if he knew the answer. He brought her here to have a safe, stable life. Had turned his back on being a cop – not so much from the danger because CID was hardly high-risk duty, not like Elizabeth's undercover work – but because the hours were terrible. He wanted to be there for his daughter and chasing villains was a time absorbing occupation. Look at tonight. Half an hour with his daughter while he drove her home and then out until lord knew when.

"I met the victim," he explained. "You read about her in the paper, I know, and she probably sounds very strange."

"She sounds like a ho," Sophie opined bluntly,

217

repeating her judgment from the previous morning. Cavendish suppressed a smile.

"Perhaps she was. But she was also bright, troubled, foolish and misguided." And not the first person he'd seen die before their time, everything they were destined to be and do erased while their lives were still in the rough draft phase. "And the owner of the home where she died – Mr. Lance, he asked if I could look into it, too."

"And you like his rum!"

"Yes, I do like his rum," admitted Cavendish, turning onto the patch of gravel in front of the gates. It was more like a layby on the road than a driveway. He walked around the car and she waited for him to pull the gate open on its squeaky wheels. From this vantage point, you only saw the top floor of the house.

They went inside and she set herself down at the kitchen table, unloading her books. Cavendish kissed his mother-in-law on the cheek and explained that he was going to miss dinner. She looked at him with a frown. "You getting yourself mixed up in this business with the dead girl?"

Cavendish found himself looking down at his feet, a grown man shamed in the face of Sophie's stern grandmother. He shuffled his feet like an errant kid, trying to think of a way to explain.

Sophie answered for him. "Yes, Grandma, he is." Her tone was both matter of fact and protective. She hopped up and kissed her Dad on the cheek. "You need to shower, and then you need to go."

He looked down into her eyes, and there was no sarcasm or anger that her Dad was bailing on her. Just love and pride, and Cavendish found his own heart filling with shame and pride of his own, followed by the danger of embarrassing emotion. He gave her a peck on the forehead and dashed downstairs to his room and a shower.

Letting the hot spray cleanse away the dirt and sweat of the day's exertions, Cavendish retraced those events of the evening at Lance's that he had witnessed himself. He knew

Pennington and Buxton might have a reason to kill each other, but to kill Amber? Amber got around. Could she have been with Pennington? He seemed like the sort that would fool around on his wife given the chance. Did Pennington think Buxton knew, and Amber somehow got caught in the crossfire?

Or Martine could have caught her husband with Amber and blown a fuse. Maybe she even summoned the dark forces of the beyond to choke the life out of her.

Deirdre Lance. Violently jealous of the girl and even imagining Amber could be Marvin's illegitimate heir. How jealous? Was the jealousy unfounded? Lance did take a lot of interest in the welfare of Amber and Mia. Did he care for other staff members so attentively?

If Ross Buchanan hadn't been jailed, he would have been an easy pick for a suspect, but there was also his wife. She hadn't been banging room service waiters all night. Could she have decided to revenge herself on Amber? Finding her wouldn't have been hard – the newspaper published Amber's connection to the Marvin Lance estate. It hadn't published her picture, so she would have needed someone to point her out, though. Then he gave himself a mental slap. Some helpful samaritan had slipped a picture of Amber inside Lorna's morning paper.

Megan Shepard? He seemed to know the least about her, and what issues she might have with the other members of the production team, or if she had any issues with Amber. She seemed a less likely suspect because she was keen to make money from Amber's story – although that could be a bluff, or if she had a motive to kill Amber she could probably do so and still make her movie.

≈

Showered and dressed in fresh tan linen slacks and a royal blue sport shirt, Cavendish turned into the Lance estate just as the sun was getting low enough in the sky to drape a veil of orange light across the sea and landscape.

Despite the news coverage the scandalous femme fatale Amber Geranabby had garnered, Cavendish was surprised by the small media circus camped directly outside the Lance gates. There were four television vans – and St. Lazarus only had a single television station. The isle's notoriety must be spreading. Would the governor welcome the publicity or hate the reason for it? Either way, Cavendish imagined the pressure being put on Chief Constable Boxer to resolve the case promptly must be intense.

There was a police constable standing outside the gates, just loitering quietly, and keeping an eye on the TV crews. Doubtless he was also charged with recording comings and goings. Standing inside the gates were three private security guards.

As Cavendish nosed his car through the gate he was stopped twice. Once by the copper, who insisted upon seeing his driver's license and making notes on a clipboard. Next a security guard stepped forward. Clearly Marvin Lance had been true to his word about making his property more secure. After comparing the license to his clipboard, the security guard returned the identification and waved Cavendish through. He was on the list.

The production crew for Martine's show had not returned and the lawns bordering the gravel drive up to the main house were empty. Cavendish glanced towards Pamela Geranabby's cottage and wondered how she was bearing up. First the revelations about her daughter's work habits, then losing her daughter. Then the nosy spotlights that would be shone on her family because of her daughter's choices, and the manner of her passing. It could be crushing.

There were no police vehicles inside the yard. A small force like the St. Lazarus PD did not have the resources to leave sentries all over the place. The man at the gate – and maybe there would be a man on the crime scene. Or at least the part where the body was found. Had they confirmed if Amber had been killed at the pool or merely dumped there? His money remained on the latter.

He didn't have to ring the doorbell – the door swung inwards just as he reached the top of the three steps to the porch.

It was the same lady who had greeted him when he was summoned in the aftermath of the newspaper article about Amber. She seemed no less dubious about him today.

"I am invited," he realized he sounded like he was defending his presence of being there, self-conscious that he was one of the players prolonging the cruel drama. "For dinner."

She opened the door a little wider for him. "This way." She led him down the hallway to the drawing room. She blocked his path while she leaned into the room and announced skeptically: "Mr. Lance, this gentleman says he is invited."

"Which gentleman Mary? I can't see him."

She moved aside to allow Cavendish forward. As he looked inside the drawing room, the doorway framed the scene inside like a tableau. Lance had a drink in his hand and stood almost in the center of the room. He looked tired and even from here Cavendish could see his eyes were bloodshot. Sitting in one of the chairs to Lance's right was Deirdre. She looked smug and a little angry – which Cavendish had determined was her natural countenance – the glass that dangled from her fingers was almost empty. Behind Lance, looking like they had not been participating in the broader conversation, Megan Shepard, Martine Letourneaux and Peter Pennington formed a closely-knit triumvirate. A cigarette smoldered between Megan's fingertips, and she looked mildly miffed that the conversation had been disrupted. Was Pennington angry or just irritated? Hard to gauge. In contrast, Martine gave a clearer impression, one of general sadness. Over Amber? How well did she know her? Amber had been nineteen and Martine had been off island for fifteen years. Pamela had moved away from that street before Amber was born, so it wasn't likely that Martine had ever met Amber. Or was he misreading Martine's sad countenance? Were there troubling events closer to home? Cavendish stepped into the room and found Hoyt Buxton was also present, but in a chair next to Deirdre's. He did not look like he had been engaged in any conversations the way the others did. He stood aloof, a tolerated outsider. Like the others, he had a drink. He looked like he needed it more though. He looked tired; his eyes weighed down by dark bags.

Cavendish said to the maid: "Thank you, Mary."

Mary grunted and walked away.

Lance welcomed him with a nervous handshake. "Mr. Cavendish, welcome."

"Archie. Please call me Archie, Mr. Lance."

Lance looked as if he hadn't slept in weeks. Whatever his feelings for Amber, innocent or not, he had woken up with a corpse in his pool. Whether she was alive or dead when she went into the water, it had happened right under his slumbering nose. Did he feel guilty he slept through it, was he afraid it made him look guilty? Was the fact of a murder on his property enough to wear him down? Or could he have put her there and was now haunted by guilt or fear of discovery?

"Archie just keeps turning up here," noted Deirdre with a sniff.

"I asked him to come," said Lance.

"I assumed you did," she drank from her glass in gulps, not sips.

"How is Pamela doing?" asked Cavendish.

Megan and Pennington exchanged glances. "Who's Pamela?"

"Amber's mother," said Martine. Cavendish hoped he could talk to Martine about her knowledge of Pamela. How well had they known each other as children? Thinking again of the pictures on the website narrating Martine's life, Cavendish speculated that Lydia Montrose was the older woman, the mentor, in the picture, and the youngster with Martine might have been Pamela herself. What different trajectories their lives had taken from that shared beginning on the street where Tyree lived.

Deirdre downed her glass and went to the bar for a refill.

"I asked Mr. Cavendish to look into what happened to Amber," Lance explained. He seemed a smaller man than the one Cavendish had met just two days ago.

Deirdre poured equal measures of whiskey and soda

into her tumbler, clanking bottles against glass. She reached for the Lance rum and looked at Cavendish. "This is your preference, I think?"

Cavendish nodded. "With Coca-Cola, please. Mr. Lance, I am happy to talk to you and your guests, but the police are better equipped to investigate. They have the resources – and the authority."

"While it's true the police here are not the typical corrupt island cops of a lot of tropic ports, they are under enormous pressure to wrap this matter up. Media have been coming in from off island since the newspaper article about Amber's … activities. The governor froze all her assets before she died, and now that she is dead it just enflamed the story more. I don't doubt their resources or their integrity. But I doubt they will be given the room to investigate properly."

"I thought all publicity was good publicity?"

"The governor seems to disagree. He is not happy about the image of St. Lazarus as some modern-day Sodom and Gomorrah where wives have to worry about their husbands being lured onto the rocks by a siren."

"It might not be a complicated case for them to wrap up, Mr. Lance. For all we know, they already have a bead on a prime suspect," Cavendish accepted the drink Deirdre had poured him. She had poured his portions as generously as her own. She clinked her glass against his, pursing her lips in the kind of flirty expression angry wives use to provoke their husbands. Lance noticed.

Cavendish said: "I don't want to take your money under false pretenses."

"Your honesty is appreciated."

"So, what's the deal," interjected Pennington. "We all have to talk to Sherlock Holmes here? We all talked to the police already. Isn't it against the law for us to talk to you about an ongoing investigation?"

"No. It's not against the law for you to speak to me. I just can't compel you to do so like the police can."

Lance interjected with what turned into a little speech:

"But I hope you will speak with Mr. Cavendish. I know you have all had a long day, a long and stressful day – but I would like Mr. Cavendish to follow up on the efforts of the police. You only know of Mr. Cavendish as a private investigator, but he is a former Scotland Yard detective. He was a Detective-Inspector in the C.I.D," Eyebrows perked around the room. Except for Megan.

Megan's instincts smelled a story. He found the look she gave him a little unsettling. "A Scotland Yard detective working as a two-dollar gumshoe in a tropical backwater? How did that happen?"

"London is cold and rainy." He felt suddenly awkward and exposed. The curious eyes discomfited him, and he sipped his drink self-consciously. Like most people who ask questions professionally, he hated having the tables turned on him.

"Whatever he was," Pennington griped. "I don't see the point of him doing the job the cops are supposed to be doing. We already told the police everything. None of us saw who came in and killed that girl."

"Came in and killed her?" queried Cavendish.

"It must have been one of her johns coming for revenge," Pennington concluded decisively.

"Interesting theory. But the only john that was on the island (that we know of) with a motive was Ross Buchanan, and he was in jail."

"Did you read the paper? She did this to a hundred guys or more,"

"Yes. Who paid up then went home. As long as their secret was safe, why kill her?" Cavendish pondered.

"Fear of it coming out. Tired of being blackmailed," said Pennington. "They can't all have been suckers – some of them might have been biding their time, waiting for the chance to get rid of her."

"Amber never bled them for more than the initial payment. She wasn't stupid," said Cavendish. "She knew the risk of provoking a dangerous response."

"Just because she said she didn't, does that mean she

was telling the truth?" insisted Pennington. "And it doesn't mean all of her victims believed her. I wouldn't."

"And it doesn't mean that one of her victims wasn't afraid that she might not come back for more," added Megan helpfully. "You believe she was a girl of her word? Maybe so. But would her victims trust her not to come after them for more?"

"What if one of her victims was running for mayor or Congress or something?" added Deirdre. "They might send someone to clean up the skeletons. Or if her tastes get more expensive. Or when she gets a disease or gets old and skanky and they don't want her anymore, she might have changed her mind and gone back to earlier victims. Blackmailers always go back for more. Just watch the movies." She downed her drink and moved towards the bar.

"You all raise valid points, but it would be a bit of a co-incidence that they do it right now, the day after her story hits the newspapers. It doesn't seem likely that a victim could get here that quickly if her exposure made him fearful, and anyone already working on their revenge would be hitting the coincidence of the century to kill her the day after her well-guarded game was made public," rebutted Cavendish. But he didn't want to answer their questions, he wanted to see what he could pick up from them. "Did the police say anything about whether she was killed in the pool or put there after she died?"

Lance shook his head. "They didn't say anything. I saw bruising on her throat – but Chief Constable Boxer did not mention it or anything else about her to me when he questioned me."

Cavendish nodded, and the others indicated that they had similarly unenlightening experiences with the Chief Constable, at least as far as the state of Amber's corpse was concerned.

"I assume the police took your security camera recordings?"

Lance nodded. "But its DVR. My security man sent them a copy. I'm having my guy go over the footage to look for intruders. I can get you a copy."

"Thanks."

"But Mr. Cavendish doesn't think it was an intruder that killed poor demure, slutty little Amber," said Deirdre, swirling her drink dramatically. "He thinks it was one of us."

CHAPTER EIGHTEEN

"I think it's too early to make any assumptions, or disregard any possibilities," said Cavendish.

"Maybe my husband raped her and dumped her in the pool." Deirdre's voice was downright coquettish as she presented her hypothesis.

"Deirdre!"

"You were asleep in a chair right next to where her body was floating. Seems a bit incredible that you could sleep through a girl being murdered," observed Deirdre caustically.

"I'd drunk way too much. I was unconscious. God knows I regret it, but I didn't hear a thing!"

"If you could sleep through a murder, what else could you have slept through?" persisted Deirdre. She plucked at her lower lip pensively: "Although, to be fair, you never seem to notice me coming and going from our bed. No matter how long I'm away from it."

Cavendish saw the evening degenerating rapidly and wondered how many glasses Deirdre had consumed before he'd arrived. Or maybe her anger at Lance simply ran that deep. Lance was looking sheepish and wary. It made Cavendish reconsider some of Deirdre's allegations concerning her husband's relationship with Pamela.

He looked at Pennington and Megan, both feisty and bristling at the idea of him nosing around. Unlike Buxton and Martine who were quiet and withdrawn. Cavendish thought about his encounter with Martine – was it only last night? – As he was leaving the property.

"How long until dinner?" he wondered aloud.

Lance glanced at his watch. "Another fifteen minutes or so. I told chef 6:30."

"Martine, could I speak with you privately for a few minutes?"

She gave him an acquiescent look, but Pennington stepped in front of her. "She doesn't have to speak with you."

"It's all right, Peter. I don't mind speaking with him."

"He has no authority – "

"But he has very sharp insight. And he cares about the truth," she replied. Cavendish bit back the temptation to ask if the spirits were unveiling these character traits to her, but he didn't want to burn through the good will she was showing him.

"You can use the study," Lance volunteered.

≈

Cavendish decided not to sit behind Lance's vast and intricately carved desk. He did not want a barrier between himself and Martine that would invent some form of artificial authority. She had made the overture and he wanted to build on that. There were two chairs on the visiting side of the desk. He took one and motioned an invitation for Martine to take the other.

"You went to check on Amber and Pamela after the argument with Deirdre last night," he began. "I was a little surprised you would take such an interest in Mr. Lance's servants."

"It's not because of that," explained Martine in a soft voice, almost a whisper. She seemed smaller. "It's not really a secret, either. I grew up here, you know that. You may not know that I grew up three houses away from Pamela."

Cavendish felt like Martine was zooming in on him with her eyes as he reached into his pocket for his small notebook and pen that he'd filched from the Conch Shack. She smiled.

"But you knew about that, too."

He tried not to reveal an answer through his eyes, he didn't want to shift control of the interview to Martine.

"I understand you knew Pamela since you were both little girls?" he based this guess on the photograph on her website, and his belief that it captured Martine and Pamela together with Lydia Montrose.

"Yes. We're actually the same age. We worked together as maids at a hotel, even after she moved away. Maybe you know about her stepfather?" Cavendish nodded. "I don't know why she didn't want to keep moving forward. She stayed as a maid, at the hotel. I wanted a different life – and I had my gift. I left the island and we lost touch with each other. I had no idea what happened to her until I came back – not even for a few days after arriving because I didn't see her around the house. I was really excited to see her when I did. Pamela, not so much.

"I think maybe she felt awkward or embarrassed – she's here as a maid and I am on TV and everything or," she hesitated before divulging the 'or,' like it discomfited her. "Or she might not have wanted to see me because she doesn't approve of me."

"What would she need to approve of?"

"She believes in my gift. She doesn't believe its right to get rich off it. Madam Lydia lived in a shack all her life."

Madam Lydia just needed a better agent, Cavendish was sure. "And are you very rich?"

"No. for all the TV and public appearances and private readings – no, surprisingly I am not very rich. Very comfortable, to be sure, but not rich. My husband thinks it's Hoyt's fault. That he doesn't fight to get me the best deals."

"What do you think?"

Martine's serene face cracked with a melancholy smile. "I think Megan is right. Not so long ago, being a psychic medium and helping people connect with the other side – that was enough. Lisa Williams, John Edward – we were all the rage. Everybody wanted to speak with a medium or see them. But now it's not enough to have the gift, you have to have a gimmick. Teaching psychic kids or solving crimes with your powers. Even that might soon lose its luster.

"That's why Megan brought us here. A gimmick to try and boost the ratings. A mix of my readings and sessions with exploring my home and investigating haunted places."

"It doesn't sound like you like that so much."

"I don't like doing gimmicks."

Cavendish sensed she was wrestling with the compromises she was making to sustain her celebrity. "I see. And how do you feel about being back here on St. Lazarus?"

She thought about this, turning over different emotions, considering them individually before settling on an answer. "Indifferent. I don't know what I expected. I thought I would feel glad to be home, but it's changed so much that there's no feeling of homecoming. It's almost like visiting a new place. It's just a warm and pretty island. But I don't feel like I've come home."

"Is this the first time you've been back since you left?"

"Yes," said Martine.

"You didn't come back for Lydia Montrose's funeral?"

Martine shook her head. "And she was very upset about that."

Cavendish wondered if she meant the deceased was upset. He decided to bring the conversation on point. "So last night, you went to check on Amber and Pamela because of your friendship for Pamela?"

"Yes. We had tea. We talked. Not much - you passed me when I was on my way back to the house, so you know how long we talked for. She wasn't really interested in renewing our friendship. I think she was pre-occupied about Amber's situation – although she didn't speak to me about Amber at all."

"Do you remember what time it was that you came back to the house? I know you passed me, but I want to get your recollections from your own perspective."

"I think it was about nine o'clock."

"And what did you do next?"

"I headed for my room, but I ran into Megan in the hallway. She asked after Amber. Did you know she is going to produce a movie of the week for her? And she was talking about a book deal." Martine stopped short. Maybe she realized she was describing Amber in the present tense. Maybe she was realizing that it looked like Megan Shepard was getting ready to move on unless she gave in to the producer's demands to add gimmicks to her performance.

"Do you know many television producers Mr. Cavendish?"

"You have me calling you by your first name – you can call me Archie. And no, I don't."

"I suppose it takes a certain kind of person to be one and to be good at it. But Megan is a mercenary creature. She will throw Amber in the spotlight for as long as she can be a money maker, then she'll move on. I think Amber thought she was going to get rich. I'm sure she would have made some money. But rich? I doubt it. And I felt like Megan's interest in Amber had nothing to do with her as a little girl, and even if Pamela doesn't want to be my friend anymore," she sounded genuinely troubled by that, "I feel that I'm her friend and I feel a little protective of Amber. I now have experience in this world that Amber does not, and I feared Megan would take advantage of the girl. I scolded Megan a little." Martine paused and her eyes drifted inward as she reached for a memory the way she might have listened for a voice from the other side.

"It made her angry. She talked harshly about my success, how fleeting it could be – listed the psychics that had gone off television. That if I wasn't willing to adapt to the future then she had to explore other options. She didn't yell but she was very mean and I didn't say very much. I'm not very good when someone is yelling at me – luckily Peter showed up and put her in her place."

Cavendish sensed that putting people in their places was a frequent indulgence for Peter Pennington. He thought about Pennington's attack on him over Hoyt Buxton, and Buxton's fear that Pennington wanted to squeeze him out.

"Your husband doesn't share her concerns about your career?"

"Concerns yes, but he disagrees about the solutions. He thinks Hoyt isn't aggressive enough as my manager."

"And Megan?"

"She thinks she should run some different kinds of shows. Or come up with new angles for me – I think Peter agrees we need to come up with new angles, but he doesn't think I need to become Martine Letourneaux: Psychic Investigator."

Martine's manner did not reflect a person worried about her career or disagreements about how it should move forward. As a psychic medium, maybe Martine had already heard from the spirits that everything would work out fine? Maybe it was just a sense of the lesser relevance of a career when measured against the murder of a young girl.

"You seem very casual about your career, about your future, just now."

Martine thought about it, as if analyzing her opinions on the subject for the first time. "Well, I grew up in a shanty with only one pair of shoes. I was only allowed to wear those shoes to school and to church. Now I have three houses – all paid for, wardrobes full of clothes. I travel all over the world and ride in nice cars when I get there. I am a guest in a house where I could have only aspired to be a maid when I was a child –" this thought seemed to trip her up for a moment, and her eyes retreated from the present. Comparing her fate to Pamela's? She dove back into the present, summing up: "Not bad for a girl from the island's dingiest shanty town. If it all stops today – I have more than most people ever hope for. Not bad for a little girl from St. Lazarus."

"So, it's enough? If it all stopped today, you would be fine with that?"

She rolled her head from side to side as if to say: *Well I wouldn't go that far.* Aloud she said: "I love my career. But everything has its time and if I wasn't all over television anymore, I think I would survive just fine. Still I think that Megan is counting me out too soon. Peter has some really good ideas about how to help me stay on top without compromising who I am."

"How about Hoyt? How would he fare if your career started to fizzle?"

"I guess he would get some other clients."

Cavendish wondered how Buxton would feel about that. By his own words, he wasn't much of a business manager. He might be more wary of his gravy train rolling into the boneyard than Martine realized if his anxiety about Pennington sidelining him was any indication. People measured success differently. What Martine counted as abundant bounty, Hoyt – or Pennington for that matter – might regard as just a stake at the table. It seemed apparent that Megan would be fine. She was already looking for other baskets to supplement her psychic income.

Cavendish was curious about Martine and Pamela. "And you didn't see Pamela until…"

"Last night, when I returned to the house and walked in on you all in the drawing room, I was shocked." So shocked that she had fainted.

"Was it a pleasant reunion?"

Martine nodded. "For me. When we were girls, we were best friends. But so much happened – I have a house in Bel Air and she's a maid. I feel – it's almost like survivors' guilt. I am the one who did so well. She could have done it too, I'm sure. She just didn't want to use her gift to make money. She thought it was dishonest - … that's not what she chose."

"But you left St. Lazarus." Cavendish imagined a different outcome if they had left together. "Did the two of you consider leaving together, even if she didn't want to be a professional psychic?"

"We talked about leaving together, but she just decided not to. For a lot of years, I thought she was the smart one. It wasn't until a few years ago that I really started to have a career."

"And last night, you went to check on Amber."

"She looked so much like her mother. When I first saw Amber, she and Pamela were arguing. It was like looking into the past – Amber looked so like Pamela at that age. They were arguing when I got to the cottage, too – I only ever saw them arguing with each other – poor Pamela. She was devastated by what Amber was doing, and the trouble she brought to Mr. Lance's house. So much anger and shame and embarrassment."

"Did you talk to Amber yourself?"

Martine shook her head. "She went into her room. Pamela made me some tea and we talked. About the old days, about the paths our lives had taken."

"Was Amber still there when you left the cottage?"

"She never came out of her room."

"And then you went back to the house, and you talked to Megan. And after Peter joined the conversation?"

"I was a little upset. He asked me if I wanted a drink – I said no, I was just going to get some air and then I would head up to bed. Then I said something bitchy to Megan – something along the lines of 'I may be fading in fashion, and maybe she can go make a billion more dollars, but *I* was her big break.'"

"I went outside, I walked by the pool. I saw Mr. Lance – he was sleeping on a lounge chair, and I started walking around the house. I was following the same path you took to your car; I think. As I came around the corner of the house I ran into Hoyt. He was nervous and fidgety, and he wanted to talk," she anticipated the next question and seemed to have no reservations about sharing. "It was all about his fear that I will let Peter fire him. How much he values me, the good times we've had, he supports my wishes to stay true to who I am in my career."

"Are you going to fire him?"

Martine sighed. "Peter thinks I should. And it seems like Hoyt doesn't know what to do. All he talked about was the past – not what he was going to do for the future." Something occurred to her. "We were standing by the corner of the house. And we heard someone coming up the path from the workers cottages. We both heard it. I didn't see who it was – but Hoyt thought he saw her."

"Her?"

"He thought he recognized Deirdre walking back to the house."

234

CHAPTER NINETEEN

When the conversation with Martine started to cross back over itself, Cavendish wrapped it up so that he could digest it and get on to interview the other people in the house. He wanted to continue mapping out the previous evening. Lance popped into the study as soon as Martine had stepped out. He looked edgier and more tired than he had twenty minutes earlier if that was possible.

"How did it go?"

"Mr. Lance, I don't think you should be expecting any grand revelations tonight. I barely started talking to people – and I don't have any of the information related to the victim's - to Amber's - body. No time of death, no physical examination – I don't think I will be able to get access to the post-mortem report."

Lance thought about this. "I might be able to help you there."

One of the wealthiest, if not the wealthiest, islander, Cavendish didn't doubt that Lance might have the connections through the governor to get that kind of access. It would be most helpful if he could and would prevent Cavendish from trying to put his friend Hardy Swain into a compromising position.

"That would be helpful," he conceded.

"Right. And who did you want to speak to next?"

Cavendish wasn't sure if Lance was casting himself as a secretary or a Mr. Watson to his Sherlock Holmes. Or just trying to stay close to the investigation. "I think Ms. Shepard."

"Right. I'll send her in. Would you like another drink? Dinner will be about another twenty minutes or so."

Cavendish demurred. He didn't think his cognitive processes would benefit from further lubrication. Lance withdrew and within a few moments Megan Shepard was stepping over the threshold. Of the party in the house, she was the one he felt he knew the least about. For the first time, he made a thorough appraisal of her.

Her hair was bobbed short and shaped such that her face was framed in three-sided square of dark hair. The straight cut of her bangs and cornered bobbed was reminiscent of a flapper, but on her it looked more severe than the carefree girls of that superficial age. Her skin was naturally fair, but she was red from Caribbean sunshine. Cavendish guessed she had burned early in her visit and the red was just now starting to soften.

Her movements were purposeful and graceless. She was more interested in what was on her mind than in the image she conveyed through her body, which was clad in loose fitting clothes. If her burn extended beyond her face and arms, the loose clothes might have been a necessity for comfort, and not a choice of style.

Megan carried a full martini glass in her hand that threatened to spill when she slumped into the same chair that Martine had gracefully insinuated herself into earlier. She looked at Cavendish inquisitively.

"Well, are you going to probe me for information?" If she was aiming to sound flirtatious, it fell flat. She couldn't hide the wheels grinding behind her eyes. Images of *Life Channel* movies and true crime dramas danced in her head, and if she was trying to mask them, she was failing miserably.

"The last time I saw you last night was right before Mr.

Lance and I stepped out onto the patio," he began. "What did you do after?"

"I had a drink with Hoyt in the drawing room."

"What did you talk about?"

"I told him he needed to help convince Martine to be open minded about some of my ideas if he wanted to get her career going. We talked – he's been trying to get her to see my way of thinking, but her husband disagrees," there was no reticence in her delivery. She seemed quite sanguine to share her movements, her conversations, her thoughts, and her deeds with Cavendish.

"Peter thinks she should stick with what she's doing?"

"Yes."

"How much interaction did you have with Amber before the newspaper story about her business activities was published?"

"I saw her. Coming and going. By the pool. Acting like the world owed her something. Took me a couple of days to realize she was a servant's daughter, the way she strutted around like a queen. I thought maybe Marvin was fucking her," she sipped her martini. "Then a couple of days later I read the newspaper and found out that everyone but Marvin was. Well, maybe he was, too. I guess the jury is still out on that one?"

"And your first impulse was to talk her into selling you her story when you read the newspaper story?"

"Damn straight. Poor island girl whoring herself out to build a better future for herself and her mom AND doing it like some avenging angel, blackmailing men that cheat on their wives. Movie of the week and a book, and maybe a speaking tour. It would have been a goldmine," gushed Megan with conviction.

"You talk like that ship has sailed?"

"She never signed anything. I am putting together something, but its public domain stuff now. Ripped from the headlines. Not her personal story. It won't have the edge of being her own story – anyone could do it, so I won't get top dollar. It's not 'in her own words!' anymore. And there might be copycats. Again, without that unique edge, her story loses value. But at least I should have the inside track since I have the good fortune to be here, right at the heart of the story."

"Lucky you."

Her eyes hardened. "A girl has to make a living. You're only as good as your last show."

"I'm surprised you didn't get her to sign something right away," said Cavendish.

"That was dear Hoyt's helpful input. He had a little chat with her, told her not to sign anything without letting an agent or someone who would have *her* interests at heart take a look at it. So helpful of him."

"He thought you would have made her sign something that was not to her advantage?"

"He's an idiot. If I screwed her out of a fair deal, word would get around. You don't always get ahead by tricking people into signing bad contracts. But he wanted to host an auction that could have squeezed me out completely."

"But wasn't his advice to her sound? Have an advocate for her interests?"

Megan snorted impatiently before grumbling: "If he wanted to negotiate with me to give her a good contract, I wouldn't have been irritated. What bugged me was that he wanted to shop her story around after implying to her that I would screw her over. My show is what got his client famous and bought him his Malibu house. He should have been a little gracious about landing Amber. We both could have benefited from her, instead, we're both assed out. You've met him. He's a sad sack. He fluked into this. Even if he doesn't think he owes me one, he could have been a little gracious."

"Why wouldn't he see it that way himself?"

Megan shrugged impatiently. "How the hell should I know?" Then she flashed a quick grin. "So, if Hoyt had been murdered instead of the girl, I would be your prime suspect?"

"Did you ask him why he was trying to undermine you last night?"

"What does this have to do with Amber's murder?"

Cavendish was surprised that Hoyt would have tried to negotiate around Megan. He seemed like a man who chose the path of least resistance. If he was afraid Pennington might steer Martine away from him, and he couldn't afford to lose her, it seemed like he would have been interested in any deal he could get. Why not bind himself in an alliance with Megan?

"How long did you speak with Hoyt?"

"I don't really remember – we going in circles. It was a while. Finally, he headed outside, I followed him and realized that I was trying to drag out a pointless conversation, so I turned back and came inside again. I went upstairs to my room."

"You didn't see Amber at all for the rest of the night?"

"No."

It was the first answer she'd given without looking him directly in the eye.

CHAPTER TWENTY

The cycle of interviews was interrupted by dinner, and Cavendish found himself in the bizarre situation of breaking bread between two of his potential suspects and across the table from several others. As a policeman, this would never have happened, such a breach of the rules of evidence and objectivity. As an investigator, he thought dinner might afford opportunities to learn more about his suspects. Who exchanged nervous looks? Who seemed a little too comfortable? What suspicions might his table mates be harboring and sheltering about one another? If the murderer was at this table and unless the murderer was a hardened serial killer, it was unlikely they would be cool enough to hide all their tells.

Deirdre and Marvin occupied opposite ends of the table, as before. Martine and Peter sat on one side of the table, facing Cavendish, Hoyt Buxton, and Megan. Cavendish was between these last two. Buxton was almost physically exuding heat and drops of sweat were beading on his forehead. His brow was so furrowed that the sweat was trapped along each ridge. If looking guilty was the leading indicator of who had committed murder, Cavendish would have slapped the cuffs on him there and then.

Megan seemed calm, but in her line of work, exuding

calm was probably a well learned skill. Deirdre looked sullen and irritable, imagining the shenanigans her husband may have gotten up to with the victim's mother. Martine Letourneaux spooned her conch chowder with a quiet serenity that kept her from the proceedings, but Cavendish was coming to see this serenity as artifice.

While everyone but Martine seemed to be in a state of anxiety or curiosity or simmering resentment, Peter Pennington was fomenting in a vat of hostility. He glared daggers first at Buxton and then at Cavendish. Defiance or challenge? Cavendish wondered if he knew Buxton had come to see him, had tried to put him on Pennington's tail. Cavendish was sure that Pennington would only need to squint at Buxton to gain a full confession of every sin Buxton had ever done or thought of doing. And why was Pennington glaring so fiercely at Cavendish? Was there something he thought Cavendish had already unearthed? And when he wasn't looking at Cavendish, he was aiming a lot of looks at Megan. Megan was pointedly *not* noticing his glances.

The soup came and went unaccompanied by any table conversation. Lance's guests were probably uncertain about the etiquette of eating with an investigator. They ate and ignored him or ate and glared at him. He noticed that Lance was also observing his guests thoroughly.

As the soup bowls were swapped out for salads, Cavendish tried to eye the two servants working the room. What was going on in their minds? They must have known Amber fairly well. Loved, liked, or hated her? How did they feel about their employer and guests sitting down to dinner tonight, the same day her waterlogged body was pulled from the pool, just as they had dined the previous evening? As if nothing had changed to mark her passing. Did they mourn her or think she had made her own fate? Perhaps one of them had even been a victim of the young blackmailer. Possibly even murdered her.

Cavendish decided to put the cat among the pigeons if he could. He had no official authority to hold over them or compel them to give honest statements. But he could shock, scare, and challenge them. See how they reacted to some bragging and boasting.

"Mr. Lance, you mentioned earlier that you might get me access to Amber's postmortem report."

Lance replied without hesitation. "Of course, I'll make the call after dinner."

Pennington glanced between Lance and Cavendish skeptically. "The police will really show some private detective all the evidence they have on a murder case?"

It was the first time Cavendish had seen Lance actively wield and display his power. His eyes were as cold as a snake's as he told Pennington: "If I ask them to. Yes. They will show a private detective whatever he wants to see. If I ask them to."

Pennington tried to play it off, grinding his knife against his plate unnecessarily as he sheared off an oversized bite of steak. "If I was your governor, I would resent having a rich guy putting more faith in a divorce detective than the police." He eyed Cavendish menacingly. "Yeah, I looked you up." Meaning: Pennington had spent thirty seconds scanning Archie's website and drawing conclusions.

"Darling, Mr. Cavendish is more than qualified to solve this crime," said Pennington's wife. She regarded Cavendish with something bordering fondness. "And I truly hope you do. Whoever ended the life of that poor girl is a monster."

"The spirit world hasn't given you any hints about who killed her?" He knew he was unkind to speak to her this way when she herself had spoken kindly. But Martine had done as much co-operatively as he could expect, so he could afford to rattle her cage and try to shake out anything she was holding back. He was being rude, but he didn't care if she was his friend or his ally. The only person he cared about was the one laying alone in a refrigerated drawer in the morgue who was depending upon him to find justice for her.

Martine dropped her eyes, the jibe not bouncing off her as easily this time. "It doesn't work that way. The spirits only bring forth what they feel they must –" Then her spark returned. She raised her eyes and leveled them at him mischievously.

"Perhaps they share my confidence in you, and don't believe you need any help."

Cavendish smiled at her smoothness, and Deirdre looked at him with a glimmer of newfound respect after her endorsement. But he had forgotten Deirdre, for all her sullen streetwise attitude, really believed the guff that Martine Letourneaux shoveled at the masses. If Martine told Deirdre the spirit world trusted Cavendish, she would believe it. He filed that away, wondering if it could be useful later.

"If the spirits could have less faith in me, it might be more helpful," he said ruefully. "Mrs. Lance, have you asked the spirits to answer the questions that plague you? The questions about Amber?"

"Are you trying to be delicate, Archie?" Her hair was breaking free from her do and she was looking a little disheveled. "The spirits won't tell me if my husband ever fucked the little whore's mother. And neither will my husband."

"Deirdre!" barked Lance. "I have told you a hundred times I was never, ever with Amber's mother. I am not her father."

"But you sure did fawn over her a lot," observed Deirdre, using an archly conversational tone. "If you are her daddy you should have taught her not to be such an evil slut – AAGH!"

Deirdre yelped and jumped from her chair, a glass of iced water had just landed in her lap and Mary, the girl serving the table, was already saying "oops!" and apologizing to her for the mishap. Cavendish sensed it wasn't a mishap – Mary clearly liked Amber. At least one member of the staff seemed to care for her, despite her shortcomings.

Now standing, Deirdre pulled her arm back and slapped the maid a stunning blow across her cheek that made the woman stumble to hold her balance. At the same instant Lance was also on his feet and yelling at his wife, while Deirdre screamed in her turn at the maid. She turned her glare on her husband when she realized he was chastising her, not the maid. Mary clutched at her cheek. It wasn't that she was too shocked to respond, her face glowed with rage that she was keeping in check. She was doubtless weighing the importance of her steady paycheck against the pleasure she would derive from striking back at Deirdre, and probably knocking the spoilt trophy wife on her ass.

"Fine!" Deirdre grabbed her salad plate and hurled it like a Frisbee at her husband, he deflected it with his arm and it spiraled against the wall, shedding lettuce leaves and cucumbers like shrapnel before exploding into ceramic shards on impact.

Everyone sat in stunned silence – including Cavendish. This was not a direction he had imagined the evening would take.

Deirdre and Marvin stared at each other with eyes it was hard to imagine ever sharing love for one another. They looked like two cobras ready to strike. Deirdre broke the eye lock first and looked at Cavendish.

"Mr. Cavendish, at some point, you are going to ask me where I was last night during the hours in question or something equally melodramatic. I was screwing Henry the security guard in his booth," she looked again at her husband. "His endowments may not be of monetary value, but they are eminently satisfying!"

She shoved her way past the maid and stormed out of the room, giving her husband the finger as she passed.

Lance remained on his feet but looked suddenly deflated - trapped somewhere between the states of rage and being gutted. He didn't say anything for what seemed like a long time but was probably just a few seconds after the sudden period of high drama. No one at the table moved to break the silence. Finally, gathering himself together, he looked at the maid who stood frozen in place where Deirdre had struck her.

"Are you okay, Mary?"

The woman nodded.

"Carry on with your duties, please, but we'll talk tomorrow. I apologize for my wife and we'll discuss how I can make it up to you," he lowered himself into his chair slowly. Everyone was waiting for him to react to what his wife had said.

He looked like he could hardly breathe. He sat very, very still. Cavendish was watching him but heard Martine whisper to her husband that they should go. No one was eating any longer, and the second maid was hovering nervously, wondering if this meant she should start taking plates away.

Lance looked at her. "Please send for Henry. And make sure he doesn't know about what my wife just said if you value your job. Bring him to my study."

Cavendish could feel the evening deteriorating rapidly. "Mr. Lance -"

"You can do what you want, Mr. Cavendish," Lance pushed back from the table again, stood up and left the room. "I need to attend to Henry's termination."

There was a pregnant pause while everyone sat numbly wondering what to do next. Megan was the first one to find her tongue.

"I think he's going to kill Henry."

It sounded like she wished she had a camera to capture the moment, not like she felt bad for Henry as she matter-of-factly predicted his death.

It seemed ludicrous that a businessman like Lance would act so rashly, but Cavendish thought she might just be right. There was something unsettling about the choice of word and how he had said it. Termination. He left the room and quick stepped it to the study.

≈

Lance was pacing like a caged animal behind his desk, fists clenched tightly, face grim and thin lipped.

"Mr. Lance, you don't want to do something you'll regret," said Cavendish, rounding the desk to stand next to him.

"What? Kill the bastard that was with my wife?"

"You don't want to kill anybody... or assault them. Besides, your wife is jealous of your fondness for Amber; she might have made the whole thing up to provoke you. If you do something foolish you will make yourself a target – Henry would be able to sue you," Cavendish was thinking Lance was violently angry, but there was still a gap between violence and murder.

What Lance said next made Cavendish re-consider just how angry Lance really was.

Lance rounded on him, and Cavendish saw menace in the man's eye for the first time. He spoke melodramatically but the emotions underscoring them were pure in the perfection of his anger. "You know what happens when you provoke a rattlesnake? You get bitten. You can make a citizen's arrest when I'm done."

There was a knock at the door. It must have been Henry – a tall, relatively fit looking black man wearing black slacks and white polo shirt. "You sent for me, sir?" He looked positively hapless as Cavendish turned to appraise him.

The next moments passed in a flash. Cavendish's attention had been on the man framed in the doorway, so he heard rather than saw the desk drawer open. What signaled the warning to him was the sudden look of alarm on Henry's face. He spun his attention back to Lance and saw the pistol coming out of the desk and leveling up towards Henry's chest. He threw his arm out and up, deflecting Lance's own arm towards the ceiling. Lance squeezed the trigger, but it was an instant too late, Cavendish had succeeded in redirecting the gun upwards. The bullet tore into the ceiling and Lance and Cavendish were both showered in a small snowfall of sprinkling white plaster.

Lance was trying to lower the pistol to line up a second shot. Henry seemed frozen in place – Cavendish had a hand on Lance's gun arm, resisting the downward pressure and keeping it aimed high. He stepped closer and with his opposite leg he kicked at Lance's knee. Lance yelped with pain and crumpled as Cavendish's foot hooked behind the back of his leg and pulled it out from under him. Cavendish was able to snare the pistol from his hand as Lance fell and neatly deposited him into his chair. Cavendish promptly flicked the release catch to drop the magazine and pumped the gun – it was a Smith and Wesson semi-automatic, 38 caliber – to make sure there wasn't another round in the chamber. He dropped the emptied pistol on the desk.

Cavendish grabbed at his ear because it was ringing

painfully from the proximity of the gunshot and he cussed under his breath as he collected his thoughts.

He looked at Henry. The ringing in his ears made him shout.

"Henry, what time were you with Mr. Lance's wife last night? And don't lie or I will reload the pistol and give it back to him."

"Um - she got to my booth about nine o'clock and stayed until after midnight. She left before my shift ended at one," he was too stunned to think about the option of lying.

"I think it's safe to say you are fired. I would get off the property and arrange to have someone send you your things," said Cavendish.

Henry didn't need to be told twice. He spun on his heel and skedaddled, charging through a cluster of bodies that had gathered in the hall in response to the gunshot. Cavendish glimpsed the faces of Martine, Pennington, and Megan... He scolded Martine with a yell: "The spirits couldn't have given us a heads up about this?"

Megan interjected. "The spirits didn't need to. I told you... he had the same look as a writer I knew..."

Martine smiled sweetly. "Again, you seem to have it under control." She spoke gently and Cavendish squinted to read her lips.

"Huh?"

Lance was adjusting himself in the chair, struggling to regain his feet and Cavendish gripped his wrist tightly to restrain him. "You need to stay in that chair before you do something that costs you a lot more than you can afford to lose. Get a hold of yourself."

There was a new arrival. Deirdre hacked her way through the doorway full of people and stopped short as she tried to comprehend the scene. "Did I hear a gunshot?"

A Greek chorus of house guests and staff affirmed that she had and ran it down for her in overlapping verbal ejaculations. Cavendish heard the snippets: "Henry ran for the hills!", "He tried to kill Henry!"; "Archie stopped him!";

"Marvin pulled the gun and shot at him"; "If Mr. Cavendish hadn't interceded…"

Deirdre's attention quickly fell on her husband, sitting awkwardly in his chair as Cavendish held him in place by his wrist. Lance's face was a composition of rage and despair, each fighting for dominance. In a blur Deirdre was on her knees beside her husband, grabbing for both of his hands. Cavendish sensed Lance lose a little focus on his anger and relaxed his grip but watched closely to be sure he was really going to calm down.

"You crazy bastard, why are you shooting at people?" but for the first time since he'd met her, Cavendish heard love in her voice and as he watched her ministering her husband he saw adoration in her eyes. Lance had tried to kill the man that she had slept with, affirming his love for her. "You dumb ass, I'm not worth going to jail for!" She was kissing his eyelids and then she was breaking down, crying, kissing his face tenderly and apologizing and telling him she didn't blame him for hating her and begging him to forgive her in a breathless explosion of words…

Lance seemed a little bewildered by the whole turn of events and said nothing, just accepted the kisses, stopped trying to get up and put his hands on her arms as she kneeled in front of him. The anger had not ebbed from his eyes, he could still see the rage boiling right on the surface, but Cavendish suspected that eventually Deirdre would be forgiven, as she clearly had already forgiven her husband for his misdeeds, be they real or imagined. Apparently trying to kill a man in a jealous rage helped restore imperiled relationships. As the moment passed, Cavendish couldn't help grinning at the absurdity of it all.

Only Peter Pennington voiced the obvious: "Um – he just tried to kill a guy. Shouldn't somebody be calling the cops?"

CHAPTER TWENTY-ONE

Archie's ears were ringing from the gunshot going off so near his head. The noise was louder than a bomb explosion in such a confined space. He had the handgun away from Lance and unloaded, and he didn't care if the police were called or not, so he plonked himself in one of the guest chairs and waited for the next few minutes to play themselves out. He thought about Henry and wondered if he had even paused to pack. He would have to track him down to interview him about Amber later, and that would be a pain, especially if he had killed Amber at Deirdre's venomous behest. He had corroborated Deirdre's statement about her movements, and he was surely too shocked to do anything but sputter the truth in that moment where he confronted his mortality, and that was something.

The cluster of people gathered at the door pressed so closely to it that they started to pop into the study one by one, like soap bubbles squeezing through a crack. Martine first, looking non-plussed but concerned. She fluttered to Deirdre and Lance. Megan came next, leaving Pennington and Buxton to force their way through shoulder to shoulder, oblivious to each other until they were on the inside.

Megan seemed less concerned about what was happening in the here and now than the others. Probably weighing this as a potential television drama. She pointed at Cavendish: "you just saved Henry's life." It was a casting judgment, not an accolade.

"It was Mr. Lance's life I was thinking about," said Cavendish. "If he's going to kill the man, he needs to make sure he can't be connected to it."

Megan annoyed him, with her pigeonholing and story building. If it was pouring with rain and she told him so, he would find a way to argue it wasn't that damp at all. Which wasn't very professional. But he wasn't a cop anymore, and one of the small comforts was the freedom to color a little beyond the lines of professionalism when you felt like it. You could allow your emotions to seed your conversation, as long as you kept them out of your judgment.

Lance and Deirdre were on their feet.

"Mr. Lance, why do you keep a loaded gun in the desk?" asked Cavendish.

"Not by habit. But after that madman rampaged in here yesterday – and I wondered who else would come looking for Amber."

"And naturally, you put a loaded gun in your desk," Cavendish shook his head. He thought only Americans considered keeping a gun handy the solution to all their problems.

"If you'd killed Henry you could've gone to jail," Deirdre admonished him. "Don't ever do something stupid like that again."

Cavendish thought it indelicate to suggest that sleeping with other men might minimize the chance of her husband snapping into a jealous rage. His stomach growled. He wondered if they could return to their main courses now.

"Well, since everything seems resolved now, shall we go back to dinner?" he suggested.

"We should just go back and eat like nothing?" Pennington was incredulous.

Megan shrugged. "I'm still hungry."

Deirdre declined. "I couldn't..." she took her husband's hand. Lance looked at her searchingly while she said. "We have a lot to talk about."

Lance nodded, and without breaking his dark eyes from Deirdre's blue ones he promised Cavendish: "I'll make sure the police give you access to all you need tomorrow."

Deirdre and Lance made their goodbyes and went out the rear door of the study.

Pennington was almost dancing with rage. "That's it?"

"Peter," Martine asked gently. "Have you ever even noticed Henry before?"

"No. But we were all in the hallway behind him. That madman could have shot any one of us. If Archie hadn't stopped him, he could've pumped us all with lead."

"But he didn't," said Megan, shepherding him and Martine ahead of her. "Let's go eat."

Cavendish sensed an opening. This could be the only time when Peter Pennington would actually be receptive to a chat with Archie Cavendish. "Peter, I could really go for a drink. Join me?"

Peter broke ranks in a heartbeat. A drink, he thought, was just the ticket. The rest went back to the dining room, and Cavendish motioned for Pennington to follow him. They went through the rear door of the study and out to the poolside bar. The sky was pitch black and the stars difficult to see because of the lights around the pool.

Cavendish had watched Lance do enough pouring in the last few nights to know where everything was – Pennington opted for a Lance Rum and Coke so Cavendish filled two ample tumblers with a mix that was nearly half and half. He poured the rum first, added the ice and then topped up with the coke.

He offered one to Pennington and then gestured that

they should clink glasses. Peter seemed uncertain – perhaps the hostility he felt towards Cavendish was lurking in his thoughts – but they had been interacting sociably for several minutes now and it would be awkward to switch off instantly. Almost grudgingly, he said "cheers" and he clinked his glass obligingly.

Cavendish sipped; Pennington swigged.

"Just another day at the office for you?" wondered Pennington.

Cavendish shook his head. "Most of my work is divorce related. Taking pictures of cheating spouses."

"Seems like you're in the same game as Amber was."

"I don't blackmail people but, yeah, I make a living off taking pictures of people doing things they aren't supposed to." He looked at the pool where Amber's corpse had been bobbing just this morning. How had she gotten there? Was she murdered in the pool? Had she been dragged there? He looked up at the roofline slanting downwards from beneath the second story windows. She could even have been killed upstairs and tossed out the window. Her body would have rolled, and when it plunged off the edge its overhand was near enough the pool that she would have made it into the water.

Pennington took another swig. He tapped the glass with his fingers, the angry man who accosted Cavendish before displaced by a man still on edge, but less openly hostile. Buxton thought Pennington was up to no good. Pennington thought Buxton had hired him to dig up skeletons in his closet. Did his angry reaction mean that he did have skeletons, or was he just angry that Buxton was trying to discredit him to his wife? Had Amber stumbled upon those secrets? It seemed unlikely that she would have access to anything in Pennington's past. What about his present?

"The day we met you thought Hoyt Buxton had hired me," Cavendish reminded him, watching the glass empty, and getting ready to prepare another strong one. He wanted Pennington to talk, and he could certainly handle him if he became unruly. He nursed his own drink slowly and when the time came to make fresh ones, he poured the cola first to hide the disparity in rum portions between Peter's glass and his own.

"He doesn't like having me around because I know what a useless weasel he is. He takes ten percent of everything Martine makes and does nothing in return. He's on a free ride."

"And you were angry that he hired a detective because assuming I dug up something from your past it might make your wife look at you differently?"

"There is nothing in my past," glowered Pennington defiantly. But Cavendish was sitting so relaxed, perhaps that calmed him down because he next spoke more evenly: "I just hate that he is such a busybody and a snake and instead of working for a living and earning his money, he'd rather spend it trying to make me look bad."

"What work do you do for a living, Mr. Pennington?"

If he felt Cavendish's barb, he rolled on without revealing it. "There is no time for me to do anything outside of supporting Martine. She's too damn busy. I work supporting her and trying to advise her," thrusting his glass towards the house he indicated Buxton. "That's why the weasel wants me out of the picture."

"Is it true you met your wife at a book signing? You were a fan?"

"Why are we talking about me and Martine and Hoyt Butthead? What does this have to do with Amber?"

"We know she blackmailed people. What if she stumbled upon a secret and tried to blackmail one of the people in this house?"

"There's nothing she could blackmail me about."

"What if she could prove your wife was a fake?"

"You're just throwing mud around. My wife is the real deal."

"Of course she is. And Buxton. How have you tried to discredit him to your wife?"

"Her show is losing popularity — that's why we're on this gimmicky trip. It's not enough to be a psychic anymore. Its psychic ghost hunters, psychic cold case investigators solving murders... Martine needs to change, or she will be irrelevant.

She doesn't like that, but it's what she needs to do to sustain her career. Buxton acts like he doesn't see it. Just agrees with her on everything because he doesn't want her firing him."

"How do you change a psychic gift? If hers doesn't work in a particular way, how can she retool it?"

Pennington wasn't drunk enough not to notice Cavendish's sarcasm and the implicit but unspoken: "oh yes, because she's faking," tagged to the end of his sentence.

"I'm not going to try to explain a gift you don't understand or believe in."

"Still, it's quite a story, you two meeting at a book signing. How on earth could fireworks start from such a brief encounter?"

"We met at the book signing the first time. But we met again later. I went to one of her readings. You know how the spirits guide the mediums to talk to different people in the audience… they guided her to me…"

"You struck up a relationship from the audience?"

"There was a third time," harrumphed Pennington. "Martine went for a walk late at night, and by fluke I was walking around the same area. Some guy jumped her and tried to mug her. I fought him off. She was pretty shaken. I took her for coffee, and we talked, and we agreed it was weird to meet three times like that. Like the universe was telling us something. And we've been together ever since." Such a lucky happenstance made Cavendish think Pennington had a confederate stage the mugging and the rescue. Probably not a hunch he'd ever be able to prove.

"And last night. Last night what were your movements after dinner?"

Pennington laughed. It was a grudging sound. "It's a good thing Hoyt wasn't the one killed. Because I was talking to him immediately after dinner, and we had an argument."

"About what?"

"About him trying to ruin my marriage. About him trying to get rid of me – and he gave it back to me about me trying to run him off. I was kind of impressed. He's always been such a little weasel of a man, but he came at me guns blazing. First time I liked him a little bit. If only he brought that much anger to managing Martine's career." He paused to deliberate something, then added a query: "Have you talked to Hoyt yet?"

Cavendish shook his head. The pause lagged but Pennington ultimately decided to share more. "Hoyt will probably tell you himself. I got him by the shirt front and slammed him against a tree. I was mad. But you must be able to understand that – you can imagine what it's like when someone is trying to take away your life."

Cavendish could imagine, better than Pennington knew. He wondered whether Martine was Pennington's life, or the lifestyle her success was able to furnish him.

"What time was that?"

"Eight – or a little after. I went for a walk to think. I got back to the house – I don't know what time, but I was going through the downstairs hall and I heard Megan and Martine talking. They were arguing over Martine's career – but not like Hoyt and I were arguing. There was no grabbing and slamming into walls. Just two very passionate women standing by their views."

Cavendish wondered if Martine would appreciate her husband characterizing her producer as passionate. "Martine wants to stay true to herself, and Megan wants her to get gimmicky?"

"Yes. Megan wants her to change her format. Martine – it's not a format to her. It's her gift. Even though she's made a lot of money from her gift, she feels - she feels like how she is using her gift is pure. That if she starts doing one of those cheesy crime solver psychic shows, it will cheapen her. Like selling out."

"And your view?"

Pennington didn't need to think about it. "I think she should do the gimmicks. That's just how she earns the money – she still has complete freedom to help people however she wishes. In fact, she could use the gimmicks to maintain a high profile and then reach out to as many people as she wants to help. She should just do the show as a way of financing everything – but that's what I think, I could tell Martine was tired, so I joined the argument and backed her up to Megan. We went to bed after that."

"And you didn't see Amber at all that evening?"

"Nope. Not after her mother took her out of the house."

Cavendish had run out of questions. It was time to wrap up and excuse Pennington, but that plan was interrupted by Hoyt Buxton literally hurling himself onto the patio and jabbing at Pennington with a vengeful finger.

"HE killed that poor girl, Mr. Cavendish!"

CHAPTER TWENTY-TWO

Pennington looked dumbfounded. At being discovered? Called out? Falsely accused? Or simply mystified that Hoyt Buxton was literally in his face, spitting accusations at him. A far cry from the mousy man he normally was, Hoyt was clearly fortified by alcohol. It sweated out of him in rancid beads. He had been sweating drunk during the conch chowder and that was a good ninety minutes ago. Cavendish was reminded of a line from Sophie's favorite Disney film, *The Aristocats*. "He's not drunk, he's marinated!"

Pennington reacted first but did not bother rebutting the accusations. His face darkened and he glowered down at Buxton. "Get out of my face, weasel!"

"You killed her. I know you did. And I can prove it!"

Pennington seemed struck dumb, anger displaced the incredulity that was writ on his face in boldface letters and Cavendish guessed the wheels were turning in his brain and turning towards an act of extreme violence against Hoyt Buxton. First Lance tried to shoot the man who cuckolded him, now

Pennington plotting violence against Buxton. Cavendish didn't want the evening to degenerate any further into a series of violent confrontations. He pulled Hoyt away from Pennington by the shoulder.

"Mr. Buxton you can't just walk up to people and start hurling accusations."

"He's a liar and if he doesn't take that back I am going to break him in two!" Pennington's wheels had ground to their familiar and nearly inevitable conclusion. An act of violence.

"You won't be able to break me in two from jail, you, you …. Monster!" Buxton quivered with rage and Cavendish was forced to grip the little man by both shoulders to keep him from turning to confront Pennington again. He was slippery as a greased pig. Cavendish gave him a shake.

"Stop it!" he spoke over Buxton's shoulder to Pennington. "Maybe you'd better excuse us, Mr. Pennington."

"Don't believe him, he's a damn liar. I didn't hurt a hair on that kid's head, I swear it!"

"Don't listen to him, Cavendish. You work for me, remember?"

Cavendish groaned inwardly. This was a fact that he had kept off the table so far. It would taint any further effort to talk with Pennington, even if he could later convince Pennington it was a lie.

"You told me you weren't working for him?" Pennington started angrily.

"When you asked me, I wasn't."

"So, you *are* working for him? Or maybe I should be specific. Did he ask you to do something? Did he give you money and did you take it and tell him you would do what he asked to you?"

"I told him I would make some inquiries for him."

"About me?" Cavendish didn't have to answer. Pennington slammed his now empty glass down and stormed off, throwing a "Fuck you!" over his shoulder.

"Don't let him go, Mr. Cavendish. He's the murderer!" Buxton was still wriggling like a cat. Cavendish immobilized him with an arm-lock that kept his right arm twisted slightly behind his back. Enough to keep him restrained without hurting him – it had been a useful grip when he walked a beat and dealt with drunk and disorderly calls. He waited for Buxton to relax his resistance a little and then spoke quietly into his ear.

"And if he is the murderer, you stupid little man, and he thinks you can prove it, do you want to spend the night in this house with him? Wouldn't that make you the most likely next victim? And if you're wrong, won't making crazy and false accusations be just the thing he can use to convince his wife to fire you?" he pushed Buxton toward one of the patio chairs. Luckily, it was wide based and wicker so that Buxton's momentum didn't knock the chair over and leave him on his ass on the concrete. Buxton did wobble though and put his hands on the arms to steady himself, looking dumbly at Cavendish.

"But I'm sure he did it." Now he sounded like he might start crying at the indignity and unfairness of it all.

"There can be quite a journey between being sure of something and putting a man in jail," Cavendish admonished him.

"Maybe I shouldn't stay here tonight," Buxton quietly observed. Looking warily at the house and thinking about Pennington murdering him in his sleep.

"No, he might put a pillow over your head and smother you," Cavendish agreed. He was mistrustful of even interviewing Buxton in this setting now, lest Pennington decide to lurk in the vicinity and eavesdrop. And if, by chance, Buxton did know something and Pennington was the murderer, Cavendish had never encountered a murderer who wasn't willing to add a second victim to his list in the interest of getting away with the initial crime. The only upside from a police perspective was that the second crime was usually poorly planned and improvised out of necessity, which created much more likelihood of incriminating mistakes. Maybe he should get whatever he could out of Buxton now and confront Pennington with it immediately. Or, if it was credible – take it straight to Chief Constable Boxer.

He dragged a chair away from the table and pulled it close to Buxton, plopping himself into it so they were knee to knee. Cavendish felt like he could become intoxicated from the sweat being pumped out of Buxton's skin. He saw fear and shame in Buxton's eyes.

"What do you think you know?"

"He killed her. I know he killed her because it's my fault he killed her."

"Your fault?"

"You know the authorities froze her accounts. She can't – couldn't - get at her money."

Cavendish knew this, but Amber hadn't seemed to care because she was banking on her movie deal and she was enough of a fighter to assume that would give her the resources to hire a lawyer and regain access to the rest of her money. Assuming she needed it after the movie of the week, the book tour, and the lecture circuit warning other girls about the dangers of picking the wrong path. Or selling them on the benefits thereof.

"I knew she couldn't get her money, and I wanted to prove to Martine that her husband is no good."

Cavendish thought he saw the picture coalescing, but let Buxton continue.

"I told her I would give her money if she could have sex with Peter. I wanted pictures, or I wanted Martine to walk in on them. Then she would see what a scoundrel he is, and she would leave him, and I wouldn't have to worry about him getting rid of me!" His voice rose at the end and he stopped suddenly, looking around with instant fear that Pennington might be ready to silence him. "At first she said no. She was mean about it. She called me names."

Cavendish smiled at the thought. He had known Amber a brief time, but long enough to know something about her personal code. She was no prostitute renting herself out, she saw herself as a predator snaring the dark souls in a trap she lined with their own sin. The payment she extracted from them, the blackmail payoff, was retribution. She wasn't one to put herself under the thumb of another man as a hooker for hire, especially a man motivated by his own craven weaknesses.

"And she slapped me."

Cavendish suppressed a chuckle.

"But she changed her mind. She came to me later that night. And we spoke. And she told me she would do it, that she was going to go and do it. I asked her if I – I tried to plan. Should I get Martine to come at a certain time, should I bring the camera and take pictures or what? She told me if I wanted to get my jollies, we'd have to do that another time. She used that word. Jollies. I didn't know what she meant," it sounded as though he had learned subsequently.

Cavendish wanted to pin down the timeline. "You asked her initially and she refused. When was that?"

"Yesterday afternoon. She was by the pool, lounging. I'd heard her talking to someone on the phone. She was mad; she was talking about getting a lawyer… I waited until she was off the phone and then I went and asked her."

"Do you know who she was talking to on the phone?"

"I didn't hear her call them by name. And I wasn't really close – I just heard things when she raised her voice once or twice."

"Did it sound like a friend? She was talking about getting a lawyer, so you didn't think it was a lawyer?"

"I'm not sure if it was a friend. It wasn't that casual. She was angry on principal; it was more like she couldn't control her anger. Not like she was venting. Oh! She did tell them she would look forward to getting the e-mail."

Cavendish wondered if the police had taken her computer. If not, maybe she had an e-mail account with a web service provider, like Hotmail or Gmail. Maybe her sister would know the password. More things going on the mental list.

"Did you ask her straight out or did you dance around the houses?"

"I asked her straight… well, no. I guess I didn't. I was nervous. I could only even finish asking her because I was that desperate."

"What made you ask her a second time?"

"Oh, I didn't. She just found me and told me she would do it. Maybe she found out it was going to be harder to get her money back after all."

"When did she tell you she changed her mind exactly?"

"About ten – right before I took Martine for a walk. I was reading in the library, Amber storms in and tells me she'll do it. She looked mad. Really, really mad. I told her that was great, I thanked her – I asked her how we should do it, if I should get a camera – and she just spat instructions at me. Take Martine for a walk; keep her away from the room. She said she would get pictures. She said keep Martine out for fifteen minutes and after that it didn't matter when she came back. If she caught them in the act, great. If not, it didn't matter. She would make sure there were pictures. Then she was gone."

"Just like that?"

"Yes, just like that."

"How much did you offer to pay her?"

"That was the weirdest thing. We didn't talk price. Ever. I guess she just trusted me to be fair with her," suggested Buxton fecklessly. Yes, thought Cavendish caustically. Because that would just be so like her… She wasn't doing it for the money. She had an agenda. If this happened at ten o'clock, it was after Buchanan had been to the house, after the confrontation in the drawing room, and after she had gone with her mother back to the cottage. After all that, she had come back to the house. What made her rent herself to Buxton? Had her Mom laid into her angrily and sparked this defiant act?

"Did you see her after that?"

"No. I didn't know if I was supposed to look for her or not. I went for a walk with Martine. When I got back, I parted from Martine and said I was going to bed because I wanted her to go to her room. But she ran into Megan and I heard them talking- arguing, more like. Then Peter was there, and I was worried because I thought Amber hadn't gotten to him. I wasn't sure what to do. I went upstairs to my room."

"And what time did you head upstairs?"

"By this time, it was very late. About one o'clock. I

thought maybe she'd got pictures and would meet me – but when I got to the top of the stairs, I ran into her Mom instead," the memory unnerved him. "She gave me a look – I felt sure she knew what I'd asked her daughter to do and I felt so guilty and ashamed I said something asinine - I think I just said 'hello' and she told me I looked like I seen a ghost. I told her I had a lot on my mind. She told me I should focus on my work. That's what she did when she had a lot on her mind. And I have to say, she looked like a woman with a lot on her mind. I told her I was really sorry that she was having such a tough time because of her daughter and she said, 'thank you'. She was carrying a basket and said 'please excuse me, but this basket is getting heavy'"

"Basket?"

"Dirty laundry. And she looked at me. And her eyes got narrow like she knew… and I just ducked into my room."

"Did you see Amber again?"

Buxton shook his head.

"And that's why you think Pennington killed her? Because you pointed Amber towards him?"

Buxton nodded. "Who else? He has the temper and he would have the motive if he realized she was setting him up."

"You know who else has the right temperament for murder, Mr. Buxton? A man who would enlist a nineteen-year old girl to engage in a sexual romp with his rival for the purpose of blackmail. If you go that far for your self-interest, how much further would you go?"

"I didn't kill her," Buxton sounded more confused than upset by the allegation.

"But there's nothing in your theory to hang a hat on Peter Pennington. You expected her to be in the house, but you don't even know if she still was. She could have been in the cottage. She could have been asleep. She could have been off the property. And who knows if Pennington had the opportunity? He and Martine share a room. What if he was there and she could never intercept him? He might still have no idea that you were conspiring with Amber to make a honey trap for him. There are witnesses for a lot of his movements last night…"

"But it must have been him!"

"Maybe it was. But if it was him, you just made yourself a target. You gave him a warning to cover his tracks carefully, and if it wasn't him – well, we covered that ground already. But you have not told me one thing that I can take to the police and get him arrested for."

Buxton looked perplexed. Cavendish wondered if he had ever once watched a crime drama. Cavendish looked at his watch – it was getting late and he had met with all the guests. He would take a crack at the staff tomorrow. He looked back to Buxton who was shifting his weight from side to side, as if the swaying might pull forth a damning fact he could share. Cavendish gave him more than a moment. Buxton looked terrified now.

Cavendish sighed. He couldn't leave him like that. "But now you've told me everything you know, and you haven't offered any evidence, I can make sure Pennington knows that you talked to me. There won't be any point for him to kill you now."

Buxton gasped with relief. "You don't think he'll kill me now?"

"Well, if nothing else, there is no need for him to…"

Buxton reached forward and grabbed Cavendish's hand between two clammy palms. Seriously – how could he be sweating yet be cold and clammy on a balmy Caribbean night?

Cavendish slipped past him and didn't look back. He felt worried eyes following him and heard in a small voice: "If I lock my door, I should be fine…"

CHAPTER TWENTY-THREE

Despite his late night, Cavendish woke early the next morning. He wanted to get back up to the Lance house to interview the staff, and he wanted to call Lance and see if the promise to get him access to the police file on Amber's death had come to pass. He hoped that the truce between Mr. and Mrs. Lance had survived the night, and that she wasn't the killer because it would dampen their road to a better marriage significantly. He assumed that Buxton was still alive because he had fulfilled his promise to seek out Pennington and assure him that everything Buxton knew was now on the record with him. And this morning he wanted to drive Sophie to school.

Sophie and his Mother-in-law, Glenda, were in the kitchen. His father-in-law had left earlier to get his 1980s vintage boat, a fifty-four-foot Bertram, ready to haul tourists on deep sea fishing adventures. As he dolloped HP sauce into the nicely runny yellows of his eggs, Sophie peppered him with questions. She had fully digested the news about Amber's little pornographic blackmail ring as well as the limited news on the murder. She was sure a policeman had sold the story to the paper for a little extra money (Cavendish agreed her theory was sound) and that the wife of Ross Buchanan had killed Amber in a jealous rage. (A tempting theory, but Cavendish wasn't sure how

Lorna would have gotten to Lance's house and back.) Maybe the security cameras would catch somebody coming or going.

"Amber's sister is in my class," Sophie observed. "I hope nobody's mean to her because of her sister."

"I'm sure they will be. People like to blame people for things they can't control – like what their families get up to."

"Now there's a positive thought to put in your daughter's brain," scolded Glenda. "You just be nice to her yourself young lady, and don't be minding what others do."

"Yes, Gramma. Do you think you can crack the case, Dad?"

He shrugged. "I hope so. But if I don't the police will be all over it, so I'm sure one of us should crack it."

"You'll crack it first because you're from Scotland Yard and Bobbie Simkiss says Scotland Yard has the best detectives in the world."

This was the first Cavendish had ever heard of Bobby Simkiss and he wondered if he needed to worry about him. "Local coppers are often underrated. Borden Boxer is no slouch. And you know Hardy and Jenny – don't they seem pretty smart to you?"

She allowed that they did.

His mobile phone rang, and he stepped away from the table to answer it. It was Lance, sounding happy. Very happy! So, the restoration of his marital bliss must have endured through the morning. Good as his word, he had spoken with the governor who in turn had spoken to the home secretary – for a little island there seemed to be lots of government and bureaucracy. Of course, the home secretary was the governor's younger brother. St. Lazarus was not quite a banana republic, but it had not forsaken its heritage as a place where there was a closely knit network among the elite. The upshot was the Home Secretary had called Borden Boxer and the Chief Constable would give Cavendish his full and complete co-operation. Cavendish felt a little ashamed feeling smug about it. A few years ago, he would be – in fact, he had been – as dismissive of private gumshoes as Boxer had been. In Boxer's shoes, he would have been furious.

He keyed the "end call" button and summoned his daughter. "If you want a ride grab your bag. We'd better get on our bike."

"Coming, Detective-Inspector!" she downed her juice, grinned, and ran for her backpack. His mother-in-law watched her go fondly and he wondered why he felt uneasy. Glenda's eyes held him and when he met her gaze she seemed to read him and grow sadder in the same moment.

"She's reminding you of Elizabeth," she said simply, gathering the plates to clear the kitchen table. Cavendish nodded. She had so much of her mother in her, and it scared him deeply.

Sophie was all questions about the case on the drive into town. Cavendish answered some of the peripheral ones and didn't yet know the answers to the big ones, so he didn't need to dodge those. He could honestly express his ignorance. He wasn't worried about Sophie blabbing around at school, his reticence to divulge too much was more about preserving her innocence as long as he could. He knew the world would come at her with sucker punches soon enough – he wanted her to have a big cushion of innocent memories to seek shelter in when those times came, and when he wasn't there to make her some cookies (well, okay, to open the packet) and give her a hug.

Sophie's school was only a couple of blocks from the waterfront and the streets started backing up a good ten blocks away as shop workers, waiters, bartenders, and guides poured down the hillside into Port Rose to tend the day's tourists. The air was sticky and clingy despite the early hour, and the engine exhausts from the long line of cars tainted the tropical air. They joined a queue of cars passing the front gate and unloading pupils into the school. Cavendish watched a big black Lexus he had seen at the Lance property a few cars ahead and Mia Geranabby hop out of it. She struggled to get her oversized backpack out of the car and on her back. One of the teacher's working as a monitor helped her, and she lurched unsteadily towards the school building. Sophie had seen her too.

"There she is. Poor Mia. She's in my class," she looked at her father knowingly. "I will be extra nice to her today - I wonder why she even came to school?"

"Surprised to see her going to school the day after..." he didn't know how to characterize the death gracefully. His policeman's mind was about to say, "*the day after Amber went for a swim.*"

"The day after her big sister *didn't* go for a swim?" Sophie wondered with a cheeky grin that faded as she thought of what Mia must be going through. "She must feel awful. I can't believe her mother made her come to school."

"Some people feel strongly that the best thing to do is maintain the routine no matter what," Cavendish observed.

By now their car was lined up with the school's front path and Sophie gave her dad a kiss before hopping out and charging into the maelstrom of uniformed youth. Normally the main door of the school was her target, but today he could tell she was looking through the clusters of uniformed students for Mia Geranabby.

≈

He proceeded to his normal parking lot, walked to Starbucks and then to his office. One of his suspects was Lorna Buchanan. She had a corroborated sexual encounter with a member of the hotel staff, but that didn't account for her movements all night. She seemed an unlikely suspect because she needed a way to get to Amber. He had contacts at the car rental agencies, so he spoke to some and left messages for others to find out if either Ross or Lorna Buchanan had a rental car. Then he rang around the taxi companies. The island didn't yet have a Lyft or Uber presence. The contacts that were available immediately told him that the Buchanans didn't have a car. The taxi companies had several pickups at their hotel, but all the destinations were restaurants, bars, or clubs in Port Rose. There weren't any drops at or near Swallows Peak Drive.

This task complete, Cavendish walked to the police station. He introduced himself to the desk sergeant who waved him upstairs with little interest. The squad room was barren, but with a media grabbing murder case filling the news, that was to be expected. Everyone would be on the job. He spied Borden Boxer's gargantuan shadow in his corner office. Between Cavendish and the office there was just one uniformed man who was awkwardly typing an incident report two fingers at a time.

Boxer faced the squad room, so he saw Cavendish approach him, and tracked his approach with the withering glare of a helicopter searchlight. Since Cavendish was not of the private investigation school that thrilled in antagonizing the police, he responded to the glare with what he hoped was a charming, contrite, and ultimately disarming smile. In the closing feet of the trip to the office he added in a friendly little wave by way of greeting. He stopped in the doorway and said good morning, waiting for the invitation into the office that should be forthcoming. Boxer looked him up and down and grudgingly invited him to come the rest of the way into the office with a grunt and a shrug towards one of the guest chairs.

Boxer's desk was clean and clear. The only items were a solitary family photograph – children, wife, and grandchildren all in the same frame – no inefficiencies there – his computer, a marble pen set and a single manila folder. As usual, he wore his uniform. In the few times he'd seen him, Cavendish noticed the Chief Constable seldom dressed in plainclothes.

Boxer pushed the folder towards him with one of his massive paws. "This is for you to look at." Boxer's eyes dared him to look at it.

Cavendish crossed the threshold – it seemed that being told to look at the folder was as close to hospitality as he was going to get. Boxer didn't grumble about being forced to disclose the file, or about Marvin Lance pulling strings to get this civilian interloper access to it. Probably thought it would diminish him. He'd been told to share the folder, and he was doing it.

Cavendish scraped the guest chair back from the desk – self-conscious at the sound, and sat down, turning the file toward him. He flipped open the cover. Photographs were clipped to the left-hand side and notes and forms on the right.

He unclasped the photos and flipped through them. As he did so, he glanced up at Boxer to see if he was going to say anything. He thought of expressing gratitude, but he didn't think Boxer would want it. They sat in uncomfortable silence as he looked at the photos.

The first ones were of her body by the pool, where Lance had dragged it from the water. Her body laid on it's back wearing only underwear. There were close ups of the bruising on her neck. There were also pictures of her face – she had an almighty shiner on one of her eyes. A fight before being choked? Cavendish considered the bruising. It looked to him like manual strangulation – the bruising was consistent with hands wrapped around the girl's slender neck. A chain or rope would have left more of a straight line. The close ups did not show any marks or patterns like he would expect from a chain. Moreover, the bruising had a mottled effect, indicating inconsistent pressure at the different points of contact. He could almost imagine the thumbs pressed into her throat and the palm and fingers wrapped around the neck. One of the pictures was a close-up of her eyes, lids pried apart. The lifeless eyes were bloodshot where capillaries had exploded as the act caused a rapid increase in her blood pressure. What had the killer seen in her eyes? Fear? Anger? Defiance? Surprise? Cavendish remembered that look – the surprise in the eyes of a man who thought he was bluffing. That he wouldn't go through with it. Anger and defiance had given way to surprise and then fear when he realized he was actually dying. Had that been the phases Amber passed through before her body went limp at the killer's hands?

He laid the photos on the left side of the folder and turned to the forms. It was difficult to prove drowning as a cause of death, usually coroners eliminate every other possible cause of death and once that is done, settle on drowning when it is the only remaining option. A drowned body and a corpse thrown in the water will both have lungs full of water. The coroner seemed convinced she was strangled to death or near the point of death and her body put in the water. There was a chance she was alive when dumped and the water finished the job, but it was a slim chance. Cavendish considered it most likely the killer believed her to be dead when he put her in the pool, or when she fell into it, otherwise why not make sure?

He glanced over the top of the folder at Borden Boxer who sat watching him like a gigantic house cat. Cavendish tried not to shift self-consciously in his seat as he read through the coroner's comments on the same things he had observed in the photographs. He focused on being very still himself, ignoring the Chief Constable's discomfiting stare as best he could while digesting the information before him.

The coroner also noted mild bruises and bumps on the body. Due to the apparent lightness of the marks he did not think they were the result of being punched or pummeled, but more consistent with the body being dragged or moved. Shoved through a window and rolled down a pitched roof?

Again, Cavendish wondered where she was killed, and how far she was moved to the pool. It didn't, according to the coroner, look like she was dragged to the pool over ground. No abrasions or scrape marks consistent with being dragged. Cavendish kept thinking of the second-floor windows opening onto that pitched roof and felt like she was killed upstairs and then allowed to slide or roll down the roof and tumble into the pool. He continued reading. No sign of sexual assault, the coroner did not believe she had been in the water long enough to hide all evidence that would be left by such an attack. No bruising on her wrists – no sign of an extended struggle. Nothing under her fingernails. This didn't mean she hadn't fought, just that she didn't scratch at her assailant. Even a chlorinated pool wouldn't remove all the skin cells embedded under her nails. Nevertheless, it occurred to him that it would behoove more killers to dump their victims in chlorinated pools. It was good for removing some specific physical evidence.

He read on. Stomach contents and toxicology reports were still pending. He closed the folder and put it down on the desk. Boxer was still sitting there like a brooding mountain.

"Thank you for letting me see this," Cavendish thought that it was worth being gracious even if Boxer had no choice in the matter. The Chief Constable dropped one of his big paws on the folder and scooped it away from Cavendish. "How is your case developing?"

Boxer spoke without hostility in his tone. "I was told to show you this file. That's all we are going to talk about – unless I need to question you about anything."

Archie wanted to offer an olive branch. He had no interest in beating the police to a conclusion, no desire to steal their thunder. His only interest in the case was catching Amber's killer. He knew Boxer was getting ready to kick him out of his office, so he just leaned back in his own chair and said: "I spoke with several people in the Lance house last night."

Boxer nodded. "My officers told me you were there."

"I thought you might like to hear what I heard, just in case they told me something they neglected to say to you or your men," said Cavendish.

Boxer chewed this comment over at length before deciding to reject the olive branch. "I know you came from Scotland Yard and all that, Mr. Cavendish, but my island police force is competent and professional. We don't need an ex-CID man to show us the light."

"I didn't say you did. I'm just saying that maybe I'm privy to information you don't have. I could be totally wrong – but witnesses forget things when they give their statements or remember things when they revisit the same statement. Or they hold things back from the police that they let slip to someone who seems less official. If I thought you were anything less than competent, I wouldn't offer to share what I know because I'd be afraid of you cocking up the investigation. Honestly, I'm not trying to compete with your investigation. I am trying to supplement it. And please call me Archie."

"I have trouble trusting a man who is in CID at Scotland Yard one minute, and a private investigator working unfaithful spouse cases in a Caribbean island the next. Such a dramatic career change makes me suspicious."

Cavendish's olive branch wasn't going to extend to a full biography for Chief Constable Boxer's enjoyment. Besides,

Cavendish could see the glimmer of suspicion in Boxer's eye went beyond the sudden career change. He may have heard some of the stories. Instead Cavendish said: "One day over a drink at the Barefoot Buccaneer I will tell you my story, but it wasn't a snap decision and it didn't turn my brain or my observational skills to mush. It had to do with losing my wife and the life I needed for my daughter and the kind of father I wanted to be for her."

Boxer leaned back in his own chair. Cavendish felt that olive branches ought to be met with some modest measurement of appreciation, and he was growing impatient with Boxer, staring at him through a shroud of skepticism. Boxer offered an olive branch of his own. "I know about your wife. I suppose I can understand that might have prompted ... changes."

Cavendish moved back to the investigation into Amber's death. "I am just talking about reporting what I heard – that's the same as a witness giving a statement and you can take or leave the information I give you as you would any other witness."

"You're not a witness to the crime."

"But I am a witness to the interactions of your suspect pool. Before and after the crime."

"Who have you spoken to outside the people in the house?"

"What suspects are there aside from the people in the house? Ross Buchanan was locked up. That leaves his wife and Tyree Fick. His wife was busy having revenge sex with the room service staff at her hotel. I've made some inquiries and it doesn't look like she had a rental car or a taxi to take her anywhere near the Lance estate. As long as the men aren't married you can probably dredge witnesses – as for Tyree Fick, maybe he could have gotten in and out of the property unseen – maybe. I don't think he is a good fit for the homicide." He was a good fit for something else, but they would get to that in a moment.

"It could have been a hundred other angry men out for revenge – or their women," prompted Boxer.

"And if you can figure out who those men and their

wives are and check the comings and goings to the island you can include or exclude them from the suspect pool," agreed Cavendish. "But I don't think it's going to be one of her previous victims. How likely is it that they would kill her vengefully on exactly the same day that she is exposed? If they were here waiting to kill her, would they go through with it when she was caught up in all this publicity? How could they get to her on the Lance estate, and why? Why not go back where they themselves were picked up, or the apartment where she filmed them? I feel sure that it matters very much when and where she was killed." He pressed his palms to his eyes and rubbed them as he thought more about Fick.

"Fick has a pretty strong motive. Amber gave him zero access to the blackmail material, and he wasn't clever enough to make his own copies. When she got shut down, he was left out in the cold. A kid with nothing to lose and no prospects of his own, doesn't take him long to go shake down the meal ticket he thought he had – but I don't see him planning to kill her by manual strangulation," he jabbed the folder. "Although an altercation or argument could have escalated, I suppose…."

"If it was Fick, he made it into the Lance property without getting caught on camera," said Boxer, metamorphosing from a granite figure to a gentler one of basalt. Maybe he was disarmed by the casual shoptalk. Maybe he was curious to see if Cavendish really had something useful to contribute.

"He could have been there before," suggested Cavendish. "Know his way about." Except he was feckless and careless. Cavendish could see him losing his temper and killing Amber – he could not imagine him being stealthy enough to circumvent the gate and cameras. "No signs of sexual assault – no bruising or scratching in her nether parts, though any fluids would have been washed away…"

"Why would she be raped? She was giving it away."

"Not to everyone. Not to Fick, for one – which he hated. And maybe someone came back for more. But she wasn't naked. She was in her underwear. If you rape her and kill her, would you put her panties back on?"

"There have been serial killers that dress their victims afterward," said Boxer.

Cavendish shook his head. "Have you had any other murders like this here? Or you think this might be the serial killer's first?"

"God, I hope not," sighed Boxer. "But it doesn't look like that to me. I think whoever killed her found her in her underwear."

Cavendish didn't think Fick was the murderer. "Fick confuses me. On the one hand I think he had feelings for Amber – affection, infatuation, maybe love – but he also told me he encouraged her to go back to former victims and continue blackmailing them. She refused. She said it was smarter to let them go and he thought they should squeeze as much money from them as they could. He claims he was on a fixed salary and that he told her to go back to the original victims for more money to achieve her financial goals faster."

"He could have killed her to get the material to go back to those victims and get more money – money he could keep for himself," pondered Boxer.

"Except he claims that he didn't know where any of the blackmail material was. Amber kept that from him," said Cavendish.

Boxer volunteered police information for the first time. "He said the same to us. About his salary, about urging her to blackmail the original victims more, about her rejection of the idea and about not having access to the material."

"I think he gave the story to the newspaper," said Cavendish.

Boxer's eyes widened. "Why would he do that?"

"To stop Amber from sleeping with multiple partners. If I'm right about his feelings for her, that might have been eating him up. To force her hand and need him as more of a partner? Give her no choice but to revisit former victims because now every man stumbling drunkenly off a cruise ship will recognize her? Maybe because he felt like an emasculated man and wanted to take action. Maybe because he got money from the newspaper – but Lorna Buchanan received a copy of the newspaper and photographs from the apartment delivered with her morning breakfast. There was no reason for Amber to do that – and the only one that could have gotten loose pictures of Buchanan with Amber was Tyree Fick. That paper had to have been delivered personally by him."

"Why?"

"Amber controlled the blackmail material very closely. Except when Ross Buchanan fought, things got chaotic. Pictures fell on the floor and they lost track of some of them. When I went there, I found a picture. But only one, and I searched the apartment for anything I could find," explained Cavendish.

Boxer nodded. "So there were no pictures for the police officers to pick up and give to the newspaper."

Cavendish nodded sheepishly. "Because I withheld my picture when I was brought in."

"Since that clears my officers of possible corruption, I will ignore that," said Boxer. "But that doesn't mean he gave the story to the newspaper."

"The newspaper printed a picture of her and Buchanan. They had to come from the same place."

"I don't see how that eliminates Tyree as a murder suspect?" said Boxer.

"Doesn't eliminate him, but where is the motive to kill her? To make more money? He really doesn't seem *that* ambitious... I think he wanted her to stop seducing tourists," concluded Cavendish. They sat in silence for a moment, both thinking about Tyree Fick, probably the more convenient potential murderer. A petty thief that could be arrested, convicted, and incarcerated with no fuss or muss. But Cavendish was sure he was innocent of murdering Amber. He was thinking about his theory about Amber being killed upstairs and then dumped.

"Where was she killed?"

Boxer shook his head. "Don't know yet. No drag marks

in the gravel... she could have been carried and dumped. Or Lance could have killed her and dumped her in the pool – he was right next to it."

"And moving heaven and earth to get the case solved – including getting me put on the case, is his clever way of throwing suspicion away from himself?" said Cavendish dubiously.

Boxer narrowed his eyes. "Getting you on the case could be his way of torpedoing my investigation."

"Touché," allowed Cavendish. "But why would she have wandered to the pool in her lingerie? Why not wear a bikini if she was going to be seductive?"

"Maybe she came to him dressed and he did assault her, but only got as far as removing her outer clothes. She fought him and he fought back too hard and killed her. Then he panics and throws her in the pool."

"And goes back to sleep by the pool until the morning? Pretty cool cucumber."

"After hiding her outer clothes – unless you found those?" queried Cavendish. Boxer shook his head negatively. Cavendish frowned at the file: "And no other marks on her body. No sign of struggle."

"She was wearing panties; lot of girls wear that for sleep. She could have been killed in her bed in her cottage and then the body moved," thought Boxer.

Cavendish decided it was time to fill Boxer in on Buxton's plot to entrap and disparage Peter Pennington. Boxer whistled when he was finished. "So much drama!"

Boxer leaned back in his chair, which squeaked ominously under the shifting load. He folded his arms across his bearlike chest and scanned Cavendish. Cavendish thought he was going to say something, but he seemed to be on pause. Cavendish had started to worry their détente had expired; it took so long for Boxer to speak. When he did, it was to extend a surprising olive branch of his own.

"Let's get a cup of coffee, and you tell me about your conversation with Mr. Lance and his guests last night."

CHAPTER TWENTY-FOUR

Sophie Cavendish sat in the second to last seat in the third row from the left. She liked being at the back of class because she could watch the other students, and Sophie Cavendish was a nosy twelve-year old. Today she was particularly interested in the girl who sat in the second seat two rows to Sophie's left – Mia Geranabby.

As soon as she disembarked from Daddy's car that morning, she had sought Mia. Like most of the students, Sophie was surprised to see Mia in school the day after her sister was murdered. She looked like she had not slept; she was ghostly pale with inky sacks hanging below her eyes. Students had dogged her with questions and comments. Sophie tried to approach her and talk to her, but her efforts were thwarted by the throng of interrogative classmates. Mia put her head down and pushed through them and asked Mr. Hammer if she could go inside before the bell, and he allowed it. Mia and her oversized backpack disappeared inside. Sophie was left frustrated in the schoolyard.

Seeing Mia looking so sad had given Sophie a second motive for wanting to talk to her. (The first being her ambition to help her Dad's murder inquiry) Sophie knew that for some people, plunging back into routine was the best medicine for a grieving heart, although it was hard for her to fully believe it. After her mother died, she had been a robot zombie with zero interest in any of her normal routines. Sometimes she still felt a bit that way. She felt something else, too. She felt like she might be able to use her experience surviving (so far) the loss of her mother to help give Mia some guidance or advice. She regretted that she and Mia weren't already friends. They had always been casually sociable, but Mia was a solitary book worm who kept to herself and Sophie wasn't exactly an outgoing social butterfly herself. She had two good friends and that was it.

Looking at Mia in class, Sophie could not believe she was really absorbing any of the lesson. Her pen was in hand and resting on her notebook, but it did not move once during the lecture. She was just sitting there robotically. The other thing that caught her attention for the second time was Mia's backpack. It was very full. Usually, her backpack was all folded up like a fresh vacuum cleaner bag on top because she switched out her books between every class with obsessive compulsive regularity. But not today, it was stretched to the seams. Sophie noticed stuff like that. To Sophie Cavendish, daughter of two police officers and granddaughter of an island busybody, this backpack discrepancy was howling like a fire alarm at her.

The lesson flew past Sophie's closed ears as she chewed her pen cap and pondered the possibilities. She had read the newspapers. She knew what Amber had done; she could guess why she had been killed. This prompted a theory about what might be in the full to busting backpack, and she was going to test that theory as soon as the bell rang for recess. She wasn't sure exactly how – she knew Mia enough to say "Hi" and ask how she was doing. It might seem strange for Sophie to be acting all friendly to her now. Or worse, with half the school gaggling around her in mock friendship now that she was a minor celebrity – "Terrible about your sister." – "I am here for you... how did they find her body?" – Sophie would just be pushed away as yet another cloying trauma groupie. She would be able to access neither the backpack nor Mia's confidence, and would be catalogued with the shallower end of the school's personality pool. But one thing Sophie had gleaned from her conversation with her Dad in the car was that Amber kept all the pictures and blackmail items to herself, and no one knew where they were. It probably wouldn't occur to grown-ups that a girl would risk giving that stuff to her younger sister, but it occurred to Sophie there was no one else she could trust *but* her little sister.

The bell chimed the class change and students gathered up their books. Those with bags stuffed binders and notebooks inside; others just bundled their books into their arms. Mia did the latter – despite having a backpack. Because her backpack was already stuffed. No room for more books.

In seventh grade, although students moved from class to class they moved as a group. So Sophie and Mia were in the next class together, but Sophie still felt self-conscious. Even though they were going to the same destination, she felt conspicuous because in her mind she was shadowing Mia, not wanting to lose sight of her. Sophie waited until Mia went to the bathroom before she went, and then she hurried as fast as she could to be out of her stall first so that Mia wouldn't give her the slip. Math, English, and Social Studies blurred by and Sophie was at a loss to account for one second of the lessons. But she knew Mia had scratched her brow four times, had gazed out the window of room 12 at an iguana in the tree for a full ten minutes, absent mindedly dragged her sleeve across her nose once and chewed the ends off two pencils.

Following her from class to class, though conspicuous, was one thing. How could she shadow Mia without being anything but obvious at recess? The bell rang before she had reached any useful conclusions and it was too late to plan. She just had to wing it. Students were still hovering around Mia like a dust cloud, so Sophie felt if she kept her distance, she would go unnoticed. Mia had her arms folded tight against her chest and kept her head down, looking uncomfortable at all the attention.

The solution to her quandary came in the form of boys. Sophie was learning that you could never underestimate the capacity for boys to be mean and nasty, and today she learned that sometimes these characteristics could be helpful. Three boys, eighth graders, moved into the group with the easy confidence of wolves swaggering through a flock of sheep. The middle-sized boy, Jeff, was the spokesman, and he gave Mia an invasive but uninformed appraisal from head to toe. The kind of look a boy gives a girl when he wants to undress her with his eyes but wouldn't really know what to do with what he found underneath.

"Sorry about your sister, Mia," said Jeff.

"Thank you."

The girl groupies were still around Mia, and Sophie hung back a way, in the shadow of an intersecting corridor.

"Sounds like she was really friendly," he said with a leer. "Wish I coulda known her better."

Mia said nothing, so he continued, reaching out for her chin. "Are you friendly like your sister?"

The moment his hand touched her chin, her leg rocketed up, and Sophie remembered what Jeff should have: That Mia was in cheerleading. Her knee struck swiftly and decisively. Sophie saw Jeff's eyes cross before they closed. He doubled over and dropped to his knees. The other boys were watching their friend, the girls were stunned silent and Mia was sprinting for the exit. She caused a wind as she swept by Sophie, who sucked in a lungful of air and launched into pursuit. Not to catch up, just to follow. Some inner instinct told her not to try to catch Mia as she hurtled through the front door of the school and down the steps.

St. Lazarus schools were not like London schools, which were barred and gated like prisons to keep the child abductors out and the students in. St. Lazarus was still a pretty safe community, recent murder notwithstanding, so school security was not a major point of concern. There was no one on the front path to stop Mia or Sophie as they left the building.

The front yard of the school was open but not vast, and the street where parents flowed through and dropped off their children each morning was narrow. Buildings two and three stories tall lined the street across from the school ground. A left-hand dogleg at the school gate, followed by a thirty-yard dash, then a right-hand turn and you had vanished from the sightlines of the school.

The school was a couple of blocks inland from the waterfront, and Mia's direction led her farther still from the bay. Pedestrians were sparse on the side street Sophie shadowed Mia along; they passed only two in three blocks, and there was just one heading in the same direction as the two girls. Sophie kept him between her and Mia. Mia did not look back – she didn't seem worried about being followed.

It was a quiet morning in the residential and non-touristy part of Port Rose. Many of the buildings were old and their stone and masonry construction seemed to help cool the hot and heavy air in the old lane. Sophie still found the intensity of the heat and thickness of the air a little strange after her earlier years in London.

Mia made a left, and so did the man. The first time it did not surprise Sophie that the man made the same turn. She paid closer attention when he made a right that kept him on Mia's trail, and she realized that as she was maintaining a consistent distance from Mia, so was this man. Sophie paid more attention to him. He was following Mia.

He was wearing what Americans called a wife-beater and the English called a vest. He was not a heavy man or broad shouldered and beefy, but his arms were muscular and slightly out of scale with his gangly frame. He wore shorts down to his knees and tennis shoes. When Mia paused to be sure of her route, he paused too.

Mia's turn took her down an alley, and now he quickened his pace. Unsure what else to do, Sophie quickened hers too.

≈

Over coffee drunk in the Chief Constable's office, Archie Cavendish and Borden Boxer talked, if not as friends, at least as grudging colleagues. Cavendish relayed Hoyt Buxton's effort to hire him to discredit Peter Pennington, and

Pennington's angry outburst when he accused Cavendish of trying to prove his unworthiness to Martine Letourneaux.

"So, Pennington wants to control Martine's career?" queried Boxer.

"But he insists he wants it for her good, not because he fears Hoyt will uncover a dark secret. Martine doesn't want to change her act to keep up with the times. Peter and the producer Megan Shepard are pushing her to move in new directions, and Buxton refuses to do so. Martine is content to let her career wind down from its celebrity status. Pennington and Megan want to keep the gravy train rolling."

"What reason could they have to kill Amber?"

"Hoyt put her up to seducing Pennington. She said no at first and then changed her mind," recounted Cavendish. "Imagine she was successful. The quietest wife can be moved to violence if she walks into an intimate moment shared between her husband and another woman."

"So that gives Martine a motive. What about Megan?"

"None that I see. She was going to make a movie of the week about Amber. She'd be killing a meal ticket," Cavendish opined.

"Deirdre Lance hates – hated - Amber because she thought she might be Marvin's daughter?" Boxer was turning over the facts as Cavendish had recounted them.

"Yes. And Amber may have pushed her buttons on that issue. Amber liked pushing people's buttons. She had a helluva lot of anger in her. I don't know if Deirdre is capable of committing murder, but Marvin Lance is," Cavendish had not yet told him of the shooting episode the prior evening and proceeded to do so now.

Boxer shook his head angrily when he learned that his officers at the gate did not respond. "As soon as I find out who was on the gate, I am going to have his ass kicked three times around the island."

An almost instinctive loyalty to fellow officers, even if he wasn't in the same department (or any department anymore) motivated Cavendish to push on quickly, hoping to divert

Boxer's attention from the laxness of his men:

"Marvin Lance – he could have been a blackmail victim. Any of the men could – although I don't know if Buxton has a wife or girlfriend who would care if he was with the girl. I don't buy Lance as the murderer. Why put himself in the position of discovering the body deliberately and not giving himself an alibi? Why move the body to where he was sleeping?"

"She always pretended she was underage, so even an unattached man could be her pray," observed Boxer. Still mulling over Buxton he added: "But Buxton knew her age, so that wouldn't apply to him."

He turned his cup on his desk, retreating into his inner thoughts for a moment before asking: "What about Pennington? If Buxton was trying to make him look bad to his wife, it stands to reason that Pennington would be trying to dig up dirt on Hoyt Buxton."

Cavendish nodded. "And I don't think Buxton could afford to lose Martine as a client. He is her agent and business manager. He is terrified of losing her as a client. What agent have you ever heard of that travels with a client and spends several weeks with her in a particular location on a particular project."

Boxer scribbled *Buxton's finances* on the white writing tablet before him. It was hard to imagine a mousy and timid human being capable of murder, but Cavendish had seen the most wretched of people moved to the most hideous of crimes by their fears of facing through the challenges being dealt them by life. Murder is sometimes the way of the coward, not just the wicked.

Then his mobile phone chirped. He pulled it from his belt to see who was calling. It was Sophie, so he said, "excuse me" to the Chief Constable and answered. The ice in his daughter's whisper chilled his very soul: "*Daddy I need your help!*"

CHAPTER TWENTY-FIVE

He was flying through the office door before he knew where he was headed, motioning to Boxer in the hope the policeman would follow, but heedless of whether or not he did. His daughter's tone ripped at his insides.

"Don't say anything Daddy because he'll hear you. He's after Mia – I'm afraid he's going to hurt her."

As rage, terror and fear rippled in shockwaves through every nerve and sinew in his body, a realization poured over him like ice water. Mia's backpack. Today, she could barely lift it. The last time he saw her get out of the car it was light and she flung it across her shoulder like nothing.

How had he not seen that!?

≈

The street had become little more than an alley, and the man had sped up, narrowing the gap between himself and Mia. The little girl had finally become aware of someone behind her. She looked back with a start and took a moment to decide if he was a threat or not. A moment was ample time for him to draw abreast of her.

"Don't run. I knew your sister."

He was blocking Sophie's view of her so she couldn't gauge Mia's reaction. She didn't know what else to do, so she kept trying to close the gap between herself and the man, but she now did so keeping herself as close to the walls of the narrow street as possible. Her instincts advised her to get as close as possible but remain unobserved. It was old construction so there were ample doorways and nooks and crannies to gain partial cover as she advanced. Enough cover to stay out of the street, but not enough to stay hidden if he looked back with purpose.

"I don't know you," Mia told the man. She stepped away from him backwards, he kept moving forwards, matching the pace of her retreat.

"I wasn't the kind of friend she brought home … I was a work friend," he explained. "You know the work your sister did."

"What do you want?" Mia was looking nervous.

"Your sister was a good friend to me. A very good friend. I was very sad and angry over what someone done to her. But when she was alive, she asked me to do something for her. In case anything happened to her, she asked me to do this thing. Like a final wish. You understand?"

He was answered with silence. Sophie held her ground during the pregnant pause – she tried to move only when Mia and the man were talking. When the man spoke next, instead of moving closer she quietly let her own backpack slide from her back, and she lowered it to the ground. Her mobile phone was in a sleeve on the side and she extracted it and held it in the palm of her hand. Feeling the man's focus was secure on Mia, she made the call to her Dad and whispered her SOS. She turned the volume down all the way – she couldn't risk his voice being heard.

"A final wish is the most important wish a person ever makes. If someone asks you to do a final thing for them, you must do it. You just have to."

"Yes," Mia agreed hesitantly.

"You know what Amber did for her work for her

286

money, don't you?"

"I don't care what she did," Mia replied protectively. "She was my sister."

"Of course. You are a good sister for loving your sister no matter what. A very good sister. Now here is the thing – you know what she did, and you know that there are many men that would want to hurt her. She always planned insurance. She planned for if anything ever happened to her, she would send pictures and videos to the wives of the men she did her work to. So that whoever hurt her would be punished."

No answer this time from Mia. Sophie had gotten to within about twenty feet, but each step closer tightened the knots of fear in her stomach. He was not a huge or brutishly built man, but Sophie doubted the chance of two twelve-year-old girls, spirited though they may be, to take him on successfully. He was also right next to Mia – he could knock her down and then it would be him and Sophie. She was trying to be very quiet, but she knew the closer she drew, the higher the likelihood of discovery.

"I think you know where she hid these pictures and things, Mia. And I need you to bring them to me. Her last wish to me was to make sure these men are punished for what they done to her."

Another pause. Sophie wondered what was going through Mia's head, what the man was thinking, and why her mind was running all over the place instead of reaching any practical determinations of her own. Frozen to the spot, she waited.

The silence was ruptured by the scuffling sound of Mia's feet spinning in place and trying to accelerate away from the man. But while she had to turn and charge, all he had to do was grab and he did so. He grabbed her by the backpack and yanked her backwards and she lost her balance and fell in a heap like a turtle. She rolled away from him onto her side and would have rolled onto all fours to regain her feet, but while she was on her side, he leaped over her and kicked her a winding blow right into her belly. Sophie heard a gush of air expelled from

Mia's lungs, and the fear in her gut turned to terror because until she saw this man kick a little girl in the belly she hadn't realized how dangerous their circumstances might be.

Only now, the man looked up and down the street, checking for onlookers. Sophie pressed herself tight into a crack between two buildings and held her breath. Her heart raced as he started walking towards her. He passed right by her hiding place without seeing her, but the minute he turned around to return to where Mia lay, she would be exposed. Hastily, she shoved her phone down the front of her uniform skirt so he would not see her one lifeline to safety, and she kicked herself mentally as she realized what had drawn his attention.

She had carefully and silently unencumbered herself of her school bag – but she had laid it down in plain sight. She was so busy being silent in her movements that she forgot to conceal her trail. Her mother would not be impressed. And her father… ooooo … he was going to kill her if she survived the next hour or so. He was going to kill her bad. She said a quick prayer that he would have the chance.

Somewhere inside her she felt amused that she could be having such thoughts even as terror clouded around her, and she felt a voice telling her she had to do something. Anything.

Any second now he would turn around and see her. Discovery was inevitable, so there was no point rooting herself to the ground like a vegetable. She could run for help, but she had no idea how far from her help might be. Mia could be dead or dragged God knew whereby the time Sophie found the cavalry and brought them back to this spot. She would not abandon Mia.

She broke cover and sprinted to where Mia lay in a wheezing heap in the street and pulled on her arm.

"We have to go!" She heard the man yell something in her direction, but she was focused on pulling Mia up. The girl's backpack weighed her down, it must have weighed a ton and she tried to slide the straps off her shoulders.

Blanched with fear, Mia nevertheless grabbed at the straps to hold the bag in place and shook her head fiercely. Mia was in a sitting position on the ground, Sophie stood facing her trying to pull her up, and she felt the man come at her like a blur on her left. He ripped her left arm from Mia, and she found herself involuntarily spinning to face him. Fear dissolved to surprise when she watched the clenched fist racing at her face. Even though she had seen him kick Mia, she was still surprised he was going to punch a girl.

His fist was flying at her. She tried to duck to the left, but that only changed it from a punch straight on her nose to a punch glancing against her right eye socket. It was a forceful blow and she was off balance – she felt herself falling backwards after the sting of the impact. As she hit the ground, she had the flash of hope that her head wouldn't smash against the pavement and knock her out. It did hit the pavement, and her vision blurred as she lay there, dazed, and inert despite a voice inside her yelling at her to get up.

She heard a yelp and thought Mia must have been hit again, and she tried to sit up, but the world was too wobbly to support her. She felt fingers go down the back of the neck of her blouse and felt herself being dragged backwards, like a kitten being carried by the scruff of its neck. She kicked at the ground and tried to make herself harder to move. The hand let go of her neck. She was sitting upright on the ground willing her vision to clear and suddenly her view was filled with the face of the man she now thought might kill her. His breath was putrid, like something had crawled into his mouth and died. She thought it toxic enough to make her pass out. Maybe that was his plan.

"You stop fighting me. I just need what I need and if you give it to me, I'll leave you and your little friend and go. But you fight me ... I will ruin you for life, you hear me?" He underscored his point with a heavy backhand that knocked her on her side. Now her ears were ringing too, and she felt herself being dragged from light into shadow. She looked around her surroundings, vaguely aware that she should see and remember everything she could. Big doors, two of them, closed. Empty work benches. A hole in the ground aligned with each door. She was in an abandoned mechanic's shop, and the big holes were the bays under the cars where mechanics worked.

She heard Mia being dragged a short distance from her, and light slaps, as if he was trying to revive her.

"You gotta tell me little girl now because it's all gone too far, and I am going to have to get away from here. I can't do that without those pictures, and I know you the only one Amber would trust with them because she never trusted nobody. She would never trust me no matter what I did for her. I woulda just taken them and gone away, and I still will. But if you don't help me, I got nothing to lose and I am just gonna have me one last fabulous party and you are gonna get hurt, you hearing what I am saying?"

"My head hurts," complained Mia.

It was then, his attention focused on Mia, that Sophie snuck her phone from her waistband. The line had been disconnected during the scuffle. She quickly texted her Dad and gave him the clues that she could. Service station, somewhere in an alley off Durham Street. Her backpack was probably nearby. She would buy as much time as she could. Then she dialed his number, ensuring her volume was low and left the line open. If the man found it, all was lost.

Whether he got what he wanted or not, he could kill both girls and their bodies might go unnoticed for days. Sophie had a vision of her rotting body being discovered in the bottom of one of the two service bay. *Stop that!*

Her father would come. Of that, she was certain. He would find her and save both of them - but he wasn't superman. He couldn't teleport here; it would take him time. It was her job to buy him that time. It was all she had to do. She told herself that she had the easy part.

She cursed herself for her impetuosity, and remembered watching her father grieve her mother. She determined that she was not going to be the reason he fell deeper into the pit. She quietly pulled herself to a kneeling position, looking around for any tool that might have been left behind that she could arm herself with. There were no conveniently placed wrenches or spanners. A few rotting cardboard boxes were strewn about, but she hardly had time to go rooting through those.

The man – she would learn later his name was Tyree – was appealing to Mia with the same mix of pleading and threats. "I know she had to be with the men, but otherwise we took all the same risks, did all the same work. We both would have gone to jail – we should have been partners. We could've made more money and I could have gotten her away from that life. I could've gotten her away from those men," he pinched the bridge of his nose with his fingers and Sophie squinted. Was he… was he *crying?* "I think maybe she liked being with all those guys. But she wouldn't even go on a date with me… I hope you won't be like that when you grow up. If you grow up."

She looked at the two service bays in the floor. She was in between the two of them, while Tyree and Mia were near an interior door that may have led to an office or toilet. Sophie got to her feet. Sophie cleared her throat loudly.

Mia and the man both glanced her way.

She mustered all her strength to sound casual because she thought that would throw him off more than a scream or fearful shouting: "So Mia, I'm just going to go get some help, okay? I'll be back in a few minutes."

The man lunged to his feet and ran for Sophie. Uncertain of her balance and with her ears still ringing, she ran around the edge of the service bay, trying to keep the hole in the floor between her and the man. He was stronger, but she was smaller and nimbler. Like a child's game she changed directions rapidly to keep him on his toes. He tried to outthink her and pick which way she was going to turn, and he was pretty good at it, but she was better at turning on a dime. She kept reversing her course – sprinting first one way, then skidding to a halt and sprinting the other. Her greater agility was her only weapon, and she had visions of tiring him out with her game of this way and that… but then what? After a few moments, her head still spinning, she was getting dizzy and she paused. They were still on opposite sides of the pit.

"I don't want to hurt you, little girl."

"Yes, you do," she hissed at him defiantly. "But if you were smart you would take off right now. You don't look smart though," she felt her fear mingling with something else in her bloodstream as her body pushed away the pain in her head. He lunged to the right and she went the opposite direction, still keeping the bay between them.

They stopped again. "How long do you think you can keep this up girl, running this way and that, you ain't never going to escape like this."

"I'm not trying to escape," she said, surprised to find she was speaking through a grin. She added coyly: "I don't need to. Help is coming."

He looked confused by the remark, and now they were moving left to right slowly, like swordsmen circling each other. Evaluating, measuring. Looking for weaknesses and opportunities.

"No one's coming," he seemed to decide she was bluffing. "Even if someone does – she's dead," he motioned towards Mia. He shrugged. "Do what you want."

He left the circling of the pit and went to where Mia was sitting on the floor. She had been watching but now she tried to back away, pushing herself along the floor in her seated position.

"You need her, she has what you want," Sophie reminded him, shrill with alarm. He walked up to her and knocked Mia backwards with a foot to her chest, then picked up one of her feet and started dragging her to the service bay.

"Amber always said I didn't think ahead. But I'm not planning to kill her…I'm just going to drop her in that hole. How many bones you think she gonna break?"

Mia started squirming furiously as she realized where she was headed, and Sophie ran for the man. She had no choice. She couldn't let Mia be thrown into the pit. Her image of her own body rotting down there fired her belly. She ran at the man and hurled herself the last few feet. She hit him square in the belly with all the force she had; he fell backwards onto the ground, with Sophie tumbling on top of him and then rolling off. It was not a controlled roll; she was not a trained or natural combatant and she didn't really have a next move in mind.

She was on hands and knees and he was on his back — he lashed out with one of his hands and yanked her supporting arm and she fell with a thump to the ground. She felt her chin bounce against the cement floor and was disoriented for a moment. He got to his knees and flipped her on her back and put his hands around her throat and started to tighten his grip. "I am going to kill you, you little bitch!"

Sophie's throat started to hurt, and she felt his breath on her and saw spit in the corners of his mouth and tried to think of something to do. It occurred to her that he must have killed Amber. It sounded like he loved her and hated her at the same time. She would have to ask Mummy to explain that to her. She was running out of air; her head was feeling strange. She heard Mia yelling at him to stop. Then something about pictures, and she heard the sound of something heavy landing on the floor.

He released his grasp on her and she lay there choking and gasping and trying to pull air back in her lungs and wondering what had made him stop. She looked sideways and saw he'd opened the backpack. It was full of manila envelopes. Part of Sophie's mind in the back corner of her consciousness felt pleased that she had been right. But she also knew that they were about to die now that he had what he wanted. Mia had given him what he sought, thinking it would buy their survival. But it was too late. Sophie knew it would do no such thing, but maybe it was buying them time. She had to hang on a little longer.

She wanted to get up, but she couldn't. She was trying to see where Mia was. Trying to think of something, anything, to buy a little more time. She felt so tired yet filled with a strange sense of calm. She tried to get up, but she couldn't. A woman's voice whispered in her ear about how brave she was and how strong, and how she had done it and she could rest now. The woman told her *Daddy will take it from here*.

That was when the door facing the street exploded

inwards.

The man who wanted to kill Sophie Cavendish and Mia Geranabby looked up with a start. He didn't recognize the man silhouetted in the doorway. Thinking it was a homeless guy in search of shelter he barked confidently: "Get outta here, you!"

The silhouette ignored him and stalked into the garage, like a leopard approaching its prey, sizing it up. Tyree stood up slowly as he began to recognize the shape.

Archer Cavendish surveyed and analyzed the scene. His daughter, blood sparkling on the side of her face, lying oddly on the ground with one leg folded back under her but a strange dazzle in her eye. Mia, cowering next to one of the service bays. The bag with bulky envelopes strewn around it.

More men streamed in behind him, but Cavendish was oblivious. His focus was squarely on Tyree and he could no longer see anything else. Seeing the look on her father's face Sophie suddenly felt bad for her assailant.

Cavendish advanced on Tyree who stood immobilized, his eyes darting between Cavendish and the policemen. He might have thought he was under arrest and that was that. But then, Tyree was not a father. Cavendish walked up to him and shoved Fick into the pit. Tyree cursed as his body impacted the uneven floor of the service pit. He landed, twisted sideways, and fell, feeling his ankle snap underneath him. The sound of it echoed like a breaking branch in the service pit as he collapsed to the ground with a howl of pain. Cat-like, Cavendish leapt into the pit and loomed over his prey.

"I think I broke my ankle," Tyree was on his back, rocking left and right. Cavendish was incapable of caring. Seeing his daughter on the floor, knowing the danger she was in. Every switch in Cavendish's psyche had been flipped. He came down on top of Tyree, kneeling on his chest, his hands around the throat. Tyree's yells were muffled as the air flow was sucked out of his lungs and Cavendish lifted his head off the floor by his neck and smashed it down.

Cavendish was given over to the rage, consumed by it, part of it. There was nothing in the universe except his hurting daughter and this easily extinguished piece of waste that caused her hurt. He felt a strange rushing in his ears and was insensible to hands grabbing at his back and the boots of policemen landing on the floor all around him. He just kept smashing his fist into the wailing man's face. Like a child dreaming he was floating, Cavendish felt himself lifted bodily off the floor and out of the bay while Tyree lay there choking and spluttering beneath him. Cavendish couldn't move. He felt hands on his legs and arms. People were yelling and he was being hauled out of the pit like a sack of potatoes as darkness clouded the edge of his vision.

Tyree was coughing and yelling that Cavendish was a crazy bastard and to arrest him.

He heard Boxer, an unlikely ally: "Don't know what you're talking about. You must have dazed yourself when you tripped and fell into the pit and hit your head."

Then came shame, and the rage was chased away by panic and he was worried about Sophie again and looking around for her. She was bending over Mia, rubbing the girl's back and then he felt pride and admiration and anger and fear and shame all over again. She looked up at him and smiled and started toward him.

"I told him I didn't need to escape. I knew I just had to buy you enough time to get here," and she buried her face into his chest, and they embraced and clung tightly to each other. Only then did they both start to sob quietly together.

CHAPTER TWENTY-SIX

The hospital. Boxer asked Cavendish not to discuss what had happened with his daughter when he followed her into the back of the ambulance. Cavendish respected this request. It was the least he could do. At the hospital Cavendish earned a strange look from a nurse when he stayed in the exam room with his daughter. Since it was apparent she'd been beaten up, Cavendish supposed without rancor that they had to consider the possibility he was the one who hurt her. After the nurse took her vitals and snapped a cold pack for Sophie to hold against her face, father and daughter waited in silence.

Sophie held the cool pack to her face and avoided his eyes, looking for points of interest in the linoleum. Cavendish felt more relieved than angry, and a little scared because she had charged into a dangerous situation with a jarring enthusiasm that wasn't altogether unfamiliar to him.

"I was scared. I was scared about both of us," she told him at last.

"I'm not surprised. He could have killed both you girls."

Sophie shook her head impatiently. "I was scared for you and me. Not Mia and me. I was scared of what would happen to me and what would happen to you if…"

"We have a lot to talk about. But let's just get you

checked out and then we'll let Boxer get your statement. We can make sure Tyree Fick spends a long time in jail."

The doctor came in, determined that nothing was broken, but not before pressuring her to speak to him without her father around. She refused. The doctor asked how she'd gotten injured and she told him she couldn't discuss it until the police came to take her statement. He had tried a couple of other different approaches – "Did this happen at home?", "Did someone you know do this to you?", and "Are you afraid that if you tell me someone will hurt you?"

"She told you. She's a witness in an ongoing police inquiry," Cavendish interjected. "Put your questions to Chief Constable Boxer."

The doctor huffily scribbled a prescription for painkillers that they could fill in the hospital pharmacy. Her medical needs tended; a policewoman came into take her statement. It was not Jenny Singh, one of the police officers Cavendish had more than a casual acquaintance with. Instead it was PC Muwambe, a stolid middle-aged woman with a tough chin and warm eyes. Since she was a minor, Cavendish was allowed to stay in the room with his daughter. For the first time, he heard her explanation of the suspicions she'd nurtured about Mia's bloated school bag – That it was filled with photos ready to be mailed to Amber's blackmail victims, any of whom could be her killer. He didn't know if he should be proud about her deductions or furious that she hadn't shared them with him at the time. Perhaps both, but he'd withhold his anger for the moment.

Cavendish had been kicking himself for not worrying more about who had the pictures and other evidence of blackmail. There was no one else for Amber to trust. Mia was the obvious candidate and if he had thought about it in time – if he had recognized the discrepancy of backpacks in time - this whole episode might have been averted.

His blood pressure worsened as she explained chasing Mia into the streets, shadowing her and then realizing she wasn't the only one. He felt afraid for her all over again even though she was sitting safely on the examining table in front of him. He felt pride as she explained rationally her decision to abandon concealment and the tactics she employed to survive, and blanched at the thought of what might have happened if he had taken more time than she had bought him to get to the service station.

He felt sick when the policewoman asked if Fick had taken her clothes off or touched her intimately. And laughed inwardly when his daughter acidly replied: "Did you see me throwing up anywhere?"

The drive home was quiet, and when they pulled into the driveway, he turned the car off and they sat in idle silence, both staring straight ahead. Sophie broke the silence.

"I'm grounded, aren't I?"

"Oh, yes," Cavendish looked at her young and fragile face, swollen and bruised on one side of her nose. "If I wasn't so glad you were safe, I'd be slapping the shit out of you right now. Don't ever, ever do that again. You don't try to help me out on a case. If you see something, you call me and tell me and then you mind your business."

"What if I was wrong? I would've wasted your time for nothing."

"I can afford to waste time. I can't afford anything to ever happen to you," Cavendish reached an arm around her shoulders and pulled her to him. "You were smart and brave today, but you would've been smarter to stay out of it. You're too young to be chasing people down alleys. Be a little girl – AT LEAST until you are 16."

"Sixteen? That's old…" she rolled her eyes.

"Go inside," he instructed. She unlatched the car door, hopped out and ran into the house with far more energy than a little girl who'd had such a day should have left in her. Cavendish sat by himself in the driveway wondering how scared he should be that his daughter was so like her mother. Part of him was proud, but the other part of him thought of his wife's fate and prayed Sophie would be the exact opposite of her. Was that so unrealistic? And so much for bringing her home to St. Lazarus and raising her away from London and away from police work. So much for protecting her from losing any more parents and assuring her a safer, stabler life while he puttered around doing cheating spouse investigations.

When Cavendish got out of the car, he was dragging his feet like they weighed a thousand pounds apiece. Such a contrast from his daughter's springy steps. Could he blame her for acting like her parents? Had his own choices laid down a trail she would inevitably follow?

He stood outside the kitchen door, hearing Sophie excitedly recounting her day to her grandmother. Lord, what that poor woman must think of the man her daughter married! The gusher of words subsided the moment she heard the doorknob turn, and she suddenly became very interested in the plate of food in front of her.

Later, when Sophie was taking her shower and Cavendish sat at the kitchen table, still stirring cold food around his plate, Glenda plonked herself down across the table from him.

"Get used to it, Archie."

"To what?"

"Worrying about her. And I am not talking about normal parent worrying. I am talking about worrying because your child is crazy. She is her mother's daughter through and through and it scares me what she'll get herself into. Part of it makes me smile to see my Elizabeth alive inside that girl but the other part has nightmares about where that will lead her." She shook her head in a gesture that bundled optimism and regret together. "Sometimes our children don't want any of what we are, and they go a different path, and sometimes they are like little clones. Who knows which to wish for? Sophie's still young. She might not be a clone of her mama – or you – or be totally different - but with her genes I'd be getting used to the idea of worrying about her a lot."

Cavendish looked up from his plate bleakly. "A man tried to kill her today."

"I know it. And I hope you ground that girl 'til she

twenty-four for being a damn fool, I'm not saying you shouldn't. But looking forward: don't get mad at her for being like my daughter and trust me I'm saying that even though I'm wanting to beat her senseless but – she did what her mama would have done today. It's in her nature. Damn foolish girl!" she grabbed at his plate, ending the subject and leaving Cavendish wondering if the foolish girl of her reverie was Sophie or her mama. "Let me heat that up so you actually eat it."

Cavendish still ate half-heartedly and felt Glenda's eyes on him even as she scribbled her way through some papers with a red pen. Years of teaching and she could keep track of twenty students and her desk – one gloomy parent stirring mashed potatoes around his plate must be supervisory child's play.

He glanced at his watch. Even with the events of the day, the wait at the hospital, the interviews, and statements – it was barely seven o'clock. He wasn't going to go back over to the Lance place tonight. He decided to go have a shower and sit by the pool with a rum and coke. As he passed his daughter's room, he had to look inside to make sure she was breathing. She was strewn carelessly across her bed, sleeping. Early, but a helluva long day for her. He went into her room and laid the back of his hand against the softness of her cheek – the unswollen one.

He whispered: "Dad doesn't always get there in the nick of time. You have to be more careful with yourself."

A deep and contented intake of breath was the only answer she gave him, so he let her be. Maybe the words would infiltrate her dreams.

The shower washed away some of the guilt and trauma of the day, and a second rum and coke numbed it a little further. He looked out over the sea and felt the wind coming off the ocean, fresh and bracing. The island sloped away below the house and stretched about two miles to the beaches, dotted with a house here and there so it was very dark and on a clear night you got a brilliant view of a star-filled sky.

He thought about the murder – it took his mind off Sophie – and mulled the conversation he'd had with Borden Boxer, enjoying the tentative understanding they had reached.

Guilt seeped in again though because Boxer had covered for him with Tyree Fick and he felt bad to have put another police officer in a position where he felt like he had to cover for him.

He watched the sky darken – the house faced southeast, so the sun was setting the other side of the mountain behind him. He thought of his daughter and her brush with death, and Amber's death, and how Pamela Geranabby must feel. How would Mia's near-death experience affect her? It could be enough to push her over the edge. Now he felt guilty for taking a break from trying to find the man who killed her daughter. He tossed back the dregs in his glass and wandered inside. He checked on Sophie again.

≈

The next morning Cavendish rose early, showered, and donned khaki canvas pants and a loose-fitting Tommy Bahama shirt over a white muscle shirt. At breakfast, Sophie was downright effervescent and unbowed by her grounding. Her bruises were hurting her, and she complained of aches and pains but Cavendish, Glenda and his father-in-law all indicated the pain would remind her to make smarter choices in future. Sophie's primary concern this morning was whether or not her facial injuries would leave a scar. It secretly pleased Cavendish that he had the only little girl on the planet who thought it would be really cool to have a scar from a fight on her face.

After breakfast, he called her school and tore into the principal for letting his daughter wander off campus so easily. It probably wasn't fair of him, but the fact no one had called him to warn him his daughter had roamed spoke poorly of the school's attention to its students. It also gave him somewhere to vent the latent anger he still felt, so he vented. He wanted to keep Sophie home from school, but Glenda talked him out of it. Better to keep her in her routine, she counselled. Not to mention a day at home from school was a reward for misbehavior. He dropped Sophie at school and then headed up to Lance's house for what he hoped would be the last day of his inquiries.

There was still an officer at the gate, but he was just

making a log of the comings and goings, he did not question Cavendish on his reasons for being there or try to impede him from going in. Cavendish pulled his car into the gravelly parking area and headed to the doors of the main house. A maid opened the door for him.

"Is Martine Letourneaux in?" he asked.

"No, she's out somewhere, Mr. Cavendish."

"Filming?"

"I don't think they're filming today. She just went for a walk - she headed out from the other side of the house."

"Mr. Lance?"

"He and Mrs. Lance took the boat out." Ah, the second honeymoon of the once hate-filled couple.

"How about Mr. Pennington?"

"I ain't seen him today." It was quickly shaping up to be an empty house.

"Do you think it would be possible for me to go upstairs and have a quick look inside their rooms?" he wondered. "You're welcome to come with me to see that I don't take anything."

The maid was a grizzled old bear of a woman, but there was still some softness in her eyes that you could catch a glimpse of.

"You think you going to find out who killed poor Amber?"

Cavendish nodded – and it surprised him that he did so with honesty. There was the familiar feeling of knowing the end was in sight, even if its details remained obscured. Like the solution was stalking him, ready to show itself at any moment. He felt like he had all the pieces in hand now. It was a matter of assembling them.

"Come on then."

She led him upstairs and opened the first bedroom door on the left. There was no exterior lock, the occupant could lock it from the inside when they were in there, but there was no keyhole to lock it from the outside.

"This is Mr. Pennington and Ms. Letourneaux," the

maid explained before expounding with a disapproving sniff: "I guess she kept her name because she makes the money."

Cavendish preceded her into the room. "You don't approve of a wife earning more than her husband?"

"I don't look down on it if he does something with himself, whether it's a job or taking care of the house or the kids. Seems he just liked to spend his time trying to boss his wife around."

Cavendish smiled at the maid's immediate familiarity with him and her enthusiastic confidence sharing. The room was not huge, but it was comfortably sized, about fifteen by fifteen with an *en suite* bath. He went to the window – it was big and old fashioned, with panes that swung wide open to admit the ocean breezes. A ceiling fan agitated the air overhead, but the room was very chilly because the air conditioning was also functioning at full tilt. He leaned out the open window and found himself looking down the slope of the eaves that created a shade for the patio and ended in line with the pool.

Cavendish turned his attention back into the room. Hoyt had sent Amber to seduce Pennington. Had she completed the task? Had Martine caught them in the act? It was unusual but not unknown for a woman to strangle someone to death, and Amber was not a big girl or thick necked one.

What would the plan have been? This wasn't her homemade video lab, there didn't seem to be a convenient place to hide a camera here. There was no closet – just a large wardrobe with heavy doors and no openings where a lens could peer through conveniently. If Hoyt had barely convinced her to sleep with Pennington on the night she was murdered, how could she have figured out a place to hide a camera on such short notice in a room that lacked any obvious hiding places? He prowled the corners of the room, looking for any discreet recesses that could have given a camera the right view while keeping it out of sight of its subject.

His ponderings were disturbed by scuffling noises. He turned in the direction of the sound and was startled to see a shadow looming in the window.

"Pennington?" Cavendish was too surprised to worry about being caught in the man's room. He was far more intrigued by what on earth Pennington was doing on the roof and why he was coming into his own room by way of the window?

Pennington, balancing carefully on the slope of the roof was clearly as startled to see Cavendish in his room as Cavendish was to see him outside it. He reeled back from the window, and suddenly his arms wind-milled wildly as he tried to regain his balance and then he was tumbling backwards. One second, he was there, the next minute he was gone. Then there was a terrific splash.

Cavendish jumped to the window, leaned out and looked to his right and saw the head and bared shoulders of Megan Shepherd leaning out of the adjacent window. She was looking in the direction of the splash and was doubtless drawn to the window by it. She looked at the point where Pennington had disappeared with surprise.

"Megan?" this whole turn of events was capturing Cavendish somewhat unprepared. Wide eyed when she saw him, Megan disappeared back into her room.

Reflecting on the thickening plot, Cavendish pulled his own head inside the room and headed for the hall to go and make sure Pennington hadn't killed himself. He noticed the maid who had helped him into the room was pulling the sheets off the bed.

"Tell him I was making the bed and you came into ask me questions," she said helpfully, and probably as afraid for her job as for Cavendish getting heat from Pennington. He smiled at her and went downstairs and out the back where Peter Pennington was pulling himself out of the pool, coughing and spluttering.

He lay prone next to the pool in a manner eerily reminiscent of Amber's corpse, and Cavendish saw his back already turning scarlet from the impact with the water. The hit must have knocked the wind clear out of him. He lay there coughing and wheezing and gradually pulled himself up to a hands and knees position, darting an angry look at Cavendish but still unable to get words out.

Cavendish knelt beside him and said, "So. You and Megan, huh?"

Pennington ignored him and got to his feet and started for the door. Cavendish trailed the wet footprints into the house and followed Pennington upstairs. He was wearing only boxers and he was bee lining for his room. Cavendish followed him, eager to follow up on this new line of inquiry. It could have been Megan who killed Amber in a fit of jealousy. This could also be the secret Pennington was afraid he was going to unearth for Buxton, the secret Buxton coveted as leverage to ruin Pennington's relationship with Martine.

Had Amber discovered the affair when she went to seduce Pennington? Had the discovery cost her everything?

Near the landing at the top of the stairs the maid was stuffing sheets into the laundry chute ham fistedly, and when Pennington hove into her line of sight she told him helpfully. "I make your bed Mr. Pennington."

Yeah, that didn't make her look guilty. Cavendish found himself chuckling inwardly as Pennington went into his room, plucking his sodden boxers away from his skin. Cavendish passed his room – he knew the door was going to get slammed in his face if he tried to follow and he wasn't fussed about getting access right now. He rapped his knuckles on the next door, Megan Shepherd's room.

"Who is it?"

"Archie Cavendish, Ms. Shepherd."

"Go away."

"You don't have to let me in, Ms. Shepherd – but you should know the first thing I am going to do is telephone Chief Constable Boxer and tell him I just saw Peter Pennington sneaking from your room to his."

She must have been standing at the door because it swung inwards with a snap. She stood glaring up at him in a robe with the Lance monogram on it. "Why would he believe you?"

"Why wouldn't he believe me? I have a corroborating

witness. And how long do you think it will take me to catch you again, now that I know what I'm looking for?"

"You are not a nice man, Mr. Cavendish. You don't even know anything about us, and you want to ruin Peter's marriage?"

"And your partnership with Martine?" he shook his head. "That's the least of it. You just gave me a whopping big motive for murdering Amber."

"Are you crazy? I don't have a motive for killing her."

"She was in the house the night she was murdered. She could have seen you and Peter together – its public record that she has a penchant for blackmail. She could've blackmailed you and Peter. You decided you didn't like being blackmailed and let's face it – there are many men with strong motives that could have done it. You strangle and toss her in the pool – the chlorine in the water taints most of the physical evidence on her body. You're off scot free."

"It's a good job you're not with the police because a policeman would know better than to throw half-assed accusations around," she retorted, clawing her robe tighter together across her chest self-consciously. "Martine's stock is falling, if she doesn't change with the times, she won't be worth anything to me anyway."

"Unless Peter convinces her to change with the times? Still a good enough reason to kill a nosy interloper," he was looking at the window. "May I come in your room for one minute?"

Grudgingly, she stood aside. He went in and she started closing the door.

"Um, no, leave it open please," he asked. "I've seen enough films not to be shut alone in a room with an angry woman in a bathrobe."

He went to the window and leaned out. The eaves sloped down sharply, and he could see the pool but... He clambered through the window and balanced himself carefully out the window. There were no signs on Amber's body of being dragged over gravel or cement... And if she was rolled out of this window there was a fifty/fifty chance she would have landed in the pool or splattered on the patio.

Pennington's window though – he had fallen neatly into the pool. Looking at the run from window to roof edge and down to the water, odds were comfortably high that anyone coming out of his window would fall into the pool.

Megan looked at him through the window. "What are you doing out there?"

Cavendish clambered back into her room. He was oblivious to her as a series of images and recollections started strobing through his mind. He thought about the maid shoving sheets in the laundry chute and was reminded of the maid he'd seen at Lorna Buchanan's hotel, doing the same thing. The two memories linked like a catalyzing string that pulled all the other pieces together into a properly ordered image. Amber had been murdered in the room Peter Pennington shared with Martine Letourneaux, the room where she had gone to seduce Peter Pennington, and was then shoved out the window. Parts of the puzzle were still blurry; one part was almost inexplicable. But the math seemed to work. He was turning this way and that, as if the images converging in his mind were manifesting physically in the space around him where he could see them and touch them. Facts fell into place.

No one had found her clothes. If she'd been murdered inside the house, where were her clothes? She was wearing only underwear in the pool. Of course, the murderer would have known they had to be disposed of completely. Who knew what evidence might cling to them? They had to be gotten rid of. His thoughts came back to the two laundry chutes. He rounded on Megan.

"The night she died; the night Amber was murdered- Peter came to you here?"

Megan shook her head. "Martine doesn't need to know."

"Just tell me if he was here or not, after you came upstairs.:

She nodded. "Until about midnight. Martine would

think he went for late night walks."

Cavendish looked at the wall that separated the two rooms. "I assume you two are quiet?"

If Pennington and Megan were in Megan's room – and Martine looked for Pennington in his and Martine's room – she wouldn't have caught them. She could have spied Pennington sneaking into Megan's room – but they were associates. Would she have thought anything of it?

The laundry chutes poked at his mind again. Suddenly, he knew exactly why.

He brushed past Megan and through the doorway and charged downstairs. He was blocked by the evidence, or the lack thereof. He paced impatiently in the downstairs hallway, almost dithering in the way he marched ten paces one direction before spinning and retracing his steps. He needed to force a confession through a confrontation, but he didn't have the authority to take the suspect into an interrogation room and try to break them down. He didn't know if it would work anyway.

He stopped abruptly. He would ask the spirits to help. He charged back upstairs and banged on Peter Pennington's door. He heard noise inside and Pennington hauled open the door. "What?"

"Can you call your wife? I need to speak to her."

"Are you insane?"

"Oh," Cavendish waved his hand airily. "Not about this. About something to do with Amber's death. This … this will all come out later and she'll divorce you and kick you out of her life without a dime, and you can hope that Megan likes you enough to take you in. But that's not what's important to me right now. I need your wife to speak to someone on the other side for me. I want her to ask Amber to tell us who killed her."

CHAPTER TWENTY-SEVEN

The big ceiling fan churned the air in the drawing room with stolid determination, sending the draft down in lethargic pulses. All the suspects were gathered, and the room had the melodramatic air of the final pages of an Agatha Christie novel. With the particular problems of the case in hand and the lack of official authority, Cavendish understood why Poirot used this mechanism for the final confrontation with the murderer.

Megan Shepherd had made a point of sitting on the sofa next to Hoyt Buxton, maintaining a decent distance from her lover, Peter Pennington. Pennington was leaning on the bar, his face bleached white with fear and anger swirling in competition with each other. He knew Martine didn't know about him and Megan yet. He had made one plea to Cavendish to keep it between them. Cavendish had been non-committal, but he had a client that had specifically paid him to dig up dirt on Peter Pennington.

Marvin and Deirdre Lance stood close to each other, so different from the couple they were just a few days ago. Maybe that was the only thing potentially positive to come out of this whole mess: one salvaged marriage. Their proximity led to her laying her hand on his forearm, and Lance laid his own hand over hers. Hopefully, their reconciliatory spirit would last beyond the conclusion of this mystery.

Buxton looked nervous and he fumbled with his glass and sipped from it often. Big bags hung from his eyes and Cavendish wondered if he had slept a wink since the idea was planted that Pennington would kill him the moment he closed his eyes.

Martine looked serene, fully in character, as she hovered at the edge of the group. She was at the end of the room such that the others would have to raise their voices to speak with her, thus her distance created a natural barrier.

"What are we waiting for?" Pennington wondered aloud, his nerves pushing him to bring on whatever was about to happen so he could deal with whatever fall out he was about to feel.

"Pamela Geranabby," replied Cavendish. "I think she has a right to be here when her daughter's murderer is revealed."

"You know who did it?"

"I know we'll all know the truth tonight."

"How?"

"Ms. Letourneaux may give us some insight."

Deirdre's eyes gleamed with enthusiasm. "The spirits told her who murdered Amber?"

"I think she may feel some helpful vibrations," said Cavendish in what he hoped was a broody and otherworldly tone. Martine narrowed her eyes at him in an uncharacteristic scowl. Cavendish didn't need to be psychic to know he was being scolded for over selling it.

"Do you even believe in the other side?" Buxton, despite his nerves, was suspicious.

"It's been an eye-opening week," said Cavendish cryptically.

Just then Pamela Geranabby materialized in the doorway and paused, wary of coming all the way in. Lance went toward her. "It's all right Pamela, come in. There's been a development."

Huge bags haunted her blood shot eyes, and Cavendish imagined his own life if something worse had happened to

Sophie yesterday. He wasn't sure he would want to keep on living, and Pamela looked as if she was running out of steam just moving herself forward. Knowing how close she had come to losing her second daughter right after losing her first must have cut deeply.

Megan self-consciously gave up her seat and motioned for Pamela to sit in her place. She stood next to the arm rest.

Martine moved towards the group at a slow and graceful pace that made it seem like she was wafting across the room, more of a spectral vapor than a person.

"I've been reaching out for Amber," she explained in a hollow voice that had a monotone edge to it, like a Buddhist monk's chant. "Finally, today I felt something."

Megan arched an eyebrow at Cavendish. "You can't be serious."

"You don't believe in Martine's gifts? You make a living off them," pointed out Cavendish. "You all do – except the Lances and Pamela, of course."

"Martine – don't mess with me," warned Pamela. "This is my daughter we're talking about."

"This is real," Martine promised her. "My gift was never as strong as yours and yes…" she looked guiltily from Deirdre to Peter – "I – um – supplement my gift on television. But this is real. I feel Amber," she tapped her chest. "I feel her in here. I know what happened to her. I feel the life being squeezed out of her and she wants to tell me something about how it happened…"

Deirdre was hung up on the possibility that Martine was not the one hundred percent real deal. "You're a fake?"

"I'm not a fake, my dear. But the truth is that spirits reach out to you when they reach out to you. They don't always reach out twice a night and for a matinee on Saturday. Sometimes you must use your insights to fill in the gaps or figure out what people need to hear so you can help them and be the voice they need to hear. One of the things Miss Lydia taught us was how to fill in the gaps."

"Fill in the gaps?" gasped Deirdre, shattered.

311

"Fake it, Mrs. Lance," added Pamela quietly. "She taught us to fake it. Fake it to pay the bills. Never seemed right to me. Filling people up with hope on the back of nothing. Making them hear what they want to hear. Gleaning their hopes and reflecting them back towards them. But it's a lie. It's all lies. God knows I've heard voices in my time, and I would give anything to hear Amber's now. If you are gonna try and fill in a gap for me now, Martine, I won't thank you. My daughter deserves better than being your circus act."

"Not fill in a gap Pamela … I feel her. I feel her anger," Martine assured her, eyes focused on a vague spot in the room where nothing was.

"You never felt anything real. It was all filling in the gaps for you and then you run off and take a lot of money from a lot of gullible people and that's their problem if they want to give you money but don't tell me my daughter would reach out to you and not me. I'm her Mother," Pamela was shaking a little bit, her stolid reserve finally cracking under this latest insult.

Marvin Lance looked betwixt the two women. "Martine, perhaps you shouldn't."

"You never believed, Mr. Lance. And that's okay," said Martine, opening her hand towards him, palm up.

"Oh, thank you," he said facetiously. For once Deirdre did not challenge his skepticism.

Cavendish leaned over Pamela and looked into her eyes. "Have a little faith, Pamela. You scared me to the verge of believing with some of the things you told me the other morning. Why would it be hard for you to believe Amber might be communicating from the other side? Does it bother you that she reached out to Martine instead of you? Policemen aren't allowed to investigate crimes involving their family, doctors can't treat their own family members – all because they are too close to be objective. Maybe it's the same with the spirit world."

"I don't think so."

"Or maybe it bothers you that she reached out to a fake instead of to someone that has real powers?" suggested Cavendish.

"I don't want Martine's hocus pocus to make anyone think my daughter is really communicating with her."

"Why? Because she's a fake – you didn't try to discredit her the whole time she's been here – why now?"

"Because she's pretending she hears my daughter."

"What if she did? What if she did hear your daughter? What would your daughter tell her?" he rose and paced away from her. "You sacrificed so much for her. You could have had the life Martine had – but it's not an honest life, is it? A glorified con-woman, wouldn't you say that's what Martine is? You're better than that, aren't you?"

"Cavendish don't talk about Martine that way," Peter interjected angrily.

"Shut up Pennington or I'll throw you in the pool again," Cavendish barked the rebuke without paying attention to him.

Martine looked at Pennington quizzically and Cavendish said to Lance: "Would you pour me a drink? Some of your most excellent dark rum and coca cola, please?" Lance nodded and went to the cocktail cabinet, his eyes oozing with curiosity.

Pamela said quietly, "Yes, Martine is a con woman. It's cruel, lying to people. Offering hope when there's none to be had. I wanted my daughter to grow up with good values. To be honest."

Cavendish nodded sympathetically.

"Then after all the sacrifices you made for your daughter, Pamela, it must have hurt you like hell when you found out what she'd been up to. You cleaned other people's toilets and she repaid you by becoming a blackmailing whore. You fought with her when I brought her home, then I think you let it go and you even stood up for her when Ross Buchanan was here. Then you fought in your cottage, and you probably thought you'd said your piece and she'd said hers and imagined things would look better in the morning. So what must have gone through your head – how must it have absolutely stabbed you in the heart - when you came up to the house and found her in Peter Pennington's room – after all you did for her, after all she had done *to* you -Then when you tried to forgive her she spat in her face one more time. And worse, doing it in the home of the employer you respected. To the guest of his wife who resented you? The guest you knew in childhood – you never mentioned knowing Martine in childhood when we spoke. I found out from Amber's accomplice, Tyree, that you and Martine knew each other. That's how Amber found out too. Found out what her life might have looked like."

"You don't know what you're talking about."

He went back to Pamela and squatted in front of her. "It's a terrible thing to lose a child. How long do you think you'll be able to bear it? The guilt. I know where Amber was killed. And the night she died; Mr. Buxton saw you coming downstairs with a bundle of sheets. There is a laundry chute at the top of the stairs – I saw a maid shoving sheets down it earlier today – yet the night of the murder you were carrying a bundle of sheets in a basket. Why was that?"

He watched her, studied her eyes for signs the weariness would make her cave into his allegations. "I think that Amber's clothes were rolled up inside those sheets – you were taking them away from the scene of the crime. Removing the evidence."

Marvin Lance froze in the midst of his drink preparations. "Cavendish, do you know what you're saying?"

Cavendish ignored Lance, unwilling to avert his focus away from Pamela as he bored in: "A lifetime of cleaning toilets and making beds, teaching your daughter to live right – yet she grows into what – a whore? After everything you sacrificed. It was for nothing. She learned nothing.

"And when you confront her with your sacrifice, what does she say? Thank you? Or does she get angry when she thinks of the life she could have had. Does she hate you because you didn't make money off your gift as Martine did? Which was it Pamela? What finally pushed you over the top – I know Amber was good at pushing people's buttons. Tell me. Tell me what made you so mad that you wrapped your hands around your own daughter's throat."

He reached out and put his own hands loosely around her throat and peered into her eyes. He heard Megan or Deirdre gasp behind him, but Pamela's eyes widened with pride and defiance. "And what made you squeeze."

He let go and stepped away from her.

"You can't think I killed my daughter," Pamela looked at him like he was insane. She also looked around to see if anyone believed him.

"Yes, I can. I think you killed her and then you rolled her dead, half naked body out the window and down into the pool," he shook his head. "I really don't know how you could do that."

"She told me, Pamela," said Martine insistently. "She knows you were disappointed in her. She understands she drove you to it. She's asking you to forgive her."

"You're lying!" Pamela shrieked; the weary calm shattered by hysteria. "You're a fake! You don't hear her voice; you don't hear anyone's voices and my daughter would never, never ever talk to you from the other side!"

Pamela was face-to-face with Martine in three strides. She raised a hand to strike the medium, but Martine faced her unfazed, exuding the serene air she seemed always to adorn herself with.

Martine didn't even seem to notice the hand ready to swing at her; she just stared into Pamela's eyes and repeated her mantra: "She forgives you."

Pamela froze, her arm still held high and ready to swing, but she seemed to have lost all momentum.

Cavendish had followed Pamela when she moved towards Martine. Now he gripped her raised arm and spun her towards him. She turned easily – no resistance – and stood facing him. The weariness in her eyes had turned to exhaustion and defeat, tears welling at their corners.

"You won't be able to hide from this – I can't believe you would want to. You murdered your own daughter." He looked into Pamela Geranabby's eyes and saw emptiness.

"She said I was a stupid… she called me a stupid… bitch, that we could have had everything. That if I had just used my gift like Martine, she never would have had to have sex with all those men," the allegation seemed to bewilder her. "She said it was *my* fault she did what she did…. I could take a daughter being embarrassed her mama was a maid, I could even take her wanting to be rich. I understood her not understanding my choices – not understanding why I raised her like I did – instead of getting rich. I can understand all that. But when she said I was the reason – she said she was a whore because of the choices I made for her… she said it was all my fault for being a stupid goody two shoes. … I didn't want to be a crook and a thief and teach her to work honestly - I chose a life cleaning toilets in other people's houses to show her the right way to live – while you," - she pointed her finger accusingly at Martine. "Swanned off to Hollywood and cheat and steal from people and my daughter thinks you are the good role model. You are what I could have been – should have been! And she blamed me for everything she'd done. I was so, so angry at her. And hurt. Humiliated. She'd brought shame to the house; she'd spat on Mr. Lance's kindness over the years - I was so angry… I grabbed her and shook her by the shoulders, and she spat in my face.," she sounded stunned, like she still couldn't believe it. She repeated it, like she was turning the memory over in her hand, still unable to process it.

"She spat in my face. I told her I should wring her neck," her voice grew very, very small. "Then my hands were around her throat."

The weight of the confession made the whole room feel darker. Now that she had spoken those seven words, Pamela seemed ready to share more.

"She said 'mama, please'," Pamela started to sob as the memory of her anger bled into remembering the horror of what she had done. "She said 'Mama please don't' – she looked surprised and scared - but it was too late, I didn't even realize what she was saying until afterwards and then … and then… I thought she had just passed out. She went limp and I put her on the floor. I slapped her cheeks and tried to breathe into her mouth, and nothing happened, and nothing happened and then… Then I realized what I had done, and I got scared. I thought about Mia. I had to protect Mia. She couldn't know what I did. I didn't mean to ki..." The word seemed to get stuck, as though her mouth couldn't bring itself to form the brutal single syllable. "I didn't mean to hurt her - but Amber called me stupid and hated me for choosing a hard life, when I chose a hard life to be a good mother! She said I was stupid because I could have given them a better life. She blamed me for all the wicked things she had done herself. And I was so mad - she– "

Pamela was quivering, the moment and all the intensity of her fury pulsing through her body in physical tremors that echoed the moment when her bottled rage exploded. "I was just angry and furious, but I didn't mean to… kill her… I just wanted to punish her."

Tears were streaming down her face and she made no move to wipe them. No one offered her tissues or handkerchiefs. They regarded her with a mix of fear and horror.

Her tears just riled Cavendish up. "Why did you throw her body out the window like yesterday's garbage?"

"To try to hide where it happened. I didn't know if the police would find evidence – I thought if I put her somewhere else…and they found her – that way – they would think one of the men killed her - and I took her clothes but I needed to hide them so I wrapped them in the sheets and re-made the bed."

Cavendish considered her weeping eyes coldly. "You showed a lot of presence of mind for someone who just killed her daughter."

"Once I knew there was no hope…"

"How did you know? How did you know there was no hope? You could have called the paramedics. You could have fought to keep her alive!"

"I felt her spirit go."

"You felt your problems go. No more ungrateful daughter to deal with," Cavendish accused her scornfully.

She stepped up to him and slapped him sharply across

the face. It stung like the dickens and snapped his head sideways. "How dare you. I loved my daughter, despite what she was. And I had to think about Mia. Mia needs her mother!"

Cavendish condemned her flatly: "You killed Amber in a fit of anger and calmly covered your tracks, cool as a cucumber. Don't put it on your other daughter that you hid the murder of the first. Don't make her carry that guilt when it was you that did this. Mia needs to be kept as far away from you as possible – God help her if she disappoints you too, someday. I can understand killing to protect those you love but ... not killing your child."

Pamela looked around the room at all the stunned faces. If she had registered anything Cavendish had just said, she did not show it. "Where are the police? Are you going to arrest me?"

"They're in the next room. Mr. Lance kindly allowed us to put recording devices in this room to monitor what transpired. I was hoping for your confession." He didn't add that with such scant physical evidence he was truly dependent on it.

As if on cue, the door to the drawing room swung open and Borden Boxer led Constables Swain and Singh into the room. Pamela looked around with rising desperation.

"I can't go to jail; my daughter needs me."

Deirdre looked at her husband and then at Pamela, then stepped over to her and put a comforting hand on her arm. "Marvin and I will take care of Mia. She'll live here like our daughter. She'll be fine, I promise you."

Cavendish wondered if this was purely generosity of spirit or if Deirdre was indulging in a small measure of vengeance on the woman she'd felt such jealousy towards.

"You can't take my daughter away from me!" Pamela cried out, eyes darting from Deirdre to the police.

Cavendish wondered coldly how she could care about a second daughter when she had thrown the first one away.

"I'm just saying we'll take care of her," said Deirdre reassuringly.

Like the United Kingdom, St. Lazarus had no Miranda

law; the policemen just cautioned Pamela that anything she said could be taken down in evidence. They handcuffed her, while Pamela muttered over and over again that she had given up everything for her. And that she was so sorry.

"My daughter needs me," she insisted, but her voice grew weaker with each protest.

Hands now secured behind her and Jenny guiding her with a grip on her upper arm, she was taken from the room.

Cavendish searched his heart for sympathy, but he thought of the light in that poor troubled girl's eyes going out and found none. He just felt sadness for the burden this would lay on Mia's young shoulders, knowing her sister that she had loved had died at the hands of the woman she was supposed to be able to trust above all others. Whose love for her sister had made her accept the task of mailing out the blackmail packages. Who could have died while faithfully discharging the last request her sister had asked of her.

Boxer gave Cavendish a smile. "I think I owe you a drink. Come by the station after work tomorrow..." then he paused. He watched Singh and Swain taking Pamela away. "I need to know how you figured out that the mother killed her own daughter."

Everybody expressed their curiosity. Cavendish shrugged self-consciously. "It was different things, coming together. Being outed in the newspaper seemed to precipitate the events that led to Amber's murder. It could have been Ross Buchanan, who'd lost everything – but he was in jail. It could have been his wife, but that seemed unlikely because there wasn't a way for her to get here without leaving a trail. She'd have to pay for a taxi or car rental. Not likely she would hitch hike. It could have been Marvin Lance but if you were one of her victims, why seek revenge now? Why set yourself up to discover the body? Why work so hard to have me dig into the case when you could have easily used your influence to bury it? It could have been you Deirdre – but again, why now? Why do it on your own turf? And how and where would you find her wearing only a t-shirt and underwear? And what happened to

319

the rest of her clothes? And then I saw the maid putting clothes in the laundry chute, and I remember Hoyt telling me that he ran into her on the stairs – she was carrying a laundry basket full of bed linens. Why carry that in a basket? Why change the linens after ten PM at night? That's a morning chore. Then I realized: Because the rest of Amber's clothes were in there – the clothes she had taken off in preparation to try to entrap Mr. Pennington. Or maybe Pamela removed them herself to make it look like a sexual crime. The clothes she had to hide and destroy after she killed Amber. She smuggled them out in a laundry basket. And that dove-tailed about something else that had been bothering me – Both Martine and Pamela talked about Martine's visit to Pamela the night of the murder. But Pamela concealed the fact that she knew Martine from childhood. She claimed Martine's interest in her situation was seeing Amber about the place. Why hide the fact they'd known each other as children? Unless she was concerned where it would lead."

Martine looked deeply saddened. "I felt so sad for her when I visited with her - but after that, it's hard to believe it - she killed her own daughter."

"That's why I don't want kids," observed Megan. "That woman sacrificed everything for her daughter. And what did she get? She got it all thrown in her face."

Martine, for once looking less than perfectly serene, looked at Mrs. Lance. She looked like she smelled a foul odour. "Deirdre, I hate to change the subject to a personal matter, but could I be moved to a different room? I'm leaving my husband."

Peter looked like a volcano that didn't know which way to erupt. His eyes dashed between Martine and Cavendish. "What? Why?"

Martine looked at Megan whose hand had flown to her neck as if she was pulling a robe tighter. "Megan, if you want him, keep him. As soon as we finish our current contract we are done."

Cavendish closed his ears to Megan's apologies and Pennington's denials. Martine seemed not even to hear them. Hoyt almost jumped out of his chair, elated. Martine pointedly ignored her producer and husband and looked at Hoyt Buxton with sad affection. "I'm sorry, Hoyt. I don't know what my career is going to look like. I am reconsidering a lot of things."

Buxton's enthusiasm evaporated.

Cavendish thanked Lance for the drink. "I think I'd better be going."

"Thank you for everything, Archie," Lance handed him an envelope from his inside pocket. Cavendish accepted it gratefully. He would look inside it later.

Pennington was storming out. Megan had the decency to seem embarrassed by her behavior as she said to Martine: "I understand. And I'm very sorry."

Martine smiled sadly as Megan left. "I can empathize with his charms."

After Megan and Peter were gone – consoling each other? Strategizing a way to ingratiate themselves back into Martine's good graces? – she said to Hoyt: "I have a suggestion for you. This whole situation has been such a terrible scandal. I'm sure you could get a book contract or a movie of the week. You should try to speak to Pamela as soon as possible. Maybe you can represent her and help her get some money to put aside for her daughter."

Buxton nodded, "I can give that a try. But you're still my client. However, you want to work, that's how we'll work."

"Thank you, I appreciate that."

Pennington might need to find a new wife to support him, Megan might need to find new shows to produce, Martine and Hoyt were reinventing themselves – and Pamela might even make money selling the story of how she murdered her daughter to put her other daughter through college. All these lives moving forward, except for Amber's. Cavendish looked at Boxer who seemed to understand what he was feeling – two policemen, in tune with each other's thoughts. Boxer shrugged as if to say, "what can you do?"

The sense of triumph at solving the crime, the momentary satisfaction of bringing Amber's killer to justice – even if it was tainted by the horror and sadness of learning it was her mother – began to pass. Because what justice was there here for Amber? She couldn't move forward or reinvent herself. Her future had stopped.

He headed for the door. Martine grabbed his wrist as he passed her looked up at him with a depth of kindness in her eyes that took him unawares. "You look sad, Mr. Cavendish. But no one can hurt her now. She's happy and she's at rest, and she's grateful to you."

That serene face had recovered from the bad smell of her husband's infidelity and manager's betrayal and now seemed so genuine and warm that Cavendish understood the appeal it held for the punters. He wanted to believe that he had helped Amber. He wanted to believe that Martine had heard from Amber those very words.

"I wish I could believe in your gift, because it would be nice to think I helped her rest in peace."

"I know you don't believe in my gift. I wouldn't have bothered telling you. It's only because Amber was so very insistent. She says you're not the only one who doesn't know when to shut up."

He knew Martine could have overheard many of their conversations here at the house. He knew she was a fraud. But he wanted to believe her, so he decided that he would.

"Tell her she's welcome. And I'm glad to have known her."

The End

of

A CONSEQUENCE OF SIN

Archie Cavendish will return

in

THE MAN WHO HAD IT COMING

ABOUT THE AUTHOR

Frederick James is a Historian by training and a mystery novelist by vocation. The Archie Cavendish novels were inspired by his enthusiasm for the genre and a lifetime of travels to the Caribbean.

James and his wife live in Southern California where they are parents to a one-eyed cat who thinks he is a dog. To keep posted on the future adventures of Archie Cavendish and for information about Frederick James' other mystery series, visit:
www.frederickjamesmysteries.com and follow him at
https://www.facebook.com/FrederickJamesMysteries

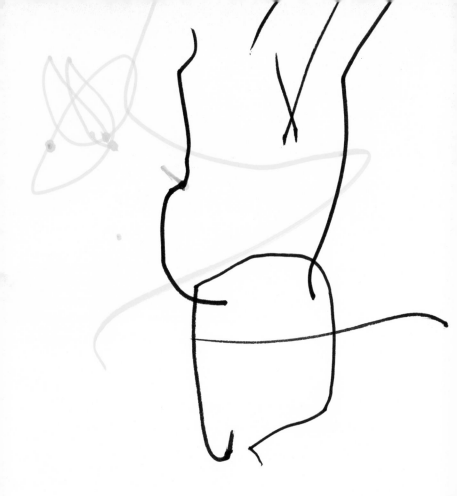

Made in the USA
Las Vegas, NV
11 December 2020